DARK FATHOM

Also by Tom Morrisey

Turn Four

Yucatan Deep

Deep Blue (A Beck Easton Adventure)

TOM MORRISEY

A BECK EASTON ADVENTURE

DARK FATHOM

BOOK 2

ZONDERVAN™
GRAND RAPIDS, MICHIGAN 49530 USA

ZONDERVAN.COM/
AUTHORTRACKER

ZONDERVAN™

Dark Fathom

Requests for information should be addressed to:
Zondervan, *Grand Rapids, Michigan 49530*

Library of Congress Cataloging-in-Publication Data

Morrisey, Tom, 1952–
Dark fathom / Tom Morrisey.
p. cm.—(A Beck Easton adventure)
ISBN-13: 978-0-310-24408-0 (softcover)
ISBN-10: 0-310-24408-0 (softcover)
1. Divers—Fiction. I. Title.
PS3613.O776D37 2005
813'.6—dc22

2005015815

All Scripture quotations are from the King James Version of the Bible.

Excerpt from *Wild by Nature: True Stories of Adventure and Faith*, by Tom Morrisey. Grand Rapids, Mich.: Baker Books, 2001. Used with permission; all rights reserved.

The website addresses recommended throughout this book are offered as a resource to you. These websites are not intended in any way to be or imply an endorsement on the part of Zondervan, nor do we vouch for their content for the life of this book.

Interior design by Beth Shagene

Printed in the United States of America

05 06 07 08 09 10 11 • 18 17 16 15 14 13 12 11 10 9 8 7 6 5 4 3 2 1

For Marilyn Watters,
who has all eternity
to read the perfected edition
of this book.
We love you, Mom,
and we'll
see you soon.

I will be surety for him;
 of my hand shalt thou require him:
if I bring him not unto thee,
 and set him before thee,
then let me bear the blame for ever.

GENESIS 43:9 KJV

PROLOGUE

MAY 6, 1945
49,000 FEET ABOVE THE NORTHWEST TERRITORIES, CANADA

"Captain, fuel pressure's dropping—number-two drop tank."

The flight deck, illuminated only by the red instrument lamps, was full of the sound of the engines, a background noise too loud to ignore and too monotonous to notice. Not even the leather flight helmets with their padded intercom headsets could cancel it out. It was like sitting under an avalanche with cotton stuffed in one's ears.

"Captain?"

Luftwaffe Captain Ernst Grüber glanced at the altimeter; his aircraft was nearly fifteen kilometers above the dark and frozen earth. He was cold, his feet nearly numb despite the rabbit-fur-lined flight boots, his fingers thick and wooden within silk-lined, shearling-cuffed gloves. He switched on a red-lensed flashlight, checked the flow from his oxygen bottle, and turned it up. Almost immediately, his head became clearer and feeling crept into his limbs. He turned to the flight engineer.

"How long since we emptied number one?"

The engineer, a lieutenant, pushed up his jacket sleeve and glanced at his watch. "Five minutes, sir."

Grüber nodded. The designers from Horten had said that the wing tanks would run dry within seven minutes of one another. That prediction was turning out to be accurate, just as all of their predictions had turned out to be accurate, beginning with the outrageous pronouncement that an aircraft such as this—with no vertical stabilizer, no rudder, and no fuselage to speak of—would fly at all.

"Watch the fuel pressure," Grüber said. "Tell me when it hits zero."

He was tired. Dog-tired already and only six hours into what was scheduled to be a twenty-two-hour mission. Fatigue was edging the Dahlem accent back into his German, a guttural undertone that he tried to hide from the high-blooded Berliners on his aircrew. But if anyone noticed, they did not show it.

"Zero now, sir."

"Very good." Grüber put both hands on the control yoke. He'd logged a hundred hours in training on this aircraft, but it still felt strange to have no rudder pedals beneath his feet. "Eject on my mark ... *now*."

The engineer pulled a pair of levers. There was a distant, metallic *thunk* as the two huge, twenty-kiloliter, aluminum tanks dropped away into the night. The instruments registered the change—the airspeed rising, the altimeter creeping higher.

Grüber allowed the aircraft to climb and seek its own equilibrium. To give it the range required for this mission, the bomber had not been equipped with the belly guns, nose guns, or tail-cannons that had been part of the original design. The ball turret behind the flight deck had been replaced with a simple Perspex dome from which the navigator, who was also the radio operator, could make star-sightings every fifteen minutes, guiding them on their journey with the same technology used for centuries by ships under sail.

With no guns, no armor to speak of, no weapons other than the single bomb in its bomb bay, the bomber's sole means of defense was altitude. It could not outrun most Allied fighters, but it could outclimb them; its service ceiling and range were a full two kilometers higher and 10,000 kilometers farther than any other aircraft in the world. That was the beauty of it.

That was the horror of it, as well.

The Horten Ho-18 *Amerikabomber* was unlike any other aircraft. It was a true flying-wing design, powered by six BMW 109-003 jet engines, capable of reaching well in excess of five hundred miles per hour in level flight. Sixty meters wide from wingtip to wingtip, the airplane was beautiful, a design seemingly snatched from some future time. With no nose and no tail, it was a shallow, batlike chevron in the evening sky. There was nothing about it that did not seek the heavens.

But that was also its principal flaw: one that Ernst Grüber had spotted within moments of first seeing a scale model of the aircraft.

"It has no vertical stabilizer," Grüber had told the Horten representative who'd first briefed him.

"The side-to-side motion of the airplane, the yaw; it is controlled by the thrust of the engines, yes?" The Horten man had smiled as if what he'd just said was supposed to be obvious.

The thrust of the engines. The jet engines. And Grüber knew about jet engines. They were more powerful than piston engines, and much more efficient at altitude, but they could also be amazingly fragile. He'd been standing on the flight line in Cologne a year earlier when one of the new Me-262 jet fighters was being run up. A line mechanic's glove had been sucked into one of the intakes; that was all it had taken to disintegrate the engine in rather spectacular fashion.

Which was why Grüber had asked his next question:

"And what happens when the thrust falls out of balance?"

That had gotten Grüber a look. "Then you must rebalance it, of course. We used this design on a fighter prototype last year. If the thrust goes out of balance and is not corrected immediately? Then the aircraft will spin. Quite violently, in fact. You would not be able to recover."

That had gotten the Horten engineer a look. "I'm flying this aircraft into combat," Grüber had told him. "It sounds a bit delicate, does it not?"

The engineer had shrugged. "For a fighter, yes. But for a bomber?" He'd shrugged again. "Just stay high, so they don't shoot you."

"Let us remember Dresden," Hockheim, the bombardier, said from his ready seat.

Grüber did not answer. There were five Germans on the *Amerika* this late spring evening; none of them had been home for the better part of a year. They had shipped out on June first of 1944, five days prior to the Normandy invasion, leaving Norway on three U-boats loaded with aircraft components, plans, and machine tools, as well as a cadre of Horten Aircraft Company designers, engineers, and skilled tradesmen.

Since then, they had been living in Japan, initially in the port city of Nagasaki, and more recently in the tiny town of Okha, on the country's northernmost island, the optimal takeoff point for a Great Circle route east over the Arctic.

They had been in the eighth month of their deployment when news had reached them of the fire-bombing of Dresden. Unprotected by antiaircraft batteries and swollen with refugees fleeing from the advancing Red Army, Dresden had been attacked by the Allies with enough phosphorous bombs to turn the medieval city's center into a veritable tornado of white-hot flame. Newsreels flown in from Germany had shown the aircrew the carpet of ash and rubble that a single night's bombing had produced. An SS intelligence officer had described to them how the intense heat had created winds so strong that pedestrians were physically swept off their feet and hurled, screaming, into the inferno.

Told once, the story would have been terrible news from home, another horrifying example of man's inhumanity to man. But Grüber and his aircrew had been told it again and again. Yet Dresden had been blanketed with more than 700,000 bombs, while the *Amerika* carried only a single weapon. That made Ernst Grüber's blood run cold. After all, what manner of bomb was it that a single one could possibly make up for the destruction of Dresden, of Hamburg?

And why was it that Hockheim – an SS officer educated as a physicist – had been pressed into service as the *Amerika*'s bombardier, rather than any of the legions of battle-trained Luftwaffe officers who were available?

"A penny for your thoughts, Captain."

Grüber blinked. He turned and looked at Colonel Kenjo Matsushida, an experienced heavy-bomber pilot and the only non-German on the aircrew. The stoic Matsushida had been presented to Grüber and his men as window-dressing, a Japanese national to sit in the right-hand seat as the *Amerika* streaked down its steel launch track.

But the Japanese pilot had been a quick study and was easily the equal of Schmidt, the regular Luftwaffe copilot assigned to the mission.

"I'm thinking of revenge." Grüber kept his eyes forward, on the empty black sky.

"Revenge." Matsushida spoke in perfect Oxfordian English, the only language that he and the German aircrew had in common. "Of course; I understand."

No – no, you do not. Grüber touched the Bible tucked inside his goatskin flight jacket. It had been a gift from his old pastor, Martin Niemöller, on the eve of Grüber's departure to begin his military training, a joyous occasion because Niemöller himself was a decorated veteran of the First World War: a winner of the *Pour le Mérite*. That was before Niemöller spoke out against Hitler's state religion policies, was arrested, held eight months, and then fined 2,000 deutschemarks and released from jail ...

... After which the Gestapo had seized the pastor and put him into the camps: first Sachsenhausen, and then Dachau.

Grüber had cut the dedication page out of the Bible, cut it out and burned it, it and the signature that tied him to an enemy of the state. But he had kept the Bible itself, kept it and had even left his Luger behind in Okha so he could carry the worn book on this flight and still make his weight. It was, after all, the only tie he had left to the man who had led him to his Savior, even though the only things that would distinguish it from any other Bible were the three verses that Niemöller had underlined in the twelfth chapter of Romans:

Do not take revenge, my friends, but leave room for God's wrath, for it is written: "It is mine to avenge; I will repay," says the Lord. On the contrary:
"If your enemy is hungry, feed him;
if he is thirsty, give him something to drink.
In doing this, you will heap burning coals on his head."
Do not be overcome by evil, but overcome evil with good.

Overcoming evil with good—Grüber wondered if that was even remotely related to what he was doing here.

Eleven hours later, the *Amerika* was closing in on the distant, dark void of Lake Ontario when the call came over the flight-deck intercom: "Navigator to pilot. Target in one hour, Captain."

"Understood: one hour out." The amphetamines prescribed by the flight surgeon were kicking in now. The whole crew had taken them half an hour earlier.

Grüber felt no better about what they were getting ready to do. Try as he could, he could only see two things good about it.

The first was that they were doing their duty.

And the second was that, once they had the big, strange, single bomb clear of the bomb bay, he and his crew would have a way out of the airplane.

The giant aircraft had no landing gear; it had taken off on rocket-assisted carriage units that had dropped away at the end of the launch rail. For training purposes, fixed gear had been mounted in false drop tanks, but for the mission, wheels had been exchanged for extra fuel room. It was the last word in commitment, a single-use airplane; once airborne, the *Amerika* could not land.

The plan all along had been to bomb the target, fly on to a rendezvous point in the Atlantic, and then parachute into the water, where a U-boat would pick them up and carry them to Venezuela and safety. But mannequin tests had shown that the slipstream would bash a man against the aircraft if he tried to jump from the crew door. The only safe jump point was from the bomb bay, which had its own front airfoil when the doors were completely open. And that exit was only usable when the bay was empty.

"Forty-five minutes."

"Very well." Grüber turned and looked over his shoulder. "Mr. Hockheim, prepare to arm your weapon."

There was movement to Grüber's right as his copilots exchanged positions for the third time in the mission – Schmidt moving back to the bomber's single narrow bunk, and Matsushida sliding easily into the right-hand seat.

Grüber could see lights ahead of them now. They had nearly cleared the lake. The *Amerika* was now in the airspace of the country for which she'd been named. Grüber glanced behind him; Hockheim was pulling on an extra pair of coveralls and donning a lead apron.

That was another thing that worried Grüber. Everyone else on the crew had left behind fountain pens and pocket change to conserve weight, but Hockheim was carrying a lead apron. And when Grüber had asked why, Hockheim had not answered.

It was just after ten in the evening, local time. They were closing in on half an hour away from target – time to arm the bomb – when the navigator got on the intercom.

"Message coming in on the radio, Captain. It's encrypted."

"Arm the weapon," Matsushida said. "We can decrypt the message later."

Grüber shot the Japanese officer a look.

"Disregard that last. Bombardier, arm your weapon. Radio operator, decrypt the message."

"We don't have time." Matsushida tapped his wrist, where his watch was, under his flying gauntlet. "We're only thirty minutes from target. We need that man to navigate."

"Encrypted traffic takes priority; we can circle, if we need to. And you and I can navigate the rest of the way to the target. All we have to do is aim for the lights."

He nodded at the slightly bowed horizon ahead of them. Through the curved nose canopy, a dim concentration of yellow-white light indicated the presence of a major city.

Matsushida said nothing.

Five minutes later, Grüber felt a hand on his shoulder. He turned and the radio operator handed him a sheet of paper with the square Enigma type running across it. Grüber switched on his red-lensed flashlight and read it. He read it again. Then he touched his throat mike.

"Pilot to bombardier."

"Bombardier."

"Safe your weapon."

"Repeat, please?"

"Safe your weapon. We're scrubbed."

"Yes, sir. Understood. Safing the weapon."

"Wait." It was Matsushida. "What are you talking about?"

Grüber handed him the signals transcript:

REICHSKANSLER DEAD. BERLIN OCCUPIED. TRUCE STRUCK. CEASE HOSTILITIES IMMEDIATELY. DO NOT REPEAT DO NOT ENGAGE. DISARM WEAPON AND JETTISON AT SEA. PROCEED WITH ALL HASTE TO RENDEZVOUS.

JOHL, GEN'L

Matsushida ripped the order into shreds. "We never received this," he said.

Slowly, Grüber slid his hand down to his hip, to his holster.

It was empty. Of course: he'd left the gun in Japan. He hoped the others were still plugged into the intercom.

"Kenjo ..."

"*Colonel.* I am a colonel, Captain, and I outrank you."

"Very well. Colonel – the war is over."

"Your war may be over. My war is not."

"But this is a German aircraft."

"Assembled on Japanese soil and dispatched from a Japanese base. Your flight path will make that obvious. No one need ever know that this was a Luftwaffe attack. Japan will claim responsibility. We will say it was our aircraft, our weapon. It will do for us what it could not do for you – break the wills of the Allies. Allow us to sue for a more advantageous peace."

The light on the horizon was rapidly gaining strength.

"Colonel ... I have been ordered by my supreme commander to stand down."

Nodding, the Japanese officer unholstered his sidearm, cocked it, and very deliberately aimed at the center of Grüber's head.

Grüber swallowed. "There are five of us on this aircraft, Colonel."

"That is not a problem, Captain. I have six bullets."

"You can't release the bomb from the flight deck. That takes a second man, down below, in the bombardier's station."

"Then I'll shoot the bombardier last."

The sound of the six jet engines came flooding back in. Grüber's mind raced, trying to come up with a way to deal with this very placid madman.

As it happened, he didn't have to. In the very next instant, there was a suggestion of movement in Grüber's peripheral vision, a blinding flash, and then Grüber fell forward against his seat harness as the world faded into silence and blackness.

He blinked himself awake. His head throbbed. Above him and to his left, wind was roaring in through a thumb-size hole in the Perspex canopy. To his right was a tangle of men – Schmidt and the radioman, struggling with Matsushida; both had hold of the Japanese officer's right arm, in which he still gripped the pistol menacingly. Still groggy, Grüber reached out and twisted the gun from Matsushida's hand, turning it toward the man's palm, just the way they'd shown him in the pitifully brief hand-to-hand combat course during basic training.

Amazingly enough, it worked. Grüber depressed the thumb latch to release the pistol's magazine. Then he worked the action to eject the round from the chamber.

Done. That was done. What next? Still blinking stars away from his eyes, he scanned the instruments. Both throttles had been shoved all the way to 110 percent power in the scuffle, and the aircraft was in a bank to the left, nose down 30 degrees, losing altitude rapidly. Already they were dipping beneath 10,000 meters. Coming rapidly awake now, Grüber took the yoke in both hands and pulled back.

Nothing.

"Pull him back!" He was shouting at the top of his lungs, struggling to be heard over the scream of the engines and the wind roaring in through the punctured canopy. "Pull him back – he's up against the yoke! We're diving."

The struggle continued. Grüber peered at the struggling, red-lighted forms, judged which of the three heads was the Japanese officer's and brought the pistol barrel cracking down upon its crown. The struggle ceased, and he tried the yoke again – it was heavy from the wind pressure, but it moved. He reduced throttles to 50 percent and kept applying back-pressure. Slowly, over the better part of a minute, the big bomber pulled out of the dive. By the time the *Amerika* leveled out, the altimeter was reading a bare 5,000 meters. Ahead, through the concave curve of the Perspex nose, Grüber could clearly see a shimmering arrowhead of electric lights, punctuated by landmarks familiar even to a German who had never seen North America before: the silver stiletto of the Chrysler Building, the Empire State Building dwarfing everything around it and, off in the blackness, all by itself, the patinaed form of the Statue of Liberty.

New York.

The city they'd almost bombed.

"Put him back in the ready bunk." Grüber looked to make certain that his orders were being understood. "Strap him in. And give him an ampoule of morphine. I don't want him running around."

Pulling off his flying gloves, Grüber felt the top of his leather helmet. There was a shallow groove there, where the bullet had scored him. But his hand was not sticky – no blood. So it had been close, but not too close.

Rolling the throttles forward to 100 percent power, the Luftwaffe captain positioned his yoke for its most fuel-efficient rate-of-climb, and the city lights dropped out of view. The big bomber passed 8,000 meters, then 10,000, and Grüber was just about to ask Hockheim what the weapon they were carrying would have done to the target when several loud bangs sounded against the underside of the aircraft, followed quickly by two more. Then metal and Perspex were clattering around the flight deck, the thumb-size hole in the canopy was joined by one large enough to accommodate a man's head, and wind was whistling up through a hole in the metal decking next to Grüber's feet.

Two seconds later, an aircraft went flashing by in the moonlight. Grüber had a glimpse of two engine nacelles and twin tail booms.

"Fighter! A P-38." Grüber started to give the firing coordinates – "Ten o'clock hi ..." – and then stopped himself. His aircraft had no gunners, no way of shooting back. He only had one defense.

Altitude.

Shoving all four throttles forward to their stops, he waited ten long seconds until the turbines reached speed, and then he pulled back on the yoke, aiming the aircraft up, at a gibbous moon, frigid air pouring in on him through the shattered canopy.

“I need flying goggles up here.”

Someone – he didn’t look to see who – handed him a pair of goggles, and he pulled them on, blinking to clear his eyes. Schmidt was strapping into the right-hand seat, helping him hold the yoke back, scanning the instruments for signs of trouble.

Grüber heard the trip-hammer sound of more rounds striking the bomber, and someone called out in pain on the intercom, but he didn’t have time to ask who it was. He was busy, keeping the big jet bomber at its maximum rate of climb.

Forty seconds later, he could see lazy arcs of tracer fire off their left wing. Then they were passing 14,000 meters, well above the service ceiling of their propeller-driven adversary. The wind howling through the broken canopy was freezing, but the controls all seemed to work, and the engines appeared undamaged – all producing equal thrust, and all within 50 degrees of one another in temperature.

“Navigator, give me a heading to rendezvous.”

“Make your heading one-four-three true.”

Good man. He’d had the heading ready, had kept his head through the attack.

“Who’s hit?”

“Hockheim.” It was the flight engineer who answered him. “It looks bad. We can’t stop the bleeding. Oh – and Matsushida took one through the chest. He’s dead.”

“Give Hockheim morphine, then. We’ll make the best time we can. They’ll have surgeons on the sub. Engineer – just as soon as we're over deep water, clear the bomb bay. And for goodness sake, check with Hockheim before you put him out, and make sure that thing's not armed."

"Yes sir."

Ten minutes later, the engineer was kneeling on the flight deck next to him. Grimacing against the cold, Grüber pulled back the ear-cup on his helmet.

"What is it?"

"Sir, it's the bomb bay doors. Two of the hinges are jammed – hit in the attack, by the looks of it. We can't open far enough to drop the bomb."

The cockpit seemed to swim for a moment, and Grüber began to sweat.

"Can we open them enough to bail out? Crawl past the bomb – do it that way?"

The engineer shook his head.

"No, sir. I can only make a gap of ten or twelve centimeters. It's not enough."

"Can you close the doors, then?"

The engineer nodded. "I can snug them up with a chain hoist if I have to."

"Make it so, then."

"Yes, sir."

Teeth clenched, Grüber touched the Bible over his heart.

The submarine rendezvous was set at 60 degrees west longitude, 35 degrees north latitude – well out into the Atlantic Ocean and far from regular shipping lanes. The plan was to put the bomber over those coordinates with several hours of fuel left – but that plan presumed that the *Amerika* would arrive undamaged at the pick-up point, with her bomb bay empty. Self-healing fuel bladders had kept the fuel loss to a minimum, but there had been loss, nonetheless. And the bomb added 4,000 kilograms of dead weight. They would have reserve fuel, but very little.

The navigator told him when they were half an hour out from their pick-up point, and Grüber, half-frozen in the windswept pilot's seat, nodded wearily.

"Very well. Get on the radio; see if you can raise the sub."

This should have been a pro forma. U-boats ran submerged only when hunting, or evading an enemy. There would be no other ships in the area of the pick-up – that was why it had been chosen – so the submarine would be on the surface, circling slowly, its engines making just enough turns to charge the batteries and run the air vents. It would have a radioman on watch, and a signal from this altitude would come in strong and clear, with no interference from the horizon. But five long minutes passed, and then ten.

"Radio – any progress?"

"No, Captain. I've tried the primary frequency and both secondaries. There's nothing."

Grüber turned and looked at his copilot.

"Schmidt – your thoughts, please."

The copilot pursed his lips.

"Perhaps their radio is out. If that's the case, I suggest we overfly the pickup point and try signaling with lights."

"I agree."

Grüber put the giant airplane into a slight nose-down attitude. It would get him closer to the surface of the sea, but there were no fighters or antiaircraft guns to worry about this far out, and putting the aircraft into a shallow dive allowed him to maintain airspeed with the engines throttled back. He could feel the doubts nibbling at him.

Twenty minutes later, they were circling. Four sets of eyes peered down at the moon-washed sea. The telltale white feather of a wake was nowhere to be seen.

"Schmidt – lights, please."

The copilot leaned forward and used both hands to activate the aircraft's running lights and forward searchlights—what would have been its landing lights, if it had landing gear. On for three seconds, off for three, on for three, off for three. He repeated the sequence ten times, and then Grüber banked the airplane to give himself a panoramic view of the sea below.

Nothing.

He leveled off, opened the flare box at his feet, and took out a pistol-like launcher with a red distress flare.

"Schmidt—take the yoke, please."

Finding an aperture from which to fire the flare was easy. Grüber simply stood, stuck the muzzle of the flare gun into the large shell-hole in the canopy, and pulled the trigger.

A brilliant red light streaked away in the slipstream, and Grüber reloaded and fired quickly until three red flares were drifting down toward the sea below.

One by one they winked out, and still there was no answer from the moon-burnished ocean.

"Perhaps they ran into trouble," Schmidt said.

"Perhaps."

Grüber did not say what was on his mind: *Or perhaps they were ordered home, so we could crash into the North Atlantic and take with us every trace of this mission.*

He looked at his fuel gauges. Perhaps they had forty-five minutes more, if they were careful.

"Navigator—where's our nearest land?"

A red lamp came on behind them, over the tiny aluminum chart table.

"Bermuda, Captain. We're less than 650 kilometers away."

"Very well. Give me a heading."

"Make heading 241 degrees."

The copilot looked Grüber's way.

"Ernst, we aren't going to try to land without gear, are we?"

Grüber shook his head.

"No. We'll have to ditch. But we may as well try to make it within swimming distance of shore."

Thirty minutes later, they could see the distant shadowed shape of land and, on the far horizon, a cluster of lights, which the navigator identified as the town of Hamilton.

"It might be defended," Grüber said. "What's on the southwest side of the island?"

The navigator checked his chart.

"Not much, from what I can see here."

"Fine. Then we ditch off the southwest shore, close as we can. Let's overfly it first."

They came in low, only a thousand meters up, and all hands looked as the water flashed by beneath them. It looked clear, with no telltale white foam, no indication of rocks or reefs.

Grüber touched his throat-mike.

"Crew, strap in. I'll come in as shallow as I can, but this is going to be rough."

He cut the big jet bomber around in a wide circle, barely banking, giving everyone time to get secured. They completed the circle and came in low, the sleeping island a dark shadow off to their right.

"Three hundred meters, Captain. Two fifty. Two hundred meters."

The copilot called out the altimeter readings. From what he could see through the shattered windscreen Grüber could be a thousand feet above the sea, or he could be a hundred – he simply couldn't tell.

"Fifty meters."

They were a bit low, and Grüber wanted to touch down closer to land. He rolled on the throttle, adding thrust.

A vague shadow of black crept in from the land side.

"Schmidt – lights."

The copilot turned on the searchlights and a hundred spots of fluttering white appeared, just in front of the plane.

"Birds! Help me pull up."

Both men pulled back on the yokes, but the bomber streaked on into the flock of startled herring gulls.

There was a muted pop from the bowels of the aircraft, and the plane yawed swiftly to the right.

"Bird strike! Number One's out. Two's out. Three."

Grüber pulled all six throttles all the way back, reducing the thrust to nothing, but he knew as he did it that it was already too late. The sea was wobbling crazily and coming up fast in the lights, the aircraft canting, spinning like a giant boomerang.

He touched his Bible and squeezed his eyes shut.

BOOK ONE

CANANDAIGUA LAKE

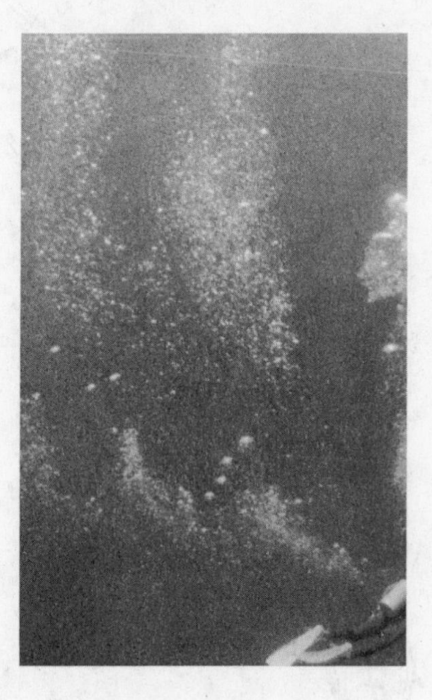

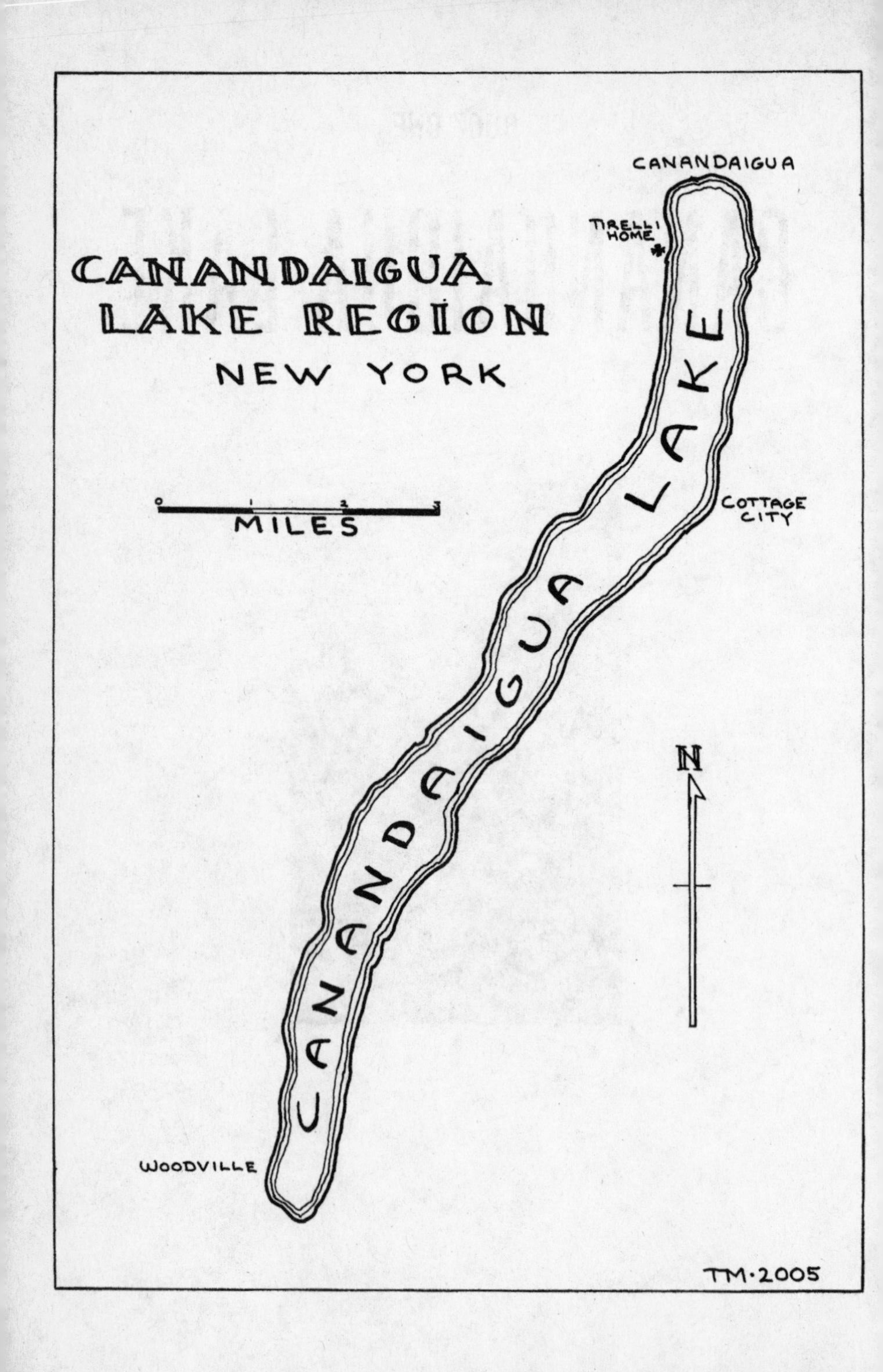
CANANDAIGUA
LAKE REGION
NEW YORK
CANANDAIGUA
TIRELLI
HOME
0
1
2
3
MILES
COTTAGE
CITY
CANANDAIGUA LAKE
N
WOODVILLE
TM·2005

CHAPTER ONE

DECEMBER 24, 1999
OUTSIDE AQUADAS, COLOMBIA

Sprawled in rotting leaves and moss at the base of a banyan tree, camo greasepaint on his face and a ghillie suit covering his body, Beck Easton blinked the sweat from his eyes and marveled at the fact that even drug lords celebrated Christmas.

At least this drug lord did: Raul "Gato" Ortega, also known as "Gato Gordo," although never to his face, convicted in absentia on seventeen counts of murder, three of them Colombian judges. And those were just the marquee crimes, the ones a Colombian court had deemed serious enough to merit his departure from the land of the living. Easton had seen Ortega's full jacket: extortion, bribery, theft, kidnapping, fraud, assault, and enough instances of trafficking to fill up several pages of single-spaced type. It was an amazing list; one had to wonder how, in just thirty-five years of life, the man had found the time to break that many laws. Then again, with the single exception of Ortega's marriage, duly licensed and recorded in Columbian records, virtually nothing the man had ever done was legal. It made Easton wonder whom he'd killed to get the house.

The house, a sprawling, terraced Frank Lloyd Wright–style villa, was perfectly situated on a rapids-dotted bend of the Rio San Sebastian, 587 laser-range-findered yards upstream from where Easton and his partner lay. So still, so perfectly camouflaged that a man could walk within six feet of them and never suspect they were there, the two men had been watching the place since well before dawn. Every once in a while the glass patio doors on the house would open and someone – a servant or a couple of women or a pair of giggling teenagers – would step out, and the barest hint of "White Christmas" or "Feliz Navidad"

would waft down the lush, green river valley. But other than that, there'd been nothing but birds and insects for eight hours. In two hours more, the light would be too low to see through a 20X spotting scope.

Sweat trickled down Easton's temple, into the crease at the corner of his eye. He blinked but did not rub, did not take the chance of putting a flesh-colored streak into the jungle greasepaint.

"Maybe he's not home," said Alvarez, Easton's partner, the one with the rifle, an M40A1 hand-built by the Marine Corps Weapons Training Battalion in Quantico, Virginia. It was the same weapon issued to Marine Corps snipers, only Alvarez's rifle bore none of the WTB's markings, not even the Remington serial number on the original Model 700 action.

"He's home." Easton let his voice nod for him. "This is his chance to show off. Lord of the manor."

"Well then, maybe he's not coming out."

"He'll come out. We've got it from two sources that he's afraid the house is bugged. His people sweep it twice a day. But on a day like this, lots of people coming and going, he's worried that maybe somebody leaves a pair of ears behind. Not just the law; the man's got competitors. So if he wants to discuss business, he'll do it out on the patio, let the river noise mask the conversation. And he always discusses business at these parties. That's why everybody shows up. You don't show, you might miss a nice, fat deal."

Alvarez stretched, slowly, no quick movements. "So what's keeping him?"

His voice was low, hardly a whisper.

"It's Christmas Eve," Easton said. "He's drinking eggnog."

The sun was setting behind them when a glint of light showed at the back of the patio. A man walked out, followed by another, and Easton bent to his scope.

"Okay," he said. "Man leading is Number One, and man following is Number Two."

The distant figures paused, Number Two lighting Number One's cigar. Easton thumbed on a ruggedized iPAQ Pocket PC and checked a surveillance photo on its screen, comparing it to the first man on the patio.

Identical.

Easton's chest tightened. He said nothing.

Low light. Distance. Simplest thing in the world to claim no positive ID. No ID, and no shot, and no kids lose their father on Christmas Eve.

"Still checking," he whispered.

Then what happens? Another team has to infiltrate, run all that risk. And some other kid might lose a father – a kid who's not the child of a convicted murderer.

Off in the jungle, a tree frog trilled, signaling the coming evening. Easton shook his head just a touch, throwing the sweat from his eyes.

"Number One is our – our primary," he finally whispered. "Stand by. Checking Number Two."

He tapped through a series of head-and-shoulder photos, stopping on the fourth one. "Two is – a secondary. Cousin of Ortega. Okay – they're tight. He'll move toward him when he falls."

Alvarez didn't reply. Easton could hear him inhaling and exhaling in long, slow drafts, slowing his heartbeat, getting ready.

"Checking the range," Easton said, his voice steadier now. He bent to the scope again and looked at the telltales, two strips of brown nylon tape hanging from bamboo poles that he and Alvarez had placed at 250 and 500 yards the night before. The first tape was hanging slack, and the second was lifting and falling in a light southerly breeze.

"Wind's same as before," Easton told his shooter. "Range is hot. When you're ready."

Alvarez bent to the ten-power Unertl on his rifle, and Easton returned to his spotting scope.

Despite what the movies would lead one to believe, the man behind the rifle was almost always the more junior member of a sniper team, and this case was no exception. This was Alvarez's fifth mission, but Beck Easton's fourteenth. And because it was his fourteenth, he could hear the hundredth of a millisecond beat between the trigger break and the rifle report, and when he heard the report, he did not jump.

He stayed at the spotting scope instead, following the tiny, fleeting gray contrail of the .308 caliber bullet as it rose, fell, and drifted a full seventeen inches to the left on its journey downrange.

"One is down," Easton said, and Alvarez was working the action already, breathing in and holding it as the rifle cracked again. Sure enough, Number Two turned, moved toward his fallen cousin, and walked directly into the path of the second round.

"Two is down," Easton said, his voice still low. "Time to move."

Spotting scope and rifle in their arms, the two men slithered slowly backward, melting into the foliage behind them. They did this until the house was no longer visible. Only then did they rise to their feet and stow their ghillie suits in a rucksack on Easton's back.

They did not run. They took turns moving until they reached a trail. Then they moved swiftly, one after the other, Easton leading. They came to a faint rub mark on a tree and turned off into the undergrowth, following a compass heading to a second trail.

The two alternated between trails and cross-country. Behind them, they heard the shouts of men searching, but these faded quickly, and they covered the last twenty kilometers in silence, moving steadily, pacing themselves.

They got to the landing zone at midnight and slept in shifts until morning, when a Colombian Army Huey came clattering in from the south. Easton popped purple smoke as planned, the helicopter settled for the briefest of instants, and the two green-clad men swung themselves aboard. Moments later, they were skimming the jungle canopy, hurtling toward Bogotá.

As the helicopter slowly gained altitude, Easton closed his eyes and settled back against the grimy web netting of the seat. There was a tap on his knee, and he looked up.

It was Alvarez, hands cupped around his mouth. "Hey! I just thought of something!"

"What's that?"

"It's the twenty-fifth," the sniper said, tapping his day-and-date watch. "Merry Christmas."

CHAPTER TWO

DECEMBER 26, 1999
THE INSTITUTE FOR HOLOCAUST STUDIES, BERLIN

Walking through the darkened halls of the Institute's research center, Ysrael Gröen noticed a light burning in a study carrel at the back of the archives.

These young people. The retired sociology professor shook his head. *They walk off and leave the lights burning with never a thought to the expense.*

But his irritation vanished when he neared the carrel and saw the familiar dark mop of hair, capped by a simple black yarmulke, much like Gröen's own, bowed over a yellowed, weathered set of papers. Gröen cleared his throat, and the thirtyish man in the carrel looked up, his bearded smile instantly warming the old man's heart.

"Dr. Gröen," the younger man said, scooting back his chair.

"Sit, Yusef Mendel. Please, sit. And how many times do I have to tell you? To a scholar such as yourself, my name is Ysrael Moishe. We are colleagues, after all."

"I live for the day when we shall be," the younger man said, the barest traces of a Munich accent still there in his university-refined German. "But I have many years of study before that shall be the case."

The old professor smiled. So deferential a young man—how many of his peers could take a lesson from this studious young Jew, who not only attended *schul* every single *shabbes,* but joined Gröen's own minyan every weekday morning when the young man's studies found him in Berlin? The tefillin at the break of day and the yarmulke all day long: those were the things that reminded a man who he was, the marks of a man who took his faith seriously.

“You are working late,” Gröen said.

“You know what they say: ‘A good Sunday makes a good week.’ ”

Gröen nodded. Growing up, he had heard his father and uncles say the same thing. “So tell me, Yusef Mendel, can Rachel and I expect you for dinner on *shabbes*?”

The younger man looked genuinely crestfallen.

“It will be my loss,” he said. “I will be in the north on Saturday, at my uncle’s.”

“More research on the aircraft factories?”

“Yes.” The young man nodded slowly. “The more I find on this, the greater the tragedy becomes. So many of our people died underground, in factories that never saw the light of day, just to give cheap labor to the Nazis.”

“Not just us,” the old professor said. “Gypsies too, and university men, and even some Christian pastors.”

“Of course, you are right. But they forced us to build the very tools with which they intended to destroy us. It is a story that must be told.”

And it would be, Gröen knew. Among the close-knit community of Holocaust historians, Yusef Mendel Benjamin was becoming recognized as a well-published, rising star. That was why institutes such as this opened their doors to him, gave him free rein to access their archives as he saw fit, to requisition state records as his research required.

“Well then,” Gröen said, “perhaps next week?”

“God willing.” The young man smiled. “God willing, I will be there.”

The man in the carrel sat, waiting and listening, heard the distant latch of the stairwell fire door and mentally counted the steps—down the stairs, through the ground-floor fire door, across the lobby, and through the double-door entryway.

At the end of a double row of file cabinets, there was a narrow pillar-window, and he went there now, standing back from the window as he watched the old professor stop at the curb, look both ways, and then cross the quiet street. The old man walked to the corner and waited. Three minutes later, a streetcar made its stop; he got on, and he was gone.

Moving quickly now, the younger man returned to the study carrel, moved aside the papers he had spread on the desk, and picked up three old, tattered, manila envelopes, each stamped "STRENG GEHEIM" in ornate red script. He switched on the monitor on a computer workstation he already had running, having watched the administrative assistant type in her password late in the previous week, and spent the next hour scanning the contents of the envelopes into a temporary directory that he'd created on the desktop computer. Then he copied the contents of the directory onto a set of five ZIP disks, deleted the temporary directory, and shut down the computer and scanner.

That finished, he hefted the three envelopes, thinking—trying to gauge what posed the most risk.

The envelopes each had catalog numbers, identifying them as being among the more than 500 kilograms of documents that he had requisitioned from the Bundesarkiv. If some fastidious German clerk audited the collection upon its return, the files would be missed if he removed or destroyed them.

By the same token, if he replaced the files there was a chance that someone might discover the same things he had, hidden among the documents preserved from Hermann Göring's wartime Luftwaffe headquarters. Yet, in the more than half a century since the war ended, no one else had, which meant that it was a prudent wager that no one else would, at least not in the next year or two.

And that was all the time he needed. A year. Two at most.

He returned the files to their cardboard shipping boxes, initialed the chit that authorized their return to a warehouse outside of Aachen, and put the ZIP disks in his valise. Then there was only one thing left to do.

He turned out the lights before leaving the office.

He took a streetcar to the edge of the financial district, to what had once been Berlin's Jewish quarter back in the 1930s, before Jews had first been encouraged to leave, then threatened, and finally forcibly removed. A few of its old residents had returned after the war, and he lived above the business of one of them, a bakery that kept his tiny studio apartment smelling faintly of yeast and, from five in the morning until nearly noon, of freshly baked pumpernickel and rye.

He had chosen the apartment partly because people would think it quaint that a Holocaust researcher would choose to live where the Jews used to live. But mostly he had chosen it because the apartment next door was rented by a merchant sailor who was gone most of the time, away on a ship somewhere in the Adriatic, the Bosporus, the Mediterranean.

The first thing he did was to back up the ZIP disks onto the hard drive of his laptop—the only computer he owned, because he traveled often. The five disks took up five gigabytes of memory, nearly half the hard drive's total space, and almost all the memory available to him, but they fit.

He thought absently about this as he padded shoeless into the apartment's kitchen area to start the tiny espresso machine brewing. All the computer magazines said that larger hard drives for laptops were just around the corner. Twenty gigabytes, thirty—maybe even more. But that was how these computers were. You bought something, and something new popped up, and then you started to hear about something even better on the horizon. He suspected the manufacturers did it intentionally—planned obsolescence, the old automakers' trick. But for now it didn't matter. The files fit on the hard drive. He could take them with him when he traveled. That was all that mattered.

He put the ZIP disks into an old-fashioned steel floor safe, spun the dial to lock it, and went back into the kitchen, where the espresso machine whistled and steamed as if about to burst. He had friends whose imams said that drinking caffeine was a violation of the will of God, but he didn't have an imam at the moment and hadn't even unrolled his prayer rug in more than a month. That would be very hard to explain – a Jewish Holocaust researcher on his knees on a Persian rug pointed toward Mecca. So he didn't worry about the coffee. Besides, Muhammad had never written a word about coffee – it hadn't been known in the Prophet's time.

The researcher took a sip and nodded to himself. He liked coffee. He liked lots of things that would have gotten him a raised eyebrow, maybe more, back home where the words of the Prophet formed a wall that encompassed one's whole world. That was well and good for those within that warm, safe womb. But out here, to the soldiers who lived among the unfaithful – for that was how he thought of himself, as a soldier – one did what one had to do to blend in. And if what one did brought the added benefit of some pleasure, some comfort? Then what of it? God was good.

Sipping the hot, thick espresso, he sat at his computer and clicked the icon for Internet access. That was another advantage of where he'd chosen to live – it was close enough to the business district to have access to a T1 broadband cable, giving him the same high-speed access enjoyed by the banks and corporations of the city's center. He had no phone line in this apartment – just the cable, which also brought him television, and a Qualcomm digital mobile phone for those rare events when he wanted to make a call.

His Internet home page popped up – it never ceased to amaze him just how fast these broadband signals were – and there, as he expected, was an Instant Message from Mohammed, his cousin and his contact back in Saudi Arabia.

Ahmed bin Saleen, the little box on the screen read in the elegant filigree of Arabic script. *Are you there?*

Ahmed bin Saleen tsked. He was not overly worried about electronic eavesdropping; the encryption program running in the background of his instant-messaging service was supposed to be state-of-the-art, used by brokerage houses and banks. But even so, any fool could have broken in here, hacked past his password on the laptop, seen this message box waiting for him, and wondered, "What sort of German Jew reads Arabic? And what sort of German Jew has a name like 'Ahmed bin Saleen'?"

It was sloppy fieldcraft, but Mohammed was older than he, and it would be impertinent of him to point it out. So bin Saleen set his demitasse cup aside and typed, *Here my cousin. Here and well. And you?*

I am well, by the grace of God, came the reply. *But worried about you. You are late.*

Bin Saleen rolled his eyes. That was so typically Mohammed – tapping his foot and pointing at his watch, even when he had to use a keyboard and a satellite to do it.

I was delayed, bin Saleen typed. *But I have news.*

And then he told him the news: what he had discovered in the archive materials, and what the implications could be.

He finished typing and waited nearly a full minute before a reply began scrolling down the screen.

Ahmed bin Saleen, are you certain of this? Do you have it from another source, as well as the one you have discovered?

Bin Saleen sighed.

I had another that I was cultivating, but have not yet gotten close enough for confirmation, so ...

Bin Saleen sighed again.

No, he typed. *I have only this source.*

The screen stayed still for half a minute.

Two sources would be more reliable.

Bin Saleen's sigh became more of a grunt.

And our children's children could be in Paradise by the time we wait for other sources to materialize. This is from Göring's own files. From the top-secret files taken from the offices of the Field Marshall himself!

This time, the reply did not take long at all.

You have searched long and hard for such information, my cousin. And if this thing exists, as you say it does, we still do not know where it might be. For it to be of use to us, we must determine the disposition of your discovery. Certainly further investigation is in order. Why not pursue your second source?

Bin Saleen closed his eyes. He hated it when his cousin was right. *As you wish*, he typed. *But to date, all of my contact with this person has been by email, and I believe that I have gotten as much information as I can in that fashion. To learn more, I will have to return to America.*

New type came up on the screen. *Do you need new papers?*

Bin Saleen shook his head as he typed. *Just give me the set I used last time. I have no reason to believe they have been compromised, and the identity matches what I have used with this contact. Make certain that my American account, the Visa card, has plenty of funds available. And have our people leave me an American-licensed car and some clothes ...*

He leafed open a world atlas and checked it ... *at the airport in Toronto*, he finished.

I will do that, his cousin typed back. *But be careful in the land of the Great Satan, my cousin. Guard yourself well, and go with the peace of God.*

His peace to you, bin Saleen typed back. *Pray for his faithfulness.*

He paused for a moment and added one more line.

Allahu akbar.

God is great.

CHAPTER THREE

DECEMBER 28, 1999
SAN FRANCISCO INTERNATIONAL AIRPORT

It had been a long, hard day of travel for Beck Easton—first a midnight jump by military Citation jet from Bogotá to Guantanamo Naval Air Station, in Cuba; then ninety minutes of debriefing, done over chow in the commandant's private mess, only it hadn't really been chow for him, because he'd been talking the whole time. After that had come a shower and a change of clothes, then a spine-rattling ride on the jumpseat of a C-130 from Guantanamo to Pensacola, followed by a hop on an unmarked Bell Jet Ranger helicopter from Pensacola to Mobile, where he got on a Pinnacle Airlines commuter flight that arrived in Memphis at 7:26, just as the sun was coming up. By then, Easton had been ready for lunch, but that was two and a half hours too early for the airport's Interstate Barbecue joint, so he'd settled for coffee and a bagel at the WorldClub, a thoroughly unsatisfying trade. Then he was back on an airliner, NorthWest Airlines this time, stopping over in Minneapolis, where he was able to grab a fast-food breakfast sandwich before catching the flight into San Francisco.

Altogether, it had been travel of the most fatiguing sort, a total of six flights and four time zones, lots of bony airliner seats (the web jumpseat on the C-130 had been little more than patio furniture), and the lady sitting next to him from Minneapolis had coughed and sneezed as if determined to infect the planet.

Easton did not have to join the cattle-call in the bag-claim area; that was one consolation. He had one carry-on and his laptop case, and the carry-on contained little more than the clothes he'd been wearing when he left San Francisco. Everything he'd worn in Colombia had come from a United Nations of military

clothing—French Foreign Legion combat fatigues, Spanish combat boots, the ghillie suit made with British materials. At least the Italian underwear had been comfortable, a quantum leap from the Austrian army skivvies he'd worn on a previous sortie, durable boxers that felt as if they had been designed by teams of automotive engineers. But none of it had been American, and none had been marked with his name.

He walked directly to the black-suited man with "MR. EASTON" hand-lettered onto a small dry-erase board, shook hands, and walked out with him to a waiting Lincoln Town Car. The black-suited man put the carry-on bag in the trunk while Easton did the egalitarian thing and got into the front seat.

Neither had spoken yet. That didn't happen until the driver had gotten behind the wheel and started the car on its way, down San Bruno Avenue and then south on US-101.

"How'd it go?" The driver asked it without taking his eyes off the road.

"Principal and a secondary." Easton stretched and gazed up, through the sunroof, looking at nothing. "Bogotá's happy."

"Yeah. I got that much from the briefing summary." The driver took his eyes off the road, glanced over at Easton. "Rough trip?"

Easton nodded.

"How'd Alvarez do?"

"Who?"

"Alvarez. Your shooter?"

"Oh. Fine. He's thorough, competent ... Good field skills."

They passed a pair of leather-clad bikers on chopped Harleys, engines rumbling as the Lincoln swept by. The driver glanced at the motorcycles, and then at Easton.

"I think I hear a 'but' coming."

Easton yawned, ran both hands back through his hair, and shook his head. "It's not the kid, Bill. It's me. When the target appeared? When I was confirming him? I almost didn't do it. I almost called the mission."

"Not enough light?"

"No . . . I had enough light."

The driver shot him another look. "Then why?"

"Because there wasn't any distance there, Bill. Because it felt like murder."

Now the driver took his eyes off the road and really gave Easton a look. But he didn't say anything, not about what he'd just heard. He reached into the pocket on the back of Easton's seat, instead, taking out two file folders. One was plain beige. The other was stiffer, edged with black-and-yellow panic tape. Moving into the left lane, setting the big, black sedan on cruise control, he handed the folders to Easton.

"Here's the deal you negotiated in Alabama."

Easton opened the plain one first, glancing over two identical sets of contracts and signing both in the same place, just above the notary seal. He put one in the document pocket of his laptop case and left the other one where it was. Then he opened the other folder, the marked one, and took out a picture of an African-American man who looked to be in his late forties.

"This the guy I met with?"

"Yeah. Name's Tony Grogan. He's CIO for a company called Dixie-Tel. Mobile telecommunications startup that just landed a big federal service contract. Your deal with him is for three years, with an option to renew for a second three at the original fee plus twelve percent. Software and a support package, exactly what your strategic team developed, only the renewal percentage is a little sweeter than what anybody'd hoped for. Not a bases-loaded home run, but a home run nonetheless. You're a hero."

"Again." Easton's voice came out even flatter than he'd intended.

The driver gave him another look, then reached down, turning down the air conditioning.

"So." Easton tapped the picture. "Where'd I meet with this guy?"

"His offices on the twenty-third. Then you got together yesterday at Snearly's, a local steak place, to have lunch. Receipt's in the folder. You shook on the deal there and went back to his place to sign so his notary could witness it."

"I prepared the documents myself at the business center in the Courtyard?"

The driver nodded. Their "legend"—the complicated cover story that covered practically every aspect of Beck Easton's overt life—always had Easton staying in a Courtyard by Marriott, ostensibly for the airline miles, but actually because the floorplans tended to be similar from one location to the next.

"Okay." Easton closed the folder. "What did I do on Christmas Eve and Christmas?"

"You rented a car and drove over to Pensacola, went diving with some old Marine buddies."

"Don't I wish."

"You've dived there before, right?"

Easton nodded.

"I did some system evaluations there on my way back from the Bahamas a couple of years ago. If anybody asks me, I can talk about enough dive sites to account for the time."

"Good." The driver looked at Easton again. "You know it isn't, Beck."

"Isn't what?"

"Murder." The driver said it as he merged onto Route 85 south, the signs saying, "CUPERTINO/SANTA CRUZ." The country was getting hillier.

Easton looked at the driver.

"I don't know, Bill. When I first went to Annapolis, I had these glorious ideas about combat. Then I heard from people who had seen action, and they assured me that it was never glorious. Then I got my commission and I went in the Marines, and I learned what an advantage the element of surprise could be, especially for a small land force. Then I went to Coronado, and they taught me that the best action is the one where the enemy never gets the chance to respond – that, if somebody has to die, you want all those somebodies to be on the other side. And that all made sense to me. But in what we're doing now? Dressing up in some other country's fatigues and going in and shooting a guy – probably an unarmed guy – on his patio during his Christmas party? I mean, I can understand the rationale for it, and I can see that the world is a better place without him. But when we pulled the trigger, it felt like murder, just the same."

The driver's knuckles whitened visibly on the steering wheel.

"You're tired," he said.

Easton nodded. "Roger that. But there's more."

The driver said nothing. He glanced up at the rearview mirror and then to the left, at his sideview. Easton glanced back, over his shoulder. The road was clear.

"When we landed at Gitmo, we went into the base commander's mess for a debrief, and there was this young Company case officer, a guy who couldn't have been more than twenty-four or twenty-five. Which is perfectly all right with me – you've got to give green people field time if you don't want them to be green forever. But this guy was mouthy, and he was pronouncing things like 'Santa Fe de Bogotá' in this silly university Spanish with this Castilian lisp that would get the tar beaten out of you if you ever tried using it in Cartageña. You know what I mean?"

The driver snorted and nodded.

"Anyhow," Easton said, "I was getting to the part where I was describing how we extracted, when this kid speaks up and asks, 'Wait. You shot and then you left?' So I tell him, 'Yes, sir. After the second subject was down, we immediately began our egress, as we were only about half a kilometer from the residence, and Ortega had a number of security people on site.' And then this kid asks, 'Well, then how did you know that your mission had been accomplished?' So I tell him that I watched both hits through the spotting scope. And *then* this guy tells me, 'Well, Major, spotting scopes foreshorten; you can think you have a good hit, but the bullet might only be halfway there. They drop on the way there, you know. It might look like you've got him, but maybe you only hit him in the knee.' Can you believe that?"

The driver shook his head. "A guy who was sitting in his daddy's rec room watching *The Simpsons* when you started doing this stuff ... and he has the nerve to lecture you on ballistics?"

"That's apparently what some of the senior staffers thought. They're trying to get back to the debrief, but this kid has to keep hammering on it, going, 'I just want to know why *he* thinks we got the guy.' 'We.' As if he'd even been in the same country when it happened."

Easton exhaled and watched the landscape rolling by.

"There's a protocol for things like this, Bill. A civilian wants to go all stupid on you, you call him 'sir' and let him go stupid. And that's what I should have done. But I didn't. I leaned over the table and got right in his face, and I said, 'Tell you what, junior. You see Gato walking around at any time? Now or in the future? You just let us know, and we'll go back and whack him again for free. No extra charge.'"

The driver looked Easton's way, eyebrows high. "'Whack him?' You said that?"

Easton nodded slowly. "Oh yeah. Which, in my mind, makes me as much of a jerk as the company kid. And the worst part is that, in a brief over coffee and eggs, this guy did what five years of getting shot at never did. He got me to lose it—lose it so bad that the senior OIC sent everybody out of the mess and apologized to me. A two-star—apologizing to *me*."

The Lincoln's air conditioning came on, its fan going up a level.

"I know," the driver finally said. "I, uh—I got a report."

"Well, there you are."

The driver thumbed a button on the wheel, fiddling with the cruise control. "We've been pushing you over the last year. Maybe you need some time off."

They rode in silence for five miles.

"This used to be all orchards," Easton said. "You know that?"

"The Santa Clara?" The driver nodded. "Sure. My old man was born out here. Talked about a blossom festival they used to have here, back before the war."

Easton looked at the office parks and housing tracts skimming by on either side of the road.

"Maybe you're right. Maybe I need some time off."

The driver shrugged.

"You deserve it. Take a few weeks."

"I was thinking of more than that."

A green sign went by. White lettering spelled out WINCHESTER BLVD., 1 MILE, KEEP RIGHT.

"Okay," the driver said. "Take a month. The division can work around you for a month. Your company can too. You deserve it. That's a pretty fat contract you're bringing home there."

Easton looked down at his laptop case. That was another part of his "legend" – his cover story. A businessman of Easton's stature – a businessman of Easton's *supposed* stature – wouldn't travel over the holidays unless the payoff could justify the inconvenience. So the contracts explaining his absences tended to be higher at times such as Christmas, Easter, the Fourth of July. The cover trips weren't always sales calls. Sometimes, if the agency knew about a mission far enough in advance, the story back at Easton's company would be that he was teaching an applications seminar. Other times, they'd be told that he was trouble-shooting a system for a customer.

Easton thought about the seven-figure contract in his case. He pictured the face of the man he'd supposedly met with to earn that contract. Then he thought of the faces that were really responsible for this windfall – the faces of the men he'd watched die through his spotting scope.

Easton pursed his lips. He tapped his fingers on the armrest. "Actually, Bill, I'm thinking of taking more time than that."

"Sure. How long do you need?"

"I don't know. Maybe the rest of my life."

"What?" They were on the exit now, and Bill appeared task-loaded, trying to drive and look at Easton at the same time. "Come on. You don't mean that."

"Believe it. I'm serious as a heart attack."

"You've been doing this a long time," Bill admitted. "Longer than I was. You want out of the field?"

"No." Easton shook his head. "I want out of the whole deal."

"You're not serious."

"No?" Easton looked at him as they made three quick turns – Winchester, then Lark, then University. They were headed toward a low building: gleaming glass walls and modern curves. "Did you notice how you didn't ask me why, Bill? We both know why. I want my life back. I want to do work that means something. Something positive. I don't – ever – want to build another hide, never want to call another shot, never want to debrief another action. I'm done, Bill. Finished. I'm cashing in."

They pulled into a lot dotted with cars – Japanese imports, mostly, but a surprising number of new Oldsmobiles. The Town Car pulled in next to an older but well-polished Land Rover Defender 90.

"Listen." Bill put his hand on top of Easton's seatback, a gesture that seemed kindly, rather than territorial. "You're tired. You said so yourself. It's been a tough sortie. Why don't you call it a day, go home, and just kick back until after New Year's? Enjoy what's left of the holiday, maybe go down to Monterey and get in a dive or two. You know how that always gets you back on keel."

Easton ran his fingers back through a thick shock of sun-streaked brown hair.

"This isn't fatigue, Bill. It's more like ... I don't know. Disgust. Really, it's time to bail."

The two men got out of the car and stepped to the back. Bill, obviously the older of the two in the sunlight, got Easton's bag from the trunk and set it in the Land Rover.

That done, he turned to Easton and cut short a sigh. "I'll check in with you after the New Year, okay?"

"I'm not changing my mind, Bill."

They shook hands; not another word passed between them.

For a moment, standing there, watching the shiny black car drive away, Beck considered doing just as his National Security Agency "handler" had recommended: get in the Land Rover and go home, pick up a fresh quart of milk on the way, and just fall into bed, 3:20 in the afternoon or not—sleep off the fatigue of the day.

But he couldn't shake the truth that the kid in the debriefing had brought to the surface: the fact that he hated his job.

Scratch that.

Hated his life.

Which didn't seem like much of a note to go home on. So he decided to go on into the office for a while. If nothing else, he had a contract in his case that needed to be logged in, or stuck in a safe, or something.

CHAPTER FOUR

The company was called "Blue Corner Technologies." It was named after a dive site in Palau – named at a time when expectations were high and hope was buoyant, and it had seemed appropriate to Easton and his two partners to name their new company after the most beautiful place they'd ever seen.

Easton and his partners, another Marine and a Navy SEAL, had all been requisitioned by the National Security Agency for assignment to their Special Operations Division, all three ostensibly moved to the reserves of their respective branches of the service and dotted-lined to the Central Security Service, an NSA sister agency that routinely employed active members of the armed services.

While the three men had been strangers to one another at the outset, they'd been as alike as brothers. All had field and underwater experience, all had been to sniper school, all had pilot's licenses, all were accomplished divers and small-boat operators, and all spoke at least one foreign language. And once with NSA, all three had been given world-class educations in computer software architecture with an emphasis in cryptography and information security.

The company had been needed as a cover. Nothing more. Just a company from which the three of them could, one at a time or en masse, very occasionally leave for a day, or two, or three – on business.

Like being in Mobile, closing the deal on an Internet security package with a cell-phone company, when you were actually in Colombia, killing a couple of drug dealers.

Profitability hadn't been a priority when Blue Corner had been founded. Realism had, though, so the three military men had each been sent off for additional schooling. For Easton, it had meant a very intensive year at Berkeley, studying C++, Java, Smalltalk, Objective C, and software systems design – everything needed to not only pass as, but function as, a senior commercial software architect.

That was one of the cleverest parts, actually. Blue Corner Technologies – a corporation that helped businesses keep their information systems secure – created the sorts of cryptography and security that the NSA broke daily in the pursuit of *its* mission. And given their excellent training, their native intelligence, and the fact that their livelihoods had hinged not one iota on the success or failure of their cover project, the three partners had taken any number of measured business risks. This had quickly established Blue Corner as a leader in its field, and made it one of the few dot-com startups that had not only survived the Bubble, but thrived.

That was the good part. That was before the first of Easton's partners had died, ostensibly in a rail accident while away in Europe on business.

There'd been a problem with the will in that case, and a third of the company's stock had gone to the man's ex-wife. Easton had asked the agency to intervene; cover or not, he'd grown to care about the company, and it irked him to see part of it go to an outsider over what amounted to a legal accident.

But once they'd done the usual painstaking background check on her, the planners at NSA had actually liked the way the ex-wife had seemingly shown up out of the blue. It had, they'd told Easton, the appearance of real life – as if, simply because they'd started the company, nothing about it could actually be real – and it added a valuable layer to the cover story. And in their opinion, Blue Corner was still firmly in the hands of its agency operatives.

Not a major problem, they'd told him – two-thirds of the stock had rested with Easton and the other founding partner.

Who went missing fourteen months later.

A previously undiagnosed aneurism was the official version of events and, as so often happened in the field, poor judgment came back to haunt the operation; this time it was a brother who got the stock. A brother whose attorney was a law-school classmate of the ex-wife's attorney, and the next thing you know, using the weight of a 66.6 percent vote, they hired a Wharton MBA who didn't know Java from jumper cables to come in and, for all intents and purposes, run the company.

Easton walked up a broad sidewalk to the bronze-glassed doors and stepped inside, where the receptionist greeted him by name and added, "Rodney has been asking for you."

Rodney.

As in "Rodney Vanderbilt."

The MBA.

Easton forced a smile.

"Well, let him know I'm here, please."

He walked across a lobby with a sunken conversation pit lined with beanbag chairs, past another set of glass doors, and into a large area full of cubicles, some decorated with Christmas lights, some with fabric kites suspended above them, one with a department-store mannequin peering over its top.

Programmer country.

Easton passed a cubicle where a young man in sweatpants, a T-shirt, and flip-flops was strumming furiously on a Fender Stratocaster guitar. The guitar was not plugged in, but Easton could barely make out the sound of Dick Dale's surf-guitar classic, "Miserlou."

Easton didn't stop to ask why the programmer wasn't working, because he knew that, appearances aside, the programmer *was* working. Folks who wrote code marched to a very different drum, like the guy at the other side of the building who couldn't fix a particularly pesky bug until Easton had gotten him a wooden Piper Cub propeller – a wooden propeller from that particular model of that particular airplane – to hang over his computer monitor.

Things like that drove conventional businesspeople, like the Wharton MBA, nuts. But things like that were also one of the reasons that Blue Corner was solidly in the black long after many of its Silicon Valley neighbors had dried up and blown away. As the ornate, gold-scripted sign on the wall of the programming group's lounge proclaimed, "HGWSC" – Happy Geeks Write Superior Code.

Easton walked into his office, switched on his computer, and checked his email. He had just over two hundred new messages, the majority of them from Rodney. Then he lifted his phone, heard the stutter-tone that indicated he had messages waiting, and dialed his access code.

"Your mailbox is full," a female voice said flatly, and he put the phone back in its cradle.

Officially, the office was on holiday, although there was a skeleton crew working through on a couple of crash projects. Easton typed up a quick memo outlining the parameters of the account that he had supposedly just landed, and sent it out to his senior programming staff, together with a notice to meet on the project on their first day back in the office.

He'd just done that when there was a quick triple-tap on his doorjamb. He looked up.

One thing you could say about Rodney Vanderbilt; he *looked* like a Rodney Vanderbilt. Hair combed back in a Prussian-blonde swoop from a high forehead, glinty blue eyes, a nose that looked as if it had been drawn with a ruler. He was in his "casual" uniform: cashmere turtleneck under an open sport coat, pleated dress slacks, small silver cell phone clipped sideways on a skinny leather belt, and Italian loafers with little brass beads on the lace-ends. He was wearing one of those wafer-thin wristwatches, and he looked at it pointedly before he spoke.

"Beck." Rodney liked to speak in a near-whisper, make people lean forward to catch the words. "We've been trying to reach you."

"Oh, I'm sorry." Easton tried his best to actually look sorry. "My cell battery died the first day away. I forgot the charger."

"Well, don't you ever check voice mail?"

Easton tried to picture himself dialing up Blue Corner on a satellite phone from the snipers' hide, checking his voice mail.

"You're right," he said. "I should have. Sorry. This new client took a lot of hand-holding."

Rodney brightened. "Oh, that's right. Mobile. How'd that go?"

"Great. We hit our numbers, and then some." Easton tapped his laptop case. "I'll have Gloria make you a copy of the contract when she comes in on Monday."

"Excellent." Rodney took out a small silver PDA and scribbled on the screen with the stylus.

Easton watched him for a moment. Then, clearing his throat, he asked, "So what was it?"

"Pardon?"

"Why were you trying to reach me?"

"Oh—yes." Rodney tapped on the PDA display and slipped the device back into an inside jacket pocket. "We've got a workspace designer coming in today. I'd like you to meet with her."

Easton took a deep breath. "A what?"

Rodney walked further into the office and sat without being asked. "A workspace designer. Ergonomic interior office design. Someone who plans the overall workspace, selects the office furnishings, and arranges them in the most productive manner."

Beck clicked his mouse and closed Outlook. "So we're hiring people to buy desks now?"

"She's provided as a service by the architect."

"The architect?"

"The one we hired to add the new programming wing."

"I see." Easton slid the folder out of his notebook case and put it into the side drawer of his desk, the one that his assistant would check for pending contracts on Monday. "So we're going ahead with that anyhow."

"Beck– "

"We don't need it, Rodney. That's overcapacity–it wastes money, and it kills companies."

"Beck ..." Rodney had this almost comically perturbed scowl that he adopted when he went into lecture mode. "We've been over this. The board has decided ..."

The board. Meaning the windfall twins–the Marine's ex-wife and the SEAL's brother.

"... the board has decided that we need to show we have the capacity to expand as our business grows. It's a measured risk."

This coming from a man whose idea of risk was mixing fabric textures, or wearing burgundy shoes with a tan belt.

"Well," Easton said, shutting down his computer. "I don't agree. And I've already shot most of my holiday on business, so I'm thinking of calling it a day. If you don't mind, I'd rather you deal with the interior decorator."

"Designer."

"Hmm?"

"Workspace designer. There's a difference."

"Sounds as if you've got a handle on it," Easton said as he got up.

"But you're the chief software architect. Surely you can better direct her than I."

"Rodney ..." Easton stepped around the desk and went to the door. "The woman's designing offices that are going to stay empty for the foreseeable future. How much direction could she possibly need? Please. Just–handle it."

"But I– "

"And Merry Christmas, Rodney."

The man blinked. "Oh, of course. Happy holidays."

Easton nodded and left. He wanted to vent, but he'd already done enough of that. And besides, he couldn't blame Rodney;

the man was a weasel, but he was a weasel following orders. The plans to take Blue Corner public had been drawn up by its absentee owners, and there was nothing that Easton, with his thirty-three-and-a-third percent ownership, was going to be able to do about that. Nor did he much care anymore. He had signed a non-compete agreement, turned down successively larger bonus offers to lock himself into a key-man contract, and now he was just waiting for the day when Blue Corner went up on NASDAQ, so he could sell out, cash in — or at least cash in to the extent that the SEC would let him cash in — and walk away.

Easton kept walking. The programmer in sweatpants had set his guitar aside now and was keystroking furiously, his nose a mere three inches from the computer monitor. Easton went down the carpeted corridor, opened the glass doors into the lobby ...

... and stopped.

Standing at the receptionist's desk was the most beautiful woman he had ever seen: long, chestnut hair, warm green eyes, and a smile that made him forget he'd just traveled the better half of a hemisphere in a single morning.

"Mr. Vanderbilt?"

"No." Easton crossed the lobby to shake hands. "I'm Beck Easton."

"Oh." Her smile went up a notch as she shook his hand. Her hand was small, warm, and gentle. "Of course. You started all this, didn't you?"

Easton just smiled.

"My name is Angela Brower," she said. "I'm the workspace designer. I know that Mr. Vanderbilt was hoping you'd be able to join us today. Does this mean you will?"

"It does," Beck said. He quietly slid his keys back into his jacket pocket. "I can't tell you how much I've been looking forward to this. Come on back."

CHAPTER FIVE

NIAGARA FALLS, NEW YORK

The watch list of the day included white Ford and Chevy vans, horse trailers, and a flatbed load of coiled steel. The vans were probably being used to smuggle some sort of contraband, cocaine and heroin being at the top of the list, while the horse trailer and the steel load were no doubt reported stolen somewhere in Ontario and presumed to be headed south. Which was only logical as, once one reached a certain point in Ontario, the only thing north was howling wilderness.

Lori Calderazzo had been working the United States Border Patrol's Peace Bridge customs station for six years. That was long enough to have learned to ignore the fact that one of the seven natural wonders of the world, Niagara Falls, was just a stone's throw west of the station. It was also long enough to have figured out why certain things got posted on the daily watch lists, and which vehicles would merit inspection beyond the cursory once-over that most vehicles got at the world's longest open border.

And the blue Toyota Celica pulling up to her inspection booth raised no red flags with her at all.

Its headlamps were not on in the waning daylight, which meant that it was not a Canadian vehicle – Canadian law required daylight driving lights, low-powered headlamp bulbs that would remain illuminated whenever the ignition was switched on in the car. But it also lacked a front license plate, which meant that it was not a New York vehicle, either. Probably Michigan, she guessed, and she looked up at the wide-angle mirror on the end of the island in front of her booth.

Sure enough, it was a blue plate with white reflective numbers. A Michigan plate. The kind you got if you didn't want to

spring for one of the special theme plates that so many states were putting out now. State university plates, lighthouses, state birds, Olympic teams, special causes – it seemed as if every state in the Union had at least half a dozen commemorative license plates. Lori's brother, who'd just started with the state police earlier in the year, griped about it because he couldn't tell at a glance, as they'd done when they were kids, where a vehicle was from. But after six years on the eastern end of the Peace Bridge, Lori could tell the lion's share at a glance, even backwards in a convex mirror. And the standard Michigan plate was so common that it was an absolute no-brainer. There was a decal in the rear window as well: YTIƧЯƎVIИU ƎTATƧ ƎИYAW.

That would be Wayne State, which Lori vaguely recalled as being near Detroit. Maybe *in* Detroit ...

The driver looked somewhat Semitic, but that didn't ring any alarm bells, either. Lots of Lori's daily traffic looked somewhat Middle Eastern, somewhat East Indian, somewhat Asian. When you lived in the melting pot of the free world, you got that.

The driver rolled down his window and smiled. Lori didn't smile back. It was part of her training – get the traffic to take you seriously.

"Good afternoon," she said. "Place of birth?"

"Ypsilanti, Michigan." Pronounced correctly – "ip," not "yip."

"What was the purpose of your visit to Canada, sir?"

"Just passing through. I'm on my way to my girlfriend's place, in Rochester."

Lori paused. It was another part of her training. Give 'em a moment; nervous people would say something just to fill in the silence. But this one just sat there, waiting.

"Did you buy anything while you were in Canada, sir?"

"I got a hat at the Falls." He got it off the passenger's seat and showed it to her: a red, beretlike thing with a symbol on the front that was half star and half maple leaf. "Other than that, just gas and fast food."

Now she allowed him a smile.

"Thank you, sir. Drive carefully."

Ahmed bin Saleen drove the Toyota away from the border station and reminded himself that he was in America now: the speed-limit postings would be in miles per hour.

Americans. They were so smug, so cocooned in their pathetic Disney-fantasy country. It still amazed him that he could just waltz in from Canada without showing so much as a driver's license. It was the same throughout most of the West now. Especially if one presented oneself as a citizen, the border checks had become laughable and, in some cases, nonexistent.

And yet, even if he had been entering a country that still took borders seriously – someplace like Israel, for instance – he was used to such things, and his reaction would have been much the same as it was now. He wasn't breathless, his skin wasn't clammy, and his heartbeat was completely normal. To be any calmer, he'd have to be asleep.

Under normal circumstances, he *would* be asleep. It would have been ideal to have flown first class, or even business class, on the three air legs that had gotten him to North America – to catch some good, solid sleep on the planes. But he always flew coach – flight crews tended to remember their business- and first-class customers. Bin Saleen had left Berlin at five in the morning, taking the train to Cologne, where he'd spent twenty minutes in a studio apartment he'd rented there, leaving all traces of his Yusef Mendel Benjamin identification, exchanging it for that of a British engineer on temporary assignment to Ford of Europe's headquarters.

From there, he'd caught a mid-morning KLM CityHopper from Cologne to Amsterdam, followed by a regular KLM flight to Heathrow. After that, he flew Air Canada to Toronto, where he left his British passport and wallet in a luggage locker, along with the luggage he'd brought from Cologne.

The key to the car had been taped to the top of the left rear wheel well, just as it always was. A wallet containing his American identification had been left in the console, along with a Canadian twenty-dollar bill for the parking-lot fee and three hundred dollars in circulated American currency. Bin Saleen had driven the Queen Elizabeth II Way – what Canadians called the QEW – down to Niagara Falls and crossed at the Peace Bridge because it saw so much tourist traffic. He had actually been glad for the fatigue – it had given him that authentic look of a traveler who'd been behind the wheel all day.

The hat had been the icing on the cake, as he'd known it would be. He pulled into the New York State welcome center, just after the currency exchange and the duty-free store, got out, souvenir hat in hand, and walked up to the highway map posted there in a glass bulletin case. The route he'd planned back in Toronto still looked like the best one. He had two hours to get to the appointment he'd set up by email, and he could drive that in the allotted time, easy.

He was one step closer.

Almost.

Ahmed bin Saleen dropped the hat into a trash bin and got back into his car.

CHAPTER SIX

BLUE CORNER TECHNOLOGIES
LOS GATOS, CALIFORNIA

"... full-spectrum halogen task lighting."

"Full spectrum?" Easton cocked his head.

"Sure." Angela Brower nodded. "You know how people look so sickly under fluorescent lighting? That's because most fluorescent lamps are discontinuous spectrum – they have very little red in the light, and red is the color that brings out flesh tones. So full-spectrum lighting creates a much more inviting work environment, and using task lighting, rather than depending on overheads, relieves eyestrain for your programmers. Actually, it's a good recommendation for just about anyone who's looking at a computer screen most of the day."

"Interesting."

Easton glanced out the window as she looked up.

"Well." Rodney Vanderbilt drummed the table lightly with his fingertips. "You two seem to have everything well in hand. If you don't require any further assistance from me ..."

"Thanks, Rodney." Easton forced a reasonable facsimile of a smile. "I think we're fine."

"Then ... if you'll excuse me, I'll be going. I've an early day tomorrow with the accountants."

"Oh." Angela looked genuinely distressed. "I hope we haven't kept you too long."

"Not at all." Rodney was up and moving toward the door. "Beck, thanks for staying for this."

He left and the conference room door shushed shut behind him. From narrow vents around the perimeter of the conference room, air conditioning began to sigh down on Easton and the designer.

Angela Brower glanced over at Easton. "Am I keeping you from ...?"

He shook his head. "No. You're not keeping me from a thing."

"But Rodney just said ..." She studied Easton's face for a moment and then broke into a blush and a smile, both at the same time.

"Oh, my ..." She fanned herself with her hand and then glanced at her watch. "Wow. It's after six, isn't it?"

She smiled at Easton and began collecting her papers. "I'd—uh—better be going too. I have to meet with the people from Herman Miller in the morning; they're on short hours over the holidays."

"So are we. What would you say to continuing our talks over dinner tomorrow night?"

She canted her head ever so slightly. There was a small lake behind the Blue Corner building, a lake with small pines planted around it, and the low sun was playing off the water. It set a bright halo around Angela's hair as effectively as any fashion photographer's key lighting.

She opened a Franklin Planner and tapped on a page.

"Uhm ... Friday morning, I have a meeting with your architect at six." She smiled. "Fortunately, I'm still running on Eastern time. Still, I think I'd better just do dinner in my hotel room Thursday."

"All right. Friday, then."

Her smile got larger. "Friday's New Year's Eve."

"It is." Easton smiled back. "Are you previously engaged?"

"No. But aren't you guys going to be up manning the screens or something? You know. Guarding against that Y2K thing everyone's talking about?"

Easton laughed. "Some of our clients might have trouble getting into their offices Monday morning if they didn't upgrade the microprocessors in their door locks. But as for their PCs and their mainframes?" He shook his head. "If they're clients of ours, they were ready six months ago. And if they aren't, there's nothing we're going to be able to do for them until they're back in the offices next week, anyhow."

Angela lifted her head. She brushed her hair back and her eyes met his. "And this dinner is to talk about ..."

"The office."

Now it was her turn to laugh. "And this isn't something we can handle with a memo?"

Easton did his best to look as if he was mulling that over. "Well, it's pretty hard to have a dialogue via memo."

"Yes? And we need dialogue?"

"Sure. Up until five minutes ago, I didn't know what full spectrum task lighting was."

Angela rolled her eyes. "I'm not sure you do yet."

"All the more reason."

"All right." She laughed and made a note in her planner. "Six o'clock?"

"Seven."

She glanced up. "I'll need to make this an early evening."

"That's fine. My need to greet the sunrise on New Year's died several years ago."

"All ... right." She made another note in her planner and then paused, pen still on the page. "Where should I meet you?"

"You're staying at La Hacienda, right?" It was where the company put all its business visitors. "I'll pick you up."

She took a breath and looked up at him.

"It'll save you the hassle of finding a cab," he said. "Los Gatos isn't like New York. You can't just flag one down. And I'll know where we're going."

"Where *are* we going?"

"We're, uhm ..." Easton scratched his head. "I'm sure I'll know that by the time I pick you up."

Angela's face got serious. "I'll need to know what to wear. All I brought with me for evenings is your basic little black dress."

"Trust me. Your little black dress will be fine."

CHAPTER SEVEN

Beck Easton had never been married and had no need for the residential trappings of married life: a lawn that needed mowing, shrubs that needed trimming, and a roof that might eventually leak. But he was well past the point where he wanted to hear bass tracks coming through the wall of a neighboring apartment. So, despite the fact that it added yet another layer to a yuppie image that he detested, he had a condo: two bedrooms, one and a half baths, a great room with fireplace, a finished basement with storage space and his exercise equipment, and a deck overlooking a lily-dotted pond that the developers optimistically referred to as a "lake."

Easton reached up to the old Land Rover's visor and keyed the tiny remote. A growing rectangle of light appeared as his garage door, last one on the drive, crawled smoothly upward. He glanced up at his place as he pulled in, saw the red eye of the smoke detector in the guest bedroom, and stopped the car.

The condo faced south. The afternoon sun faded the bedspread. So Easton kept the blinds in that room closed. All the time. And his cleaning lady knew that.

Easton pulled the Land Rover into the garage, debated leaving the door open for a quick escape, and decided against it. If somebody was in his house, he wanted to know who it was, not give them an easy way to bolt. He touched the remote again and the overhead light flashed five times before the door came sliding back down.

Easton got out and left the SUV's door open. He didn't keep a gun: not in the house and not in the car. California was not the most NRA-friendly place on the planet and a pistol would be too hard to explain to the authorities if the place ever got burgled; gun ownership didn't match his carefully constructed agency legend.

He opened a cabinet in the garage, pushed aside a gas-grill cover and two quarts of motor oil, and put his hands on a Ka-Bar in a sewn and stapled brown leather sheath.

Twelve honest inches of black Parkerized steel and stacked leather grip, the Ka-Bar was the traditional fighting knife of the United States Marine Corps, a crude and nasty brute of a weapon, and the closest thing to a sword that any member of the American armed forces had carried into battle for the better part of a century. But it wasn't illegal, not even in California, and it was widely available to civilian purchasers. Lots of traditionalists thought of it as the ideal camping tool.

Leaving the sheath in the cabinet, Easton turned the knife around and carried it pommel forward, the flat edge of the blade resting against the outside of his forearm.

He unlocked the door with his left hand, stepped into the darkened kitchen, and checked the control panel for the burglar alarm.

It was still armed; Easton keyed in the pass code but left the kitchen lights off. He removed his shoes and walked stocking-footed, heel-to-toe across the tile floor, pausing at the door to the great room to look for reflections in the glass patio doors and listen for anything out of the ordinary. But all he heard was the ticking of an electrified ship's clock on the mantle and the hum of the refrigerator behind him.

Crouched low, Easton took a step into the great room, heard a footstep on the landing above him, and froze. The lights snapped on, there were footsteps on the stairs and Bill Spalding, Easton's NSA handler and his "driver" from the afternoon ride in from the airport, stepped out into the room.

"Man ..." Easton stood up and let his hands fall to his sides.

"I guess I should have left you a note or something," Spalding said. "It's been a long day. When I saw you weren't coming right home, I went upstairs and racked out in your guest room for a while."

He looked at Easton's right hand.

"Is that the way the jarheads are teaching knife-fighting now? You think something's hinky, you just carry the knife in a blocking position? Don't you think it would work a little better if you held it pointy-end first?"

Easton set the knife down on the dining-room table: on the center cloth, where it wouldn't scratch the wood.

"I have a new policy," Easton said flatly, turning back to Spalding. "I don't kill more than two people a week."

Spalding walked past him, into the kitchen, switched on the lights, and began filling a small carafe from a drinking water spigot on the sink. He spooned coffee into a basket, put the basket and the water into a small black espresso machine, plugged it in, and switched it on.

"Make yourself at home," Easton told him.

"I thought Alvarez was the trigger-man down in Aquadas," Spalding said, squinting at the espresso machine.

"I ID'd the targets. I was the one who gave him the green light to shoot."

"Way I look at it, neither one of you guys killed squat," Spalding said as the little black machine emitted a mechanical sigh. "Ortega as much as killed himself when he offed his first judge. You don't pull stuff like that without expecting consequences. And his first judge was something like 1973. Since then—even if you don't count the dealers who kill one another back here and the crackheads who OD—the man's been personally responsible for the deaths of literally hundreds of people. He was way overdue. Mother Teresa would have capped this guy, given half the opportunity."

He opened the refrigerator, got out a quart of milk, sniffed it, and poured some into a measuring cup.

"We've already had this conversation," Easton reminded him.

The espresso machine began hissing and roaring in earnest, and Spalding steamed the milk, building up froth in the clear Pyrex cup. He got a couple of regular coffee cups out of the cabinet, divided the milk between them, poured the espresso in, and then spooned the milk froth on top. He picked one up and handed the other to Easton.

"What? No demitasse?"

"I didn't know you had any."

"You seem to know your way around. I would have thought you'd have brought some with you."

Spalding took a sip of his coffee and shot Easton a look.

"I'm a brown-water squid. Perked coffee in plain white mugs with a pinch of salt. You tell anybody I'm drinking this stuff, you may never be heard from again."

Easton didn't remind Spalding that the NSA man was the only person who'd ever used the espresso machine in Easton's condominium. Easton had never even plugged it in. It was part of the furnishings some agency detailer had equipped the place with as part of Easton's supposed Silicon-Valley background.

"Let's sit down," Spalding said, walking past him into the great room.

"Gee, boss, you don't mind if I take my coffee in there?"

Spalding either didn't catch the sarcasm or he was pretending not to notice. Probably the latter, Easton decided as he followed the NSA man into the living room.

"So ..." Easton settled into a sturdy leather armchair as Spalding sat on the sofa. "What happened to 'I'll see you after the New Year'?"

Spalding turned the coffee cup in his hands.

"Something's come up."

Easton set his coffee aside and shook his head. "What was I doing in the car, Bill? Talking to myself? I told you; I'm getting out."

"I respect that. And this is a good step in that regard."

"What 'step'? I'm not interested in steps."

"You still hold a commission from the Corps."

"Don't give me that. I'm not deployed. I can resign anytime."

Spalding tapped the rim of his coffee cup. "Right. I know you better than that."

"Meaning what?"

"Meaning that you aren't a hothead—aren't the type to go storming off when there's a more orderly way of doing things. And there is, Beck."

Easton looked at the cold, dark fireplace for a moment and then turned back to Spalding. "All right. I'll listen. What've you got?"

Spalding nodded, picked up Easton's remote, and turned on the TV, which came alive with a plain blue screen. Then he put a hassock next to the TV, got a notebook computer out of a black nylon case that had been sitting there, and used cables to connect the notebook to the game ports on the front of the TV. He opened the computer, and as it woke from hibernation, an image appeared on the TV screen: an Arab man, bearded, wearing a genteel version of Bedouin dress—white headscarf held in place by a black corded headband.

"This is Mohammed al Fadli, a suspected senior member of the Shura Majlis."

"The governing council of Al-Qaeda," Easton said.

"Exactly." Spalding nodded. "He's a Saudi, same as Osama bin Laden. Only unlike bin Laden, al Fadli still lives in the Kingdom. He's a distant relative of the royal family and, as he hasn't personally committed any acts against us or a cobelligerent nation, it would be a diplomatic faux pas to try and extradite him."

"I detect a 'but' coming," Easton said.

Spalding nodded. "We have reason to believe he's a planner. At least a planner, and maybe a treasurer. We've got innuendo linking him to several embassy attacks, which is enough to pick him up if he ever comes to the United States for medical treatment or decides to hop a jet and go shopping at Harrods. But so far our boy Mohammed has been pretty smart about not leaving the Kingdom."

Spalding advanced to another PowerPoint image, this one of al Fadli in a business suit. He was wearing a gold Rolex, the wrist bracelet loose. His hair was black, with not a trace of gray, and he was smiling, showing rows of even, white teeth.

"About three months ago, we learned that al Fadli was replacing all the computers in his Jedda residence," Spalding said. "And it's some residence. The dude not only got a Dell; he got a truckload. We intercepted the shipment in Amsterdam, and while it was too many machines to do the full Monty on 'em, we were able to put a fly on his wall. We put in an interceptor chip that records every keystroke he makes into his computers, and then uses his broadband signal to relay them back to NSA in batches at night, while the screensaver's on."

"What'd you learn?"

"Besides the fact that somebody in his house is into porn, and he's skimming the profits on his father's oil business?" Spalding winked. "We've been intercepting regular IMs – instant messages – that he's been sending to someone with a European MSN account. Pretty smart, really, since IMs are so fleeting that they don't regularly get monitored by the major agencies. If we were CIA, we would have missed it. But we aren't the CIA, and we caught the IMs, the outgoing portions, at least, and the recipient has been on the trail of some sort of strategic asset – that's basically what they've been calling it in Arabic – ever since we began eavesdropping. But since we only get al Fadli's side of the conversations, just who he was talking to was a mystery ... until recently."

"What happened recently?"

"Two nights ago" – Spalding tapped his keyboard – "our boy went no-brain and typed the guy's name: *Ahmed bin Saleen*."

Easton shrugged, his eyebrows raised.

"I know." Spalding nodded. "We'd never heard of him before, either. Until we cross-referenced Air Force files."

He keyed his computer and a picture came up on the TV screen: a clean-shaven young man in a military uniform, looking straight at the camera. Under the uniform hat, his hair seemed a bit shaggy—à la John Travolta in *Saturday Night Fever.*

"Our boy is Saudi Air Force, or he was, and he got flight-trained," Spalding said. "And as is the case with most of the Saudi sticks, we trained him. This is the base ID shot we took when he was here, June through November of 1989, and as far as we can tell, this is the only picture that any Western intelligence service has ever gotten on him. The Mossad has files on the leading families from just about every Muslim nation in the world, and they have a ton of information on his family: oil money, two European shipyards, they own a mall, and they're major benefactors of the university there. Bin Saleen has seven older brothers, and some of them play at going to offices, managing their managers. But none of them really need to work to earn their keep. They mostly travel and party. The family has enough cash to keep them in Mercedes SUVs and vacation homes from now to doomsday. So we have to figure the kid, here, has beaucoup bucks too. But neither we nor the Mossad have records on him since he came here to play Steve Canyon. It's a dropped-off-the-face-of-the-earth scenario. The Israelis figured he was dead."

"And now you want me to make him that way for real?"

Spalding shook his head. "You want away from that end of the business; I can understand that. But you've picked up a lot of skills along the way. Not just observation and fieldcraft but a sense for what's in the air. We want to use that. Al-Qaeda is up to something. We can smell it. Now we want you to zero in on this bin Saleen character and learn what it is."

Easton sighed, leaning back in his chair. "It's a big world, Bill."

Spalding nodded and shut the TV off with the remote.

"It just got smaller. We have enough details from al Fadli's end of the IMs—dates and times of transmissions, proximity of IP addresses, and so forth—to narrow the start of your search to Berlin. CIA's got a guy over there in our embassy who thinks he has a lead."

"And he's not following it because ...?"

Spalding shook his head. "Doubtful that this one is gonna stay in-country over in Germany, Beck. Al-Qaeda isn't just one organization; you know that. The name means 'The Database.' It's a support network holding up more than two dozen highly organized groups in more than fifty countries, all over the world. And between his family's money and what al Fadli has been skimming off the company books, bin Saleen has the resources to travel just about anywhere. Including here, where the CIA can't scratch its nose without a letter from the president. But you are not similarly constrained. And I've got a feeling you're gonna rack up some frequent-flyer miles on this one."

Spalding stopped talking and there was a click, followed by silence, as the notebook's hard drive parked itself. The NSA man leaned forward and clasped his hands.

"Beck, if you don't want to do the job anymore, then you have the gratitude of the agency, and of the nation, if it only knew the half of what you've done for it. But there are two ways out of this thing, man. You can take your ball and go home, or you can withdraw gradually. The second route has a heck of a lot more dignity, you know? And it doesn't leave bridges smoldering behind you. Take the assignment—it looks like it might last a bit—and I'll clue the powers that be that you want to call it a day."

Easton sat, arms folded, and thought about that for a moment. "That's all you want me to do? Track this guy down? Find out what he's up to?"

"That's it. No guns, no gear, no engagement. First step is to make a hop to Berlin and meet with the CIA station chief there."

Easton nodded. He hated accepting this, but Spalding was right. Life was like war that way – the organized withdrawal was almost always the better option.

"How soon do I leave?"

"We've got you on a flight leaving San Francisco at oh-six-hundred Saturday."

Easton looked up. "That's New Year's Day."

"What's the matter?" Spalding was smiling. "You got yourself a hot date for New Year's Eve?"

Easton raised an eyebrow. "I could've," he said. "But not with a curfew like that, Dad."

CHAPTER EIGHT

CANANDAIGUA, NEW YORK

"Mister Tirelli?" Ahmed bin Saleen smiled and extended his hand. *You're supposed to be American—act garrulous.* "I'm Andrew Sasri."

Anthony Tirelli looked to be in his late twenties, maybe early thirties: ample pot belly under a Rochester Institute of Technology T-shirt that was too small for it, several days' growth of beard, bushy eyebrows, and black hair sprouting out of his head in thick fingers, as if he had a palm tree somewhere in his lineage. His grayed jeans were gone to scruffy white fuzz at the hems, and he was wearing scuffed Minnetonka moccasins that had thread on the tops, suggesting the presence of beads at some point in the past. That was about all there was to see in the darkness of late evening. There was no porch light burning and the entry-hall light was behind him.

A smile split Tirelli's shadowed face at first, and then his mouth changed to a thin, straight line.

"Uh, no offense man." He shuffled a little as he said it. "But do you have any kind of, you know, ID?"

"Identification?" Bin Saleen touched a finger to his lips. Then he reached inside his jacket. "I have my driver's license. Will that do?"

He slid the Michigan license out of a thin black eelskin card case and handed it over.

The other man held the license up so the light from the entry hall would hit it, looking alternately at it and his visitor.

Bin Saleen let him take his time. He knew that the license looked absolutely genuine, from the picture of the Mackinac Bridge on top to the outline of the state imprinted in reflective gold across its face. There was no reason it wouldn't look genuine; his people had hacked into the Michigan Secretary of State's computer system to get it for him.

"Says here you're from Dearborn," Tirelli said. "The newsletters say you're from Detroit. Where's Dearborn?"

"Suburban Detroit." Bin Saleen smiled a little and shrugged. "Where Ford Motor Company is headquartered."

"Oh, yeah?" Tirelli handed the license to him and stepped back, holding the door open. "Well, sorry to hassle you, man. But you know how it is. I only know you from our emails, and ... newspapers, the government – there's lots of people who'd like to get a look at my files."

"I'll bet."

Bin Saleen stepped inside. The house was old and well built: varnished beams holding up the ceilings, dentate moldings running around the tops of the walls. The furniture all looked to be from an earlier age: upholstered wingback chairs and legged sofas.

But the place was a mess. Magazines and beer cans were piled everywhere, there were pizza boxes stacked in the corner of the living room, and crumbs and threads littered the rugs as if they had not been vacuumed in months. Paper plates, glasses half-full of cola. It wasn't the kind of mess you had after a party. It was the kind of mess produced by a slob, someone who just never picked up.

"You'll have to excuse the place," Tirelli said as they walked back toward the lake side of the house. "It's not mine. Belongs to an old couple who live in Florida nine months out of the year, only come up here for the summer. I'm the caretaker, like Jack Nicholson in that movie ... what's it called?"

"*The Shining.*"

"There you go. *The Shining.* So, you want something to drink? A beer or something?"

"No, thanks." Bin Saleen smiled. "I'm good."

He was willing to sacrifice his dietary laws for the cause. In fact, he liked drinking. But he didn't like beer, it was late, and he couldn't for the life of him imagine eating or drinking in this pigsty of a residence.

"I've got a long drive ahead of me," he said. "Do you mind if we just cut to the chase?"

It was one of his favorite Americanisms. His language teachers had all been instructors at the KGB school that had once readied SVR operatives for foreign postings, and that was their key to success: a practiced and common accent—Midwestern English, in this case—together with the judicious use of slang phrases. That was how you passed for native.

"Oh, sure." Tirelli nodded. "That's right. You're driving down to the city tonight, right?"

He led bin Saleen back to a guest room, where a hollow-core door had been laid across trestles to form a table for a Gateway desktop computer and printer. Several file cabinets had been moved in as well, and this room actually looked rather neat: the bed made, things put away and in their place.

"Let's see, your email said that you wanted to do a newsletter piece on the V-E Day sighting." Tirelli took a folding chair out of the closet and set it up for his visitor. "And if that's right, you've come to the right place ... Uh, what do I call you? Andy?"

"Andrew," bin Saleen said.

"Oh. Sure. Andrew. Well, like I said, you've come to the right place. What do you want to see first?"

"Amaze me."

"You got it." Tirelli put a CD into his computer, moved his mouse, and opened files, talking as he clicked. "Actually, 'V-E Day Sighting' is a misnomer—it happened the night before. But I guess 'V-E Day Eve Sighting' just doesn't have the same ring. You know what a flyway observer is, Andrew?"

Bin Saleen shook his head.

"They're birdwatchers," Tirelli told him. "They track waterfowl migration. What they do is, if there's a decent moon showing, they stay up all night, watching it, and count the number of ducks and geese they see crossing the face of the moon. I guess there's some formula they must use, figuring that, for every bird they see crossing that little bit of sky in front of the moon, that represents 'x' number of birds that were migrating that night."

"Sounds like a snooze." Another Americanism.

"No joke." Tirelli made a final click and brought up a series of thumbnail photographs. "Anyhow, some of these folks set up cameras with telephoto lenses and photograph what they're counting. And all these pictures are scans of black-and-white photographs taken by a flyway observer who was watching in Peterborough, Ontario, on May 6, 1945. I guess he was trying to count snow geese on their migration north or something. His photos looked like this."

Tirelli clicked on one of the thumbnails and brought up an image. It showed the moon, about 90 percent full, and two geese were clearly silhouetted against it. They were flying one above the other, and they covered nearly the entire face of the moon.

"Hmm." Bin Saleen nodded. "That's actually a very nice image, isn't it?"

Tirelli laughed. "It's not typical. Mostly they get ducks' tails, heads, maybe some wings flapping up in front of the moon. This particular guy had rigged up a clockwork mechanism to advance his film, kind of like the World War II version of a motor drive, you know? Guess it gave him a higher number of usable images. And what's cool from *our* perspective is that it gave him this ..."

He brought up an image that showed the same gibbous moon, but had just missed perfectly framing a solitary goose, its head already past the illuminated face.

"Do you see it?"

Bin Saleen bent nearer to the screen. He *did* see it: off to the left of the moon, there was the faintest suggestion of ... something. He could see a tiny speck, like light reflecting off metal or glass.

"It's not very conclusive," he said.

"It isn't. But this is."

Tirelli clicked on the next thumbnail. In this picture, only the tiniest bit of a goose's tail was showing at the bottom of the moon. But that didn't matter. In the center of the moon was what looked like a backward check mark, and behind it ran two gray lines, so close together that they could almost have been one.

"That's amazing." Bin Saleen wasn't acting in the slightest. It *was* amazing. "Can you ..."

"Way ahead of you, Andrew."

Tirelli clicked again and brought up an image that concentrated on the anomaly. This time you could see that it was a chevron-shaped craft of some sort. There was a dot of light at the head of it, and the lines behind were now clearly contrails.

"Did you have it enhanced?"

Tirelli chuckled. "Great minds ... yeah. I have a friend who computer-enhances aerial photography up at Kodak. I asked him to take a crack at it, and this is what I got."

He clicked and the photograph resolved into a crisp image. This time, the dot of light at the head was clearly moonlight refracting through a nose-dome or canopy, and bin Saleen could see the suggestion of turbulent vapor in the contrails—six distinct contrails, he noted.

"You know," he said, "there've been aircraft like that."

As well he knew.

"There have." Tirelli nodded his head. "The Air Force developed some in '47, '48. But not back in 1945. And there's more. This flyway observer kept a log of all his images to the nearest five minutes. This shot was taken at 11:05 on May sixth."

Bin Saleen waited, knowing there'd be more.

"Twenty-five minutes later, an Army Air Corps P-38, being flown into Milville, New Jersey, from Chanute Field in Illinois, is diverted to intercept an unidentified aircraft coming in from the northwest," Tirelli said. "The fighter intercepted it and opened fire on it five minutes later, over Middletown, New York.

"Middletown is like 265 air miles from Peterborough. That craft had to be doing about 530 miles per hour to get there at that time. Nothing in the world flew that fast in level flight at the time. But this thing did. It got there. We've got police logs from a sheriff's deputy who heard machine-gun fire and saw the P-38 chasing something. Something big. And I got this."

He clicked an icon on his computer screen and a voice, an elderly man's by the sound of it, began playing over the computer's speakers.

"It was huge," the voice said. "Maybe ... I don't know ... maybe half a football field from wingtip to wingtip, at least. Maybe bigger. Huge and shaped like a bat. No propellers that I could see. Nothing in the way of an engine nacelle anywhere on it. Just all wing and huge. It was wartime, and we always carried live ammunition back then, even when we were just ferrying planes, so I didn't wait to report in or nothing. I knew this wasn't American, so I made two passes and I'm sure I hit it both times. But it just kept climbing, neat as you please. Pretty soon, we're at my service ceiling, and I can barely keep the nose elevated to aim, but I fired anyhow. I missed, that time. The tracers were coming out white, instead of red, which meant it was the end of the belt, and I could see them falling short. Last time I saw that thing it was still climbing. It looked like it was headed to the moon."

The little progress bar on the computer screen shrank to nothing and disappeared.

"That was Edgar Charles Wilson," Tirelli said. "He was a lieutenant in the Army Air Corps in '45, and he was the pilot who attacked the UFO. Hear the last part? 'Like it was headed to the moon.' Wow. And I got this."

Tirelli clicked and brought up a color picture of an Arctic-jacketed military man standing next to a huge, dented, silver metal object.

Horten drop tank. Bin Saleen was careful not to react, but he recognized it from the blueprints.

"This is the Northwest Territories, Canada. Some anthropologist working with the Inuits up there hears this song about a night bird that makes this sound ..." He imitated a whooshing sound, like a jet engine. "... and they talk about something falling from the sky. This guy's able to date the creation of the song back to five nights after the fourth full moon in 1945, which is close enough to May 6 for jazz. And last year, the Air Force released this photo of unidentified wreckage found near that old Inuit village."

Bin Saleen just kept waiting.

"Nobody brought anything back, apparently, but they said that the metal was lighter than steel and definitely not aluminum."

Titanium. "You're sure these things are related?"

Tirelli arched his bushy eyebrows. He got up, walked to his bookshelves, and came back with a globe, which he set on the floor between the two of them. He held one end of a rubber band in the Northwest Territories.

"The wreckage was found here," he said. Then he stretched the rubber band to a point just northwest of New York City. "And here's Middletown. A line drawn between those two points passes right over Peterborough, Ontario."

"And your conclusions?"

Tirelli arched his eyebrows even higher.

"Remember the Doolittle raid on Tokyo? How they had to launch bombers from an aircraft carrier to be within range? Well, bomber range got better during the war, but it didn't get *this* good. There wasn't a plane in the American arsenal that could have flown from the Northwest Territories to New York without stopping, and Canada was practically nothing but wilderness back then. Still is. There was no place an airplane *could have* landed to fuel, so my guess is that this is no airplane. Not of its day. You've got the wreckage of … I don't know what, maybe the entry vehicle, crashing up near the Arctic, and you've got this big craft that cruises faster than the world's fastest fighter at that time. And just four, five years later, we've got the Air Force test-flying craft that *look* like this."

Bin Saleen blinked. "How do you tie those two things together?"

Tirelli leaned forward.

"Roswell." He whispered it, as if he was afraid the house was bugged. "Teflon, Velcro, the Space Shuttle tiles … we've always figured that was alien technology, reverse engineered. And now we've got the proof. The missing link. I've got proof that we modeled some of our experimental planes after alien spacecraft."

What an idiot. But bin Saleen didn't say it. Instead, he nodded at the computer. "I notice all these files are on one disk. Are you getting ready to make a presentation?"

Tirelli nodded. "Good eyes, Andrew. Yeah, I've got them saving some time for me at the MUFON Symposium's morning session, next month in Palm Beach. I haven't told 'em what it is yet. Just that it would be big."

That could be a problem.

Tirelli cleared his throat. "You won't put anything in your newsletter until March, right? I mean, I'll want to announce this stuff first by myself."

"Oh, sure." Bin Saleen nodded. "But if you could burn me some copies of those images, I'd appreciate it. Here. I brought a blank ZIP disk with me."

He didn't really need the copies. He fully intended to take the original CD with him when he left. But he needed time to think.

"It must be nice, living on a lake like this," he said as the other man opened directories and copied files.

"It's not as great as you think. Like living on a busy street. You get a lot of noise."

"Not during the winter, certainly."

The computer hummed and clicked as it copied the files, and Tirelli shook his head. "You'd think that, but in the winter it gets even worse, must have to do with the leaves being off the trees. Nothing to block the sound. It seems like there's always some dweeb running up and down the lake on a snowmobile. And just this afternoon, I had a bunch of scuba divers out there, not fifty yards off shore, making all kinds of racket with a chain saw."

"Chain saw?"

"They use them to cut through the ice so they can dive. Supposed to be a ferryboat or something sunk out there. The ice fishermen cut holes too, but just little ones. These divers, they make a racket. Seems to last forever. And when they're done, they shove the ice-block back in to fill the hole, but a night like this, with the temperature only down around thirty? It won't freeze over until morning. It's a hazard. Of course maybe, if they make enough holes like that, they'll get themselves one of those snowmobiles. Now *that's* something I wouldn't mind seeing."

Bin Saleen nodded. He was getting an idea.

"You wouldn't even think that ice could hold a person," he said.

"*That* ice? Oh, sure it could. Absolutely. This time of year, it could hold a car."

"Well, you sure wouldn't catch me trying to go out on it. You never do, do you?"

Tirelli lifted one side of his lip. Just one side. "What? You've never been out on a lake in the winter?"

Bin Saleen grinned and shook his head. "I get the willies just thinking about it."

Willies. Another of his former-KGB language instructor's words.

Tirelli stood up. "Get your coat, Andrew. We're gonna give you a whole new perspective."

Bin Saleen drew back a little. "Are you sure?"

Tirelli laughed. "Absolutely."

Good.

"Keep your eyes open, Andrew. Who knows? Maybe we'll see a UFO while we're out here. Be each others' corroborating witnesses."

Bin Saleen walked with exaggerated care. It wasn't necessary in the slightest. The ice beneath their feet was covered with an inch or more of crusty, granulated snow that offered excellent footing, like walking on a gravel path. *Corn snow*, he remembered his language instructor telling him, back in the days when he had never seen snow, except in pictures. But he rocked as he walked. He wanted this fat little American to think of himself as his protector. His hero.

The UFO crack had been just that, of course. The sky was almost completely overcast. There was no chance of seeing anything in the skies overhead. And there was little chance of anyone seeing them out here; little chance of them distinguishing anything other then dark shapes on the ice.

That too was good.

They walked across the creaking lake surface. Off to their left was a rough tripod, three wooden tree limbs leaning against one another.

"What's that?"

"That's where the divers cut their hole," Tirelli said. "They think that marks it or something. As if you'd see something like that in a snowstorm."

Bin Saleen walked nearer to it.

"Be careful." The concern was evident in Tirelli's voice. "That block won't be frozen over. And believe me, that water's deep. Deep and freezing."

Pretending to ignore him, bin Saleen walked up to the tripod. He moved his foot, the one furthest from Tirelli, and knocked one of the tree limbs away from its footing. The whole thing came clattering noisily down.

"Clumsy me," he said, stooping.

"Andrew, leave it." Tirelli was walking over to him purposefully. "Really, man. That's dangerous."

"I just need to set this back up." Bin Saleen picked up one of the limbs. Carefully settling his full weight over his right foot, on the solid lake ice, he put the left one on the ice block bobbing in the triangular hole, making it look as if he were standing on it.

"Andrew – don't step there, man." Tirelli was trotting toward him now.

Bin Saleen dropped the limb, making it look as if he was losing his balance. "Oh, no ..."

Tirelli dashed forward and offered bin Saleen his hand.

Just as the Saudi had known he would.

Ahmed bin Saleen took the American's hand. Braced himself. Pulled ...

CHAPTER NINE

DECEMBER 31, 1999
NEAR SEASIDE, CALIFORNIA

"I can tell you where we're going if you want, but it'll be a lot more fun if it's a surprise."

That's what Beck Easton had said to Angela nearly an hour earlier. And of course she had opted for the surprise.

Now she was beginning to wonder. He seemed nice. But wasn't that what everybody had said about Ted Bundy? And what did she know about Beck Easton anyhow? That he was a software architect, that he was one of the founders of Blue Corner, and that he had this air of casual charm about him. That was about it.

That and the fact that he seemed very confident about ...

... Well, everything.

It was dark outside the car now. Although it wasn't even really a car. Beck drove a vehicle that looked as if it belonged on the Serengeti Plain. Rough and ready. Although Angela did have to admit that the old Land Rover had been meticulously cared for. It looked as if it had just rolled off the dealer's lot.

And Beck was wearing a tux, simple and black—and a tailored tux at that; you could tell by the way it fit. Complete with black cummerbund and tie. Which had caused her some concern over whether the "little black dress" was sufficiently formal, although his smile and his compliments had quickly set her mind at ease.

Now she wondered if Ted Bundy had ever worn a tuxedo. She thought she could recall seeing a picture ...

The landscape was certainly causing her some concern. Beck was driving her down a stretch of highway as desolate as anything she'd ever seen. The only lights were their own headlamps.

No, that wasn't quite true. Far off to the west, Angela could see a distant point of white, almost a dust-speck of light. A ship perhaps? Could they be driving next to the sea?

"Where are we?" She hoped her voice didn't sound as weak to him as it did to her.

"P.C.H.," he said. And when she didn't respond to that, he smiled, adding, "Pacific Coast Highway. That's the Big Blue out there, to our right: Monterey Bay."

"Oh." Angela cupped her hands around her eyes and held her face close to the door glass, trying to see details, beach or waves. But all she could see was blackness, a great void with the stars overhead and, far off in the distance, the ship. "I bet it's beautiful in the daylight."

"You'd win that bet." Beck's voice sounded softer now, mellower. "A few miles further south, you start running into one of the most famous stretches of wild coastline left in California. Artists come from around the world to paint it, and it's got some of the biggest surf in the world. This your first time here?"

"Uh-huh."

"Well, welcome. Where's home for you?"

"Chicago. And St. Louis before that."

Beck moved into the left lane and passed a farm truck, the only vehicle they'd seen in several miles.

"Do you still have family in St. Louis?"

"Not any longer. We all moved north at once. My dad took a job teaching at Wheaton College, in Illinois. I'm a PK."

"PK?"

Now it was Angela's turn to smile. "'Preacher's kid.' My father was the teaching pastor at a community church down in Missouri. Wheaton's a Christian school—Billy Graham went there."

"Oh. I see." Beck reached up and fiddled with the rearview mirror. Angela wondered for a moment whether he was thinking about turning around and taking her home. That had happened once in college, when her roommate had fixed her up with a blind date and neglected to tell the guy what her dad did for a living.

But Beck didn't turn around.

"I used to live in the Midwest," he said instead. "Michigan. Little town called Lake Orion. My dad was an autoworker."

"Are your folks still there?"

"Buried there. Remember Flight 255? The one that crashed on takeoff at Detroit in eighty-seven? They were on it."

Angela felt her heart fall. For a moment, she had no words. The SUV crested a rise, and lights—a coastal town—showed ahead of them. Finally, she found her voice.

"Beck ... I'm so sorry."

He reached over, squeezed her shoulder—an electric moment of warmth as he did that—and he smiled. "Forget it. You didn't know. And we're here."

"Where?"

"Monterey."

They drove down a hill and into town. Beck turned, and Angela saw a sign that read "Cannery Row." Who was the novelist who wrote about that? Was it Steinbeck? They pulled up in front of a wharfside building, and a parking valet was opening her door. She looked up at the lettering next to the building's entrance.

"You're taking me to dinner at the Monterey Aquarium?"

Easton shrugged and grinned. "I hear the seafood's really fresh."

Easton pretended not to notice all the heads turning as he and Angela walked into the aquarium. Not that it was easy to do; they made a nice couple—her in a simple black dress that sent all the attention to her smile and her eyes, him in the tux he'd gotten for an industry awards show a year earlier, a genuine

Armani tuxedo, the only Armani anything that he owned or ever intended to own. The two of them weren't Barbie-and-Ken, but they did look right together. A nice couple.

A couple? Where was that coming from? After all, he'd known her for what? Something like three days? Or, to be perfectly frank, maybe something more like five hours—spread out over two days?

Steady, chump, Easton told himself. *You've been a bachelor for thirty years, come March. Let's keep both feet on the ground.*

"Beck Easton! Please, ease my broken heart and tell me this lovely creature is your sister."

Easton smiled at the familiar Dublin accent.

"Hello, Ian." He offered his hand. "Angela Brower, this unrepentant apple-polisher is Ian Joyce—no relation to the writer, although he will do his best to convince you otherwise. He's also our host this evening. And Ian, may I ignore your politically incorrect comment and present Angela Brower, a business colleague from Chicago?"

"Business colleague?" The little red-headed man's face lit up. "Well. Hope does spring eternal. Welcome to Monterey, Angela."

"Ian's company makes the proprietary servers used by half the dot-coms in the Valley," Easton told Angela, grinning. "And then, ten months later, he tells us that what he just sold us is obsolete, and we have to buy new."

"Well," the host elevated an eyebrow, raised a hand, palm up, and nodded toward an aquarium viewing wall: dark blue water teeming with shadowy kelp and anchovies. "Someone's got to feed the fish."

"Seriously, we appreciate your having us here for it, Ian," Easton said. "I can't think of a better way to welcome the New Year."

The Irishman beamed as he patted Easton on the shoulder and turned to welcome some new arrivals.

"He seems nice," Angela whispered. "A little over the top, but nice."

"Wrong on both counts." Easton laughed. "He's better than nice; he's outstanding. And he's not just over the top. He took the top with him."

A young woman came by with a tray, and Easton smiled, accepted two flutes of champagne, and handed one to Angela.

"Have you known Ian long?" She held the glass in both hands, the way one would hold a rose.

Easton smiled. "He was the very first supplier to come calling back when my partners and I were still renting office space at the AmeriSuites. And you know how the worst thing that can happen is when your friend leverages the friendship to open a business relationship?"

Angela nodded.

"Well ..." Easton raised his glass, paused, lowered it again. "Sometimes, one of the best things is when a business relationship turns into a friendship."

"You two lunch together, that sort of thing?"

Easton laughed. "After our company built the building? The week we were moving our equipment in? Ian and his team were there, helping us, and he and I were, I don't know, writing a backup protocol, and he started talking about climbing Yosemite ... It was the reason he came here to go to college, way back when. He knew Berkeley was just a few hours from the Valley. I said I'd like to try it sometime, and the next thing you know, we're at Camp Four, bouldering. Two months after that, I'm climbing the Nose Route on El Capitan with him."

"El Capitan." She looked down into the bubbles of her champagne. "Doesn't that take several days to climb?"

"It took us two long ones. We slept in hammocks hanging from bolts." Easton lifted his glass again and then glanced down. "Don't you like champagne?"

Angela blushed, ever so slightly.

"I don't know." She smiled. "I've never tried it. I've never tried ... well, anything. I don't drink."

Easton could actually feel his eyes widening.

"I'm sorry." He accepted her glass and shook his head. "I just put that right into your hand, didn't I?"

He signaled to one of the catering staff, gave the young man the two glasses and asked him to bring them a couple of Perriers with lime.

"So," Angela said as a *mola-mola* – a huge ocean sunfish – drifted behind her in the giant floor-to-ceiling aquarium, "this man makes you sleep in a hammock hanging from bolts, and you still give him your business?"

Easton laughed.

"I got even." He smiled at the memory. "I taught him to dive, and two months after that, he and I were shooting video of mako sharks off Catalina. Bluewater diving, and no cage. And wouldn't you know it? Ian jumped into diving with all the enthusiasm he showed for climbing. Don't get me wrong – he still climbs. But in a way, that shark dive was the genesis of this ..."

He motioned, palm up, taking in the string quartet playing in an alcove, the aquarium window-walls, and the growing crowd of businesspeople in formal dress.

"Ian's not only a diver now. He's one of the leaders in the movement to preserve Monterey Bay. And in addition to renting this place for his New Year's Eve, I can guarantee you he's making a hefty donation."

The catering person brought them a couple of mineral waters and Easton waited until Angela had tried hers. Then he asked, "Okay. What's that look?"

"What look is that?"

"The you've-got-something-on-your-mind look. What are you thinking about?"

"Oh, just that you have an interesting friend ..."

Oh, wonderful, Easton thought to himself.

"... and that *his* friend is even more interesting."

Easton found himself momentarily speechless – a rare condition for him.

"Uhm – Ian never structures these things," he finally said. "No speeches, no agenda. Until the music starts, around ten, you can sit and dine whenever you want. Shall we?"

"Sure."

So they did.

Angela was relieved to sit down to dinner. Not that she was famished, but as long as they were dining, there was significantly less chance that she'd be sticking her foot in her mouth again.

... *His friend is even more interesting.* What in the world was she thinking? Could you get drunk just breathing the vapor from champagne? Why not just load herself into a slingshot and throw herself at the man?

This wasn't her. It wasn't anything like her. She was usually contained, reserved. What was it her younger brother had once told her? "No offense, Ang, but most of the guys I know are scared to death of you."

And deep down inside, something about her liked that distant, coolly professional image. So what was there about Beck Easton that made her shed brain cells in his presence?

Dinner was seafood, the server being quick to add that they would be dining on Atlantic salmon and lobster, species not even remotely related to those on the other side of the aquarium windows.

Not that Angela noticed that much about the dinner. Beck was a polished conversationalist, which is to say that he got her talking about herself, her family, her passions, her dreams. He did not remain completely silent as she spoke, but when he talked, it was usually to rephrase what she'd just told him and then to ask a question that further drew her out.

Dessert came—one of those artistic creations with sauce drizzled in patterns on an iced plate—and the string quartet was replaced by a small jazz combo: a signal, Angela supposed, that the party was about to begin in earnest. It wasn't the sort of music one would dance to. Which was fine by her; while she didn't have any particular feelings one way or another on the subject, the churches her father had pastored in her girlhood had all frowned on dancing, so it wasn't a skill she'd ever mastered.

"It'll be nice to have a non-noisy New Year's Eve," she thought aloud.

"How's that?" Beck asked.

"Oh, in Chicago, it seems like everyone has to blow a horn or something to welcome in the New Year. At least it's not like Detroit. I visited a girlfriend from college there a few years ago. And I swear that, at the stroke of midnight, everybody that owned a gun was outside, shooting it straight up into the air. I had this vision of ducks and geese falling out of the sky. I guess I've always thought it would be nice to have a New Year's moment with no Dick Clark, no Times Square—nothing to hear but the sound of God's creation."

"Really?" Beck glanced at his watch—this big brass-and-silver, black-faced diver's thing that he wore. "What say we get out of here?"

Angela searched his eyes with hers. Part of her—the greatest part of her—felt they might be drawing closer to a my-place-or-yours moment, and dreaded it. But a very tiny part of her thought the same thing and wanted it, hoped for it. And that was the part that really frightened her.

"Sure," she finally said. Because that was all she felt she could trust herself with—one syllable.

If the parking valets thought it odd that the well-dressed couple was leaving the party well before midnight, they didn't say it.

And if Angela noticed that they headed out of town to the south, rather than north—the way they'd come in—she didn't show it. She simply sat, church-mouse quiet, as Easton drove, occasionally checking the luminous dial of his watch.

He made it to the gravel turnout with ten minutes to spare. Shutting off the engine, setting the parking brake, he got out, walked around to Angela's side and opened the door, extending his hand.

She accepted it gently, tentatively. As she got out of the car a sea breeze lifted her hair like the caress of a ghostly hand.

"Hold onto my arm," Easton told her in a low voice. "The path's a little stony in places."

They walked for a few minutes in silence under a moonless sky, the stars scattered across the heavens above them like a spray of glowing sand. Angela gripped Beck's arm a little more closely than she needed to—she'd never been one to go for stiletto heels.

When they stopped, she had the sensation of a great gulf of nothingness beneath her feet. Almost everything beneath the canopy of stars was pitch-black, although she could just barely see a pale, luminous line moving far, far beneath them.

"This is Point Sur," Beck told her, his voice hushed. "It's one of the most famous spots on the coast. The surf is breaking on the shore about two hundred feet below us, and there are these huge rocks standing offshore that it's breaking around, as well."

He raised his left hand and looked at his watch.

"And," he said, "it will be midnight in exactly ten seconds, nine, eight, seven, six, five, four, three ..."

Beck fell silent, and the soughing of the wind crept in to fill the void. Far beneath their feet, Angela could hear the surf as it crashed against the rocks and fell back upon itself. But other than the beating of her own heart, that was all she heard. There were no party noisemakers, no sound of celebration, not even a ship's horn from out on the ocean.

Nothing but the sound of God's creation.

She took it in for perhaps half a minute. Then she turned to Beck, pulled his face down to meet hers, and kissed him, gently and slowly, on the lips.

"Thank you," she told him.

In the starlight, she could barely see him smile.

"You do great thank-yous," he whispered.

So she thanked him again.

Every fiber of Easton's being wanted to see Angela to her room, to drop every hint that he wanted to be asked in. And every shred of common sense told him not to do it, that it would be the wrong thing to do.

Wrong—that intrigued him. Easton believed in ethical, if competitive, business practices, and he had the character of a career Marine officer. Still, it seemed to him that it had been years since, in his day-to-day comportment, he had seriously considered the ramifications of "*right*" and "*wrong.*" And it felt good.

So he saw Angela into the lobby and stopped there.

"I had a wonderful time," she told him.

"As did I. And we got so much work done on the floor plans, didn't we?"

She laughed. She had a pleasant, easy laugh. "Well," she said, "I suppose I'll be seeing you at Blue Corner."

"You will. And will we see each other socially again?" He could see her take a breath.

"I ..." Her voice was barely a whisper. "I would like that very much."

Now it was his turn to take a breath. "I have to leave tomorrow ... I'll be gone for ... I don't know. A few days."

“On New Year’s Day?” Her brow furrowed slightly. “What sort of job makes you travel on New Year’s?”

Easton thought about that. “One I’d like to be shed of,” he told her frankly, wondering even as he said it why he was telling her this.

“Thinking of a change?”

He nodded.

Angela smoothed the lapels on his tuxedo, touched his cheek and lifted her head toward his.

He took the hint and kissed her good night.

“Have a good trip,” she whispered. “I’ll see you when you get back.”

CHAPTER TEN

JANUARY 1, 2000
EL JIDDAH, SAUDI ARABIA

On the widescreen TV, CNN was replaying images of the previous evening's ball-drop in Times Square. Americans in pointed paper hats lifted glasses and mugged the camera as they sang.

"Look at them." Mohammed al Fadli gestured at the screen with his left hand. He would not honor the infidels by pointing at them with his right. He helped himself to another fig from the teeming silver platter between their cushions. "Their women bare their arms and faces as if they were sister or mother to every single person on the planet. And in the freezing cold, no less. How is it that God lets such animals survive?"

Ahmed bin Saleen said nothing. He knew the question was rhetorical, and he knew that when his cousin got going on the Americans, a single comment would never suffice.

Sure enough, in less time than it takes to say it, Mohammed had picked up the subject and was worrying it again.

"We waste opportunity after opportunity," he said, shaking the half-eaten fig at the TV screen, which had now switched to an image of swimsuit-clad revelers gathered on a pier in southern California. Even having such an image on one's television set could get you seventy lashes at a Saudi police station—not that there was a policeman in the Kingdom who would dare to arrest Mohammed al Fadli. "Just think what a kilo of *plastique* and a timer, set for midnight, could have done for our cause."

"It would have killed perhaps one or two hundred Americans," bin Saleen said. He shifted to find a more comfortable position on his cushion. Like so many wealthy Arabs, his cousin Mohammed had one room in his house that was decorated to resemble—however vaguely—the interior of a Bedouin tent. Heavy fabrics were

draped down from the ceilings and out to the walls, the floor was covered with a huge hand-woven rug that had been commissioned specially in Iraq, and the tables rose only the breadth of two hands from the floor. That no Bedouin prince had ever traveled the desert with a fifty-inch color plasma TV lashed to the back of his camel was a triviality that was apparently lost on Mohammed. But he did conform to the tribal concept of seating, which was a camel hair–stuffed cushion rather than a proper chair with legs and a back. And to bin Saleen, who had lived most of his adult life in western countries, it was an uncomfortable way to sit, even though retirement to a "desert room" was an unmistakable signal among Saudis that matters of business and honor were about to be discussed.

"Exactly." Mohammed let his hand fall to his thick, robed thigh with a slap. "We could show these demons that they do not enjoy nearly the level of security that they seem to feel they do. We could teach them the fear that should beset all who do not follow the teachings of the Prophet."

Bin Saleen helped himself to a fig, the sweet, heavy taste reminding him of his boyhood. "And then," he said after he had cleared his palate with tea, "they would do as the Israelis have done. They would increase the scrutiny at their borders and put armed soldiers in their airports, fortify their critical assets."

"And what of it?" Mohammed dismissed the thought with a wave of his hand. "The Israelis are still vulnerable. Hardly a month goes by that some do not suffer for how they have treated our brothers."

Bin Saleen thought to himself, not for the first time, that it took a very odd set of circumstances for an Arab to refer to a Palestinian as his brother. But he did not give voice to the sentiment.

"That is true," he said instead. "But they slay them by what? The handful? And often as not, no one dies but the martyr himself. Even so, the men are now watched so closely there that they must sometimes stoop to sending a woman to carry the bomb – as if a woman could possibly enjoy the fruits of a martyr's paradise."

Mohammed fell silent, contemplating, bin Saleen knew, the impossible prospect of a woman with a martyr's reward of forty virgins.

"So what are you suggesting?" Mohammed asked, his head cocked ever so slightly.

"That we slay the infidels in much more significant numbers."

Mohammed sat up. "By the thousands?" One could sense the hope in his voice, and bin Saleen smiled grimly.

"God willing," he told his cousin, "by the millions."

Wonder flooded the elder Arab's face. "You have found what you were looking for," he said, his voice thick with emotion.

"Not yet," bin Saleen admitted. "But I have found a place where there is a chance – just a chance, mind you – that it could be."

CHAPTER ELEVEN

JANUARY 2, 2000
THE AMERICAN EMBASSY, BERLIN

"An Instant Message is nowhere near as easy to trace as, say, a phone call," the CIA chief-of-station was saying. "That's why the bad guys like 'em. But with the help of some Army crypto assets, we were able to trace bin Saleen's end to a couple of MSN servers in central Berlin – one in the University area, and another that serves the western fringe of the financial district. So we went address by address looking for commons – I won't bore you with how much manpower that required – and seventy-six hours later, we came up with this ..."

He tapped the screen of his laptop computer and an image came up – an identification card, printed in German. The picture showed a man in his mid-thirties with the forelocks and untrimmed beard of a Chassidic Jew.

"This is supposed to be Yusef Mendel Benjamin," the station chief said. "Card's his research pass to the Center for Holocaust Studies. His specialty is war crimes – he's been working for the last seven months on documentation of Göring's use of Jewish slaves as the labor pool for his bunkered aircraft factories – the ones that were housed underground in the Hartz Mountains."

"I've heard of those factories," Beck Easton said. "They're not news."

"They aren't," the station chief agreed. "At least the plants building the Messerschmitt jets and the Henckel medium bombers aren't. But the folks who follow such stuff say Benjamin has been assembling a fairly well-supported argument that other companies, such as Horten, were coerced into using slave labor in fortified factories, as well."

"Then why didn't we know about them?" Easton asked him. "If they were coerced, they had nothing to lose by admitting what was going on."

"According to some of Benjamin's articles, Göring's SS spirited some of Horten's senior engineering staff off on a secret project, and they were never heard from again. As for the people who worked there – well, we already know that there were standing orders to execute all slave labor if a facility was in danger of Allied capture."

He clicked an optical mouse button and the picture on the screen began to change: the cheekbones narrowed, the ears and nose became smaller, the forelocks dissolved, the beard receded and then disappeared entirely, and the hairline crept half an inch forward.

"This in Benjamin age-regressed to his mid-teens," the CIA officer said. "It's not a dead-on match for the one photograph we have of Ahmed bin Saleen, but it's close enough to get our chins itching. Actually, we found no fewer than two hundred guys in the university area that were close enough to get our chins itching. But the reason we're so interested in this bird is because when we ran the home address – "

"Let me guess," Easton said. "He lives on the edge of the financial district."

"You got it. On Bundestrasse, above a bakery. We're paying a visit this afternoon at two, after the bakery closes. Want to come?"

CHAPTER TWELVE

EL MEKKAH, SAUDI ARABIA

The *kiswa*, the ceremonial, Egyptian-woven black covering, rippled in the gentle breeze blowing through the great, open-air mosque. Beneath it was the *Ka'ba*, the crown jewel of Islam, a rectangular brick building held by tradition to have been built by the patriarch Ibrahim himself.

Had their visit been a month earlier, Ahmed bin Saleen and his cousin would have arrived at the climax of the *Hajj*, the ceremonial pilgrimage required at least once in the lifetime of every Muslim able to make the journey. But bin Saleen, who had grown to manhood only thirty minutes away from the center of Islam, had made the Hajj himself only once—at the end of his university studies. He had dressed in the robes of a humble pilgrim but had been accompanied by a contingent of his father's armed bodyguards. Riots were not uncommon during the Hajj, as millions of the faithful feverishly sought to gather as much of the *baraka*—the good fortune granted by the various relics and sites—as possible.

Today the pristine courtyard around the Ka'ba was completely deserted, except for bin Saleen, his cousin Mohammed al Fadli, and one elderly *imam*, a venerable member of the sect that guarded the site.

It was not, bin Saleen knew, simply that it was a quiet hour in the middle of a workday. Like Jerusalem's Dome of the Rock, this place was sought out by a small but rising percentage of the world's 1.9 billion Muslims, twenty-four hours a day. It was a measure of his cousin's standing within both Saudi culture and the hierarchy of Islam that the man had been able—with a single phone call—to have the Ka'ba courtyard closed for twenty minutes of private prayer, a privilege usually restricted to the king and certain members of the royal court.

Walking in their stocking feet—all three men had left their shoes in the mosque's gigantic anteroom—bin Saleen, his cousin, and the imam approached the Ka'ba as, around the ancient city, loudspeakers carried the liquid, floating sounds of the traditional call to prayer. They walked to three intricately patterned prayer rugs that had already been laid on the marble courtyard in a triangle, its tip aimed at the wall containing the door of the Ka'ba. It was a concession to the *imam*, who was better than ninety years old, and too frail to carry his own rug.

Yet he led them in the *salat*, the traditional Muslim prayer, with the practiced ease of a man who had been doing so five times a day all his life. He knelt, bowed his head all the way to the wool nap of his rug, sat on his heels and stood with the ease of a man a third of his age, and his voice, which wavered in everyday conversation, was clear and strong as he chanted the ancient Arabic in a rhythm halfway between speech and song.

Bin Saleen had not prayed in a mosque since he was last in his own country. That was—he ticked off the months ... Could it possibly be four years?

It could, he decided. Four years and then some, when he had come home for the funeral of his father, a man who had burned with a desire for *jihad*, a holy war against all infidels, and especially the Americans. He'd rued the king's alliance with the Great Satan, which defiled the soil of the Kingdom with its heathen Air Force bases and its women soldiers who walked on the sacred soil of the Kingdom with their hair and arms uncovered and their legs sheathed in nothing more than men's trousers.

And although bin Saleen was far from an observant Muslim—for how could he be, living hidden, as he did, among the infidels?—and although he had consorted countless times with women dressed far more brazenly than the camouflage-fatigued Americans, consoling himself with the fact that a man was not meant to be celibate ... and although in his heart of hearts he considered talk of *baraka* and the like to be little more than superstitious mumbo-jumbo ... still, the memory of his father and the old man's zeal for the faith in which generations of his family had been raised brought tears to the Saudi's eyes. That memory, the memory of his father's wish that all the world should be brought to the faith of the Prophet—at the tip of a sword, if necessary—engendered within bin Saleen a hatred for all who opposed that holy legacy.

And when, in the dark hours of the morning, it sometimes occurred to him that he had dedicated his life to a path in direct opposition to the peaceful and hospitable elements of his father's faith, then alcohol—another recourse proscribed by Islam—was usually sufficient to drive such thoughts away.

Yet here he was, in this holiest of places. It was a complicated life.

The *imam* clapped his weathered hands together and the three men rose to their feet. The fifteen minutes of worship seemed to have passed in an instant.

"Ahmed bin Saleen ..."

He looked up at the unfamiliar sound of his given name. It filled him with melancholy—he was standing, after all, in the only country on earth in which it could be openly used.

Behind the old *imam* the *kiswa* lifted slightly and fell, as if the Ka'ba beneath it breathed in peaceful, regular sleep. The old man bore a callus in the center of his forehead, a mark of great piety, the result of regular contact with the earth in prayer. The small, pale knot of tissue moved slightly as the imam spoke.

"My brother Mohammed al Fadli tells me that you are about to embark on a journey of great importance to the faith, one that will require much *baraka*. Tell me, my son, would you care to enter the Ka'ba of Ibrahim?"

For a long moment, bin Saleen was speechless. Admission to the Ka'ba was generally restricted to a select few holy days of the year, and even then only a handful of the faithful were allowed to enter, out of respect to the great antiquity of the shrine. It was the sort of thing that had to be arranged months, or even years, in advance. That he was being offered entry on the spur of the moment spoke volumes of his cousin's standing with the mosque – and of the extremely generous donation that he had no doubt made for the privilege.

Ahmed bin Saleen had been years away from his faith. But he knew that there was only one worthy answer to such an offer.

"Most reverend *imam*," he said when he had found his voice, "others of greater worth than I will wait for the appointed day to enter the Ka'ba. I would do them no honor were I to enter before them."

The *imam*'s toothy smile and the beaming face of his cousin convinced bin Saleen that he had given the proper response.

"Then, cousin," Mohammed al Fadli said, "at least you will observe the custom and touch the Black Stone."

Bin Saleen nodded solemnly. Considered by some geologists to be a meteorite, and by others to be a large fragment of basalt, the reddish-black rock in an exterior corner of the Ka'ba had once been a single thirty-centimeter piece, but had fragmented into three parts sometime during the lifetime of the Prophet. It was now bound together with a large and oddly futuristic-looking girdle of pure silver with an aperture through which one could place a hand upon the relic. Contact with the Black Stone was said to impart special blessings, and while bin Saleen lumped such traditions with four-leaf clovers and rabbits' feet, the Black Stone was accessible to any Muslim who visited Mecca – even women – and to refuse contact with it would have been an insult. So, at a gesture from the *imam*, he approached the eastern corner of the Ka'ba and knelt on the white marble base before the brilliantly polished silver band, the *kiswa* lifting and settling silently just above his shoulders.

"Go ahead, my cousin," Mohammed encouraged him, his voice low.

Bin Saleen reached out with his right hand, and touched the silver band, the precious metal cool to the touch. Within, he could see the stone, tiny yellow and red particles flecking its surface. He reached within the opening and placed his hand on the rock, after the fashion of millions of supplicants before him.

His eyes widened.

"Yes," the *imam* whispered. "It is warm, my son, is it not?"

The stone was not only warm—it was blood-warm. And while bin Saleen reasoned with himself that the dark mineral had merely absorbed the heat of the desert sun, and was now slowly releasing it, deep inside he had another, much different impression. It was as if he were touching the warm heart of an otherworldly, living thing.

"It is a good omen, my son," the old *imam* told him. "You will have much *baraka*. It portends very well for your quest."

CHAPTER THIRTEEN

17 BUNDESTRASSE, BERLIN

The operative they used to do the door check was German, an army colonel who looked a little long in the tooth to be a FedEx delivery man, but that was all right – FedEx people on the continent wore hats, and besides, the idea behind the uniform was to disguise him as someone who wouldn't merit a second glance.

They'd introduced the colonel to Beck Easton as "Klaus" – just that, the first name and nothing else, and that bothered Easton a little. True, he would probably never see the man again after this afternoon, but this was an operation, and operations sometimes went badly, and people got killed. It seemed to him that, if a man was risking his life with them, they at least owed the guy the courtesy of acknowledging his last name.

Then again, Easton wasn't calling this show. That was the province of the field agent they'd dispatched from the embassy, an early middle-aged ex-military man named Hunter who came with a first name – Joe – and, aside from the way he treated the hired help, seemed decent enough.

Now Easton and Hunter were sitting in the center and back seats, respectively, of a Ford Transit Kombi van, binoculars to their eyes, watching the curtains in the apartment above the shuttered bakery for any hint of movement, secure in the knowledge that the solar film on the van's windows would hide every trace of their surveillance.

The CIA comms gear was so sensitive that Easton could hear the whisk of Klaus breathing as he ascended the stairs, the tread of his feet as he climbed, and the squeak of the odd board in the stairway of the old, prewar building. Fifteen steps and then eight paces apparently brought the German operative to the apartment

door, because the next thing Easton heard over his earpiece was a crisp triple-knock upon the door.

Easton and Hunter watched the apartment windows. The curtains remained still—no nervous suspect checking the street for signs of trouble.

Thirty seconds passed, and Klaus knocked again.

"*Guten tag*," they heard him call out. "*Herr Benjamin? Ist FedEx.*"

They heard him knock a third time. Then Hunter keyed his radio, saying, "Try the neighbor's—see if anybody else is up there."

They heard him do so and, when they were relatively certain that the building was empty, Hunter radioed again, "Hang tight. We'll be right up."

Easton and Hunter crossed the cobblestone street wearing white coveralls and beaked paper hats. Each man carried a wire-handled paint can. When they got to the upper floor of the bakery building, Easton stepped back while Klaus drew a 9mm Beretta from the FedEx box he'd been carrying, and Hunter knelt before the door, opened his paint can, and took out a lock pick and a tumbler depressor.

It had to be this way, Easton knew. As a member of his country's armed forces, Klaus was constitutionally prohibited from breaking and entering the home of a private citizen. So was Hunter, for that matter, but Hunter was an American, and so the German government could not be held accountable for his actions.

Both Easton and Hunter were, on the other hand, taking part in this operation unarmed. If anybody got shot as part of this visit, having a German pull the trigger kept the news in the national sections of the local papers and out of the pages of the *New York Times* and the *Washington Post.*

Spin control.

The lock clicked open, and both Americans pulled Tyvek microfiber booties over their shoes and donned latex gloves. Then, as Klaus covered them with the gun, Hunter pushed the door open and stepped swiftly inside, checking the doorframe for signs of an alarm system.

He nodded, and Easton entered as well, opening his paint can and taking out a small electronic device with a telescopic wand. Switching it on, Easton began passing the wand slowly around the perimeters of the rugs, under cabinets, and around every door and drawer in the apartment.

The studio apartment was tiny—one main room and a bath with a claustrophobically small shower cabinet, the kitchen differentiated from the apartment proper only by its metal-bordered patch of linoleum. Still, Easton worked for a good ten minutes; the device with the wand was known in the trade as an "electric dog"—designed, like its canine counterpart, to sniff out cordite, gunpowder, fulminates, and other possible explosives. It was not unheard of for Al-Qaeda locations to be booby-trapped.

But the device's needle moved only once—for a box of strike-anywhere matches in a metal box above the stove.

His sweep done, Easton waited while Hunter completed his own check for listening devices. It was only after the other American had completed his sweep that Easton broke his silence.

"So what's with this galley?" He nodded at the small kitchen area, where a small fiberboard cupboard, a portable refrigerator, and a hot plate sat separate from the regular furnishings.

"Kosher kitchen," Hunter said. "We had conservative Jewish neighbors across the street when I was a kid. You have to keep the meat products separate from the dairy, and you have separate implements for each."

Easton looked at the cupboard and moved a few things. Clean spots appeared in a layer of dust.

"Well," he said. "Either this guy's gone vegan, or this is window dressing. This stuff hasn't been moved in weeks."

Hunter opened the medicine cabinet in the bathroom, then a closet, then a dresser drawer, and then another.

"It's window dressing," he said. "He's gone out of town. No toothbrush or toiletries, there's no luggage anywhere in the apartment, and several of his hangers are empty. But look at this ..."

Easton looked. In the open dresser drawer atop a velvet bag, were two small leather cubes attached to long leather straps. "What am I looking at? Some kind of harness?"

Hunter shook his head. "They're tefellin."

Easton gave him a blank look.

"The boxes contain passages of Scripture," Hunter said. "Their function is described in the Bible: Deuteronomy, I think. Observant Jews use them during morning prayer; they put one on the forehead, and the other on the right arm. If this guy is that conservative – and the way the kitchen is set up, he's trying to make it look as if he is – he wouldn't travel without these. He needs them every day to pray."

"Maybe he forgot 'em?"

"A Chassidim? No way. They'd be the first things in his bag. He'd wander out of this joint without his pants on before he left these behind. And in the other drawer there's three *tallits* – the fringed strips of cloth that observant Jews wear under their clothes. So I doubt he's traveling with those either. No – this guy's a ringer."

"Pretending to be a Jew so he could use the Holocaust center to do his research."

"You bet." Hunter nodded. "All right. Let's see what else this place tells us."

The desk and dresser drawers yielded nothing unusual. Then Easton noticed that the rug under one chair had several depressed marks under the chair legs, as if the chair was moved and replaced often. He lifted the chair away, folded the rug back, found a loose board, lifted it, and exposed a safe bolted into the floor joists.

Two minutes later, Hunter had proved that he was as handy with safes as he was with door locks, and if they'd had any doubts about whether Yusef Mendel Benjamin was a fake, they were gone. With its slotted top removed, the shallow, oblong safe revealed not only five ZIP disks, but three EU passports under three different names—none of them Benjamin or bin Saleen—one envelope containing five thousand euros and another containing five thousand dollars, American Express and Visa cards to match the names on the passports, and two sets of car keys.

"If we can take those disks back to the embassy, it won't take long at all to copy them," Easton said.

"Let's do it, then," Hunter said, dropping the disks into a plastic evidence bag. "We'll scan the passports and the cards as well, and copy the serial numbers on the bills. And I pulled some hairs out of the trap in the bathroom sink—we'll get those in the bag back to DC, and have our lab people get a DNA print on this bird. Klaus'll keep an eye on this place until I can get back here and set things back the way they were. You see anything else you need?"

"No ...," Easton started to say. Then he noticed a notepad lying on the desk next to the docking station for a laptop computer.

Taking a penlight out of his pocket, he played the white beam across the notepad at a low, almost flat angle. As if by magic, letters appeared—the light revealing the depressions left by a pen.

"What've you got?" Hunter asked.

"Name and address."

"Whose?"

"Anthony Tirelli's," Easton told him. "At 7167 North Lake Drive, Canandaigua, New York."

CHAPTER FOURTEEN

JANUARY 3, 2000
LOS GATOS, CALIFORNIA

Except for the wooden airplane propeller suspended above his computer monitor, the man's cubicle looked absolutely unremarkable. And in anyplace but the Silicon Valley, so would he – a neat dark gray business suit over a white oxford-cloth dress shirt, a red-and-blue-striped rep tie, black wingtips, and a Wally Cleaver haircut.

So far in her interviews, Angela Brower had spoken with a woman who wore men's boxer shorts as trousers, a guy with green hair, a pale-skinned Goth of indefinite gender, and two young men dressed identically in plain pants, penny loafers, and polo shirts buttoned all the way up, the white rims of T-shirts floating half an inch above their ribbed polo collars.

Still, all of these programmers had given her the same sorts of requests: comfortable, all-day seating (the consensus seemed to be for the Herman Miller Aeron chair), indirect lighting so they wouldn't have a glare problem with the monitors, ergonomically placed keyboard trays, and easy access to shared equipment.

Not this guy.

"A B-17 bomber wing," he finally said after a full minute of pensive silence.

"A bomber wing?"

"From a B-17," he repeated. "Right up here ..."

He motioned with his hands, showing where the wing should be positioned relative to the programmers' cubicles.

Angela just sat there, pen poised over her notepad. So far, she hadn't written a thing.

"Oh, I know what you're thinking," the man told her. "The starboard wing would be completely wrong. No, no, no, no, no.

Completely. If we put a starboard wing up there, it would practically guarantee buggy code. The port's the ticket …"

"'The port?'"

"The left." He started sketching on the back of an interoffice memo. The man was actually a fairly decent artist. "Like this, see? With the propellers facing the windows. And the flaps should be set at eleven degrees."

"At eleven degrees …"

He beamed and nodded emphatically. "Absolutely," he told her. "That's the correct setting for a short-field take-off."

"Uhm …" Angela tapped the notepad with her pen. "How would you get something like that inside the building?"

The programmer furrowed his forehead in thought, brought out a scientific calculator, and did some quick figuring, looked up into the air at nothing, and figured again.

"You couldn't," he said. "Tell you what: put me down for an Aeron chair – charcoal-gray, size B."

He turned back to his monitor, and Angela got up, muttered a thank-you, and walked away, wondering whether the man had been serious about the airplane wing. Two minutes later, as she stepped into the cubicle they'd given her as a temporary office, she was still wondering.

It had been a long day. Still, programmer weirdness aside, it had been highly productive. She'd culled the possible furnishings down to a short list; she had a good grasp on how to handle traffic flow through the programming department …

… and she'd learned more about Beck Easton, all of it good.

Kind. Smart. Generous. Tuned in. Far-sighted. Intuitive. Those were the sorts of things everyone said about him. Even the Goth, who'd given mostly monosyllabic answers, had ended their interview with a rare two full sentences: "Whatever Beck asks for, do it that way. Beck *gets* it."

And everyone, even Mister B-17, had mentioned the IPO, since everyone had a stake, however small, in the company. Blue

Corner was going public soon – by mid-summer, some said. By fall for sure.

It gave Angela pause. It made sense of what Beck had said about having a job that required him to travel on New Year's Day. So he was planning to bolt as soon as the company had gone on the market – sell as many shares as legally possible and hit the road. And while that would leave him at least a moderately wealthy man, it was still a red flag.

Angela's girlhood confidante had been her great-aunt – a retired missionary who'd outlived five brothers, two sisters, and a doctor husband, and who'd had a seemingly endless supply of stories about doing God's work in Kenya, in China, and on the high mountain plateaus of Peru. The spry, straight-backed old lady had been Angela's most trusted source of information about studies, clothes, books, music, schools, life ... everything. And that had included men.

"Whatever you do, sweetheart," the grand old lady had told Angela, "you make sure any man you get interested in has the two *J*'s – the first is 'Jesus,' and the second is 'job.' Having money may seem like a nice start, but it's solid, steady employment that makes for a good husband."

Angela had first gotten that advice when she was seventeen years old. And now here she was, eight years later, falling head-over-heels for a man she was pretty sure did not have the first "J" in his life and seemed to be trying as hard as he could to lose the second.

So what would Great-Aunt Eulesta have to say about that?

"There is a line, Angela, between God's way and the world's way." Angela could practically hear the old lady's voice in her head. "And a smart Christian woman not only does not cross that line; she does not allow herself to stray anywhere *near* it."

Yet here she was tiptoeing right along that line like the Great Wallenda.

She gathered her notes, zipped them into a calfskin portfolio, and decided to call it a day.

Ten minutes later, she was parking her rental car at La Hacienda, glad that the little family-owned establishment was just that and not some big, impersonal conference hotel. The place looked practically deserted, and she was looking forward to some quiet, a nap, maybe a quick dip in the pool. She parked her rented Grand Prix in the lot and walked back to the bungalow, slipping the key in the lock and opening the door to the soft scent of roses.

The roses, a full dozen of them, long-stemmed and red, had arrived promptly at ten o'clock on New Year's Day. It had more than surprised Angela – she couldn't imagine what Beck had paid to get a florist to open up and make a delivery on New Year's or how he'd even contacted one to do it in the first place. And yet the flowers had arrived in a long white box tied with red ribbon, delivered by a smiling young woman who hadn't seemed at all put out about having to work on a morning when most of the world was home sleeping off the previous evening's celebration.

The beautiful, red blossoms had brought tears to Angela's eyes. And then the card – "Thanks for explaining that full-spectrum lighting thing" – had broken her out in a fit of giggles, right there in her room with no one to hear it.

She set down her portfolio, slipped off her shoes, and crossed to the dresser to smell the flowers. Then her fingers brushed against the leather cover of a worn black Bible. She picked it up, sat on the end of her bed, and opened the old, familiar book.

The first verse she looked at was one she had long since committed to memory – 2 Corinthians 6:14, the verse that her father had always shared with his students when they came to him, telling him that they were thinking of starting a relationship with someone who was not a Christian:

> *Do not be yoked together with unbelievers. For what do righteousness and wickedness have in common? Or what fellowship can light have with darkness?*

But that wasn't the answer she was looking for. So she leafed through the concordance at the back of the old Bible and found 1 Peter 3:1:

> *Wives, in the same way be submissive to your husbands so that, if any of them do not believe the word, they may be won over without words by the behavior of their wives, when they see the purity and reverence of your lives.*

But Angela was twisting Scripture, and she knew it. Beck Easton was not her husband, and she, if she was truly observant of God's Word, would carefully avoid any path that might possibly lead to her becoming his wife.

Becoming his wife? She was doing it again—contemplating a future with this man whom she'd only known for a handful of hours.

It worried her, and the worry brought to mind another of Great-Aunt Eulesta's sayings: "Worry, young lady, is nothing more than prayer to the devil. You have a Savior, and your Savior has made it clear what you are to do when your heart is troubled."

So, Bible still in hand and not caring for a moment what it would do to her nylons, Angela knelt at the foot of her bed and followed—at least in this respect—her faithful mentor's advice. She bowed her head and, silently and wordlessly, she began to pray.

CHAPTER FIFTEEN

JANUARY 4, 2000
CANANDAIGUA, NEW YORK

Cold wind lashed the length of the lake, sending billows of spindrift ahead of it and giving the long, wide expanse of ice the appearance of a harsh, frozen desert. To Beck Easton, clad in a sage-green Air Force survival parka, his eyes shielded from the low afternoon sun by dark Ray-Ban Cats sunglasses, it was like watching a movie. But the young FBI agent with him, a pale-faced kid named Avery, was dressed more for fashion than for climate, and folded the collar of a Burberry raincoat up against the wind as he stamped his feet on the porch of the old Victorian house.

"N-n-nobody home," he said, shivering.

"Nobody's answering, that's for sure," Easton agreed as he knocked a fourth time. "Let's take a peek around back."

They walked to the back porch, which looked directly out onto a small bay, the house having been built on a slight peninsula. Easton walked onto the screened porch and over a small drift of snow. Three knocks produced no response there, as well.

"No answer," Easton said, looking up at the porch eaves. "But the front hall light is burning, and so's this one."

He leaned close to the window.

"Light's burning in the kitchen too."

"Lots of folks leave lights on when they go away," Avery said, his voice more steady, now that he was out of the wind.

"True." Easton tried the door. The knob turned in his hand. "But do they go away and leave the door unlocked?"

He was about to step into the kitchen when the FBI agent stopped him with a hand on his shoulder.

"We don't have a warrant," the agent said.

"So we won't collect evidence," Easton told him, and he walked on into the kitchen.

Pizza boxes and empty pop cans were piled everywhere, but the thing that registered with Easton was that they were piled and not scattered. There was no sign of a struggle. It just seemed to be the home of someone who got his decorating tips from *Animal House*.

Down a hallway, a light burned, and Easton walked toward it. He heard footsteps behind him, turned, and saw Avery following.

The light was burning in a spare bedroom that had been adapted for use as an office. A Gateway PC was sitting on a desk improvised from a hollow-core door over two trestles, and the power light was burning on the CPU, but the monitor was dark, except for a small white "C:\" and a blinking cursor.

Keeping his gloves on, Easton pressed the "ctrl," "alt," and "del" keys simultaneously. But rather than rebooting, the computer went dark for half a minute, and then a message came up on the screen: "OPERATING SYSTEM NOT FOUND."

"What's that all about?" Avery asked.

"Somebody's blanked the hard drive," Easton said. "Either that, or overwritten it with Xs, which would accomplish the same thing. Whatever was on here is gone."

He looked out the window at the white lake ice, thinking. Then, just as he was turning away, he looked out the window again.

No struggle in the house. He thought of the apartment in Berlin. *And bin Saleen travels light and alone.* He turned back to the PC, pictured bin Saleen taking whatever he needed off it, and then leaving.

So what did he do with whoever was here?

Easton pictured himself in a foreign country. If he was trying to stay low-profile, he wouldn't carry a weapon.

Neither would bin Saleen. He would have had to improvise.

How?

Easton looked out once more at the frozen lake.

"Tell me," he said, turning to Avery. "The weather. Has it been this cold for the last week?"

"Not all week. We had a brief thaw a couple of days ago."

"And the wind – is it generally out of the same direction as now?"

"Yeah. I check every morning before I run. It's been westerly all week. Why?"

"Just a hunch," Easton said. "So where's the nearest place around here that you can land a helicopter without attracting too much attention?"

"A helicopter?" Avery straightened up. "Now, wait a minute; I don't have authority to call for a helicopter."

"That's not a problem," Easton said, pulling a ruggedized satellite phone out of the pocket of his parka. "I do."

The nearest place turned out to be the Air National Guard base just south of Rochester, and the gusting snow helped to obscure the fact that the Sea Stallion helicopter was Navy, rather than Air Force.

"Major Easton?" The flight-suited ensign had to shout to be heard over the whine of the turbine. "Got your gear here, sir. You want us to stand by?"

"No." Easton shook his head. "If you brought what I called for, you're good to go."

The ensign nodded and, with the help of a flight technician, carried two large duffel bags to Avery's waiting Chevrolet Suburban.

"Major?" Avery asked after the helicopter had lifted off and disappeared into the snow. But Easton just smiled, shrugged, and said nothing, just as he had said nothing during two stops on the way to the air base – once at Sears to buy a four-stroke chain saw, and once at a sporting goods store, where he purchased a plastic roll-up toboggan and, after asking Avery for his sizes, a thickly insulated snowmobile suit and a pair of felt-lined boots. Easton continued to avoid the FBI man's questions throughout the forty-five-minute ride back to the lake.

It was only after dark, after they'd pulled into a public park just across the bay from Tirelli's house, that Easton let the FBI man see what was in the duffel bags. In one was a black crushed-neoprene DUI dry suit with an attached hood and O-ring-sealed rubber gloves. In the other was a pair of swim fins, a dive mask, a scuba tank and harness, a side-diaphragm regulator, a UK1200 dive light with a red lens, a line reel, an ice axe, and a tubular, screwlike ice piton.

"You're planning to go scuba diving?"

Easton nodded.

Avery turned and looked at the dark, frozen lake. "Here?" He was getting a little worked up – his face was turning red, despite the cold. Easton could see that, even in the dim light from the back of the SUV. "At night? Under the ice? Why?"

Easton nodded in the direction of Tirelli's house as he got into the rear compartment of the Suburban and began changing into an insulated undergarment and the dry suit. "About a hundred yards off the house, there's a triangular hole that's frozen over on the ice, and three tree branches next to it," he said.

"And?"

"And the tree branches should be set up, like a tripod, over the hole. That's how ice divers warn snowmobilers and what-have-you that there's open water on the lake. But the branches aren't set up over the hole. They're scattered next to it."

"So what's the mystery about that? It's windy."

Easton shook his head. "The branches are scattered upwind of the hole. I could see that plainly from Tirelli's office – snow blowing one way, and branches strewn the other. Given that and the unlocked house and the lights and the wiped hard drive. I'm just taking a wild guess here, but ..."

Avery's eyes grew wide. "Listen," he told Easton. "If you suspect a homicide here, we have to notify the New York State Police. That's not optional."

Easton stopped pulling on the dry suit and looked at the agent. "If you call the State, we'll have flashing lights and TV cameras up one side of this lake and down the other. And the work I'm doing here calls for a little more discretion than that."

Avery's mouth became a thin, straight line. "There's procedure that has to be followed here."

Easton sighed. He reached for his parka, opened a pocket, and got out the satellite phone again.

"Okay," he told Avery. "We can do this a couple of ways. I can call up a pretty important guy in Washington, who will call your director, who will call you and tell you to cooperate. Or you can just cooperate of your own volition, and we can save the battery on my phone, and the director of the FBI won't remember you for the rest of your career as the jerk that got him hauled out of a dinner party or something. How do you want it? Your call."

Avery's shoulders slumped, just a little.

"There you go," Easton said, putting the phone away. "Now, why don't you pull on that snowmobile suit and those boots? Believe me – you're going to need them out there."

Avery had to give Easton that one thing. By the time they were fifty feet out from the shore, he was glad – extremely glad – for the snowmobile suit. With the hood up and cinched snug on his suit, and the knit collars pulled down over his gloves, the only exposed skin on his body was a small section of his face, but even there, he could feel the frigid wind cutting him like hard-frozen sandpaper.

Avery was pulling the toboggan, laden with Easton's dive equipment. Easton was walking alongside, the chainsaw in one hand and the ice axe in the other. Avery could hear the ice creaking as they walked, the sound barely audible under the soughing of the wind.

Avery wasn't crazy about being out on lake ice this early in the winter. He'd grown up in Minnesota and remembered too many stories about Christmas-present snowmobiles plunging through ice and snow in the first days of January, taking their riders with them into frigid, inky-black water. But this Easton guy didn't seem fazed at all about being out here, not even now, three hours after sundown, with Orion climbing ever higher into a hulking, black winter sky.

Then again, this Easton guy was the one in the waterproof suit.

They got to the triangular scar on the ice, and Easton said, "You'll want to stand back. This is going to get a little wet."

The NSA operative didn't so much pull the cord on the chainsaw as he held the cord-grip in his right hand and pushed the saw away from him with his left. It looked unorthodox, but it worked—the saw sputtered on the first pull and hiccupped to life on the second.

Easton ran the saw up to full throttle and then bent to his work, bringing the tip of the blade down to the ice just outside the triangular hole and raising a shimmering flurry of ice crystals. He didn't seem to be straining or pushing—he was letting the saw do the work, and within seconds water was coursing down the upper part of the blade and spilling over the surface snow in a growing, dark gray spot, as if the rapidly revolving chain had found the very jugular of the lake. Water squirted up from the hole and splashed against Easton's legs as well, but he seemed not to notice as it froze in rough sheets on his shins and ankles and covered the galoshes-like boots of the rubber suit.

It took three minutes for Easton to cut the first side of the hole, and Avery watched the shore, looking for a light, apprehensive that some homeowner was going to notice the noise, call the police, and lead to questions from his regional office that he would not be able to answer.

But no porch lights came on along the shore. No spotlights speared out from roving patrol cars, and this puzzled Avery at first, until he realized what Easton must have known all along: that, between late-night snowmobiles, and auger-wielding anglers trying to get in a little ice fishing after work, the whine and growl of small engines was probably a fairly common sound on the lake, one that would kindle nothing more than petty irritation among the few wintering homeowners within earshot.

After three cuts and ten minutes of noise, Easton killed the saw, and the low sigh of the winter wind came creeping back in. What Easton had made was not really a hole—not yet. While water seeped darkly from all three freshly cut lines, a block of ice, four feet long on each of its three sides, still floated there motionlessly.

Avery was just wondering how they were going to get it out when Easton put one foot in the center of it, stepped forward, and pushed down.

The block dipped and slipped neatly under the edge nearest to Avery, diving like some mute sea mammal into the deathlike stillness of the lake water. Moments later, he both heard and felt it thumping against the ice beneath his feet. It was too much like a living thing, seeking escape, and Avery shivered at the thought and hoped Easton didn't see it.

If Easton did, he said nothing about it. He just set the saw down and moved to the next stage of his work, picking up the ice axe and using its tip to chip a small depression into the lake ice next to the hole. Then the NSA man picked up the ice piton and turned the axe sideways, pounding with the flat of it to get the threaded piton started. After that he slipped the long pick of the axe through the piton's ear and began to twist the screwlike piton clockwise, turning the axe around and around until the eight-inch piton was securely in the hole, the ear nearly level with the ice.

Avery watched quietly as Easton slipped a loop of line from the reel through the piton ear and then passed the reel through its own loop and cinched the line snug, securely attaching the line to the solidly planted piton. Then he took the scuba tank and harness from the toboggan and set it upright next to the hole, the dive light already clipped to the harness.

It was only when Easton waved a hand in front of his face that Avery realized the man was talking to him.

"Sorry," he said. "What'd you say?"

"Hold this steady for me, would you?"

Avery held the tank by its valve as Easton sat on the edge of the hole, his legs in the water from the knees down, and pulled on his swim fins. It looked like cold work, but if the man felt it, he showed no sign. He just scooted back until he felt the harness against his back, pulled on the shoulder straps of the harness, and fastened the waist-belt. He spat into the dive mask, sloshed it in the water and then pulled it on as well, carefully smoothing the forehead of the hood over the top of the mask. Then he took the regulator in one hand and the line-reel in the other.

"Okay," he told Avery. "I should be back here in fifteen minutes, twenty tops."

Avery frowned. "What should I do if you're not back by then?"

Easton laughed. "Then, you can probably go ahead and give the state police a call."

Easton eased himself into the water, left arm raised, letting the excess air hiss out of his suit through the exhaust valve as he floated, shoulder high. He held the regulator in his mouth, but breathed around it, rather than through it, knowing that the device's internal valving would freeze open in the ten-degree air.

When he began to feel heavy in the water, he stopped venting the suit, put his hands under the ice, and pushed up. The water closed over his head, and the sound of the wind was replaced by the sound of the lake—a silence punctuated by the plink of bubbles drifting up from the folds of his suit and an odd, subterranean-sounding creaking as distant ice expanded against itself.

At ten feet, he took a breath, the first stage of the regulator hissing on the valve-top behind his head, the air in his lungs stopping his descent and putting him into a hover. The water around him was inky black, relieved only by a green radium glow from his pressure and depth gauges. He craned his head back and saw the vague, gray triangle of the hole.

Easton gave the reel a tug and satisfied himself that the line was secure. Then he switched on the light, the red beam reaching out like something solid, picking out particles floating in the water and, for five long seconds, the pale, gape-mouthed shape of a sluggish striped bass.

The red light was better for preserving night vision, and it would be less noticeable to observers on shore, but it had only about a third the power of a conventional dive light. The lake water, which Easton knew would offer only about ten feet of visibility during high summer, was eerily clear, all the microscopic life gone dormant in the shadows under the ice. Even with the dim, red light, he could easily make out ripples in the muck of the lake bottom, fifty feet below.

Above him, his exhaust bubbles were hitting the opaque ice and then quivering along it like quicksilver, separating and then recollecting into reflective ovoids that slowly crawled their way to the hole. Easton pressed the inlet valve on his chest, adding the slightest touch of air to his suit. Then, keeping the light pointed at the surface, he hovered in place and turned slowly.

He knew that only about ten percent of "drowning" victims actually drown, the majority actually asphyxiating, so strong is the aversion to inhaling a liquid. This left air in the lungs, and air in the lungs made a body buoyant. So the most logical place to look for an individual missing under the ice was at the surface, and at the surface was where Beck Easton found what he'd thought he might find: the still form of a man floating chest-up in the red beam of the light, his hands and face pressed against the underside of the ice like a browser trying to peer into a darkened shop window.

The illusion vanished as Easton drew nearer. Anthony Tirelli – that was who the corpse had to be – was missing all his fingertips. It was something Easton had seen once before, when he'd helped a sheriff's search-and-rescue team recover a scuba diver who'd died in an underwater cave. When faced with imminent death, a person would try to dig through anything – solid rock or, in this case, ten-inch ice – in a last, desperate attempt to get air.

Even in the crimson beam of the dive light, Tirelli's abraded fingers looked surprisingly pale and clean, all blood long since eked out and washed away. And when Easton turned the corpse over, the face looked peaceful, eyes closed, as if in sleep.

Easton swallowed and went to work. He turned out the pockets of the dead man's thin mountain parka, finding only an old-style Volkswagen key on an unadorned ring and a tightly folded five-dollar bill.

There was no wallet, no ID, so he turned out the jeans pockets next. He found a quarter, one of those round one-size-fits-all screwdrivers, and an inch-and-a-half square of plastic, which he turned in the beam of the dive light.

The letters "COMPACT FLASH" and "256MB" showed up clearly in the red light. He zipped the card into his belt pocket, put the rest of the items back where he had found them, and then turned and began swimming toward the hole, reeling in the line as he went.

On the ice above, Avery kept his gloved hands buried in his pockets and stamped his boots on the ice. The snowmobile boots had thick felt inner liners, but even so, his feet were beginning to numb. The tension on the guideline had not changed for five minutes, but bubbles continued to percolate into the triangular opening.

An otherworldly crimson light showed dimly in the dark water, grew stronger, and then winked out as Beck Easton's rubber-hooded head broke the surface of the water. The NSA operative took the regulator out of his mouth and looked up at Avery.

"Do we have any kind of waterproof bag or container?"

Avery checked his pockets and came up with a plastic Ziploc bag with "EVIDENCE" written across it in white block letters. "Will this do?"

"Perfect," Easton said. He did something beneath the surface of the water and then handed the bag up to Avery. It was full of water, and a square plastic card lay in the bottom of it.

"Put that inside your suit, so it doesn't freeze," Easton said as he pushed down on two sides of the hole and swung himself into a sitting position on the ice. "Let's get this gear collected and get back to the car."

Avery looked at the bag and then back at Easton. "But what about the body?" He looked at the bag again. "You found a body, didn't you?"

"I did," Easton told him. "But we'll call and get some guys out here later on, after we're underway. Right now my priority is to get that flash card to Fort Meade ..."

CHAPTER SIXTEEN

JANUARY 5, 2000
NSA LABORATORIES, FORT GEORGE N. MEADE, MARYLAND

"That's pretty cool." The lab tech looked Native American – long black ponytail, bronze skin and high cheek bones – but his accent was pure and unadulterated Brooklyn. He handed Easton two envelopes: in one was the compact flash card, and in the other was a compact disk. "How long did you say that card was under water?"

"Not sure," Easton admitted. "But the water was pretty cold. And I left the card to my PDA in a pair of jeans one time when they went in the wash, and it still worked after, so I figured it was worth a shot."

"Well, you were right. I used a light dispersant spray to displace the water, and then I blew it dry, and it seems okay. Funny thing though ..."

"What's that?"

"Well ..." The tech wrote a note on a clipboard and set it aside on the counter. "Most folks use CF cards in digital cameras, or like you did, in a PDA. So I was expecting a whole bunch of jpeg files, or date-book entry documents. But this one has only one file on it."

"Just one?" Easton looked up at the tech.

"Yeah. A PowerPoint presentation. Something for some UFO convention. Takes up almost the entire card."

Four hours later, Easton had grabbed a quick breakfast in the NSA laboratory's cafeteria, followed by a shower in the lab's visitors' quarters. He was feeling as human as one could feel after a three-hour flight on a helicopter, a half-hour debrief, and a grand total of forty-five minutes of sleep.

Now he was in one of the lab's moderate-sized conference rooms—wired, as most of them were, for video conferencing, although the big projection screen TV in this one was showing only a plain blue screen.

Bill Spalding had joined him, looking well rested and dapper, despite a five-hour flight in from the West Coast and a cancelled day at Disneyland with his grandchildren. So had an Air Force colonel in full uniform and an elderly man dressed in khaki slacks, a polo shirt, and what looked suspiciously like cleatless golf shoes.

Spalding confirmed those suspicions as he made the introductions.

"Dr. Simpson is a consulting editor with *Jane's* and was an Army Air Corps oversight contractor on the Northrop Flying-wing programs," he said. "Dr. Simpson, we appreciate your joining us here on such very short notice."

"On the second fairway, they land a helicopter," Simpson grumbled. "Just as I'm getting ready to chip. The second fairway of the Fort Myers Palms Country Club. Do you have any idea how long it takes to join a place like that?"

"And this is Colonel Merriwether, from Air Force Public Affairs," Spalding continued. "He answers queries about Project Blue Book, and he's had contact with Anthony Tirelli in the past."

The two men shook Easton's hand, even though he had not been introduced by name. Operative identities were revealed only on a need-to-know basis, and apparently both Simpson and Merriwether had dealt with the NSA often enough to know this.

The video conferencing screen went dark for a moment and then came back up with a picture of Joe Hunter and an Army captain, sitting in what Easton recognized as a CIA conference room at the American embassy in Berlin.

"Looks as if we've got a quorum," Spalding said. "Berlin, why don't you start with what you've found on your end?"

On the screen, the Army captain – the name tag on his fatigues said "Woodward" – looked at Hunter, who nodded.

"What we got off Benjamin's hard drives at the Holocaust Research Center seems to bear out what he's been publishing over the last couple of years," the captain said. "His work has all been in the direction of discovering whether the Horten Aircraft Company used slave labor in the latter years of the war, and he has accessed literally thousands of Luftwaffe and Horten files. But we've noticed that he requested a disproportionately large number of files on Horten's *nurflügel* programs ..."

"*Nurflügel?*" Easton asked.

"Their flying-wing projects," Simpson said, proving that he was listening, even though his face looked as if he was still mourning the loss of that chip shot on the second hole.

"The last day he was seen at the research center, he returned a couple of file cabinets' worth of wartime documents to the German state archives," the major in Berlin said, looking at notes on the desk in front of him. "We retrieved these, and while most were fairly innocuous, a couple raised some flags. One was a manifest for eight BMW jet engines, some prototype bombsights, aircraft instrumentation, bomb bay machinery, and some high-efficiency fuel pumps that were all delivered to a U-boat base at Kristiansand, in Norway."

"Jet engines to a U-boat base?" Easton asked, raising his voice so the table mike would pick it up.

"Late in the war, we know that Germany was using submarines to ship advanced technology and some of their better engineers out of the country," the major responded. "Some of it was headed to South America, but a significant proportion of it was geared toward equipping the Japanese with better weapons and material. So far as we know, none of it ever got through – some of the subs were depth-charged and sunk, some surrendered, and the rest seem to have just disappeared. U-boats were prone to loss anyhow, and we've never seen any evidence that the Japanese received and used German technology."

"Until now," Spalding said.

On the screen, Joe Hunter looked up. "Okay, I'll bite," he said. "Want to explain that?"

"We retrieved a PowerPoint presentation from Anthony Tirelli, the individual whose address we found in Benjamin's apartment in Berlin," Spalding told him. "Tirelli is deceased"—if this got a reaction from any of the listeners, none registered it—"but he was apparently planning to speak at a UFO convention in Florida this month and forward a theory that the programs you were working on, Doctor Simpson, were based on technology given to us by little green men."

The old man rolled his eyes.

"Um, gentlemen," Merriwether, the Air Force colonel spoke up. "As General Spalding has said, I've met with this Tirelli several times in the past and, while I'm hesitant to speak ill of the dead, the man was a fruitcake. Certifiable. In his mind, the Wright Brothers and Apollo 13 were both directly linked to Roswell and Area 51."

"And this presentation looks like more of the same," Spalding said. "But what troubles us is the 'UFO' he shows to support his theories." He pressed a key on his laptop, and the image of the Berlin conference room was replaced by an enhanced and enlarged shot of a flying-wing aircraft passing in front of the moon.

"What's the provenience on this?" Simpson asked.

"Peterborough, Ontario, just after oh-four-hundred Zulu on May 7, 1945," Spalding said, reading from the notes in front of him.

The old golfer got to his feet and moved closer to the screen.

"Impossible," he said. "The YP-35 wasn't airborne until 1947. And this definitely looks like a jet—look at how closely the contrails are spaced. That would be the YB-49, which didn't fly until late 1948 ..."

He tilted his glasses and peered at the screen.

"Six contrail roots?" The old man shook his head. "We used eight engines, not six. And besides, all the flying-wing test flights were made over and around Muroc Field – what they call Edwards Air Force Base now. This picture has to be a fake."

"One would think," Spalding said. "But in this presentation, Tirelli's notes show that he intended to claim corroborating testimony from Inuit tribespeople in the Northwest Territories, as well as a number of witnesses in New York State, including an Air Corps ferry pilot who swears he fired on it. Colonel Merriwether, that's why we faxed you the notes. Does that jibe with anything in your records?"

The Air Force officer consulted a three-ring binder in front of him before he spoke. "A Lieutenant E. C. Wilson," he said, "ferrying a Lightning out of Chanute ... reported firing on a 'bat-shaped aircraft,' and his ammunition belts were partially depleted on landing, but there was no official confirmation, and no gun-camera footage. Planes being ferried usually flew with the wing cameras empty. And by the time this report filtered through channels, the war in Europe was long over."

"What about the civilian sightings in New York City?" Easton asked. He and Spalding had already gone through Tirelli's presentation together.

"There was hardly a day during the war that someone, somewhere in the United States, didn't report a strange aircraft or ship," Merriwether said. "And some of it was legit – there were U-boats on patrol off the East Coast through most of the war, for instance. But most of the reports were dismissed as wartime hysteria. This photo puts a different bloom on it."

Simpson tapped the desk in front of him with his gnarled fingertips. "So you're saying what?" He looked at Spalding as he asked it. "That the Germans sailed a bunch of components and some Horten engineers to Japan, built a flying-wing, and flew it to New York?"

Spalding nodded. "That's what the evidence suggests."

Simpson laughed. "General," he said. "The day after both surrenders, we had people in Germany and Japan, looking for every advanced technology, including flying-wings. I ought to know – I went to Germany and gathered Horten's data myself. If the Axis built a flying-wing in Japan, how is it that we never found either the place where they constructed it or the record to show that it was built?"

There was a moment's pause, and then the Air Force officer spoke. "We know that both the Germans and the Japanese tried to destroy anything that might speak particularly ill of them after the war," he said. "And besides, if the plane or its component parts were built in either of the two major industrial centers – Hiroshima and Nagasaki – then we probably destroyed the evidence ourselves."

Simpson shook his head and continued to shake it, despite the hush that fell over both conference rooms.

"Dr. Simpson, you're still skeptical," Spalding said. "Would you mind telling us why?"

The elderly man nodded and got to his feet. "For one," he said, walking as he spoke, "Horten was going for maximum aerodynamic efficiency, so they didn't put empennage – tailfins or rudders – on their airplanes. That looked good in theory, but in actual application, it was a disaster waiting to happen. If an engine flamed out, the plane would go into an irrecoverable spin. And second, every flying-wing bomber made prior to the B-2 – German, American, or Russian – had the same failing. Our bomb runs were as much as 3,000 yards less accurate, from altitude, than those from a B-29."

He waved at the image on the screen. "Dropping a bomb from one of these things was like watching a drunk throw darts. The nose would oscillate in flight, so the bombsight picture wandered all over the map. You'd be lucky to place your ordnance within a mile of the target."

"Um ... within a mile might have been accurate enough."

Everyone looked up. The comment had come from the speakerphone on the table – the Army Intelligence officer in Berlin. Easton saw Spalding tap a button, taking the bomber image off the screen and replacing it with one of the Berlin conference room.

"The second document we discovered concerns the output of a secret reactor facility that Göring apparently constructed in the Hartz Mountains late in the war," the captain said. "First mention we've seen of it, and it looks as if even Hitler didn't know about it. Apparently he and Göring had a falling out over how to proceed on atomic bomb development, so Göring funded this facility on his own, siphoning money from other Luftwaffe projects. That must have meant cutting corners because this reactor appears to have been spectacularly crude – practically no safety precautions to speak of. But these documents claim that they used it to produce nearly a hundred kilograms of plutonium-238 oxide."

"Wait a minute," Easton said. "The Nazis never had the bomb." He remembered that much from school.

"They never had a thermonuclear weapon," the officer in Berlin agreed. "But with a hundred kilos of plutonium oxide on hand, they wouldn't need one. A conventional airburst weapon, like the ones the Japanese were developing to disperse biological agents near the end of the war, would have more than sufficed."

"What sort of damage potential are we talking about?" Spalding asked him over the table mike.

"In terms of physical damage? Buildings and such? Practically none – the weapon would detonate at 3,000 meters. But in terms of loss of life? Put it this way – a nanogram of plutonium-238 would be enough to sicken or kill everyone in a decent-sized office building. Airburst over New York? If the winds are right, a hundred kilograms could wipe out the entire East Coast. It wouldn't be quick, and it wouldn't be painless. And with a half-life of 87.7 years, it would keep the East Coast hot for centuries."

Easton looked up, scowling.

"Back that up a minute," he said. "Are you saying that this bomb would still be deadly today?"

"Well, sure." It was the Air Force officer who responded this time. "The explosive components would probably have gone inert by this point, but the plutonium would still be plenty hot. And the daughter element – the product that results when the plutonium decays – would be almost as deadly as the plutonium itself. It would still be many times more lethal than the weapons we dropped on Hiroshima and Nagasaki. I wonder why they didn't drop it."

"The time," the army officer responded from Berlin. "Germany surrendered shortly before oh-three-hundred Zulu on May seventh. They must've gotten an order to abort."

Both conference rooms went deathly still again. Easton got up and, hands in pockets, walked over to a large globe in the corner.

"So," the Air Force colonel said, "if the Axis built a dirty bomb packed with plutonium-238, and it didn't get used back in 1945 – then where is it today?"

Taking a hand out of his pocket, Easton traced a line on the globe – out of Japan, across the Northwest Territories, over Peterborough, Ontario, and on to New York City. He tried to imagine himself as the pilot of a plane, a plane carrying a payload that could only anger and provoke the forces occupying his homeland if they found out about it. He couldn't retreat along the line he'd taken coming in, because he'd already been discovered there. Turning north would take him into the ammunition-plant environs of New England, and flying south would take him toward Washington – both heavily defended areas. So his only alternative would be to go out to sea in an aircraft that had already burned up a continent's span of fuel. Tracing his finger across the blue of the globe, he looked for a landfall, any landfall.

And found one.

"I think I know where it is," he told the Air Force colonel. "But you aren't going to like the answer."

"Try me," the officer said, his face set.

"My guess is one of two possibilities," Easton told him. "The most likely is that it ditched in deep water in the North Atlantic and it's gone forever."

"You said 'two possibilities,'" Bill Spalding said. "What's the second?"

Easton pursed his lips and tapped the globe.

"Right here," he said. "The Bermuda Triangle."

BOOK TWO

CHURCH BAY

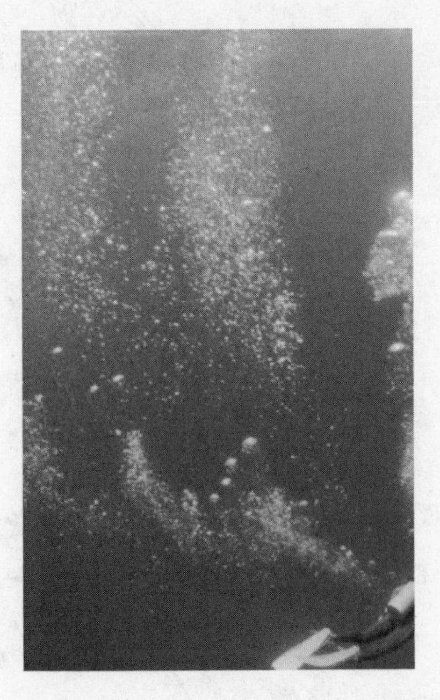

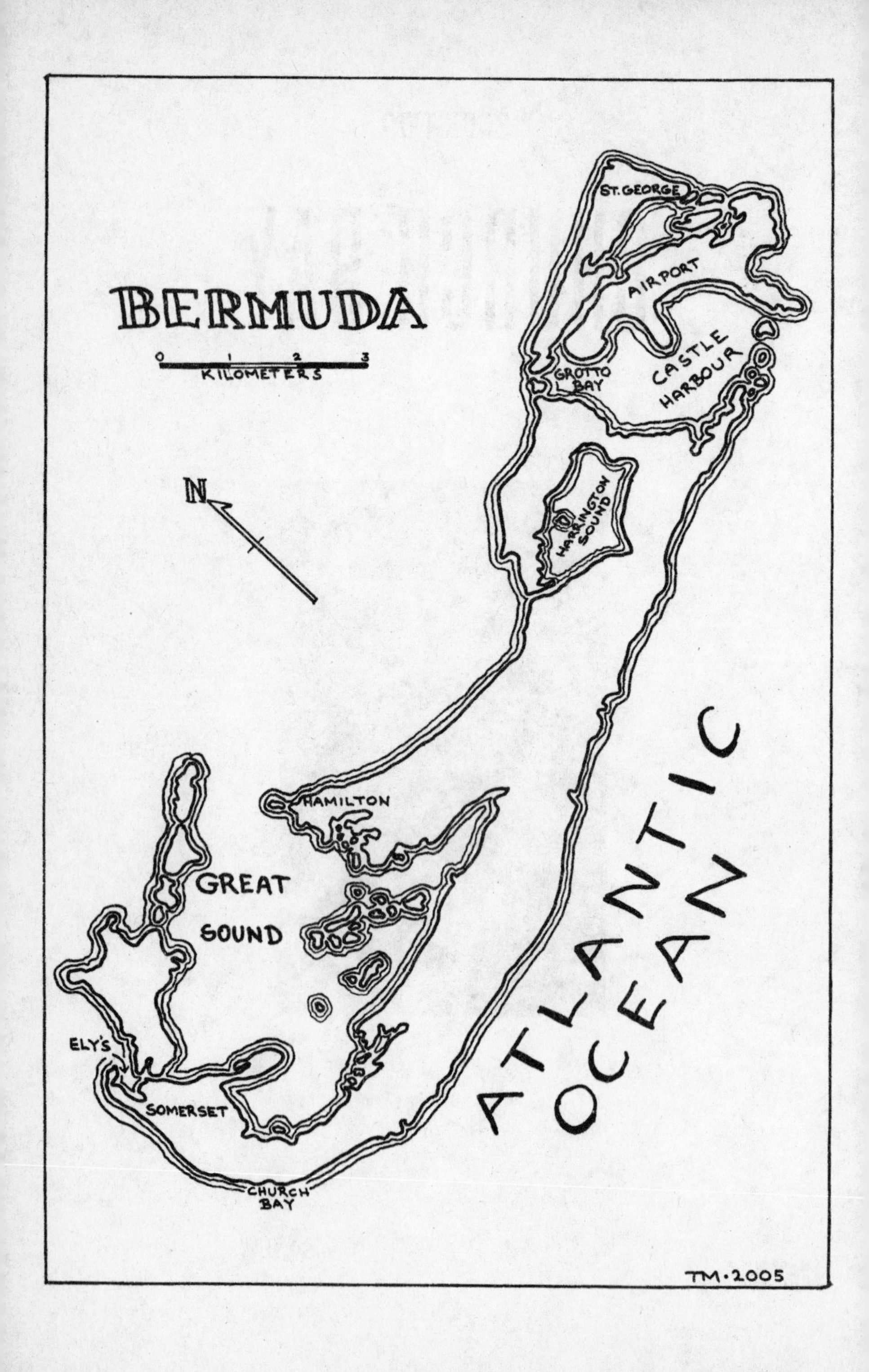
BERMUDA
0 1 2 3
KILOMETERS
N
ST. GEORGE
AIRPORT
GROTTO BAY
CASTLE HARBOUR
HARRINGTON SOUND
HAMILTON
GREAT SOUND
ELY'S
SOMERSET
CHURCH BAY
ATLANTIC OCEAN
TM·2005

CHAPTER SEVENTEEN

JANUARY 6, 2000
BERMUDA INTERNATIONAL AIRPORT, ST. GEORGE'S PARISH, BERMUDA

Beck Easton was accustomed to the idea that each time he revisited one of his old scuba diving haunts, it would be changed.

That was certainly true with Bermuda. When he had first come to the islands to wreck dive on leave from Basic School, Bermuda had seemed like a place frozen in the innocence of the fifties. Even then, Hamilton had boasted a business district, but it had been mostly reinsurance firms and banks – the sort of businesses that were all but invisible to the common man. Now, in addition to the stout Bermudian cottages and old colonial island homes, Easton could see townhouses under construction on those few plots of the South Shore available for purchase by foreigners.

As the Continental Airlines 737 made its final approach, Easton peered down onto North Road. The helmeted tourists on motor scooters were few – typical for the slow season after the holidays – and the road was still populated by Nissan minivans, Rovers, tiny Suzukis, and Toyotas. But the occasional BMW and Peugot punctuated the mix; a surprising number of cars, given the fact that only residents could drive one – all a tourist could rent was a scooter – and the government strictly limited cars to one per registered address.

The airliner passed Hamilton, and Easton looked down on more construction – century-old buildings being torn down, no doubt, to make room for modern office space.

Still, Easton didn't bemoan the change.

First, he couldn't ethically criticize it because, in a very real sense, he and his company – his legitimate company, the one he could acknowledge in public – had helped create it.

Blue Corner Technologies was one of a growing community of companies that had made it possible to do business securely on the Internet. Not absolutely securely; Easton had always made it clear to his clients that there was, strictly speaking, no such thing as absolute security. But with good encryption, properly constructed firewalls, and due diligence, a person could do business online and know that the transaction was as secure as, if not more secure than, a meeting behind closed doors at the local bank.

This made Bermuda, with its pro-business attitude and its favorable tax laws, extremely appealing to North American businesspeople in search of an offshore home. Only two hours from New York by jet, it was the kind of place a Manhattan venture capitalist could visit on a day-trip, if need be, and yet it offered businesses a degree of flexibility and freedom unheard-of in most North American cities.

So the combination of an attractive business climate and high Internet security had made Bermuda the "it" place to incorporate offshore. That in turn made the legal trade a popular one—Bermuda had more lawyers, per capita, than any other nation in the western hemisphere. The thriving legal community, together with their accompanying army of CPAs, drove up the average income and lifted the standard of living for the administrative assistants and information technology workers who supported them. And when business owners came in to visit their money, they spent some of it in the local shops, stayed at good hotels, ate in better restaurants serving the trendy new Bermudian cuisine, chartered fishing boats, and played golf: all things that helped trickle some of that economic influx down to the level of the rapidly rising middle class. The bottom line was that a tiny archipelago with little in the way of natural resources was a twenty-first-century nation with a median income that was the envy of most of the world. That was thanks in part to work that Easton's company had done.

Easton could live with that.

And the other reason he didn't bemoan the change was, he had to admit, guilt. In so many of the islands Easton had visited, the economic disparity was staggering. More than once – on trips to Micronesia and to undeveloped islands in the Lesser Antilles – the people helping Easton with his diving had been so poor, and their equipment so rudimentary, that he had left all of his dive gear with them when he came back to the States.

But in modern Bermuda, tourists bought their dining, their lodging, and their activities from people who were their social and economic equals. That made it a fairly expensive place to visit, as island destinations go. But Easton liked the idea of traveling to a place where he didn't feel as if he was taking advantage of the locals.

And he especially liked it when he was on assignment and wasn't personally picking up the tab.

The wind roared over the extended flaps, and the jet's tires chirped against a runway that would never be lengthened, because there was no real estate left for it to grow into.

Fewer than three minutes later, the seatbelt signal chimed off, and Easton reached into the overhead compartment and took out a light leather flight jacket. Unlike many visitors, Easton harbored no illusions about Bermuda being tropical. While the Gulf Stream washed its shores and kept temperatures warmer than one might expect for the latitude, Easton knew that January in Bermuda could be downright springlike. The customs and immigration officials who stamped his declaration and passport were in long trousers, and not the country's trademark shorts, and the skies outside the terminal, while not overcast, were dotted with clouds.

Easton shouldered his duffel, picked up his gear bag, and walked out of the secure arrival area.

Immediately, he saw a familiar face. It was a bearded, balding, ebony-skinned man in his early fifties, a man with tight, curling hair gone gray at the temples, weathered crinkles at the corners of his eyes, and the look of a person who'd spent a lifetime on the water. He was dressed in crisp khaki trousers and a short-sleeved sport shirt—almost glaringly casual for a Bermudian. And his hearty laugh and warm smile immediately set Easton at ease.

"Hey, Jason," Easton said, setting down his bag so he could shake the black man's hand.

Jason Belden's smile brightened by a magnitude or two. "You're looking very fit. Brilliant! Good to see you, Captain."

"'Captain' no longer." Easton grinned back. "Number one, someone at the Pentagon fell asleep and bucked me all the way up to an O-4. And number two, I'm in the reserves now." It was part of his agency legend. "So 'Beck' is not only appropriate, it's preferable."

"*Major* Easton!" Belden was a native Bermudian, but he had also been a twenty-year Royal Navy man. It was the sort of thing that didn't wash out easily. "Are these your only bags, sir?"

"Just the gear bag and the duffel. I freighted a couple of cases out from DC; they get here?"

Belden nodded. "Came in yesterday, Major. It's all secured—in the gear locker back at the shop."

"Then we're good to go," Easton told him, picking up the gear bag before Belden had the chance. "And Jason?"

"Yes, sir?"

"You 'sir' or 'Major' me one more time, and I guarantee I will put an octopus in your wetsuit the very first chance I get. Am I clear?"

Belden grinned: two rows of perfectly straight white teeth. "Loud and clear, mate. The truck's at the curb."

Belden's truck was a Ford Ranger pickup; larger than the Korean and Japanese pickups fetching cargo from the terminal, and considerably older as well. Eight gray-metal scuba tanks stood in a wire rack in back, and all had yellow caps hanging by nylon keepers from their valves.

Easton nodded toward the tanks as he opened the door to the truck cab. "You just get in?"

"Sure. Sure. Morning run." He said it "mawnin'," thirty years off-island not enough to completely cull the Bermudian accent from his speech. "You know me. A two-tank dive in the morning, and a one-tank in the afternoon, unless I've got a night dive on, and then it's just the one in the morning."

"Am I going to mess you up if I charter you exclusively for a few days?"

The Bermudian grinned.

"In January? Not at all. I've a couple of Germans coming in, but I'll just send them out with Blue Water. Not many tourists on-island now until April—half the time, the boats go out with more crew than divers. Terry will be glad for the business and I'll be glad for the change."

The two men set Easton's bags in the back of the truck. Then they climbed into the cab and Belden started the engine. He turned to Easton, all grins.

"So why would you want a charter all to yourself, Beck? You find yourself a map to Blackbeard's treasure?"

"A little more recent than that, Jason. But not far off the mark."

"Sounds very good by me." The Bermudian put the truck in gear and slipped out onto the left side of the road. "I have done nothing but take tourists out to the *Constellation* and the *Montana* for the last three weeks. My old boat could just about make the run by herself now. It is quite time for something new."

He fell silent and drove, the old truck's tires humming on the pavement, staying at the twenty-five-kilometer-per-hour speed limit, as a marine radio atop the dash sputtered bits and pieces of conversation. They made a turn and the sea, sparkling, blue, and dappled with cloud shadow, appeared to both sides of them as they crossed the causeway into Hamilton Parish.

Belden glanced over at Easton.

"You know, your cases arrived with a customs declaration," he said. His voice sounded deliberately casual.

"Uhm-hmm?" Easton hoped he was doing better at feigning disinterest than Belden.

"A Sea Scan portable sidescan sonar computer, a Marine Sonics Technology high-resolution towfish, and a bespoke magnetometer," the Bermudian said. "What you have sitting back at my shop, sir, is worth more than my Hatteras. And I imagine it is a better kit than what old Bob Ballard used to find the Titanic. Not that it is any of my business, but would you care to tell me just what it is you're searching for?"

Easton glanced at a pair of boats bobbing next to a concrete pier as Belden made the turn onto Blue Hole Road. Belden was no fool, and Easton had known he'd be asking questions, so he'd discussed the matter with Spalding before leaving Washington.

"During your time in the Royal Navy, Jason, did you ever do any work that fell under the Official Secrets Act?"

The Bermudian grinned.

"That fellow in Rome," he said. "The Pope – might he be Catholic?" He lifted an eyebrow. "Yes, sir. I have done work under the Act. More than once."

"Well," Easton told him, "this will be one of those sorts of jobs."

"Government work?"

"My government." Easton wasn't about to mislead an old friend. "But what I'm doing is in the UK's interests, as well."

The Bermudian looked at Easton as he drove, the question obvious on his face. So, as Belden turned again and made the long run up the driveway to the Grotto Bay Beach Resort, Easton told him what he knew – about Ahmed bin Saleen, about the Horten flying-wing, the plutonium, and his theory as to the bomber's whereabouts. It took a while, and Belden pulled the truck to the side of the drive to let Easton finish.

“There’s already one person dead in this,” Easton told his old friend. “So the man who started the ball rolling – this Saudi – is dangerous. Very dangerous. I think you should know that going in. In fact, your wisest course might be to just lease me your boat and let me go this alone.”

“My boat and your gear?” Belden tsked and shook his head. “No, sir. That’s no one-man job. It would take two to handle it at the very least, preferably three. But my lad, Brad, still has a week to go on his holiday leave. He’s attending Britannia Royal Naval College, you know.”

“So I’ve heard,” Easton said. He paused. “About the mission: what do you say?”

The Bermudian winked.

“I say,” he said, laughing, “that it looks as if I get to call you ‘Major,’ after all.”

Belden already had a key for Easton’s hotel room – “I stopped in and squared things away with J.P. this morning, Major ...” – so all they had to do was drop Easton’s duffel with the Grotto’s ancient, pith-helmeted doorman. Then they were back in motion, this time on Middle Road, out of sight of the sea.

Belden kept his shop and office in Hamilton, the island’s capitol, where tourist foot traffic – and the likelihood of walk-in customers – was at its highest. He also had a rigid-hull inflatable that he kept at Ordnance Island, in St. George, for reaching the East End wrecks. But his main boat, a ’64 Hatteras, was moored at Robinson’s Marina, in Ely’s Harbour, on the opposite end of Bermuda. Both sites were natural “hurricane holes” that would give protection in all but a direct blow, yet still offer ready access to the Atlantic and the seamount waters around the archipelago.

After hearing the details of Easton’s assignment, Belden nodded and plucked a microphone from its magnetic mount on the dash.

"Bradley," he asked, "you still at the shop?"

"Here, Dad."

"Let's get the Hatteras rigged. Load up those cases that came in yesterday, run them out to the dock, and start setting things up. Right? We're going to drop the empties at the shop and then I'll be right behind you."

"Will do, Dad. See you soon?"

"Soon as I can. Out."

Setting the microphone back on the dash, Belden turned to Easton. "Are you hungry, Major? Want to stop for a bite in Paget, or in Sandy's?" Like all Bermudians, he pronounced it "Sands."

"Not unless you'd care to, Jason. I've seen both sides of the Atlantic in the past few days. I'm not sure whether it's breakfast-time, dinner, or anything in between."

Belden raised an eyebrow. "Perhaps it'd be best to take you back and drop you at the Grotto, sir. Let you rest up and reset your clock. My Bradley and I can get your things rigged, if you'd like to go out first thing in the morning."

Easton smiled and shook his head, knowing where the conversation was headed. "I can catch a nap in the truck on the run out to the West End," he said. "But I'm betting you'd like to get out on the water."

Belden shrugged as he nudged the old pickup into the right-hand lane, giving plenty of leeway to a pair of white-helmeted tourists chugging along on motor scooters. "Gear like that will take two, three hours to set up," the Bermudian said. "Maybe another hour to calibrate, plus an hour to get to where you want to search. Sundown is in six hours, and I imagine that this sort of work is best done in darkness, don't you, sir?"

Easton nodded, grinning even more broadly at his old friend's enthusiasm. He leaned back in his seat and gazed out the open window as they passed Fort Hamilton and crossed into the outskirts of Hamilton proper. He tapped the old truck's metal sill with his fingertips and leaned back in his seat.

Belden was right. The search ahead of them was best done at night: less chance of another charter wandering into their search grid, and less chance of being interrupted by radio calls from the curious. And while Easton had chartered Belden's boat for the week, the man still had a shop to run during the day, so dusk-to-dawn searches were out of the question. Any way he looked at it, Easton was going to have a fair amount of downtime.

They passed a couple walking hand-in-hand along the beach road, and Easton drummed his fingers on the metal sill again. He entertained a thought, just for the moment, of sending an airline ticket to Angela, getting her her own room at another resort, all on the up-and-up. Bermuda had some wonderful restaurants, nice shops. She'd enjoy it.

What are you? Nuts? This may be a needle-in-a-haystack, but it's still a mission.

Easton chased the fantasy from his mind and thought once again how glad he would be when he was finished with his covert life.

Belden's dive shop had changed considerably since Easton had last seen it. What previously had been a montage of shipwreck photographs behind the counter was now a gigantic mural of a purple-tipped anemone hiding an orange-and-white-striped clownfish—a species not found within three thousand miles of the Bermuda archipelago. The dense racks of wetsuits had been thinned to one sparse display of colorful, polar-fleece-lined diveskins and a rack of rear-zip three-millimeter suits, equally adequate for diving and Jet Skis. The spun-copper diving helmet, once displayed in a place of honor in the front of the shop, now stood in its glass case against the rearmost wall, just a few feet from the door to the back room, as if it were gradually being coaxed into retirement.

The dive masks were still there. The boots, fins, snorkels, and shot-pouch weight belts were still there. There were even a couple of models of buoyancy compensators in various sizes, two or three models of regulators, and housings to fit the most popular models of video cameras.

But the bulk of the available floor space in the dive shop – at least 60 percent of it – was given over to T-shirts and polo shirts in every imaginable color and size, embroidered windbreakers, Nike Aqua Socks and Teva sandals, swim trunks and swimsuits, and Lycra snorkeling suits, Lycra unitards, Lycra headwraps, and even Lycra tank skins, designed to allow the user to customize a rental tank so it would blend with or complement one's outfit.

Easton glanced Belden's way as they carried the scuba tanks in.

"Now, Major, don't get me started." Belden hung his head and shook it slowly as he walked. "I know what you're thinking, and I agree. But my Becca, my eldest girl, did a study, and she showed me that, what with the end-of-the-year reductions we always made, the retail side of the business was barely staying afloat. So I gave her leave to do as she liked with the place for one high season – meaning to put her back in her place, be the wise daddy. And wouldn't you know it – she cleared more than the boat did, after expenses. Made enough to foot the payrolls, make our margin, and leave enough over for a complete overhaul on the Hatteras, and then some. Now, I have my pride, Major, but I know when I've been bested. And it's not the same crowd that comes diving these days. This lot is ... I don't know, skiers who're bored of the snow, I imagine. Nobody learns to dive with the Navy anymore."

Easton laughed. "You wouldn't have a computer where I could check my email in this neon jungle, would you?"

"This day and age? Go broke in a heartbeat if I didn't. Not that I ever touch the thing, mind you. That's my Sarah's job – my youngest. Took a first in maths on her college entrance exams last fall. Me, I'm doing well if I can make the phone work. Just set those tanks down here, and the computer is straight back, through the door."

Easton followed Belden's directions and walked into a crowded, eight-by-ten-foot office. There were two chairs, and one of them was occupied by a slender and attractive young woman with long, raven hair and honey-brown skin a shade or two lighter than her father's. She was checking off signed waiver forms and sorting them into folders.

"Pardon me," Easton said, and then he stopped. "Sarah? Is that you?"

The young woman smiled and nodded.

Easton shook his head and settled into the open chair. "Great Scott! Look at you. Wasn't it just last year that I brought you that American Girl doll?"

"It was six years ago." She laughed. "And I took her everywhere. I even had my school picture taken with her—Momma made her a uniform to match mine. It's good to see you again, Beck."

She kissed his cheek and closed some programs so he could use the computer.

Ten minutes later, Easton was rubbing his chin, thinking. There had been, and would be, no messages from Spalding or the NSA—reading other people's emails was a considerable part of the agency's business, and they knew better than to send anything over so public a medium as the Internet. Most of his mail had dealt with Blue Corner—updates on how the team was initiating the Dixie-Tel project, make-work messages from Rodney about the new programmers' wing.

But one had been from Angela. In it, she thanked him once again for New Year's Eve, thanked him once again for the roses, and said how glad she was that they had met.

Then she went on: she had just about finished her work at Blue Corner, and, as it would help keep the project under budget if she kept her travel expenses to a minimum, she was thinking of leaving near the end of the week – going back to Wheaton and finishing her drawings there. If he wasn't back by then, she wrote, she just wanted to thank him for his kindness.

The end of the week. Easton wondered if they could cover all the water they needed to in just a week. Maybe. But that would still put him in Los Gatos just as Angela was leaving.

And that wasn't the worst of it. He couldn't quite put his finger on it, but there was something in Angela's email that felt distant. Final.

As if she was saying good-bye.

Easton pondered that for a minute. He was amazed at how hollow the thought made him feel.

Snap out of it.

He walked back to the front of the shop, found Belden, and wasn't nearly as amused as he had been by the clownfish mural. Telling himself to get his mind back to the work at hand, Easton accompanied his old friend out to the truck.

CHAPTER EIGHTEEN

LOS GATOS, CALIFORNIA

The roses had now opened fully: big, beautiful, dusky, crimson blossoms nearly the size of Angela Brower's open hands. The flowers still pleased her each time she returned to her room, but the pleasure was bittersweet. They reduced the anonymity of the place and reminded her that she had a man—a wonderful and exciting man—who cared for her.

That was the good part.

That was the bad part too.

Setting her laptop case and purse on the dresser top, she turned the roses to better catch the light and stepped back to look at them, her face neutral and expressionless.

She knew that in a day, maybe less, the blossoms would begin to droop, despite the aspirin that she had crumbled into the water. The petals would fall and she would be left with nothing to carry home to Wheaton but a fluted crystal vase.

To carry home to Wheaton ... and that would happen sooner, rather than later. At least she had done the honorable thing—emailed Beck to let him know she'd be going soon.

She wondered if he would be back before she left and was stymied by the fact that she had two feelings about that prospect—each the polar opposite of the other.

The part of herself that she most trusted—the sensible, logical, Great-Aunt-Eulesta-educated part—said that it would be best if she was gone before Beck Easton returned to Los Gatos. Gone, and hidden, like some frightened little rabbit scurrying back to its warren in Wheaton, Illinois.

But the other part of her—the part that she secretly thought was really her—thought back to midnight on that bluff overlooking the dark ocean, of that kiss ... those kisses.

And that started her heart beating like a trip-hammer.

The two J's ... she could practically hear her great-aunt's voice in her head ... *not only does a Christian woman not cross that line; she does not allow herself to stray anywhere near it.*

Shaking her head, Angela opened her laptop and began revising her notes. It was early evening. She could work for a couple more hours.

And the sooner she finished, the sooner she could leave.

CHAPTER NINETEEN

ROBINSON'S MARINA, BERMUDA

Like his youngest sister, Bradley Belden had matured considerably since Beck Easton had last seen him. The once-gangly teenager had grown into an athletic young man, his Undersea Bermuda polo shirt stretched over a V-shaped torso and biceps that suggested deep familiarity with a weight bench.

"Brad!" Easton grinned and held out his hand. "How's life as a mid?"

"Grueling, sir," the young man replied, greeting Easton with a firm handshake. "And how are you, Major?"

Easton stepped back and crossed his arms. "Am I going to have to listen to this 'Major' stuff from you as well as your father?"

The young man pushed his hand back over his close-cropped black hair. "I wouldn't dream of answering for my father, Major, but I'm nothing but a cadet – *everyone's* a 'sir' to me ... sir."

"As well I know."

Brad brightened. "That's right! My dad told me; you went to Annapolis, right?"

"Back in the Pleistocene Era. So I'll tell you what. We'll observe submarine protocol. That means no saluting, regardless of cover, and no *sirs*. Fair enough?"

Brad made a show of grimacing. "I'm not entirely certain we do it that way in Her Majesty's Navy. But I'll try."

"There you go." Easton looked at the diveboat, riding high next to the dock on the incoming tide. "Wow. Looks as if you've made good progress, getting this all set up."

Brad turned and nodded at the two laptops mounted in the wheelhouse, the voltage inverter and interface mounted between

them, and the trolling outriggers clamped to the transom at the stern.

"It's pretty straightforward," he said. Then, lowering his voice, he added, "And it didn't hurt that you were keeping my dad out of my way."

"I am old, Bradley," Jason Belden said behind his son. "I am not deaf. Now, do you have the major's dive gear on board?"

"Aye, sir," Bradley stifled a flinch. "Aboard and stowed."

"Then ..." The elder Belden's voice dropped half an octave or so. "Why don't you step aboard, so you can continue your criticisms of the elderly at sea?"

Five slips down, Ahmed bin Saleen pretended to tighten the painter on a rented twenty-two-foot Boston Whaler and glanced every few seconds at the *Hog Penny*, the pristine old charter boat that belonged to Belden's Undersea Bermuda. Yesterday and the day before, both, the boat had left the dock for two charters a day, one at half past eight in the morning and one at two in the afternoon. This late in the day—the sun would be going down within the hour—he'd expected it to be deserted, unless the charter had a night dive scheduled. But it was getting ready to make way with only three people on board, and for the last two hours, the mate had been rigging the towfish for a magnetometer—and bin Saleen recognized it for what it was because he had the second cousin of the device stowed away in the Whaler's live well.

He had been in Bermuda for only three days. Only the evening before had bin Saleen managed to get his search equipment squared away. Now he was ready to start looking, to start searching for uncharted wreckage that would, the God of the Prophet willing, be that of the missing Nazi bomber. But he was hesitant to even leave the dock; he had never anticipated that he might have company in his quest.

He removed a screwdriver from a toolbox, bent over the stern running light, and watched the charter boat from the corner of his eye. The *Hog Penny* had started its engines now; gray exhaust was burbling to the surface at its broad stern. The diveboat's mate had gone forward to cast off the bow line, and the American – bin Saleen was not close enough to make out individual words, but he had heard an American accent – was casting off the stern.

It could all be coincidence. The dive boat's mate had greeted the American like an old acquaintance, so it was possible that he was a repeat client, possibly a wealthy diver who came in and booked the whole boat for himself every year after the holiday rush was over. And ships had been foundering in Bermudian waters since before the *Sea Venture* had gone down en route to Virginia in 1609.

So it was not at all beyond the pale that the American could be just another wreck diver. Most scuba divers who visited Bermuda came to dive on shipwrecks. And the more dedicated among them might bring along the gear to search for undiscovered wrecks, rather than content themselves with seeing those that had already been charted.

Still, why would a wreck hunter spend so much on equipment in this day and age? There once had been a time when treasure hunters could keep what they found in Bermuda's waters; all they'd had to do was offer the Crown right-of-first-refusal on its purchase. But those days were long gone; modern Bermuda claimed title to anything found in her waters, charted or not.

Besides, it was coincidence enough that this mysterious American would show up at a diveboat moored at a slip within sight – and nearly within earshot – of Ahmed bin Saleen's rented boat. That he would come equipped with a magnetometer was especially suspicious. Two magnetometers showing up at the same time in a place inhabited by fewer than 70,000 people? That was certainly one more than the laws of probability would allow. If he added to that the likelihood that the Berlin apartment had been compromised, as his watchers there believed, then the chances of this American showing up at this time and not being in any way related to bin Saleen's search were smaller than the Saudi would have liked.

That the American had shown up within a week of bin Saleen's appearance was of even greater concern. He had come to Bermuda assuming that he would have months in which to conduct his search and, hopefully, retrieve what he was after. Now his window of opportunity appeared to have shrunken to a matter of days.

The Saudi grimaced.

Part of him wanted to believe that this new person was just some wealthy American fool doing some wreck diving, spending his tax-free offshore profits.

But deep down inside, bin Saleen feared that his cover had been blown—that this American had, incredibly, obtained the same data and was on the same quest.

Ahmed bin Saleen's mind raced. He had to assume the worst. It was the only logical course.

And besides, even if the American was nothing but an innocent shipwreck hunter, what if the wreck he happened upon was that of the old Horten bomber? What would happen then?

Disaster.

So if the aircraft was indeed here, bin Saleen would have to get to it first. But he could not do his search during the daytime; he needed open water for that, unimpeded by competing boat traffic. And with Belden's charter boat heading out this evening, bin Saleen would not be able to search tonight either. Two vessels conducting underwater searches in the waters of a country no larger than a small city—there was no way that would go unnoticed. And while this Bermudian, this Belden, might not mind inviting that level of scrutiny, bin Saleen wanted nothing of the sort.

So at the moment, he was stalemated.

But he could try to learn more about this American. Waiting until Belden's boat had pulled away and was crossing the waters of the harbor, Ahmed bin Saleen cast off his lines.

He started the Whaler's big outboard and nosed it out into the channel, where the diveboat had gone.

CHAPTER TWENTY

Ely's Harbour is guarded by reef up to its very mouth. To reach the sea Jason Belden had to thread the thirty-two-foot boat through a series of twists and turns that he had long since memorized, but required his concentration nonetheless.

Knowing this, Beck Easton stayed out of the pilothouse and stepped aft. At the near end of Ely's, he could see Bermuda's Great Sound through the portal of Somerset Bridge, which connected Somerset Island – "up the country" to Bermudians – to the main body of Sandy's Parish.

A popular stop with tour guides, Somerset Bridge was popularly described as the "smallest drawbridge in the world," and Easton had to assume that was correct. Massive wooden support beams sprouted from stone abutments on either side of the bridge and terminated in a hinged leaf all of eighteen inches wide. At one time, sailboats passed from Ely's to the Great Sound by asking passersby to lift the leaf and make room for their masts. In an age in which diesel engines had largely replaced sail, the gap had been padlocked for years, and most vessels reached the Great Sound by going the long way around, past King's Point, on the far side of Somerset Island. But the channel under the bridge was kept dredged, and most Bermuda captains knew Somerset Bridge as a shortcut they could use to enter the Great Sound "in a pinch" – a tight fit for most modern vessels, but passable under the right conditions.

Up on the flying bridge, Easton could see the unmanned helm ticking left, and then right, pantomiming Belden's movements as he steered his vessel from inside the wheelhouse. No order was given, but Bradley Belden went to work, raising the vessel's LORAN-C and radio masts as the boat idled into the outer reaches of Ely's Harbour. Easton gave him a hand, speaking as he did, filling the young naval cadet in on the background of the missing Nazi flying-wing bomber.

"So, basically, we know it was headed this way when it was last seen," Easton said as the *Hog Penny* cleared the harbor mouth and the two of them joined Brad's father in the wheelhouse. "And we figure one of three things happened. Either it ran out of fuel, ditched, and sank somewhere out in the open ocean; or its crew ditched it intentionally and rendezvoused with a naval vessel, most likely a sub; or—and this is, admittedly, a long shot—they put the bomber down here within swimming distance of the beach."

"Which do you think is most likely, sir?"

Easton looked at the young man in the golden light of the low late-afternoon sun, the white rooftops of Somerset seesawing ever so slightly behind him, keeping time with the wavelets slapping lazily against the hull. Even in the fading light, Easton was struck by how alike father and son were—earnest, dedicated, the kind of faces one knew one could trust.

"You don't put just anybody at the controls to fly a Great Circle route over the Arctic," Easton told him. "I've got to believe that, whoever the pilot was, he must have been a pretty good stick. He wouldn't have run out of fuel unless he was so badly damaged that there was no alternative. As for a sub, if one had picked them up, you'd think we would have found out about it when Germany's vessels returned to port after the surrender. There've always been rumors of Nazi subs that ran to Venezuela after the war, but none were ever confirmed. So, long shot or not, that leaves here."

"No record of German aviators wading ashore here either, Major," Jason reminded him as he steered north, headed for the hook-shaped point at the top of the harbor. "No Germans at all—remember, we had a captured U-boat up at the Royal Naval

Dockyard for a good part of the last year of the war. Place was buttoned up tighter than a drum. And didn't the Brits and the Americans both have radar operating off the Island?"

"They did." Easton watched as a sportfishing boat idled past to their left, headed for the marina. "But the radar was mostly watching the sea. In the air, the flying-wing wouldn't have cast much of a radar signature, not even for an operator looking for it. The design is inherently stealthy. And as for why no crew were ever spotted, there's a world of difference between ditching an airplane in open ocean, with nothing else around, and putting it down next to an island surrounded by reefs, all the while trying to avoid being shot down. These folks would have had their hands full. A hundred different things could have happened ..."

"... Only one of which would have resulted in everyone wading ashore." Brad finished the thought for him.

"Well, if it's lost in the drink, I think we can rule out the waters around St. George's," Jason said. "Radar or no, jets are noisy. This lot would have steered well clear of it. The North Shore was already pretty well settled in the forties, so they probably would have avoided it as well. Were I a German aviator, I would have stayed well hidden until teatime, not shown my face until I was sure everyone had listened to the radio and heard about the surrender. I'd hide in the bush 'til then, and there would have been more bush on the South Shore during the war. Warwick and Paget didn't get built up until the fifties or so.

"And," he continued, "to get to the Sound, one would have to overfly Hamilton coming one way, and the Royal Naval Dockyard or Morgan's – which was US Navy in the war – coming the other. West End's too close to the Dockyard too, and if your airplane had gone down between Tucker's Town and Warwick, I have to believe it would have been found by now. That's Wreck Alley, from the *Rita Zoretta* down to the *Minnie Breslauer*, plus there's a breaking reef line that one could see from the air, even by moonlight."

"All that leaves is the Atlantic side of Southampton and Sandy's, from Ely's, here, down to what?" Brad asked. "Horseshoe Bay?"

"That's the way I figure it," Jason agreed.

"It's your water," Easton told him. "If you want to start at Horseshoe, then that sounds good to me."

Grinning, Jason Belden pushed the throttle lever all the way forward. The engine roared in response and the *Hog Penny*'s bow rose, the diveboat transforming itself instantly from a sleepy vessel at wallowing rest to a deft thing of beauty and speed.

As they heeled around the point and entered the open ocean, a horizon of golds, reds, and pinks opened in front of them, the sun a distant orange ball being absorbed by the western horizon under a slim bank of clouds. The diveboat began to porpoise, the waves of the true sea rolling in now against the hull and alternately lifting and dropping it.

Off to the west, the sun made its final drop into the pink horizon. Jason Belden flipped two switches, bringing up his running lights, and turned the knob on a green metal box that stood on the navigation console. An LCD screen, like the screen of a laptop computer turned on end, came bluely alive in front of him.

Easton stepped next to the charter captain. The image on the screen looked like a simplified map of the region. At the top, two bars bore white letters that read "21.7 KNT" and "172.43MAG." On the bottom of the screen, two strings of eight numbers, the last three in each string changing rapidly, kept track of current latitude and longitude. In the exact center of the screen was a simplified boat shape, its bow pointed at the top of the screen.

"Nice," Easton said. "Radar, GPS, and charts in one display. What's the story, Captain? Santa good to you?"

"No," Belden laughed. "Becca's T-shirts were. We put this in when we had the boat out of the water for the overhaul. It's good for navigation and weather both. Here—step in here and have a go."

Easton took the helm and compared the radar signature in front of him with what he could see through the windows of the open-backed wheelhouse. To the left of the screen, the darkening landmass of Bermuda was painted in intricate green contours.

He turned the gain all the way down and then brought it up again just enough to cancel out the wave return. Moving blips on the screen corresponded to two sport-fishing boats coming back in after an afternoon on the blue water. He pressed the range button three times, moving the most extreme range marker out to twenty nautical miles. The shape of Bermuda resolved into its familiar hook and he could even see some moving returns from the Great Sound—probably sailboat masts topped with aluminum radar-return targets. A blip appeared to his far right and he stared that way, out at the dusky horizon. Moments later, a minute string of lights appeared: a distant container ship, probably inbound from the East Coast. Easton pressed an illuminated button marked "MET," and gray bands appeared to the east, indicating cumulus clouds that had passed over earlier in the afternoon. There was another button marked "WAY," which Easton recognized as "waypoints"—a stored list of memorized coordinates. Easton did not touch that one; he knew that charter boat captains considered their dive site locations to be proprietary information, intellectual property that was rarely, if ever, shared.

"Very nice," he told Belden. "Does it make coffee too?"

Belden laughed, an unabashed bray.

"I would not be surprised in the slightest to discover that it does," he said. "Actually, I often run with everything off but the radio during the day. I like to use the compass and the landmarks, and sometimes it is nice not to think about satellites looking down on me and to remember when there was some skill involved in all of this."

Easton nodded.

"There still is, Jason," he said as the boat banked into a shallow turn. "There still is."

Half an hour later, only the thinnest band of reddish-gray was left on the western horizon.

Gibb's Hill Light was a waxing and waning orb off their port stern when Jason Belden began to reduce the throttle.

Easton looked to his left, toward the island. No lights showed at the waterline, which did not surprise him; he could tell by the angle to the lighthouse that they were abreast of South Shore Park with its three big public beaches.

Jason Belden flipped the switch on a smaller display next to the radar, and a bright green sonar image and black numerals came up, showing the depth to the bottom in feet.

"How shallow do you want to start, Major?"

"Clear as the water is, here? If that plane went down in less than fifty feet, I've got to think it would have been spotted by some pilot on his way into Kindley Field, at least in the first few months after it went down. So no use searching shallower than that."

He moved back into the open deck behind the wheelhouse and, a Pelikan waterproof penlight gripped between his teeth, opened the long yellow, plastic travel case containing the magnetometer towfish. Brad began setting up its ruggedized laptop display on the navigation console, plugging it into the coaxial cable and power leads that he'd zip-stripped into place earlier in the afternoon.

Easton found the waterproof placard that he'd been looking for and brought it forward to Belden.

"Says here if we run it at eight knots relative on a hundred meters of cable, the fish should ride at a depth of ten meters," Easton said. "That would give us a pretty narrow search band if we were towing the sidescan, but we won't use that until we have specific targets to look at. With the magnetometer that close to the bottom, we'll have great sensitivity."

"We'll need it," Belden said. "Lots of volcanic deposits in these waters, you know. Give you false readings on the magnetometer."

"This one's optimized for titanium," Easton said. "And we've got to start somewhere. Let's begin at the ten-fathom contour and then run an east-west grid from there to the far side of Southampton. Just run us east for a quarter mile or so first, and Brad and I can rig the tow lights and start putting the fish in the water after you've come about."

Three minutes later, the ruggedized laptop was up and running, the Peizo resistor on the towfish sending the information that it was riding steady at ten meters of depth and searching for the disturbances in magnetic fields caused by both ferrous and nonferrous metals, as well as unnatural bottom disturbances. A few minutes after that, it was registering a significant anomaly just to starboard.

"That will be the *Breslauer*," Jason Belden said, locking the helm onto autopilot at a heading of 270 degrees true.

"Then we know it's working," Easton replied. "Let's start mowing the lawn."

For the next four hours, the three men followed the same routine. Jason Belden ran a perfectly straight line for four miles, made a wide, low-speed "keyhole" turn designed to keep the towfish off the bottom without placing undue strain on the cable, and then headed back in the opposite direction on a track exactly fifty meters to the south of the one he'd just run. It was a procedure remarkably similar to running a combine though a cornfield or pushing a mower back and forth across a broad lawn.

Easton watched the magnetometer readout and recorded every anomaly, noting its exact latitude, longitude, and depth. Meanwhile, Brad stood post in the stern, training a searchlight on the cable and watching for anything that could snag the towfish.

It was going on midnight when Jason Belden broke the silence. "Major? You'd better have a look at the radar."

Easton looked up on the screen. An even pattern of vertical columns—the GPS record of the search grid—glowed in pale, luminous green lines. To the right of the screen, the Warwick beach gleamed in a darker green. And directly behind the dive-boat, at a distance of just a little over a mile, a radar blip was keeping pace with them, following the same course.

Easton backed out of the pilothouse and looked up at the stubby mast behind the bimini top, supporting the saucerlike radar antenna. Three white lights, rigged one above the other, were glowing brightly on the mast shaft, indicating a vessel performing towing operations. Maritime law called for nearby craft to give them a wide berth; following directly behind them would be out of the question.

"Might be a tourist in a rented boat," Jason said. "Perhaps he just thinks that the lights mean we're having a party."

"Bradley," Easton called, "Cut the searchlight, will you?"

The light winked out and Easton gazed directly astern. Some shore lights showed to the north, but all there was behind them was inky, jet-black water and a night sky full of stars.

"Whoever they are, they're not showing any lights at all," Easton muttered. "And I've got to think that even a tourist would know better than that."

He fell silent for a moment, thinking, while the diesel engines thrummed beneath their feet.

"Brad," Easton said, "flip that light back on and point it dead astern, right at the horizon."

The young man did as he was told and, for a matter of seconds, it illuminated a tiny, bluish-white mustache—the bow wave of a distant, following vessel. Then the mustache died away. Easton turned to the radar and saw that the blip behind them had fallen lower on the screen. But it continued to trail them.

"I cannot slow down, Major," Belden reminded him. "Not unless we bring in the towfish. Otherwise we run the risk of fouling her."

"That's all right; steady as she goes." Easton picked up the microphone to the marine radio, set the channel indicator to 13 – the international hailing channel – and keyed the microphone. "Vessel following the craft showing three white lights. Stand off and show your running lights. We have an object in tow."

No lights came on and the blip drew slightly closer on the radar.

"Vessel following, please respond, over." Easton held the microphone away from his mouth and listened.

Nothing.

He put the microphone to his mouth again. "Bermuda Marine Police, this is the diveboat *Hog Penny.* We are signaling tow in progress and have a vessel closing on our stern. Could you investigate, please? Over."

Almost immediately, red and green lights winked on behind them. On the radar screen, the blip began moving to their right. After that, they saw a white lamp – a stern light – that receded rapidly toward the horizon, even as the blip dropped to the bottom of the screen.

"Marine Police to station calling," the radio crackled. "Can you repeat, please? Over."

"This is the *Hog Penny,*" Easton replied. "Belay my last. Thank you, Marine Police. Over and out."

He looked at Jason Belden, who shrugged. "Don't know, Major. Someone who's had too many Dark and Stormies, too little training, and the keys to a boat?"

"Maybe," Easton said as the distant white light diminished to a pinpoint. "Maybe not."

CHAPTER TWENTY-ONE

JANUARY 10, 2000

Did you remember to tape the Manchester United football game for me? If so, could you drop it by my house at noon?

That was the email Ahmed bin Saleen had sent his cousin as soon as he'd gotten back to his room at the Fairmont Southampton Princess Hotel. He had sent it in English, and he had used the simplest and most break-resistant code possible, which was really no code at all. The business about the tape and the football game meant nothing, but was only there to make the message look innocuous. "Could you drop it by my house" meant that Mohammed was supposed to Instant Message him, and "noon" meant noon in Saudi Arabia which was, unfortunately, six in the morning in Bermuda. That was earlier than bin Saleen cared to rise after a night of following the mysterious American, but he would have made it earlier if he'd thought he could have coordinated such a thing with his cousin. Despite bin Saleen's numerous suggestions, Mohammed al Fadli often did not check his email until well after breakfast.

He had, however, checked it this morning, because the IM box popped up on bin Saleen's notebook computer—a brand-new machine with a brand-new IP address that would not appear familiar to surveillance programs—as the tiny digital clock in the corner of the screen blinked over to "6:01 a.m."

The peace of God upon you, my cousin, Mohammed's greeting read in Arabic.

And upon you, my cousin. The custom here would be to spend several minutes inquiring about the health of one another's family and friends. But Ahmed bin Saleen had neither the patience nor the time for that. Nor did he want to keep the IM connection

open one second longer than necessary. So without leaving his cousin a moment of dead screen time in which to reply, bin Saleen continued typing: *We have a complication. There is an American here, and he appears to be on a similar quest.*

His last sentence hung there on the LCD display, unanswered, for ten seconds, twenty, thirty. After half a minute of nothing, a reply appeared: *How is this possible?*

It was the same question that had plagued bin Saleen since the equipment arrived at the *Hog Penny* the afternoon before. In more than twenty years, Western intelligence had never been more than a distant, even abstract, concern for him, and now they seemed to be on his very heels. But it was one thing for him to be concerned, and another for Mohammed al Fadli, secure within the borders of the Kingdom of Saudi Arabia, to ask what bin Saleen saw as an accusatory question.

It could be a coincidence, he typed in reply. *There are many people who come here to scuba dive on shipwrecks, and some prefer to search for undiscovered sites. But even if that is the case, we still have a problem. He may, God forbid, find what we are looking for before we are able to do so.*

Ahmed bin Saleen clicked the "Send" icon. He heard muffled voices—a group of Canadian businessmen on a golf holiday, laughing and talking loudly in the hallway on their way out to the links.

This must not be allowed, his cousin replied.

"As if you were here to disallow it," bin Saleen muttered at the screen. But what he wrote was: *It must not and it shall not. I will see to that. But we may need to recover the item sooner than I had anticipated, and I will need special equipment for that: a ship capable of lifting at least five thousand kilos.*

Ahmed bin Saleen knew what the next question would be before it appeared on the screen: *When is this ship required?*

He bent to the keyboard.

God willing, this week.

The screen did not change for nearly a minute this time. Finally a reply appeared.

This is a great thing to ask, given the fact that the object of your search still eludes you.

Ahmed bin Saleen curled his hands into fists and clenched his teeth. He thought of any number of responses, rejecting each in turn. Finally, he typed: *Great acts sometimes require great risks. I do not ask this casually, my cousin.*

This time, the reply did not take long: *Then, God willing, that will be arranged. Do you need anything else?*

"I have the dive equipment, the lights, the radios," bin Saleen said aloud, thinking. He wrote, *Make sure that the ship has underwater torches, for cutting metal. Also, how are our contacts here for eluding customs?*

Bermuda has very close scrutiny because of the narcotics, his cousin replied. *But our contacts are good. What is it that you require?*

Get me a pistol—something easy to carry and conceal, bin Saleen typed. *Do this as soon as possible.*

You need a gun?

Absolutely, bin Saleen typed. *I need a gun.*

CHAPTER TWENTY-TWO

JANUARY 11, 2000

Over five days of searching, Easton and the Beldens had begun operating as a unit. Now that the cabling was all in place, setting up the electronics took only a matter of minutes, even in the dark.

Easton and Brad cast off the lines and then, as Brad scrambled up to the flying bridge to raise the radio antennae, Easton went into the wheelhouse, where Belden was already powering his electronics. They motored slowly out of Ely's, and Easton stood next to Jason Belden as the charter boat captain powered up his electronic navigation system.

"Can you bring up the plot of the possibles we've found so far?" Easton asked.

"Sure thing, Major." Belden punched in a pass code, then pressed a button marked "Log." A screen came up marked "Range" and the old captain selected the previous five evenings.

The screen dissolved into a detailed nautical chart of the western half of Bermuda. From an offshore spot halfway down the length of Somerset Island to a place relatively close to the beach off Warwick Parish, twenty-one glowing red dots appeared, their GPS coordinates arrayed next to them in yellow numerals.

"There is a great deal of water we've not surveyed," Belden observed. "But if you ask me, I would say that we've covered all the likely area. If it wasn't ditched here, I would say that your airplane was ditched in deep water, off in the open ocean where no one is likely to ever find it."

"I agree. So what would you say? Dispense with the magnetometer tonight and start sidescanning these sites?"

"That would be my vote."

Easton stepped out of the open-backed wheelhouse and glanced up at the moon. Fuller moons tended to be popular with divers and sportfishing charters alike. They couldn't be certain of the relatively empty water they'd enjoyed earlier in the week. But he also had the nagging feeling that time was running short; he hadn't forgotten the boat that had tailed them that first night. He took a breath – salt air – and stepped back into the wheelhouse.

"You're right, Jason. And it won't take us long to rig the side-scan. The towfish is about the same size as the magnetometer's; we can use the same downrigger, if we want."

He turned to the navigation screen. "Why don't you set a course for this site, down here off Warwick, and Bradley and I will start rigging the fish?"

"Consider it done, Major."

They rounded the entrance to Ely's, and Belden pushed the throttle forward, bringing the boat up on plane.

Running lights on, Ahmed bin Saleen kept the big Mercury outboard turning at just a few hundred RPMs above idle, gliding the Boston Whaler across the inky surface of Ely's Harbour. His one-piece Henderson wetsuit remained unzipped to the waist, a concession to the lingering warmth of the day. Behind him, bungeed to the boat's tank rack, his scuba gear was all set up and two extra tanks stood at the ready. He had a mask, fins, a snorkel, and a weight belt in a net bag, all moderately worn, and he even had a dive flag, red with a white stripe, complete with a plastic mast and a suction cup to mount it to the console windscreen.

Not that he planned on using any of those things. But if anyone in authority were to board his boat, he wanted an iron-clad reason for being out on the water in the dead of night, one that would get him out of the encounter with nothing more severe than a lecture on the dangers of diving alone.

He had been following this diveboat now for five nights, and he was no nearer to his goal than he had been when the American had first appeared. Soon it would be a week with nothing accomplished.

He let his fist fall on the boat's gelcoated console, instantly regretting the display of emotion. He was, after all, supposed to look like a tourist. If anyone was watching, he was supposed to be having fun.

He had carefully cultivated that façade, shaving his beard and having his hair streaked so he could look like the cover story his Al-Qaeda brethren had concocted for him – that of a Canadian playboy with money to burn, taking advantage of the off-season in Bermuda to pursue a protracted wreck-diving holiday.

A vacation, he reminded himself. Younger, more modern Canadians would use the American term.

He tsked under his breath. That was part of the risk one took when taking on a new identity with so little prep time. But Tirelli's absence must certainly have been noticed by now and, even though the pathetic little UFO fanatic had seemed relatively friendless, bin Saleen could not take the chance that the Andrew Sasri cover identity had been breathed to anyone. If only the man had not made plans to speak at that UFO convention ...

But that was ... what was the expression? "Water over the dam?" Was that something a Canadian would say? He supposed it was, but he wasn't sure; he'd been schooled to talk like an American, not a Canadian. He shook his head and motored on. Too many things about this project were turning out to be shaky. Too many.

Ahmed bin Saleen rounded the entrance to the harbor. Belden's diveboat was heading south at what looked to be full power, and bin Saleen decided to wait a bit, keep a healthy gap between the two of them. He could catch up once they had slowed, and do as he had done for four nights now—shadow them from shallow water, where his radar return would be lost in that of the land behind him.

He shook his head again. He, Ahmed bin Saleen, was on the defensive, and he had never before found himself in that situation. Or at least never for more than a few moments at a time. He was the planner. It was his specialty to keep others worried, trying to guess his next move. And he resented this American who had, wittingly or not, so effectively turned the tables this time around.

The Saudi swallowed and set his chin.

This was a minor setback. He would overcome it and regain control of the situation.

As God was his witness, he would.

CHAPTER TWENTY-THREE

M.V. *MARINE QUEST IV*
ATLANTIC OCEAN — 93 MILES NORTHWEST OF CORVO FLORES

Shoes off, bare feet up on the console, Jeff Slagle leaned back in the creamy white cowhide helmsman's chair and watched the chrome wheel – a drive-by-wire helm barely larger than an automobile steering wheel – creep back and forth minutely in response to the autopilot. His digital instruments were green across the board, the radar showed clear except for a supertanker a good twenty-five miles to his south, and, from six home-theater-quality stereo speakers hidden behind overhead panels and cabinet work in the spacious bridge, Tina Turner was in full fortissimo growl, asking "What's love got to do with it?"

"Beats me, Tina, baby. It sure beats me."

Slagle watched the *Quest*'s bow lift and drop in relation to the darkened horizon, spray flashing in seeming slow motion each time the graceful vessel dropped. He nodded his head in time to the music. One thing you could say about Tina: the woman had pipes.

Legs, too, if the videos didn't lie. Other than that, though, she was a little scary looking, if you asked Slagle. Scary and old enough to be his mother. She *had* to be if she and Ike had been cutting records back in the sixties, a decade that had faded into history by the time Jeff Slagle was five.

The song ended and Slagle waited to see what would be next; he had the new CD player set on "shuffle."

The music came up: "We Don't Need Another Hero."

Bummer. Not that it was a bad tune – quite the contrary. But the subject matter left something to be desired.

Slagle had just finished his evening radio call to the Walker's Port Oceanographic Institute, home to the *Marine Quest IV*, and where the 262-foot vessel was bound after a twenty-four-month refit in Rotterdam. It had been the oceanographic research vessel's first major overhaul since the *Quest* had been launched in 1979, and the ship had been gone over from stem to stern and from the hull on in. It had a new diesel-electric powerplant, new bow and stern thrusters, a computerized navigation system that could hold a position to within a tenth of a meter, new comms gear, weather radar with Doppler capability, a larger and stronger helipad, and a full galley refit.

Most importantly, the vessel's crane had been replaced with an articulated derrick that could swivel to lift up to an eight-ton submersible, either through the amidships moon pool or, counterbalanced by computer-controlled ballast tanks, from alongside the vessel.

All of which were needed if the *Quest* was to carry out its next mission, a two-month trip to explore satellite seamounts around the island of Saba and, hopefully, confirm reports of a new subspecies of six-gill shark. Eleven marine biologists had carefully coordinated their sabbaticals to make that trip, and before they could leave the vessel would have to be upfitted with a new mainframe computer that was outside the Rotterdam shipyard's area of expertise. The *Quest* also had to make sea-trials with both of its submersibles and return in time to be provisioned.

The departure date for that trip had been set: in seven weeks' time, the *Marine Quest IV*, both submersibles, and all the people with the letters after their names would be headed for the Dutch Antilles – and upfit and trials would require six of those weeks. Getting home in time to start everything on schedule was already looking like something of a crapshoot, and now the big meteorological brains at Walker's Port – the same geniuses that had told him that the tropical storm out of the Azores would be long gone by the time he crossed the Mid-Atlantic Ridge – had now gotten on the horn with him during his daily check-in call to let him know that the remnants of that same storm had apparently stalled 650 miles west of Massachusetts ... directly in his path.

No one had ordered him to change course. No one had even suggested it. Even a bureaucracy as multi-tiered and degree-happy as Walker's Port respected the age-old tradition that gave the captain the final say in the disposition of his vessel. But the "met" brainiacs had reminded him at least three times that he would be encountering high winds and thirty-foot sea swells if he continued on his present course, whereas he would encounter much calmer seas and only an additional four days of travel – ten days in all – if he diverted south to Charleston and then came back up the coast once the storm had blown out.

Slagle had told them he'd see them in less than a week.

And now Tina seemed to be weighing in with her opinion. But the *Marine Quest IV* was the most stable vessel of her size that Slagle had ever served on, and now she had an additional thousand horsepower. They'd be all right.

But a change of tunes was definitely in order. Night was coming on. Maybe some Bob Seger. Or Ted Nugent.

Yes. That was definitely the ticket. Time to hear from the Motor City Madman. Flipping open his CD wallet, he hit "Stop" on the player, and then froze, listening.

Slagle walked to the side of the wheelhouse, cracked the hatch, and listened again. His ears had not been deceiving him – there it was, only louder: the steady *whup-whup-whup* of rotor blades.

A chopper – but what on earth was a helicopter doing out here in the middle of the Atlantic Ocean?

Slagle stepped out onto the weather deck. Sure enough, just vaguely visible in the backwash from the deck lamps, a single-rotor helicopter was closing on their stern.

Slagle watched as the aircraft drew closer and whistled. Lower wing tanks, outriggers on the tail boom – their visitor was a Bell 430, just about top-of-the-line when it came to corporate helicopters.

The hatch aft of him opened and the *Marine Quest*'s comms officer emerged.

"Wilson?" Slagle called. "What's the story?"

"Mayday, Cap," she told him. "They're coming straight in. Said they have a cockpit fire."

"A fire ..." Slagle ducked back into the wheelhouse, brought the ship about into the wind, slowed to two knots and re-engaged the autopilot. He slapped the big red button to sound a general alarm, grabbed a fire extinguisher off the wheelhouse bulkhead, and raced back out to the weather deck.

The chopper was settling onto the helipad. No sign of smoke, but the cockpit glass was so darkly tinted that, between that and the failing evening light, he couldn't see anything inside. With Wilson hot on his heels, Slagle raced up the short ladder to the pad—was that writing on the fuselage Arabic?—transferred the fire extinguisher to his left hand and opened the cockpit door with his right.

He froze. Two pilots and six passengers: that's what these corporate 430s were set up to carry. But this cabin was absolutely *packed* with men in black jumpsuits, with—*what the*—were those ski masks over their heads?

"Hey!" Slagle still had the extinguisher; some part of him was still looking for a fire. "What's going on?"

The man nearest the door pressed something hard and cold against Slagle's forehead.

A gun, the captain realized. *This guy just pulled a gu—*

Khalid al-Hawsawi smiled, pushed the nearest body out of his way with his boot, and stepped from the idling helicopter. *That's the beauty of yelling "fire." You do that, everybody comes running ... and they all have something in their hands.*

"Fan out," al-Hawsawi called into his shoulder mike in Arabic. "Two of the crew are down. We have twelve to go. Mustapha, secure the radio. Everyone else, search the ship. Use the blueprints. Check every space. Nobody lives, but check your backgrounds before you fire. We need this ship in perfect condition. I repeat—we need this ship."

CHAPTER TWENTY-FOUR

JANUARY 12, 2000, 3:00 AM
HAMILTON, BERMUDA

"Okay," Bradley Belden said. "Here's Target One."

He slid a diskette into the PC, and the three men, crowded into the tiny office area in the back of the dive shop, turned their attention to the screen. An image streamed into place: a rectangle with two circles underneath it, a smaller rectangle toward the front.

Brad Belden moved closer. "What the—?"

Easton chuckled. "Is that what I think it is?"

Jason nodded. "If you think it's a Ford Model A, then yes. That's what it is. And would you look at that—it's standing upright on its wheels."

They moved on to the next target—two roughly carrot-shaped objects, next to what looked like a pile of beans.

"All right," Bradley said. "I give. What is that?"

"Cannon," Jason said. "Two of them. And Major, can you tell me what that is next to them?"

"Ballast stones."

"There," Jason Belden said to his son. "See what you can learn if you pay attention in those naval history classes?"

The next seven images weren't nearly as interesting: four were metal drums, one was a huge marine diesel engine, one showed a sheaf of rectangular sheets that Easton eventually identified as corrugated metal roofing material, and one was a pile of cast-iron bathtubs.

"All right," Brad Belden said. "Best for last."

He clicked the mouse and an image came up that, even in the high-contrast sonar imagery, was obviously a three-masted

schooner lying on its side, its chains and anchors piled next to it like discarded necklaces.

None of the men said a thing. They'd already seen this image in the paper printout on the boat, but the digital recording was considerably more detailed, showing deadeyes still attached to the rigging, and wooden barrels – obviously deck cargo – scattered in the sand next to the ship.

Finally, Easton broke the silence.

"That's it? That's all we have, right?"

Bradley nodded. "That's the lot, Major. We had some other hits, but they're all known wreck sites, known and well-dived."

"Well, then. Okay, gentlemen. Good mission."

Jason gave Easton a tired smile. "I'm sorry we didn't find what you were looking for, Major."

Easton shook his head. "I'm not. If the weapon that was on that plane has three miles of water on top of it, then that's the best place for it. I said it before – this was the logical place, but it was a long shot. Our mission was to see if it was here, and it isn't. We'll still want to transfer all our disks to Fort Meade so they can do their own analysis, but as far as I'm concerned, we accomplished what I was sent here for. Good job."

Jason nodded at the schooner on the screen. "I trust you are going to stay and take the first look at that, are you not?"

Easton cocked his head.

"Captain, don't you have a VIP list – clients who come down and dive with you a couple of times a year?"

"Well, sure, but – "

"No buts. The smart business tactic is to send out an email tomorrow morning – invite those folks to come down and dive a virgin shipwreck, as a thank-you for their patronage."

Jason's dark face softened. "Major, you are being too generous."

"Not me." Easton laughed. "Courtesy of the United States of America. They're the ones who put the shekels in the checking account. But there is one thing I'd like."

“Name it,” Jason said.

“When we’re done looking at the slide show – ” Easton nodded at the computer. “Do you mind if I use this to go online, use the Internet, maybe send a couple of emails?”

CHAPTER TWENTY-FIVE

LOS GATOS, CALIFORNIA

Angela was up before dawn, partly because she wanted to finish packing.

And partly because she hadn't gotten that much sleep, anyhow.

Her field work at Blue Corner was finished. She had done everything that needed to be done, measured what needed to be measured, completed her interviews, conferred with the local suppliers.

She was done.

She no longer had an excuse to linger, and in some strange way that saddened and relieved her, both at the same time. Her level-headed life had taken a rocking with the arrival of Beck Easton; for the first time in her life, she understood the word "smitten."

But she was smitten with a man who was, spiritually, worlds away from her.

And to that she added the seven or eight states that were going to permanently separate her from him in a matter of—what?

Twelve hours, if her flight out of San Francisco International was on time.

Beck had told her that he wasn't sure how long he'd be gone on this trip—that it all depended on the complexity of the issue he was investigating. That made sense; security software was not a simple proposition. But she'd harbored both a hope and a fear that he'd be back for one more day—one more evening—before she got on a plane and flew back east.

Angela picked up an open suitcase, put it on the bed, and sat down next to it.

She supposed that she could invent a reason to come back to Blue Corner later – to supervise the installation of the dividers or site-check the lighting or something like that.

Except that wasn't her normal procedure. It wasn't even close. She was more than competent; she was great at what she did. That was why they'd flown her halfway across the country to do this. Ambient lighting, compatibility with the building's climate-control system, adaptability to future expansion – she'd thought of everything and attended to every detail. To come back for a second trip would be extraneous. Worse, it would be dishonest.

And to come back on her own would seem like chasing him.

Even so, she found herself considering the possibility.

Angela went to the writing table next to the window. The rising sun was glazing the palm fronds outside her window with its first orange light. She looked at that for a moment and then began to pack her attaché, clearing away her pens, her pencils, her drawing pads.

Even if she *did* come back, where was the future in all of this? Beck Easton seemed to have feelings for her, but she wondered if they could even come close to what she felt for him.

Shaking her head, she set the briefcase aside and opened her small, silver notebook computer. She'd emailed her final site report to the architects the previous evening, sending a copy to Beck as her way of saying good-bye. But she always checked her email every morning, so she plugged the laptop into the LAN connection that even a family hotel provided in the technology-savvy Silicon Valley, turned the computer on, opened her browser, and clicked the icon for her email program. It was up in seconds on the broadband connection, and she selected the little blue envelope pictograph for "Send and Receive Mail."

Like dominos flipping in reverse, unread messages began to pop up on her screen: the daily headlines email from the Chicago Tribune, an after-Christmas-sale notice from Sears, a

Northwestern alumni pledge appeal asking her to "Be a Winning Wildcat," an email from her sister (who wrote her every day), and another email from

Beck.Easton@BlueCornerTech.net

Angela sat straight up and reminded herself to breathe. She glanced at the palm fronds, yellow now as the sun rose, turned back to her computer, and clicked the touch pad button. A message came up:

From: Beck Easton (beck.easton@bluecornertech.net)
Date: Wednesday, January 12, 2000, 0100PST
To: Angela Brower (abrower6@windycity.com)
Subject: Meeting

Maybe I'm thick, but I still don't quite have a handle on that continuous spectrum lighting stuff. Another meeting seems in order (maybe several) and I'm finishing up an assignment right now, so my schedule's open, if yours is. If it's not too much of an inconvenience, would you mind meeting me here? I know you might be anxious to get back to the latest snowstorm in Chicago, but I'm afraid I'm in Bermuda.

Angela blinked and turned away from the computer screen.

Bermuda! Her heart began to race. Then, just as quickly, she scowled.

Bermuda?

The thought that Beck would want her with him was enough to make her glad that she was sitting down. But then the thought that he would think of her as the sort of woman he could invite on a trip like this—that was like a damp, heavy weight on her shoulders.

She could practically hear Great-Aunt Eulesta again: *The wrong men date you, Angela; the right men court you.*

Angela put her finger on the touch pad, ready to delete the message. Then she noticed there was more. Scowling, she read on:

> Now, before you zap this and erase me from your address book, I'd like you to take a look where you'll be staying:

And after that, there was a hyperlink:

> www.willowbank.bm

This just seemed to make things worse. Did he think she could be moved from a lifetime of devotion by a few pictures of beaches and palm trees? Heart heavy, she clicked on the underlined blue letters.

A web-page opened: British-colonial-pink color bars and, sure enough, images of rooms with ocean vistas. Shaking her head, Angela looked at the text.

> Welcome
>
> Willowbank is more than a beautiful, ocean-side resort. Open since 1960, Willowbank is a nondenominational, nonprofit Christian hotel, welcoming all visitors to Bermuda. While our governing principles are firmly rooted in the historic Christian faith, throughout our history Willowbank has welcomed all visitors, without regard to religious affiliation.

A Christian hotel? Angela clicked around the website: they had a schedule of visiting pastors, regular morning Bible study, and "two of the finest beaches in Bermuda."

What was Beck trying to tell her? She clicked the mail icon in the toolbar and went back to the message.

> If your schedule allows, I will have a ticket waiting for you at the American counter at San Francisco International at five tonight.

I've routed you through O'Hare with an overnight layover so you can stop by your place and pick up some proof of citizenship and your island clothes. I am staying at Grotto Bay, at the other end of Bermuda, and I give you my word that we shall observe the proprieties at all times. Bring a sweater—Bermuda can be brisk in January.

"The proprieties at all times." Angela smiled. She recognized the line—it was from *The Quiet Man*, one of her father's all-time favorite movies. She'd gotten him the video three Christmases before.

She looked at the vase that the roses had come in, at her Bible, at the computer screen. She pictured Beck Easton. She went back to the Willowbank website and looked at it one more time.

What was she doing?

What would Great-Aunt Eulesta think?

CHAPTER TWENTY-SIX

JANUARY 13, 2000
ST. GEORGE'S PARISH, BERMUDA

Beck Easton stepped away from Jason Belden's family car, a Nissan Sonata minivan, crossed the lot at Bermuda International Airport, and glanced at the heavy Citizen Aqualand dive watch on his wrist.

He was fifteen – okay, he was twenty-five minutes early. And it wasn't as if he'd had to allow for traffic. Grotto Bay was all of maybe five minutes from the airport. He stepped to the door of the arrivals hall and looked in. He could see only the lobby area, just a few taxi drivers sitting and talking as they waited for fares. The doors to the customs and immigration area were frosted glass, impenetrable, with "SECURE AREA: DO NOT ENTER" written across them, but he looked at them anyhow, as if he might be able to materialize Angela Brower by sheer force of will. He did that for a few seconds and then stepped away.

"*Stupid in love.*"

He'd first heard the phrase when he was at BUD/S, the intensive commando-style SEAL training course at Coronado, California. It had been a couple of weeks after Hell Week; they were in the intro section of underwater operations, and one young lieutenant had managed to mount the regulator upside-down on his tank, not once, but twice. That had been sufficient to cause the blue-T-shirted instructor to erupt in richly profane wonderment, at which point one of the louie's teammates had said, "Cooper ain't himself, today, Master Chief. He got engaged last night."

At which point the chief had replied, "Well, then, I understand. Lieutenant Cooper, here, has bypassed 'in love' and gone directly to 'stupid in love.'"

And as much as Easton hated to admit it, that was exactly where he was. Stupid in love: there was no other way to describe it. True, he had managed to take Angela Brower off his mind while the Beldens and he had gone out to scour the Bermuda sea-bottom each evening, but even that was only the result of years of trained concentration and military discipline. And when that was over, from the time they tied the diveboat up at the dock to the time he reported back next day to continue the search for the mysterious German bomber, his thoughts were on the woman who had so very recently entered his life. That was especially true since he'd gotten her reply to his email:

Have sweater. Will travel.

In a way, he was very happy. In another way, he was not. This feeling, this head-over-heels feeling, disoriented Beck. He had never been a believer in at-first-sight chemistry. He had always assumed – although less in recent years – that there would someday be The Woman, the one that he would want to spend the rest of his life with. But he had likewise assumed that getting into such a relationship would be a slow, gradual process, that friendship would grow into attraction, which would, after a period of weeks, months, or years, turn to love, and that love would – in a period of time that he was admittedly vague on, although "decade" sounded about right – eventually mature, like deliberately aged wine, into a desire for commitment.

When friends of his had reported experiences to the contrary, he had always laughed, accusing them of having "microwave relationships," and told them that they were "in love with the idea."

Yet here he was, and it sure wasn't just the idea.

He looked at his watch again – now it was fifteen minutes until Angela's flight got in. Back against a light, he slid his hands into the pockets of his chinos and closed his eyes, the Bermuda sun warm on his head, his arms, his shoulders.

The seatbelt chime rang, the cabin attendant made the tray-table announcement, and Angela Brower looked down at her book, a paperback by an English woman, Penny Culliford. It had seemed absolutely hilarious when she'd skimmed it in the bookstore, but now she was a hundred pages into the novel, and she couldn't recall a word.

Pursing her lips, she closed the book. It wasn't the writing. It was the waiting. Tugging her seatbelt snug, she lifted the shade on the airliner window. The ocean, a burnished sheet of blue the last time she'd looked, had detail now—whitecaps and lines of swells.

The 737 banked, leveled itself, and extended its flaps with a low, mechanical whir. She could see land now, a long, green stretch of land dotted with hundreds of white rooftops, a few kites fluttering brightly above the beaches. Angela held her book with both hands as the airplane whirred again beneath her feet and the flaps on the wings moved further. She caught a glimpse of a runway, and the airplane banked a second time.

This is real. I am actually doing this. Angela resisted the urge to pinch herself. She had flown to Wheaton. She had picked up her still-stiff-and-crisp passport, which she'd gotten for a design conference in London two years before.

She hadn't picked up either of her two swimsuits. The first one—a French-cut bikini with a spaghetti-strap top—was so skimpy that no one, not even her mother, had ever seen her in it. She had bought that one at her tanning salon and had never worn it anyplace else. And while her second suit had seemed downright Victorian in comparison, it was, nonetheless, a two-piece, and running off with a man to an island in a swimsuit that exposed her navel just wasn't something she could see herself doing. So she'd brought the sweater, some dresses, some capris, but she'd left the swimwear at home.

Penny wise and pound foolish.

Angela reminded herself that she and Beck were staying in separate resorts that were miles apart (she'd verified that on the Internet), that hers had ordained ministers in residence, and, on top of that, she had the best precaution of all, which was her common sense.

She *hoped* she still had her common sense. It had kept her on the prudent and sensible side of this whole relationship-with-the-opposite-sex thing now for twenty-six years. She told herself that she was still acting responsibly.

Then again, if that was the case, why hadn't she told her parents where she was off to?

And why, for that matter, had she not even stopped by their house to let them know that she was back in town, however briefly?

Far beneath her seat, she heard the familiar rumble and clunk of landing gear extending and locking into place. The ocean outside her window was just a few hundred feet below her now, and it was spotted with the vague, dark shapes of underwater reefs. They passed over a sailboat at anchor, its shadow on the white-sand bottom making the craft seem as if it were floating in air.

Angela swallowed. For better or worse, she was only seconds away from touchdown in Bermuda. And minutes after that, she would be meeting Beck Easton face-to-face, on a beautiful, exotic island.

Angela could not, for the life of her, remember when she had been so apprehensive.

And she could not, for the life of her, remember when she had been so thrilled.

Unless one has frequent re-entry stamps in one's passport—or one is unfortunate enough to be selected for a random and very thorough search—customs in Bermuda is generally a relatively brisk affair. Easton knew that. Still, the second hand on his dive watch seemed to crawl as people began to emerge from the secure area. Twice he craned his neck, trying to spot Angela standing in the queue on the far side. But every time someone walked out, the doors snicked shut behind them with brisk, British-territorial officiousness.

That was the way it worked. So he stood there, smiling expectantly, until Angela finally emerged from the doors, her passport and entry chit in one hand, pulling a wheeled, tan canvas suiter.

Easton smiled broadly and reached to take her bag but never quite got there. In a flash, both of her arms were around him, and she was tipping his head toward hers, kissing him with a tenderness that convinced him fully and absolutely that he had been missed. Nothing could spoil the moment, not even looking up and seeing the customs person looking their way through the still-parted doors and grinning broadly.

Wow. The last time this happened, it took the whole Pacific Ocean and New Year's Eve.

That was what he thought. But what he said was, "Hi."

That was it. One syllable.

"Hi," she breathed back. Then, "I missed you, Beck. But I need to tell you: that's all I can do to express it. Do you understand?"

He hugged her for a moment and said, "That's pretty good."

What did I just do?

Angela felt lightheaded, like the time at her ninth birthday party, when she had breathed down three helium balloons in a row in an attempt to sing the alphabet song in an Alvin-the-Chipmunk voice.

Only this time it wasn't helium. It was that kiss, a public display of affection as foreign to her as Japanese television, and then there had been the ultimatum. Where was all of this coming from? She was normally a very graceful person; all through college the other girls had complimented her on her poise. But now she felt like the first time she'd ever worn heels.

They walked out to the van, a stubby little Japanese thing with a young black man at the wheel—at the wheel on the right-hand-side of the vehicle—and Beck introduced him as "Brad." Then he put her bag in back, they slid into the second-row seat together, and Beck smiled and asked, "How do you feel? Tired after the flight? Hungry?"

She brightened. "I'm starving."

"Can't have that. Bradley here will run your bag out to Willowbank. Let's jump out in Hamilton and get a bite."

On her trips into Chicago, going to the Merchandise Mart to look at fabric samples, Angela had always been amused by the tourists, people dressed a stage or two too casually, walking down Adams with their heads craned back, looking up at the skyscrapers.

Now she supposed she was doing the Bermuda equivalent, looking to this side and that, trying at every turn to see the sea, which looked ever so much more hospitable from ground level.

All the windows in the van were open, and Angela thought for a moment that perhaps she should have brought a scarf, but between threading around people on mopeds and motor scooters and creeping cautiously past uniformed schoolchildren on their way home for lunch, they never went that fast, anyhow. So while the breeze cooled her—an amazing thought: it had been snowing when she'd left Chicago—it didn't tangle her hair.

Soon they were passing a tiny harbor dotted with moored boats, then a playing field that Beck identified as a "cricket pitch," and after that they were turning into a section of town where the squat, pastel-colored Bermuda houses gave way to surprisingly modern-looking office buildings.

"Where would you like lunch, mate?" Brad asked from the driver's seat.

Beck turned her way. "Do you like seafood?"

She nodded. "Love it."

Beck looked up, at the driver. "Want to drop us at the Lobster Pot, Bradley?"

The Lobster Pot had stained glass murals on the inside, scenes of the sea and sailboats at anchor. It was crowded with business people in coats and ties, and Angela looked around as they were seated.

"Looking for Bermuda shorts?"

She laughed. "Yes. I read about that on the way in – coats, ties, and shorts."

"If you run by a school when it's letting out, you might see a headmaster dressed like that – they often do year-round. But for business dress, it's generally long trousers until Easter. Come back in a couple of months, and you'll start seeing the shorts, always worn with kneesocks. Trimingham's, over on Front Street, is supposed to be the place that first sold them. Rockfish is the local fish in Bermuda, by the way – I've been coming here for years, and I've never had a bad rockfish."

They ordered – broiled rockfish, twice – and then they talked about her flight in. Angela asked Beck about the work that had brought him to Bermuda, and he made some basic, noncommittal comments and then shifted the conversation back to her. Then the food came and Angela looked down at it uncertainly.

"Would you like to ask a blessing?" Easton asked.

She smiled in relief. "Lord, we thank you for this food and ask that you bless it and this time we spend together. Let it honor you. In Jesus Christ's precious name."

"Amen," Easton added.

She smiled. "Thank you. That can always be sort of awkward. Most of the time I just pray silently"

"Pray all you want around me," Beck said. "Where I was in school, the chapel was the tallest building there. We were led in grace before every meal. So I'm sort of used to it."

Angela looked up, surprised. "You went to a Christian college?"

Easton laughed. "No. I went to Annapolis."

"The Naval Academy?"

He nodded.

"So you were a naval officer?"

He stiffened a little. "Marines. Still am – I'm in the reserves now."

She looked at him with awe. "An officer and a gentleman – the things you don't know."

He smiled. "I wouldn't expect you to know. I mean, after all, the time we've spent in one another's company comes to a grand total of what? Forty-eight hours?"

"If that." She looked at him, the smile still on her face. "So 'fess up, Commodore."

" 'Major' – and don't *you* start that, please."

"Okay. 'Fess up, mister. How often do you do this?"

He looked at his plate. "Eat lunch here?"

"You know what I mean." The smile was still there, but Angela could feel it fading into a shadow of itself. "How often do you send tickets off to a woman you've just met less than two weeks before and invite her to join you on a business trip?"

Easton met her eyes. "Including this time?"

She nodded.

"Then that would be one."

She felt lighter, brighter. Then she added, "This is crazy, you know."

"I do. But I thought it over before I emailed you, and I decided that there could only be one thing crazier."

"What's that?"

Easton took a breath. "Not doing it. Not doing it and taking a chance that you'd be gone and out of my life before I could get back to you."

For a moment, all the sounds around them became especially apparent: the clatter of dishes in the restaurant itself, a woman laughing at one of the tables in the bar, one of the suit-coat-wearing businessmen saying, "Brilliant!" to something that his colleague had just said. Then Angela said – she nearly whispered it – "Yeah. I know."

Beck's face became serious.

"I know I should be saying something witty, but I'm fresh out of witty right now. This is, well ... are you telling me that I'm not the only one who's falling kind of hard here?"

"Oh, no." Their eyes locked as she said it. "No, Beck. You're not the only one at all."

The rockfish was pretty much a blur for Beck. One minute there was a filet on the plate in front of him, and the next, he was tapping his fork against empty china. Angela was sitting with her back to the window, and when he looked up, he saw her smiling eyes and, behind her, a blue Bermuda sky.

He tried to think how it could possibly get better than this.

He came up blank.

After lunch, Angela and Beck walked down to the waterfront, where a large cruise-ship mooring stood empty – "Cruise season doesn't really get rolling until April," Beck told her – and they boarded a catamaran ferry to cross the Great Sound, a twenty-minute water panorama of what Beck referred to as "the Island."

"But it's not really *an* island, is it?" Angela asked. "Isn't it a bunch of islands?"

Easton laughed. "You're right – but when I asked a local about it once, he said, 'My friend, none of our landmasses are more than a hundred yards away from the next one, and when you are 600 miles out in the middle of the Atlantic Ocean, you don't count a ditch as water.'"

The ferry ride took twenty minutes. Just when the ferry looked as if it were about to head out to the open ocean, it turned to put in at an ancient fortified installation guarding the entrance to the Great Sound.

"Wow," Angela said as the ferry pulled into its slip. "Substantial. What is it?"

"Royal Navy Dockyards," Easton said. "After the Revolutionary War, Britain lost most of its reprovisioning stations in North America, so it outfitted the Dockyards as a place to repair and resupply ships. There's also a redoubt—a fort that guards the harbor."

"To protect against pirates?"

"No," Easton laughed. "Mostly to protect against us. Britain didn't really kiss and make up with the United States until after the Civil War. The Royal Navy was in here until 1950, and the government recently renovated the place—the terminal for the really big cruise ships is here, and there are shops, restaurants, a maritime museum."

They got out and walked around the immense old facility. Angela stretched, catlike, as she walked, loving the feel of the sun on her back. In truth, the weather was not all that different from what she'd left in Los Gatos a couple of days earlier, but the nearness of the sea made it feel exotic.

They wandered into galleries and watched a painter at work. Then they walked along the water until they found a row of taxis—not cars, but small passenger vans—and Easton led her to the first one in line.

"Willowbank's in Somerset, same parish that we're in right now, and it's just a short ride. Thought you might like to freshen up."

At Willowbank, a key and welcome packet was waiting for Angela in the lobby. They followed a walk through a lawn planted with short Bermuda grass and came to a room on the end of one of the buildings. Beck opened the door for her and said, "Take as much time as you want. I'll be out on the beach."

She kissed him again, just a peck this time – a slow peck – and went in.

The sound of surf greeted her. The blinds were back, and only the screen was closed on the patio door, letting in the breeze and a view of the beach, which was right there, just steps away from her room. She slipped off her shoes and walked on the cool tiled floor to the windows, so she could look out: the sand was so pinkish-white it almost hurt to look at it, and the water was a luminous, transparent blue, living and moving, breaking over a near-shore reef with a slowness that suggested tremendous, sleeping power. For a long moment, she stood, mesmerized.

Her bag was waiting on a folding stand, and she opened it, thinking of the swimsuits she'd left home in Wheaton and blushing for a reason that escaped her. Then she hung up the things that needed to be hung, put the rest in drawers, and tucked her bag into a corner of the closet, out of the way.

She looked in the mirror, shook her head, found a pair of off-white capris, and went into the bathroom. Five minutes later, her hair brushed and pulled back into a ponytail, she slipped a pair of straw sandals onto her bare feet and, pocketing her key, went out into the sunshine.

She found Beck on the beach, standing in the sand with his boat shoes in one hand, looking out at the ocean as if he were thinking of buying it. She took off her own shoes and walked through the warm, deliciously soft, pink sand. Without a word, she slipped her hand into his.

"Is the room okay?"

"It's great."

"Are you sure? I was going to put you into Elbow Beach, or the Southampton Princess, but … well, I thought I had a better chance of talking you into coming if I put you here."

"You were right, and the room's fine. Where to now?"

Easton looked out at the sea. "Let's see: the whole country's only twenty-seven square miles, and that's smaller than an American township. We can literally be anywhere in Bermuda in about forty-five minutes. And there are caves and beaches and historic sites and parks … Where would you like to go?"

She gave his hand a squeeze.

"Someplace with you," she said softly. "Everything else is negotiable."

CHAPTER TWENTY-SEVEN

JANUARY 15, 2000
NEAR TUCKER'S TOWN, BERMUDA

"Oh, wow. That is absolutely magnificent. It looks like I don't know what – a postcard!"

"You can bet it's that," Beck told Angela. "A postcard and a calendar and a painted dish and a tea towel. This day and age, it's probably a screensaver and a mouse pad, as well."

They were standing on the beach beneath a green headland – the grounds of the "Mid Ocean Golf Club," Beck had told her – looking at a huge rock formation, barn-size, maybe larger, called "Natural Arches."

And that was exactly what it was. The rock rose from the ocean in a pair of gigantic arcs – you could walk right under them on the beach – to join the headlands above. Waves splashed around its base, a suggestion of the forces that had carved the island limestone into this shape. High above, as if cued by some invisible art director, a single gull canted and soared in a robin's-egg-perfect sky.

Angela smiled. She'd been in Bermuda for two days now, and Beck had been a perfect gentleman. She was relaxed, comfortable.

"I've often thought this is probably what the people on the *Kate* were looking at when she went down," Beck said.

"The *Kate*?"

"A two-hundred-foot English steamer that went aground on the reef, back in 1878," Beck said, pointing to the southeast, where a line of waves was breaking about a quarter-mile offshore. "Not much left that looks like a ship there anymore. Boilers, winches, and so forth – and the prop's sitting up on the reef, in twenty feet of water. The ocean got the rest."

Angela cocked her head. "You've been diving here?"

"For years and years." Easton was still looking out to sea, a slight smile on his face. "Bermuda shipwrecks are famous the world over. When I was on active duty? Stationed on the East Coast? I was known to come here even on my weekend leaves, just to get in a few hours of diving."

"Are you diving on this trip?"

"I have my gear, but no. No plans this time. Let's take a closer look."

They walked under the arches and along the broad, deserted beach, taking their time. Angela stopped and glanced back at the rocks. Voice hushed, she said, "This must be an amazing place to watch the sunrise."

Easton squeezed her hand. "I hear it is. If you want, we can come back in a couple of days – see for ourselves."

The sea rolled, in and out, and she looked up at him. "That would be nice."

The silence that followed was both magical and awkward, and Angela was glad for the sound of the waves.

The pause gave her a moment to think. This was a Saturday – Saturday morning. Tomorrow would be Sunday. There was a church service at Willowbank, and while she was certain Beck would attend with her if she asked, she was hoping that he would ask her.

Almost as if on cue, Beck cleared his throat. She looked up at him.

"Remember Brad? The young man who gave us a lift from the airport yesterday?"

"Sure."

"His family – the Beldens – have been very kind to me over the years. I'd like you to meet them. Would that be okay?"

"Friends of yours?" She found herself smiling. "I'd be honored. When?"

"Tonight?"

Angela pursed her lips and looked up at the sky. "Let's see. I think I just might be ... Yes, I don't believe I have a previous engagement for this evening."

Her face straightened. "What should I wear?"

Easton smiled. "We're going to Pawpaw's, a local place, down on South Road. It's French food and Bermudian both, but folks there don't stand on as much ceremony as they do in Hamilton. What you're wearing right now is probably fine."

Angela squinted. "Is there a Mrs. Belden?"

"There is."

"And you have their phone number?"

"I do."

She nodded. "I'll call her and discuss wardrobe."

"Understood."

The two of them turned and walked east along the beach, back the way they'd come.

They were almost back to the road, and the waiting taxi, when Angela realized that they hadn't discussed Sunday morning.

CHAPTER TWENTY-EIGHT

SANDY'S PARISH, BERMUDA

The sun, orange-red and distorted by shimmering atmosphere, sank toward the ocean. It seemed to touch the water and spread, like hot molten metal, at its base.

"Watch closely," Beck Easton told Angela. "We might see the green flash."

"Green flash?" Angela looked his way. "What's that?"

"Something that happens every once in a while with an ocean sunset. Keep looking, even after it's down. It will only happen for a split second, if it happens at all."

Angela turned her face west again. Still looking at the sun, she reached to her side, found Beck's hand, and held it.

The sun was moving visibly. It seemed to melt even further, like a flattened egg yolk, and then it contracted steadily, drawing into a distant glowing gem of red-orange, embering fire. Then that too was gone.

"Keep watching," Beck whispered.

As if on cue, a jade light, like an impossibly distant green candle flame, appeared for the most fleeting of moments and then died.

For ten long seconds, neither one of them said anything. Angela realized that she was holding her breath, and she exhaled.

"Did you see it?" Beck asked.

"Yes." Angela was still looking west, at the darkening horizon. She turned to face Beck. "What made it do that?"

"The atmosphere acts like a prism, refracts the sunlight over the horizon, and it's coming through much more air than it does when the sun is overhead, so some of the spectrum gets absorbed.

You're the designer—if red, orange, and yellow all get absorbed by the atmosphere, what's the next color in the spectrum?"

"Green."

"There you go."

She grinned. "Well. Aren't you the hopeless romantic?"

Beck shrugged. "Hey, I watch sunsets, don't I?"

Angela gave him a theatrical pout and then kissed him, a quick peck. Then she pulled him closer and repeated—more slowly this time.

Still holding hands, they walked south along the beach, the surf shushing itself to their right, lights winking on in the homes set back from the sand. A few minutes later, they were turning up onto the grounds at Willowbank, and Angela squeezed his hand again.

"All right, Mr. Easton, since you are such a font of knowledge, let's walk up front. There's something else I want you to explain to me."

"My pleasure."

Angela smiled. It was *her* pleasure—that was for sure. This day had been the happiest she could remember. For lunch, they'd gone to a place called the Swizzle Inn, over on the east end of the Island—now even she was starting to call it that—where Beck was staying. Then they had taken a cab into Hamilton, visits to studios where it seemed that half of the artists already knew Beck, another ferryboat ride across the Great Sound, this one putting in at a place called Somerset Village, and finally this long walk on the beach.

They crested the small rise from the beach, found a path, and followed it around to the front of the resort to a round arch, almost otherworldly in appearance, perfectly framing the rising full moon. As if on cue, both she and Beck stopped walking.

"I keep seeing these all over the island," Angela said. "What are they?"

"It's called a *moongate*." The two of them started walking again, up the path, slowly now. "You're right. You'll find them in gardens all over Bermuda. It's a tradition that goes back at least a hundred years."

"It looks almost Oriental."

Beck nodded. "The story is that Bermuda sea captains brought the designs back from their trips around the Horn and into the western Pacific."

They got up to the gate and Angela touched it.

"What sort of stone is it?"

"Bermuda stone is traditional," Beck told her. "It's a volcanic rock. The whole country is the top of an old volcanic seamount. Some folks will tell you that Harrington Sound, east of Hamilton, is an old volcanic caldera, although from what I've read, the magma just pushed the seamount above the surface – it never actually erupted. But there's a dense, lavalike stone that they've built with here for centuries, and that's what this is. Here in Bermuda, they have a tradition about these gates."

"What's that?" Angela looked at Beck, his face blue in the moonlight, and smiled, thinking that the tradition probably had something in common with mistletoe.

"Well, they say that if a couple ..."

Definitely like mistletoe.

"... if a couple holds hands, and walks through one of these gates, and makes a wish, then their wish will come true."

He held out his hand. "Want to try it?"

Angela took his hand and they stepped through the round gate. They stopped on the top step on the other side and turned to face one another.

Beck smiled. "So?"

"So – what?"

"What did you wish?"

She cocked her head and lofted both eyebrows.

"It's not like blowing out the candles on your birthday cake," Beck said. "I don't think telling jinxes it."

"Then you first."

He shook his head. "Not the way it works. I asked you."

Angela turned her head and gazed at the moon.

"I didn't wish," she said. "I prayed."

"Well, okay. I guess a prayer is the same as a wish made to God."

It isn't.

"So," Beck asked again. "What did you pray?"

"That ..." She turned to face him again. "... That you knew what I knew."

The smile was still there on his face. "That I knew about what?"

"About love. Not this ..." She made a small "you-me" gesture with her free hand. "But about God. The only pure love there is. I prayed that you would know about Jesus."

The smile stayed there in his mouth, but it vanished from his eyes. They stood there on the steps, her hand still in his, while the moon rose half a minute higher in the dark Bermuda sky.

"All right," he finally said. "Teach me."

"What?"

"Teach me what you want me to know."

Angela searched his face in the blue moonlight. His eyes were open, honest. Sincere.

"All right," she said. "God created us for a place a lot like this."

She waved her hand and took in the sea, the first stars, the foliage blooming next to the path.

"A garden. It's what we were designed for. It's the only environment that is totally natural to us—a place where God could shower us with his love. It's where we were meant to spend eternity."

"Sounds nice."

There wasn't a hint of a grin on his face.

"Better than nice," Angela told him. "Perfect. But something came between us and God."

"The apple?" Now there was the hint of a grin.

"The apple." She looked in his eyes as she said it. "And regardless of whether you see that as literal or figurative, that started it—a split between us and God. A gulf that separated us from him. And strange as it may seem, the more we try to get back to that feeling we had in the garden, the more that gulf widens. I mean, just think about it—a person takes drugs, a person sleeps with someone they just met, a person gets something he didn't work for, or drinks himself silly. Those all make you feel good, for a moment—and in the garden, we felt good. But when we seek that substitute, instead of the source of all goodness, real goodness, then we just move farther and farther away."

Beck wasn't smiling at all now.

"Some people," Angela said, "laugh at the idea of sin."

"Not me."

She searched his eyes again. "Okay. You understand, then, that God is holy. He can't be where sin is."

Beck nodded slowly.

"And that you can't even things up between the two of you. You can't give God anything to make your own sin go away."

Beck looked up for a second, and then looked back down, into her eyes.

"That makes sense. I mean, if you believe that God created everything ..."

She nodded.

"... Then it's all his to begin with," Beck continued. "There literally isn't anything to give him to square things up."

Angela paused. She had never heard it put that way before. But it made sense. He was getting it.

"But," she said, "the good news is that God arranged to pay that debt for you."

"Jesus."

"Yes." He was getting it. Or was he? His lips were set, drawn tight.

"I remember a conversation like this," Beck said. He very nearly muttered it. "A few years ago, actually more than a few. It was with a Navy chaplain who was helping us out in the Corps. And this is the part where I got stuck."

"Why?"

He took her hand and started walking again, back through the gate and toward the resort. "First, because I imagine that your sins have been considerably different from mine. And it doesn't seem like they would have the same price."

"But all sin has the same price. The Son of God—God himself—went to the cross."

Beck stopped walking.

"That's the other part," he said. "I'm not really sure about God. Whether he exists at all, or—if he exists—whether he cares."

He looked her in the eyes and squeezed both of her hands.

"I have seen a lot of the bad part of the world, Angela. I've seen things that gave me nightmares. And if God is on the throne, then he's not doing much of a job. I know that's not what you want to hear, but if I say something just because you want to hear it, then I would be doing something very wrong. And I've done enough wrong in my life; I won't compound that by harming you. Do you understand? I won't lie to you, even if I think the lie might please you. Does that make sense?"

It did. And while Angela had a dozen rebuttals, ready and waiting, something deep within her told her to stop where she was—to let what they had talked about soak in, and take the rest up again later—tomorrow, or when the time felt right.

Beck squeezed her hand.

"I'm not just baiting you here, Angela. If there's a way you can help me to be more like you, then I'm for it. You bring out the best in me. To tell the truth, you bring out better than the best in me. I like that. More than you can know, I like that. I long for your kind of faith, but I have to live in the world I see."

If there's a way you can help me to be more like you, then I'm for it. Angela took that, claimed it as her own. She would do that, in time.

She just hoped that the time would come soon.

CHAPTER TWENTY-NINE

Beck Easton was just pulling on his trousers when the knock came at the door.

"Brad?" He glanced at his Aqualand dive watch. He'd agreed to meet Brad Belden at the lobby in an hour, and only thirty minutes of that time had passed.

Another knock at the door. Louder, this time.

Barefooted, towel over one shoulder, he opened the door. A young man in a white shirt, tie, and a soft leather jacket was standing at the threshold, holding up a diplomatic-corps identification card.

"Major Easton?"

"Yes?"

"No offense, sir, but would you have any ID?"

Easton went to the bureau, opened it, and got out his passport. The young man scrutinized it carefully, compared the number to a small notebook, and then handed the passport back.

"Thank you, Major. I'm from the consul's office. We've had a priority signal for you." He handed Easton a white number-ten envelope with the Great Seal of the United States where the return address should go.

"All right." Easton hefted the envelope. "Were your instructions to wait for a reply?"

"No sir. Just to deliver this to you and to bring it in my own car, not a consular vehicle."

"Okay. Thank you, then. Sorry to put you through all that trouble."

"You're welcome, sir. No trouble at all."

Easton shut the door behind the man and carried the envelope to the glass patio door, breaking the foil seal as he walked.

There were two sheets of paper inside, one of them a typed, faxed memo. He opened that first.

TO: Easton, R.E., Col., USMCR
FR: Spalding, W.A., SOG, NSA
RE: Sidescan Imagery

Computer enhancement of sidescan imagery shows suspicious anomaly on your file labeled "Target # 3." Please investigate at your earliest convenience.

And under that was a handwritten note:

Beck—
This may be it.
Bill

Brow suddenly moist, Easton opened the other sheet of paper. It was the image of the bottom with the marine diesel engine, only it had mid-tones in it now, rather than the harsh contrast they'd seen on the PC at Belden's shop. Off to one side of the engine, maybe fifteen meters away, someone had hand drawn dotted lines around a vague shape atop some rows of coral formations, a shape that looked vaguely like the center section of a huge, broken boomerang.

"Oh, man ..."

Easton stepped away from the patio door, picked up the room phone, pressed 9 for an outside line, and then dialed a seven-digit number from memory. It was picked up on the second ring.

"Hi, Sarah? It's Beck. Fine, thank you. Yes, I am looking forward to it. And I can't wait to hear what you think of Angela." He listened to the reply and then asked, "Sorry to trouble you at home, but would your father be there?"

CHAPTER THIRTY

Guidebook stuck in the back pocket of his Dockers, video camera in his hand, Ahmed bin Saleen tugged the zipper a few inches higher on his windbreaker and stepped to the northeast corner of Somerset Bridge. The marina had been deserted enough during the afternoon for him to do some judicious pruning of the foliage near the bridge—just enough to give him a sightline to where the *Hog Penny* was docked.

Just down the harbor, in the dimly lighted marina, there was movement on the open afterdeck of the diveboat, and he raised the camera and aimed it at the vessel and its dock.

The camera was an older eight-millimeter model, one of those that came with a basic form of night vision as an option. Such a feature was not available on the latest models—some perverted Westerners had discovered that if they used the night vision feature during the day, and videotaped women wearing sheer or thin fabrics, the light amplification would render the fabric virtually invisible. And the reaction of Western lawmakers, rather than demanding that the brazen daughters of that nation cover themselves with something more substantial, had been to demand that the makers of video cameras cease to offer the feature—as if it were the technology, and not the depraved use of it, that was the problem.

He pretended to videotape a tranquil vista—the orderly rows of sailboats, charter boats, and pleasure craft sleeping at their moorings in the moonlight. The amplified night-vision picture allowed him to see two figures moving on the *Hog Penny*'s afterdeck. The further figure, the one sitting on the gunwale, seemed to be stretching, as if he were yawning and just waking up.

Ahmed bin Saleen touched the zoom tab on the camera, closing in on the deeply shadowed image.

The screen brightened and faded, and details resolved. It was the American. And he was not stretching. He was pulling on a wetsuit.

A wetsuit.

He shook his head slowly. Just when he'd thought that he was shed of the infidels, just when he was starting to think that he could take to the water once again in peace ... This evening's surveillance was supposed to be the same as the previous evening's – a pro forma. His plan had been to watch for three nights, make sure they were not coming back, and then resume the search himself. But now the American was putting on a wetsuit.

Meaning that this evening, unlike any of the previous evenings, the American was planning to enter the water.

They had found something. Or at least they believed they had.

The American stood and loosened the stern line from its cleat. Moments later, the sound of the boat's big diesel reached bin Saleen's ears, and the *Hog Penny*'s running lights came on, ball-like flares in the green, amplified image of the viewfinder.

Years of training kept bin Saleen where he was, panning the camera across the waters of the harbor, lowering it only after he was in profile to Robinson's Marina. He glanced at his watch, zipped the windbreaker higher still, and walked at a leisurely stroll north on the roadway, away from the *Hog Penny* and the marina.

The pace of his footsteps was slow and deliberate, but his heart was racing, the pulse throbbing at his temples. *Tonight. They are going after it tonight, right now – tonight.*

To his side, he could hear the diesel of the diveboat chugging steadily, heading toward harbor's mouth. He picked up his pace to a brisk walk and turned down the drive to the marina.

He broke into a trot. *If I can get to the boat right away, I can get to the mouth of the harbor in time to see which direction they've gone. I need the boat, the satellite phone, everything. There is not a moment to waste.*

As the *Hog Penny* came abreast of Somerset Bridge, Easton saw movement under the bridge's street lamps. Just a glimpse, but it was the rapid, hunched gait of someone going quickly. He turned where he sat on the gunwale and looked across the water to Somerset Road: a man, a billed cap, a blue nylon windbreaker—that was it, and then the person was gone.

Someone hurrying to dinner after an evening walk. Easton pictured that, and he envied the stranger, whoever he was.

Easton had tried diplomacy with Belden, suggesting that they go out first thing in the morning, and Belden had asked to go right away, as Easton had known he would.

"If that thing out there is what you think it is, Major, then I wouldn't enjoy my evening, waiting until sunrise. Church Bay's just half an hour out, half an hour back. Take you twenty minutes to have a look. If we leave right now, we can send my family and your lady friend up to Pawpaw's ahead of us, join them maybe half an hour late."

Easton had, of course, agreed. And Angela had not sounded at all distressed when he had phoned her at Willowbank, told her he had to attend to a client's emergency, and that he would see her soon.

Soon. He folded up the ankles of the wetsuit, pulled on his neoprene dive boots, zipped them, and lapped the wetsuit legs down over the boots. Just this single, quick dive, and then it would be over for sure.

He picked up his weight belt—eight pounds of lead shot enclosed in zippered pouches on a heavy, two-inch nylon belt—and draped it over his gear, the buoyancy compensator and regulator already set up on a steel tank filled with NOAA Nitrox II. Then he walked forward to the wheelhouse, squeezing Jason Belden on his meaty, broad shoulder.

The Bermudian glanced his way, smiled, and turned back to his navigation screen. "Not long, Major. Be there before you know it."

Ahmed bin Saleen returned the satellite phone to the rubberized "river bag" under the Boston Whaler's console. He took his first deep breath in several minutes, heart rate back to normal.

Things were still under control. He had his assets in position. And he had the *Hog Penny* in sight, albeit just barely.

That incident on the first evening had left him feeling chastened and stupid. How could he not have thought about the radar? He knew Belden's boat was equipped with one—the squat oval of the radome, newer than the other accoutrements on the diveboat's navigation mast, had made that obvious. Yet he had allowed himself to be discovered, had his position announced to the authorities over the air. He counted himself fortunate that he'd been able to flee along the coastline up to Devonshire Bay, hide in its sheltered waters, and then skulk back out, returning to Robinson's Marina long after the *Hog Penny* had been tied up for the night. He had been unable to sneak aboard the diveboat and have a look because Robinson's had a night watchman and the man was good, coming out ostensibly to catch his painter as bin Saleen pulled into the dock, and chatting with him amiably until bin Saleen had left the premises.

In a way it was all good, a learning experience. Ahmed bin Saleen came from that part of the world that had invented the game of chess, and one truism of that game was that, to be a master, one had to take the offensive whenever possible, yet have a strategy for defense, as well.

He was using one such strategy as he rounded West Whale Bay, the crook of Bermuda's West End, and cut the small boat in, close to shore. By using the electric hoist to tilt the outboard up, bin Saleen was able to creep along close to the beach, as he had for five nights earlier in the week, in water so shallow that the hull sometimes scraped on the furrowed sand of the bottom.

He raised a pair of rubber-armored marine binoculars and examined the distant dots of lights that were the *Hog Penny.* The vessel was not showing the three vertical lights it had displayed when it had been running its grids. And as bin Saleen watched, the white speck of the stern light faded and a red light appeared, joined a moment later by a green light.

Turning. The diveboat was coming about slowly, bow into the wind. It crept along a moment longer and then came to a halt.

Stopped. Yet this stretch of coast had a persistent west-to-east current.

So the *Hog Penny* was riding at anchor.

Ahmed bin Saleen saw a faint light on the diveboat's flying bridge. Moments later, small spotlights came on, illuminating a dive flag—a red rectangle with an ascending diagonal white stripe—flying from the top of the vessel's navigation mast.

It is happening. They are preparing to put the American in the water. Ahmed bin Saleen crept his vessel closer, the binoculars clamped to his eyes.

Beck Easton stood before the navigation screen and zoomed it all the way in, to its finest setting. The dot representing the magnetic object was about ten degrees to port and ahead of him, no more than two hundred feet west. Figuring that Brad had about three hundred feet of scope out on the line, that would put the anchor within easy visual range of the object, if an object was there at all. He fixed the relative positions of the diveboat and his quarry in his mind, and then walked aft, where Bradley was holding his gear steady on the broad gunwale of the boat.

Easton put on his weight belt and then backed up to the rest of his gear, sliding his arms back through the shoulder straps and muttering "got it" as he stood and fastened the waistbelt of his harness. He bent forward at the waist, letting the forty pounds of the steel tank rest on his back – to a man accustomed to diving steel doubles, the weight was negligible – and tugged the shoulder straps tight, fastened the chest strap, and clipped his gauge console to a stainless-steel D-ring on his harness. He fastened the low-pressure hose to the autoinflator and secured it to his shoulder strap with a Velcro keeper, spat in his dive mask, rubbed both lenses, and handed the mask to Bradley, who rinsed it over the side and handed it back.

Donning the mask, Easton walked slowly to the stern, balancing the weight of the equipment against the roll of the boat. He stepped through the open stern onto the swim platform, pulled on both fins while Bradley held him steady by the tank valve and unclipped the head of his high-intensity-display light, a lamp as powerful as an aircraft landing light, attached to a waist-belt-mounted, eight-pound battery pack via a rubber-shrouded umbilical.

Cupping the light to his chest, protecting the delicate head, Easton checked his waistbelt pocket with his other hand, making sure that the NSA Geiger counter, a cigarette-pack-size rectangle of electronics, was still there, and that the pocket was zipped completely closed.

"All right," he said. "If this isn't it, I'll be back in a couple of minutes. And either way, I'll be back within twenty."

And with that, he settled the regulator into his mouth and leaned forward, pushing up and off the platform at the last possible second, so he entered the water in a half somersault, breaking the surface with his shoulders and the rounded crown of his tank.

Sound vanished, inky blackness surrounded him, and then, as he completed the somersault under water, a haze of bubbles lifted, and the lights of the boat appeared through the shimmering, dancing surface.

Easton took a breath and rose, touching a hand to the top of his head as he broke the surface, signaling "okay" to the boat. Venting his buoyancy compensator with one hand, he checked his backup lights with the other, turning each shoulder-strap-mounted lamphead until it lit and then turning it off again. The air hissed noisily out of the BC, and then he was back into the underwater silence again, sinking as he rolled into a facedown attitude and began kicking, moving his legs and fins in great, steady sweeps, propelling himself toward the anchor line.

As he swam, Easton slid the D-shaped handle of the lamphead onto his right hand, positioning it so the lamp rested on the back of his hand, leaving his fingers unencumbered. He reached down to the waistbelt-mounted battery pack, found the rubber-booted toggle switch, and flipped it.

A spear of light, blue at first and then stuttering by stages into a shaft of brilliant white, shot out into the blackness. Easton lifted it before him and found the yellow anchor line a good sixty feet away, bellying moderately in the steady half-knot current. He dropped his head and picked up the pace, feeling the current steady against his hair as he made headway.

In less than a minute he was at the line, and he paused there, unzipping the waistband pocket and taking out the small black box. He pressed a rubber-shrouded button and a series of LED bars—green, then yellow, and then red—lit up and then disappeared, a red diode in the corner of the display the only indication that the unit was on. He pressed the box against the face of his Citizen Aqualand dive watch, and one green LED came on, registering the weak radiation coming from the radium hands and hour marks of the watch.

The scientists back at NSA had told him that anything in the green or the yellow ranges of the electronic Geiger counter was safe. It was only if it ventured into the red that the situation was harmful.

Satisfied that the instrument was properly counting RADs, Easton slipped it back into the waistbelt pocket and, using the anchor line as a flexible handrail, began pulling himself along, gliding smoothly and steadily, dropping toward the sea bottom.

Easton got to the anchor and set it, lifting it so the pronged Danforth tines would drop and dig into the coarse-grained sand of the bottom. He lifted his gauge console, checked the compass and reoriented himself.

There. The diesel we sounded should be right over there.

He swept the light in that direction. Yellow eyes glared back at him, and he aimed the light directly at them. Stingrays – they fluttered up from the bottom, sand falling from their disks, and then swam, ghostlike, away. A small octopus blushed blue and then scuttled away as well, lifting itself and jetting, squidlike, into the darkness. He continued to sweep the light, and there, just beyond where the stingrays had been resting, the off-white sand bottom gave way to something darker.

The diesel. He swam to it, reoriented himself.

Easton pulled the electronic Geiger counter from his waistbelt pocket and checked it. A single green LED winked on, then off, then on again, then off: background radiation, nothing more than the normal emissions of trace elements in the seafloor.

He swam away from the diesel, and colors began to emerge – browns and oranges and reds. It was star coral and brain coral, two species that covered much of the rock around Bermuda's reefs.

Moving slowly, working his fins with his ankles alone, Easton glided over the seafloor. It looked as if he was simply over a large coral colony, the same sort of sea life that covered so much of

Bermuda's sea bottom. He swept the beam of the light ahead of him and swam on.

Standing at the side of his boat, Jason Belden watched the distant return of Beck Easton's dive light from the sea bottom, seventy feet below. The light faded to a dim patch and Belden turned and walked back into the wheelhouse.

Instinctively, he checked his radar screen. Then he adjusted the range and checked it again.

"Hello," he muttered. "Bradley? Come have a look at this."

The midshipman was there in a second.

"Yeah, Dad?" He joined his father at the screen. "Wow, that's one huge return. What is it? Cruise ship?"

Both men looked south. Beyond the wheelhouse window there was nothing but the black of night.

"That's not right," Bradley said. "She's standing inside our three-mile range ring, but I don't see a light. And we should be able to see a dinghy at almost three times that range. Fog bank?"

His father shook his head. "If it was fog, we'd show it on the weather setting."

The younger man reached for the radio.

"What are you doing, Bradley?"

The younger Belden gestured at the window. "She's not showing lights, Paw. She's posing a menace. We have to call it in."

Jason shook his head.

"Not while the major is down on this dive, Son. That target out there isn't moving. We have some time. If she's still dark when the major gets back, we can call her in then. But I don't think we want too many questions about why we're anchored here, in the dead of night, diving on an uncharted wreck site."

"All right." Bradley leaned into the window, cupping his hands around his face. "But that is weird, is it not? What do you think it is? Is she big enough to be a cruise liner?"

Jason studied the radar return.

"No," he said. "She's not that. Besides, we're still three months away from cruise season. But she is definitely bigger than a breadbox, is she not?"

Pale bluish-tan in the bright, narrow beam of the dive light, the bottom was coming up. Easton glanced at his depth gauge: eighty feet. And while he knew he was fine – even after twenty minutes of bottom-time at this depth, he'd sufficiently be clear of nitrogen to go straight to the surface – he had this slightly off-center feeling. The feeling that his antennae were up.

He began sinking a bit, pressed the autoinflator, and added enough gas to put him into a hover just four feet off the bottom. Now he was over loose sand and could just make out the lines of tongue-and-groove coral formations.

He consulted his Geiger counter – still reading low in the normal background range – and began kicking steadily toward the low, shadowy lines of coral.

Ahmed bin Saleen ran the Boston Whaler only slightly above idle, quartering into the current so his heading was almost exactly south. His hope was that anyone watching – by radar or by eye – would mistake him for a fisherman heading out to deep water, after billfish or tuna or whatever it was that these idle Westerners pursued with their white boats and their cigars and their cans of beer and their bottles of Black Seal rum.

He looked at the horizon, where the *Marine Quest IV* was holding position in the night. It had been a calculated risk to call in the oceanographic vessel, bringing it within radar range. Yet it was as he had predicted; he had been monitoring the hailing frequencies and no call had gone out from the *Hog Penny* to the authorities.

Which meant that, right now, both of the Beldens were no doubt watching that great, hulking radar return on their flank, and not the tiny return of his little boat, creeping along a mile or so off their bow.

He opened the river bag and took out the pistol. It was a weapon with which he was quite familiar, a Glock model 29, manufactured with a bare minimum of metal. The slide and the frame were both manufactured from polymer, a substance opaque to security X-ray machines. Even so, the handgun's components had been smuggled into the Hamilton cargo terminal, distributed among six separate crewmen on two different ships.

The barrel, guide rod, and return spring of the weapon had hidden easily in the pencil slots of a briefcase, and the frame of the gun had been fitted into a void cut into a Bible, an irony that had given bin Saleen a smile. The most difficult part had been the nine-millimeter bullets, which had been secreted between the walls of a stainless-steel Coleman vacuum flask. The gun would hold sixteen rounds – fifteen in the magazine and one in the chamber – but his contacts had only been able to bring him five.

Ahmed bin Saleen looked at the lights of the distant anchored *Hog Penny*. If he cut his engine now, the current would carry him directly to the diveboat – silently, with no sound of a motor in the still, night air, and no prop noise to carry underwater. It would get him there in about twenty minutes and, if the American found nothing, he would have returned to the diveboat by then, and the Beldens would pull their anchor and be gone.

But if the American found what he was looking for, it would take him some time to examine it, to determine that what he was looking for was still there, and that it was still viable and not broken and scattered by its impact with the sea. And if that was the case, then bin Saleen would have plenty of time to do his work.

He hefted the Glock.

Five shots was more than enough.

CHAPTER THIRTY-ONE

Easton stayed in his hover, four feet off the bottom, and kicked closer to the coral.

Tongue-and-groove coral was something he had seen often on trips to the Bahamas. It looked like its name – as if someone had routed out roughly parallel grooves in the seabottom. But usually it was several grooves next to one another. This looked like only two. Puzzled, Easton took a deep breath and rose a little higher in the water column, slowly fanning the night-shrouded bottom with his light.

There were more than two grooves. There were at least seven, but there was a gap between the northern two and the ones further to the south. Or rather there was a gap between the lengthier grooves. There were shorter grooves of coral to the west – and, although he could barely make them out in the beam of his light, there seemed to be at least the suggestion of some more short grooves far to the east.

Easton exhaled and descended to the broad expanse of sand between the coral. A few seafans waved on the edge of the large plain. On the nearest, a single cowry crawled, the tan and brown bands of its shell gleaming in the beam of Easton's light, a thin trail of destruction following the tiny animal in the seafan's burgundy lacework.

Easton was turning, surveying the rest of the sandy plain, when he caught it – the briefest glimpse of dusky olive gray gliding by in the gloom.

A dolphin, he told himself as he turned. *There's an outside chance that it's nothing but a dolphin.*

But he knew that it wasn't.

Easton vented some air from his buoyancy compensator, sank to the sand, and rolled over, so he was gazing upward at about a forty-five degree angle, moving the beam of his dive light in brief, halting, ten-degree arcs.

On the third sweep he caught a glimpse of it: twelve feet long, gray, with a secondary dorsal fin and a vertical caudal fin, or tail.

It was the second two parts that bothered him. Dolphins have only a single dorsal fin and their flukes – their tails – are horizontal to their bodies.

Confirming what he'd suspected: what he had was a shark.

That, in and of itself, was not all that distressing. Most reef sharks – species such as nurse sharks or lemon sharks – were like cats, curious but skittish. Easton had been in the waters off the Outer Banks in the company of literally hundreds of ferocious-looking sand tiger sharks, a species that appeared to be all teeth and muscle. In the waters near California's Channel Islands, he had fed blue sharks by hand and even held one in his arms. Easton knew that, of the literally hundreds of species around the world, only a few were truly dangerous to man, and of those few, the three most dangerous were the great white – far larger than this one – the mako, which was not found in the Mid-Atlantic, and ...

The shark swam back into his light, passed over him, and moved its shovel-like snout back and forth as it passed through his exhaust bubbles. It continued swimming and Easton's light picked up a dusting of white on the outer curves of its long pectoral fins.

An oceanic white-tip. That was it – the third species always dangerous to man, and arguably the most dangerous of the lot. And that was what Easton was looking at. The shark swam on, and Easton's light caught a pair of clover-leaf-like ventral fins, meaning that this shark was female.

The more aggressive hunter of the species.

Oh, boy.

When Easton had left BUD/S – Basic Underwater Demolition/SEAL training – and gone on to more specialized mixed-gas dive training, his instructor had been a civilian contractor, Bret Gilliam. Gilliam was a longtime open-water depth-record holder, and one of the few advanced diving instructors with a security clearance high enough to work with covert operatives.

And one afternoon, after completing a lengthy decompression, Gilliam had told Easton about some work he had done off Andros, setting targets for high-speed passes by nuclear submarines.

Except for the depth – the divers had been working at approximately 300 feet – the work had been relatively straightforward. The divers had formed the four points of a large square and the sub, approaching at flank speed, would drive through the center of the square while a fifth diver, with a cine camera, would videotape the submarine's props and record how much cavitation, or bubbling, they produced – which was the purpose of the exercise.

That part had gone fine. But afterward, during the hour or more of decompression that followed work at such depths, white-tips had harassed the men on every dive. And they had grown progressively bold, to the point that, on one of the last dives, Gilliam had looked up to see one of his comrades being pulled away by ten feet of shaking, champing, *Charcharinus longimanus*, one of the most ancient and menacing predators on the planet.

Gilliam had gone to the aid of his friend, but not even two grown men, beating on the animal for all they were worth, had been sufficient to convince the shark to release its prey. And finally, when the other diver had succumbed to shock and stopped moving, the white-tip had simply turned tail on Gilliam and outswum him, its helpless victim still clamped within its jaws.

As ferocious and formidable a predator as the oceanic white-tip was, Easton knew that in all of recorded history there were only five recorded fatalities attributed to the species, Gilliam's unfortunate colleague being one. That was because, of all the requiem sharks, the oceanic white-tip was one of the species most rarely seen in waters frequented by swimmers or divers. It was a deepwater species, free-ranging and pelagic, only venturing into near-shore waters to breed or, occasionally, to hunt. So the chances were that Easton was the first human being that this particular shark had ever seen, and it would be naturally wary of him.

To test this, Easton waited until the shark was swimming in his direction, and then he pushed off the bottom at it, extending his light toward it like a glowing, blue-white spear. Sure enough, the shark abruptly changed direction and swam off into the darkness.

Good. Things could be a lot worse.

And then, as if on cue, they were. The shark returned, and with it was another – another oceanic white-tip, another female, another twelve-footer.

That was one more twelve-foot shark than Easton could keep his eyes on at the same time, so he kicked, smoothly and swiftly, to the nearest of the short coral grooves, and dropped into it. At the back of it was an opening – a tunnel. Knowing that a free-ranging animal like the oceanic white-tip would be unlikely to follow him into an enclosed space, he ducked into it.

At the same time, he extinguished his light. To produce its extremely bright beam, the HID light jumped a spark between two points, like an arc lamp, and Easton knew that this could produce enough electrical background "noise" to attract any number of large predators. Trailing a fingertip on the sandy floor of the passage, finding his way by touch in the total darkness, he ran a mental inventory – was he carrying anything else electrical that could draw predators? He remembered the Geiger counter, took it out, glanced at it, and stopped swimming.

The red diode was on, indicating that it was powered up.

But so was the entire column of green LEDs.

He was still well within the safe zone, but something nearby was producing a significant amount of radiation. Intrigued, he removed a backup light from one of his shoulder straps, twisting the head to produce a modest beam of light, considerably yellower and less powerful than the HID wreck-diving light. He pointed it down the passage and his heart dropped.

There, less than ten feet away and glassily reflecting the flashlight beam, was a huge, milky eye nearly three feet across.

CHAPTER THIRTY-TWO

Angela was just leaving her room at Willowbank when she felt it—an overwhelming sense of dread.

She stopped, took a breath, and looked around. There was no one nearby, as she'd known there would not be, because the dread she felt was not for her. It was for Beck.

Beck is in danger.

She had felt such sensations before. The first time, she had been barely fourteen, at a family Christmas gathering, when she had the notion that her grandfather was in danger. She had told her father, who had laughed and told her not to be ridiculous—that everything was absolutely fine.

But Great-aunt Eulesta, who had overheard the whole thing, had taken her aside a few minutes later and said, "Sweetheart, your father is a good teacher and a great man of God, but the fact remains that he is a man, and men are thicker than bricks when it comes to things like this. A woman's intuition is a sense, like seeing or hearing or smelling, and when danger comes calling, intuition is often the first sense to know. That, and it is my experience that a man is far more likely to shrug off the whispering of the Holy Spirit than a woman is. When you feel like that, God's talking, sweetheart. And when the Almighty speaks, his creations would do well to listen. We need to pray."

They had prayed together that evening, and later they had learned that, just at that moment, Angela's grandfather's car had swerved off an icy patch of roadway and landed in a ditch. Yet he and the car had been unharmed, and a young man had happened along in a four-wheel-drive pickup truck just moments later and had used his truck to pull the car back to the roadway.

Angela took a few steps toward the resort's main lodge, and the feeling hit her again, a gray wall of caution and dread. It nearly staggered her, and she walked a few steps more to a concrete bench under a post-lamp and sat down on it, unsteadily.

The paddle was nothing more than a gray plastic T-handle and a gray plastic blade, joined by a three-foot length of aluminum tubing, but it had proven sufficient to Ahmed bin Saleen's needs. With it, he had been able to correct the drift of his rented boat without starting its engine, and to bring it on a heading that would set him noiselessly on a collision course with the anchored *Hog Penny*. Now he crouched in the bow of his boat—crouched and waited. He didn't have to wait long.

"Hello the boat." The voice was Bermudian, metallically amplified over a loudspeaker. "Ahoy! Stand off. We have a diver in the water."

A spotlight played over the boat, bathing the helm and its console in stark white light, and then passing away again.

"Ahoy! Is anyone aboard?"

Ahmed bin Saleen risked a peek over the gunwale. Only a hundred feet separated the two vessels. The younger crewman was racing along the near side of the *Hog Penny*, setting out white, foam-rubber fenders.

Thirty seconds later, a jolt rocked the boat. A stainless-steel boathook clanked against the handrail above bin Saleen's head, grappling the upright and bringing the two boats abeam of one another.

In a single planned movement, bin Saleen stood, swung the paddle, and connected with the side of the younger crewman's head. The man collapsed without so much as a word.

"Hey!" It was the older crewman, the one who owned the boat. He took a step forward and bin Saleen pulled the nine-millimeter Glock from his waistband ...

Centered the Tritium sights on the older man's abdomen ...
Squeezed the trigger.

It was not an eye at all. Easton could see that now. It was a hemisphere of Perspex, the World War II precursor of Plexiglas, and it was filled on the inside with sand and silt, rendering it milky and opaque.

Forgetting the sharks, Easton swam nearer and played his light over the rim surrounding the viewing port. The rivets securing it had been hammered flat and then sanded; he could barely feel them with his fingertips. This craft had been designed to move through the air cleanly at high speeds.

He moved the light to the surface surrounding the port. It appeared to be a very tightly woven fabric of extremely fine metallic threads, painted over with a clear, yellowed sealant of some type. It was not rusted, and he doubted that aluminum could be drawn into so fine a thread.

Titanium. That was it. He was looking at an aircraft covered with titanium fabric.

The world's greatest titanium deposits were in Russia, and Easton recalled that some parts of Russia, such as Sakhalin Island, had been occupied by the Japanese during the war. So it all made sense.

This was the plane. The sandy area where he'd seen the seafans was not seafloor at all—it was the bomber, lying flat atop the tongue-and-groove coral formations and covered over with sand. He examined the fuselage. To his left, he could see a crumpled area and the bent metal strips of more riveted surrounds. The cockpit—or what was left of it. But although he assumed that the viewing port would be directly on the center axis of the aircraft, he could find no seams of any kind—nothing that even vaguely suggested the presence of a bomb-bay door. Then he understood what he was looking at: *It's resting upside-down.*

Easton continued along the dark coral groove, tracing his backup light along the aircraft above his head. There were no markings, nothing to interrupt the silver-gray surface except the seams where one width of metallic fabric overlapped another.

He got to open water and reached up, touching the edge of the aircraft above him. The edge felt crumpled and sharp, like broken fiberglass.

So it broke up when it hit. The wing-ends are missing.

Easton pictured the impact: the wing-ends breaking off, the remaining jet fuel spilling out into the ocean, seawater rushing in to take its place. Jet fuel is lighter than seawater; it would have provided most of the aircraft's flotation. In its absence, the flying-wing would have sunk immediately. No wonder Belden said there had never been reports of German fliers coming ashore. A crumpled cockpit and a rapid sinking—no one would have lived long enough to get out.

He checked his watch and his pressure gauge quickly, then searched the dark water around him with the backup light. No cruising shapes; no yellow eyes. The sharks were gone, which made sense. He had been under the bomber for almost fifteen minutes, and the white-tips were open-water predators, wanderers—if a meal was not in the immediate offing, they would move on, looking for something easier to catch.

He added a puff of air to his buoyancy compensator and rose above the sandy flat between the grooves. He could discern a subtle pattern now, like the outline of the famous Nike "swoosh," only it was huge. As it was, it was wider than a 747; with the wingtips intact, its wingspan would have rivaled that of a B-52.

Easton could discern a slight hump where the shape was its widest, and he swam there, hovering over it and fanning the sand with his hand. After five minutes, he had exposed a few inches of metal beam, fabric on one side. *The bomb-bay door—it's partially ajar.* He took out the Geiger counter and held it over the gap.

Half the yellow LEDs came alive.

So this was it. This was the bomber, and the plutonium weapon was still aboard. His part was finished; he needed to get back to the boat, get on shore, find a secure line, report what he had found, and let the Navy come in with a salvage ship and retrieve the thing.

He kicked smoothly back to the anchor and worked it free of the sand, so it began to slide gradually along the sand bottom, tracing a wide, flat depression behind it. Then, holding onto the anchor line, he lifted his console and checked his dive computer.

It showed him clear to ascend; thanks to the nitrox mixture he was breathing, he could stay down another ten minutes, easy, and still be able to go directly to the surface. So he began moving slowly up the line, venting his BC as he went, watching the luminous face of the gauge and staying at well under one foot a second, the maximum allowable ascent rate.

He had just cleared forty feet when he heard it—the rumble of an outboard motor starting up, followed by the high-pitched whine of cavitation.

Prop noise.

Easton flipped the switch on the HID battery pack and raised his right hand. In the moment or two that it took the lamp to come to full brightness, the boat had fled, but there, next to the hull of the *Hog Penny*, he could still see the white water of a wake. Someone had just been alongside the diveboat.

And Belden would never allow that with a diver down.

Easton began pulling himself up the anchor line, hand over hand. His dive computer began beeping an ascent alarm, but Easton kept on going, dark anxiety growing steadily within him. The alarm was still beeping when he broke the surface next to the *Hog Penny*'s swim platform.

"Jason? Bradley?"

No answer.

The ladder was still up and secured against the stern, so Easton grabbed the edge of the platform and kicked with both fins, pushing himself up like a swimmer climbing out of a pool.

"Jason?"

Easton pulled off both fins, tossed them through the open gate at the stern, and shrugged off his harness and tank.

When he got to his feet, the first thing he saw was the form of a young man.

"Brad?"

Easton dropped to one knee and touched a finger to the midshipman's neck. The pulse was good and strong. A goose egg was rising above and just outside his right eyebrow, but other than that, he appeared to be uninjured.

A moan arose from the wheelhouse. Easton went forward, switched on the cabin light and grimaced, despite himself.

Jason Belden was lying on the deck, both hands pressed to his stomach, and there was blood everywhere.

"S-s-sorry, Major."

"You stay quiet, Jason." A quick check showed that the captain had been gut-shot. He'd been hit twice, and he was bleeding out steadily.

Easton reached for the microphone to the marine radio. It wasn't there. He looked up: the transceiver had been smashed, completely destroyed, the navigation console beaten in, every instrument dented or shattered. The same with the first-aid kit—the red steel box was dented and open, its contents gone.

An orange Igloo cooler was bungeed to the starboard bulkhead. Easton grabbed it, opened it, and dumped the contents on Bradley Belden's head; the young man came around with a moan.

"Brad—listen to me. I know you're groggy, guy, but I need you to come around. Your dad's been shot. You need to put pressure on the wounds."

That was all it took; Brad was on the move immediately.

Easton went forward, ready to hot-wire the boat to get it going, if necessary. Then, despite his haste, he stopped cold. Despite the nearly complete destruction of the diveboat's instruments, the key was still hanging from the ignition.

Why leave the key? Why leave me alive in the water?

It didn't make sense, and Easton didn't have time to make sense of it. He flipped the switch to start the blower in the engine compartment, let it run while he ran forward and cut the anchor line with a dive knife, and then raced back to the helm and started the diesel. Ten seconds later the vessel was roaring at full throttle, the bow lifted cleanly out of the dark water, spray glazing the wheelhouse windows.

For twelve minutes, neither Easton nor Brad said a thing—there was nothing to say. Brad had the palms of both hands pressed against his father's abdomen, trying to keep his father's lifeblood within him, and Easton was running for port for all he was worth.

He was slowing to make the turn into Ely's Harbour when Bradley called forward, "Beck! No."

Easton looked back. Brad was looking up emphatically, where the moon was nearing its zenith.

"Tide's up, Beck. We can't clear Somerset Bridge. The flybridge is too high. We'll have to go around King's Point, far side of Somerset."

Beck gritted his teeth, reopened the throttle, and aimed the boat north. King Edward VII Memorial Hospital, Bermuda's only hospital with an emergency room was six miles east, in Hamilton, and he had just committed himself to a three-mile detour.

He didn't know if Jason Belden had the time for such a lengthy run.

He held the throttle hard against the stop.

CHAPTER THIRTY-THREE

Situated on a curve on South Road, tucked away in an area of upper-middle-class homes, on the northern outskirts of Hamilton, Pawpaw's was doing a brisk business as Rebecca Belden stopped the family van in front of the restaurant.

The drive down from Somerset had given Angela plenty of time to get acquainted with Rebecca's family—two younger sisters, a brother who appeared to be fourteen, and her mother, who had skin like aged mahogany and laughing eyes. They talked as they drove about how Jason and Bradley had gone out for a last-minute charter.

First Beck and now these guys. Angela nodded as the other women talked. *Bermuda's after-hours business seemed to be hopping this Friday night.*

"It's a very pleasant evening for January," Mrs. Belden said as they got out of the van. "Why don't we sit outside, here, and wait for our gentlemen?"

They gathered around a couple of patio tables and the older lady immediately assumed responsibility for the party, signaling a passing waiter and ordering fish chowder for everyone. It was brought out a few minutes later, wide bowls of a rich, thick red soup that the waiter laced with dollops of liquid from two small bottles.

Angela looked up, glancing at Mrs. Belden.

"Sherry peppers sauce and Black Seal rum," the older woman explained.

"Sherry Rum?"

Mrs. Belden waved her hand. "The chowder's served so hot that any alcohol evaporates away in just a few seconds."

"It does?"

Mrs. Belden smiled. "That's how my auntie explained it to me, dear, and I have never questioned her."

Angela tried it. It didn't taste intoxicating. Or rather it did, the mixture of tastes very nearly a sensory overload. She smiled and took another sip, and Mrs. Belden began to give her a brief history of Bermudian cooking.

Angela's earlier feelings of dread had just begun to subside when a burgundy-shirted man, the restaurant owner, waved emphatically at the table and pantomimed a phone to his ear.

Scotty, the fourteen-year-old, ran to see what the matter was, went inside the restaurant, and stayed there for about a minute. When he came back, his eyes were wide, his face drained.

"Momma," he said. "That was the police. Bradley and Dad are at the hospital. Dad's been shot."

For several seconds, nothing happened. Then the whole family was up and moving toward the Nissan van, Rebecca clasping Angela by the wrist and pulling her along.

"Beck," Angela told her. "I need to leave word for Beck ... tell him where I've gone."

"Beck is already at the hospital," Scotty told her as they moved. "He was out on the boat with my dad. He's the one who brought him in."

Easton was losing his patience. They had been at the hospital for better than an hour, and while there was absolutely nothing wrong with the medical care Jason was receiving – he had gone into the operating room within four minutes of their arrival, and the attending surgeon had seen service in Operation Desert Storm – the Bermuda police had been another thing entirely.

In a country where the mere possession of a handgun was a felony of the most serious sort, having a citizen riddled with gunfire was unsavory news, and Easton—the only foreigner within earshot—had been singled out as the subject of the authorities' scrutiny. His request that the American consul be sent for had been viewed as a stalling technique, and when he had requested that someone send round to Government House for a representative from MI-6, that had been viewed as the ravings of a lunatic.

At one point, handcuffs had been produced, and Easton was just promising a burly detective sergeant that he would be chronically unable to use handcuffs in the future if he attempted to use them now, when the American consul general appeared, taking the husky young Bermudian aside for a chat.

That settled that issue, but Easton's next request—the use of the consulate's encrypted satellite phone—had given rise to a difficulty. The consul general had left it at his residence, in Hamilton Parish, on the charger.

A driver had been sent for the phone, and Easton had taken advantage of the lull to go out and find Angela in the waiting room.

"Any word on Jason?" he asked.

"He's out of surgery, and his wife is with him in recovery. The doctor seemed happy with the way things have gone."

"Good." Easton could feel a weight come off his chest. "That's very good."

"Beck." Easton was wearing a plain polo shirt over canvas trousers, and Angela held his shirtfront as she spoke to him. "Beck—what happened? Who shot Jason? And what were you doing out on his boat?"

"I was diving. I found him shot when I came back up. Him shot, and his son knocked unconscious. Brad was better for a while, but he blacked out when we got here—concussion. We hope we'll know more when they come around."

Angela's eyes searched his.

"You were diving? By yourself? At night? Beck, what … what's going on?"

Easton looked at the wall clock and then back at her. "Listen — why don't we get you a cab back to the Willowbank, and — "

"Beck, the police have been talking to you since we got here. They didn't look happy. Tell me. What's going on?"

"I — "

Easton was interrupted by the American consul general, who was saying, "Um — sir?" and waving a phone with a bulky antenna from the doorway of the hospital conference room.

"Angie, I've got to go. Why don't you go on home? I'll talk with you about this later."

"I'm going to stay here with Mrs. Belden, see her home."

"Okay, fine. And then go back to the resort and we'll talk in the morning."

"And you'll tell me what this is all about?"

"Sir?" The diplomat was still waving the satellite phone. "Sir?"

"Angela, I'll talk with you in the morning."

He leaned forward to kiss her, and she turned slightly, allowing it to land on her cheek.

CHAPTER THIRTY-FOUR

JANUARY 16, 2000

Pushed through the early morning water by a matched set of Detroit Diesel engines, the seventy-two-foot Donzi, personal plaything of the American consul general, was a bit of overkill for three men and two sets of dive gear, but Beck Easton couldn't find anything wrong with the way she covered water. Since leaving the docks at Ordnance Island, Detective Sergeant Geoffrey Tucker—the same detective sergeant who had been so eager with the handcuffs just a few hours before—had kept the throttles wide open. Easton had little doubt that they would be making the twelve-mile trip down to Church Bay in less than half the time it would have taken to travel by car.

Master Chief Willard Johansen, chief diving officer of the naval salvage and recovery vessel *USS Grasp*, showed little indication that he did not travel by a two-million-dollar yacht every day of the week. Then again, having been lifted off his vessel by a Marine Pave Low helicopter, transported by Osprey to Nassau, capital city of the Bahamas, and then flown the final leg of his journey on a US Air Force Learjet, there was probably little left in the way of personal transportation that could elicit a comment from the stocky little fireplug of a man.

Nor had he so much as raised an eyebrow when Easton had given the Bermudian policeman the GPS coordinate of the German bomber from memory. The master chief viewed such abilities as pedestrian—he could recite unassisted the coordinates of the last seven sites his team had worked.

The sun was just clearing the eastern horizon when the constable brought the vessel off plane. As they drew abreast of Church Bay Park, Easton went forward to handle the anchor.

The consul general's Donzi had only a basic sonar, the type used for sportfishing, but even that was enough to find the coral, and Easton threw the anchor on command, set it, allowed enough slack for the moderate current, and came aft to gear up.

"I don't know if we're out of the woods yet with whoever attacked us last night," Easton told the master chief.

The Navy man looked up at the Bermudian policeman and asked, "Detective Sergeant, are you carrying a sidearm?"

"A sidearm, sir?" The policeman seemed startled by the question. "You mean a gun?"

"I mean a gun."

The Bermudian shook his head. "No, sir. We never carry them. Not unless we're on personal-protection detail."

The master chief scowled, reached into his gear bag, and came out with a .45-caliber Colt Gold Cup competition pistol and two extra magazines. The bullets on top of the magazines had a hollow-nosed, striated appearance that Easton recognized—Federal HydraShoc personal-defense rounds, not the smooth-nosed, full-metal-jacketed bullets approved by the Geneva Convention. The Navy man racked the slide on the gun, ejected the magazine, and replaced the cartridge he'd just loaded, locked the magazine back into the grip of the gun, and handed the pistol and the spare magazine to the startled policeman.

"There you go, Detective Sergeant. She's loaded, one in the chamber, and the safety's off. Anybody comes callin', you empty this puppy out at 'em, y'hear? Then you drop the mag, reload, and keep right on blastin'. Got it?"

"Sir, a gun? Please. This is most irregular."

"Not half as irregular as an early grave. Take the weapon, Detective Sergeant."

The Bahamian nodded, wide-eyed, accepting the huge, heavy handgun.

"Okay, Major." The master chief settled his mask on his face. "It's your water. Lead the way."

Going into the water with the sun rising was literally as different from the earlier dive as night and day. The two divers could see the bottom as soon as they had entered the water, and a pair of eagle rays loped along over the sand, passing a scuttling spiny lobster.

The divers descended to the bottom of the line and set the anchor. Then Easton led off, kicking toward the tongue-and-groove coral.

They were only halfway there when he sensed that something was wrong. The hump of sand covering the bomb-bay doors was missing, and there was a rectangle of metal lying on the sand bottom where no metal had been the evening before.

Heart racing, he kicked rapidly, shoulders bobbing as he zeroed in on the wreck site. When he got there, he could see that the modest depression he'd fanned into the sand a few hours earlier had been enlarged to an excavated square. The bomb-bay doors were lying on the sand, lumpy, raw metal on their hinges, testifying to the fact that they had been cut away with an underwater torch. Easton could hover right over the bomb bay and gaze down into the empty cradle.

Master Chief Johansen joined Easton and held up his index finger—crooked, like a question mark.

Easton could only shake his head.

They were too late.

The bomb was gone.

CHAPTER THIRTY-FIVE

What with the debrief that followed the dive, and the lengthy phone call to Washington from the consul general's office, it was noon by the time Beck Easton got back to Grotto Bay. Noon, and he was exhausted, having been awake for better than twenty-six hours straight. He needed to talk with Angela – but first he needed a shower, both to rinse the sweat and salt off his skin and to coax some semblance of life back into his body. So he resisted the temptation to call her from the Grotto Bay lobby and went to his room, determined not to speak with anyone until he was feeling a bit more human.

He saw it as he was walking into the room, setting the key on the dresser top: the message light on the phone was flashing. It wouldn't be the NSA – their dread of hotel message systems was just above their dread of email and digital cellular phones. And it couldn't be the Beldens – both had been sedated when he'd left the hospital earlier in the day.

That left Angela.

Angela.

Easton avoided the phone for a moment. Then he shook his head, swallowed, and pressed the flashing message button, followed by the 7 key to play the message:

"Beck? It's Angie ... Angela.

"Beck, I don't know how to ... I feel dishonest, somehow, communicating with you this way, but the resort staff called the airport for me this morning, and there's a flight back through Newark at twelve-fifteen, and I ... well, I know that I need to be on it.

"Beck, I may feel dishonest about this, but, hon ... but, Beck, I know that you have been dishonest with me. You being other

than where I'd thought you were, people getting shot, the police getting involved—I don't know what's going on, and I can't be in this, Beck. I can't be part of it.

"What's worse is that you seemed so perfect to me. I never thought it could happen this quickly, but I've fallen in love with you, Beck. And now all of this has happened, and I need to get away and go home and try to fall out of love, because we can't have a future together if there is going to be this kind of deceit.

"This is going to be ..."

There was a pause here, and Easton could hear her take a wet breath.

"This is going to be hard, because I'm still working for your architect, and I know that you have all my numbers and everything. But please, Beck—if you are even half the gentleman I thought you were, you won't call me. Please don't. I need you to leave me alone."

Another damp breath. Weeping. She was definitely weeping. Easton felt something like one millimeter tall.

"Thank you for the good time we had together, Beck. I feel stupid saying it now, but the last two days were the happiest of my life.

"I'll be praying for you, Beck. Good-bye.

"Good-bye."

I've fallen in love with you, Beck. Easton played the message over, listened to that sentence again, and shook his head. He put the phone back into its cradle and glanced at his dive watch.

It was 12:25. Angela's message had said that her flight would leave the gate at twelve-fifteen. He walked out onto his room's small patio, overlooking the startlingly blue water of Grotto Bay. Bermuda International Airport was just across the way, and as he closed the glass door behind him, he could hear the distant rumble of jet engines turned up to full throttle.

Twenty seconds later, a Boeing 737 rose from the runway on the other side of the blue water, the Continental Airlines logo crisp and distinct on its tail, even at this distance. He watched it climb and bank, knowing that he was looking at the only woman who had ever truly meant something to him, the only woman he had ever met like that in his life.

He wondered if she was looking back at him.

BOOK THREE

SANTA CATALINA

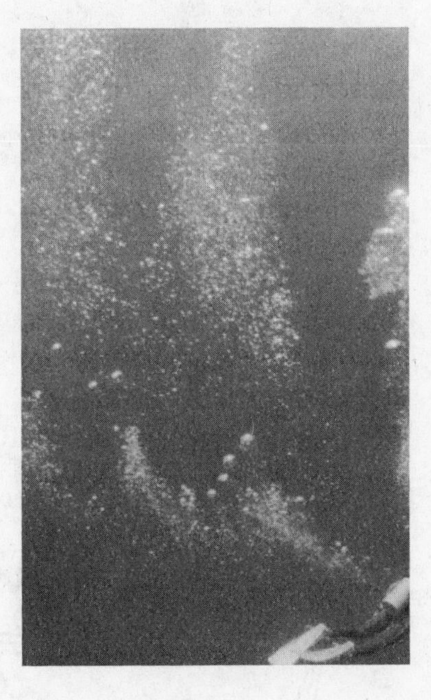

SANTA CATALINA ISLAND
AND ENVIRONS
0 1 2 3 4 5 6 7
MILES
PALOS VERDES HILLS
PACIFIC
OCEAN
WEST END
ITHMUS
AVALON
TM · 2005

CHAPTER THIRTY-SIX

FEBRUARY 12, 2000
LOS GATOS, CALIFORNIA

The Starbucks was doing a brisk business – not the episodic breakfast, lunch, after-work type of business that it would do on a workday – but a steady stream of suburbanites stopping in for a jolt of caffeine to get them through a day of shopping. A few sat and chatted at the tables in the sunshine outside, on the walk, but not many, and it afforded Beck Easton and Bill Spalding a place to meet covertly without seeming covert – a way to hide in plain sight.

"This is the motor vessel *Marine Quest IV* – an oceanographic research ship," Spalding said, handing Easton a digital color photograph that had been printed on plain typing paper. "Its owners reported it missing in the Mid-Atlantic in a storm last month, but the Coast Guard picked up an automatic distress signal from the *Marine Quest* a hundred miles north of Grand Cayman three days ago. The ship had just come out of refit, and it had been equipped with float-away emergency beacons, the kind that will activate automatically in a sinking. Apparently whoever scuttled her either didn't know about that or didn't think of it. Anyhow, this spiked some interest at Fort Meade because the *Marine Quest* was equipped with derricks and winches that were easily capable of lifting that bomb off the seafloor. She also had a moon pool – her hull could be opened to lift submersibles and the like, right through the bottom of the ship, so you could be passing right by her in another boat, and not be aware that any sort of salvage operation was going on.

"The Navy sent a submersible to the site of the distress beacon. They found the ship in 14,000 feet of water and – here's the important part – they recovered an ordnance package of several

hundred pounds' worth of World War II–vintage Czechoslovakian high explosive, which we figure to be the dispersal propellant of the bomb. Based on the shape of the ordnance package, the munitions experts at Meade think the plutonium is contained in anywhere from eight to ten lead-shielded containers, shaped like this."

He handed Easton a CAD-rendered drawing that looked like an overlong baking pan.

"What's the scale?" Easton asked.

"Big. They'll be about eight feet long. And the bad news is that they could be just about anywhere right now. If they were taken off the *Marine Quest* where she sank, they could have been put on a freighter bound to or from the Panama Canal. And for all we know, the sinking might have been a deliberate ruse. They could have offloaded these puppies in Boston, Baltimore, New York City, you name it ... and then brought the *Marine Quest* down south to sink her."

"So they're gone," Easton muttered.

"Gone, but not long-gone, thanks to you."

"I don't see how that helps."

Spalding looked up at him, held the look until Easton met his eyes.

"Don't look at this as a failure, Beck. We wouldn't even know to be looking for this stuff if it hadn't been for you."

"True, but if I'd just stayed where I was ..."

"What? You could have been around for them to put a bullet in you too when they came back? I saw the report, Beck. You didn't have a radio. You didn't have a choice. You saved a man's life. No. Don't you dare go kicking yourself over this one."

He looked up again, studying Easton's face.

"There's something else, Beck. What is it?"

"Nothing." Easton shook his head.

"'Nothing' my foot. We've known each other too long for that. Come on, Beck. It's me. Spill."

So Easton spilled. He told him about Angela, the scene at the hospital, the note. And when he'd finished, Spalding was looking at him, his expression absolutely blank.

"You poor, love-sick cow," he said. "And let me guess ... You want someone at NSA to call this woman up and tell her, 'Hey. It's all right. Beck Easton isn't a gangster; he's not a crook. He's one of the good guys. He's a secret freaking agent!' Is that it?"

Easton didn't say a word.

"I can't do that, Beck. The *director* couldn't do that. It's a violation of federal law. Maybe, just maybe, the president could do that, but I don't think he would want to write a note to your girlfriend for you. This comes with the territory, man."

Easton nodded. He knew Spalding was right. He tapped on the drawing on the table.

"I want to help you find this, Bill."

"I thought you wanted out."

"I did and I do. But not this way. Not with unfinished business. I need to clean this up."

"Well, I'll have to think about that."

"Think all you want, but put me on this."

Spalding gathered the papers and returned them to his valise.

"The nuclear people at Argonne National Laboratories tell us the key is lead," he said.

"Lead?"

Spalding nodded. "You take that plutonium out of this shielding, you're going to have to put it into something else made out of lead to handle it. And they don't think it will be left in its original shielding—puts too many limits on the ways Al-Qaeda can use it. So the Argonne folks tell us they'll need lead, about half a ton of it, to adequately shield it. Turns out there's about a million uses for lead—it's in CRTs, fishing weights, wheel weights, car batteries, glass. Black-powder enthusiasts cast bullets out of it, restoration experts use it to repair stained glass, and they even make keels for racing sailboats out of it. So we have compiled a roster of all the legitimate users of lead, loaded it into Echelon as an exception list, and now we're monitoring every transaction we can monitor for anyone buying five hundred pounds or more. If anyone unusual pops up, we should hear about it. It's not much, but it's a start."

He tapped the table. "Tell you what. Lead sounds like something the Environmental Protection Agency would be interested in. I'll have them cut you an ID—FedEx it out next week."

Easton nodded and the two men got up from the table.

"Oh, and Beck?"

"Yeah, Bill?"

"I've been married for twenty-two years, so I know a little bit about this woman thing. Monday's Valentine's Day. You send that girl some roses."

CHAPTER THIRTY-SEVEN

MARCH 8, 2000

Bill Spalding may or may not have been the world's greatest authority when it came to Mrs. Bill Spalding, but Beck was beginning to suspect that the man didn't know squat when it came to women in general. Valentine's Day had come, Valentine's Day had gone, and Beck hadn't heard as much as a peep from Wheaton. As far as he could tell, he had paid eighty-four dollars, plus tax, to have a dozen red roses shipped to a landfill in upstate Illinois. He had been tempted more than once to call and see if that was the case, but knowing that the line between "ardent admirer" and "stalker" could be very fine indeed, he had kept his peace.

He had concentrated, instead, on the IPO. Dot-coms that had survived the bubble were trading for ten times annual revenue, so Easton was bringing in all the business he could, NSA-assisted or not. Being a millionaire in the twenty-first century didn't have quite the same cachet it had when he was a kid, but if things went as it appeared they were, he was going to come out of this deal somewhere in that vicinity, and that was certainly better than coming out poor.

He was thinking about that when he pulled into his condominium complex and met the UPS truck going the other way. He got to his driveway and saw why—there was a brown cardboard box resting against his front door.

He parked the Land Rover in the garage, went in through the kitchen, and walked through the living room to open the door. The box was from a bookstore in Schaumberg, Illinois. He took it to his dining-room table, pulled a tab to open it, and found a book, a big, phone directory-size Bible, with a black Morrocan

leather cover that had his name embossed on it in gold: "BECK EASTON."

That was it. There was no card, no receipt.

He looked at his watch. It was half past four; seven-thirty in Illinois. He found Angela's number in his PDA, got the phone off its stand in the kitchen, and dialed her. She answered on the second ring.

"Hey," he said. "What's the occasion?"

"It's your birthday."

He looked at the date on his watch; so it was.

"How'd you know it was my birthday?"

"You told me over lunch at Ariel Sands. So when's *my* birthday?"

Easton thought for a moment. "I don't know."

"Uh-huh. Thought so. I would have put your full name on it, but I don't know your full name. I mean, 'Beck' is a nickname, isn't it?"

"Yeah."

"So what is it?"

"What's what?"

"Your real name."

Easton didn't say anything. Across the kitchen, the refrigerator gurgled, as if it were hiding an aquarium in it somewhere.

"Beck? You still there?"

"It's … Robert Exeter. Robert Exeter Easton."

"Robert *Exeter*? Are you kidding me?" Angela sounded as if she was having way too much fun with this.

"Robert is a family name on my father's side, and my mom read the other one in *Reader's Digest* when she was pregnant. It's the name of a school …"

"Oh, I know what Exeter is. This is too funny."

"Then you can see why I prefer 'Beck.'"

They both fell silent, and Easton looked at dust motes turning in a sun ray near the window.

"It's good to hear your voice," he finally said.

"Beck—don't go there."

"But you did send me a birthday present."

"I sent you a Bible. You *need* a Bible."

Careful.

"Listen, I don't know what you think happened in Bermuda, but—"

"Are you going to tell me?"

"Well, if it had been anything illegal or anything like that, I'd be in jail there and not here talking to you on the phone, right?"

"O.J. Simpson's playing golf in Florida—anything's possible."

Easton fell silent, thinking. "When can I see you again?"

He could hear her breathing. Finally, "I don't know."

"Then when can I talk to you again?"

"You've got the Bible?"

"Uh-huh."

"After you've finished the Old Testament."

Beck glanced at the contents page.

"That's, uh, like fourteen hundred pages."

"You can skip the footnotes."

Easton opened a page and glanced at it.

"Awful lot of *thees* and *thous* here," he muttered.

"I was feeling a little petulant, so I got you King James."

"Okay, then ..."

"'Kay. Happy birthday, Beck."

That was it. She hung up.

Bill Spalding had an expression. What was it? "Better than a sharp stick in the eye" ...?

Easton opened the Bible to the Old Testament.

In the beginning God created the heaven and the earth ...

CHAPTER THIRTY-EIGHT

JUNE 23, 2000
OAKLAND, CALIFORNIA

There are nineteen miles of waterfront at the Port of Oakland. Nineteen miles of waterfront, served by thirty-one gigantic gantry cranes, each crane capable of emptying an entire containerized cargo vessel in a single eight-hour shift. This meant that each crane does, in one day, the work that an entire crew of longshoremen would do in a month just three decades earlier. And each cargo container looked like the next, and each was locked, and that meant that, to Phil Wasserton, working at the Port of Oakland was like trying to push back the ocean with a sponge.

Wasserton was chief customs inspector for the port, overseeing a crew of forty-six people, none of whom could accomplish a tenth of what the average person on the street would consider a reasonable and prudent discharge of their duties.

Wasserton looked out the window of his shanty of an office—a "temporary" building that had stood on this spot for as long as he had held this job—and looked at cargo containers stacked like skyscrapers on the concrete dock space outside. Trucks were pulling into position and stopping for a matter of moments as cranes lowered containers onto skeleton trailers. Then they drove away, loaded with—heroin? Counterfeit Levis? Bootleg videos? AK-47s? Illegal Chinese immigrants destined for Brooklyn sweatshops?

He didn't know, and he never would know, because except for the one-tenth of one percent that he ever got a chance to take a look at, all he had to go by were the bills of lading, and for all he knew, those were as much fiction as the latest Grisham novel.

At least things were moving better now than they had been for those sixty days late in the winter, when the Defense Department had burdened him with olive-uniformed people armed with radiation-detection equipment. Wasserton didn't know what they were looking for, *they* didn't know what they were looking for, and when he'd asked why they were on his docks, risking grievances from the unions, he'd been given some story about unsafe X-ray equipment from the Philippines ...

... and *that* he was *sure* was as much fiction as the latest Grisham novel.

They were gone now, and things were back to normal. His people spot-checked cargo, processed duty, and paid extra attention to anything coming in from Colombia.

A container was being lowered onto a trailer just twenty feet outside his window. He glanced at the number and entered it into the computer on his desk. It was from Birmingham, England, it was going to Irvine, California, and it was loaded with a combination of automotive electronic circuit boards and flatware. Or so the bill of lading said, and the duty had been paid.

Wasserton watched the container drive out of his world and hoped it was nothing dangerous.

CHAPTER THIRTY-NINE

JULY 17, 2000
EL MEKKAH, SAUDI ARABIA

"One and a half billion dollars? This is outrageous."

"It is one-point-*seven* billion dollars, and it is not outrageous, sir. It is what the thing costs."

His cousin, Mohammed, was inscrutable, but Ahmed bin Saleen could barely contain his wrath. He lowered his head, folded his hands, and peered at the man who spoke so arrogantly to such an important citizen of the Kingdom.

The little Swiss physicist was a mercenary of the vilest possible sort, a sarcastic little weasel who had been beckoned by the smell of a paycheck and hadn't the sense to show proper respect once he'd gotten here.

He'd had the cheek to bring along a mousy little blonde whom he referred to as his "assistant," and whom he brought into his hotel room every evening. There they spoke English, as if that would be some sort of exotic and unintelligible dialect in this sand-strewn backwater of the world. When they spoke—and bin Saleen did not wish to think of what was happening when they did *not* speak—the physicist referred to his hosts as "wogs" and joked about their customs, their dietary laws.

Little matter. The Kingdom had a region known as the "Empty Quarter," and it would be just slightly less empty once Mohammed and he had heard what this infidel had to say.

Ahmed bin Saleen looked at the printout in front of him and read the top few items: HEPA II air cleaners, decontamination showers, umbilicaled clean suits, shielding, redundant building depressurization units. It went on for pages, and it had footnotes referring to tolerances in RADs.

"How long will it take to set all this up?" he asked the physicist.

"Set it up? You don't set something like this 'up,' sir. You construct it. You build it."

"Fine. Then how long to build it?"

"What? Do I look like a contractor? I'm sure I haven't the slightest idea. One year, a year and a half, I would imagine."

"A year and a half? That is preposterous."

The physicist shook his head and helped himself to a fig. He used his left hand, and that *did* elicit a reaction from Mohammed.

"I do not *write* the laws of physics, sir," the infidel was saying. "I am simply aware of them. And you are talking here about handling Plutonium-238, arguably one of the most poisonous substances known to man. A speck the size of a pinhead could wipe out everyone in this house. When you are dealing with a substance of that potency, you must exercise the proper precautions, regardless of the costs in time and money, or you will suffer the consequences."

"And what," bin Saleen asked, "if you are willing to suffer the consequences?"

The physicist looked at him and drew his head back, his bushy eyebrows lowered.

"Then, dear sir," he said with a wave of his hand. "All you need is an imbecile with a shovel."

CHAPTER FORTY

AUGUST 21, 2000
LOS ANGELES, CALIFORNIA

"Diego Rivera. That your real name, my man?"

Diego nodded his head. He did not know what to make of this *anglo*, if an *anglo* was indeed what he was. He looked Middle Eastern, only he had the bleached blond hair, wore too much Stetson for Men, and talked like Samuel L. Jackson in that crazy movie, the one with no beginning and no end—the *Pulp Fiction*.

"'Diego Rivera'... He was, like, a musician, right?"

"Painter. No relative."

"Well, your momma musta had some phat sensa humor. Anybody ever tell you this green card looks like it come from Kinkos, Dee-ay-go?"

Diego decided this would be a good time to feign a lack of English.

"How's the water in the Ree-yo Gran-day this time of year, Dee-ay-go?"

Diego just looked at him. He had actually walked across from Tijuana on a fake ID, but he saw no reason to apprise this strange, rude man of the fact.

"No matter, my man. This called 'the land of opportunity' for a reason. Tell me something, Dee-ay-go. You hab-lay the Ang-lay pretty good, do you?"

"Yes. I had two years of the English in university."

"Well! Look at the big brain on Dee-ay-go! That good, my man. That better than good, because these three boys in the truck don't speak a stinkin' word of it. That means *you* gonna be the foreman. So the boys in the truck gonna do all the grunt work, and we payin' them eight dollars an hour. We payin' you fifteen, and all you gotta do is tell these beaners what to do. Cool?"

The "beaners" part made Diego want to punch this strange man just a little, but he skipped past that to the important part.

"You say I will be making fifteen dollars an hour?"

"Fifteen green and that's cash money, Dee-ay-go, and we ain't gonna be makin' no deductions like they do in there." The strange man jerked his head toward the temporary agency on the corner, which had asked Diego to leave after one quick look at his counterfeit green card. "That sound good to you, my man?"

Diego nodded.

"Well, time's wastin', my man. Get in the back of the truck."

Two hours later—"It cool, my man. We payin' you for the transit time"—the truck pulled into an industrial park on the outskirts of Irvine, and Diego and his three colleagues were walking into what appeared to be an enclosed loading dock. The space, hot and close, was equipped with a small hand-operated forklift, an industrial-quality steel table, a collection of screwdrivers, wrenches, and other hand tools, and some small aluminum scoops, like you would use to portion food out for small animals.

Next to the table was the strangest barrel Diego had ever seen. It sat by itself on another hand-operated forklift, had walls that must have been five inches thick, and appeared to be clad in stainless steel. An equally thick lid sat on the table, and the lid had a hole in it that corresponded to a two-inch-thick drill rod protruding from the depths of the barrel.

At the loading dock, a cargo container was parked. Diego glanced in. Inside were a number of large troughlike items that appeared to be made of lead.

"Okay, listen up." The strange Anglo was handing out coveralls that appeared to be made out of a waxy, fibrous white paper, face masks with black filters, welders' gloves, booties made out of the same paper as the coveralls, hair nets, and goggles. The other three began putting the clothing on, but Diego just looked at his.

"What is it for?" he asked.

The strange Anglo looked at him as if he had just dropped from the sky.

"This here a clean-room environment, Dee-ay-go. We a recycling company. You see those things in that truck?"

Diego nodded.

"Well, those the stabilizer assemblies from a Cray II supercomputer, Dee-ay-go. You hab-lay Cray II?"

Diego shook his head.

"Don't matter. All you gotta know is, you put this stuff on, you take those stabilizer assemblies apart, you scoop out the powder you find inside, and you put it in this barrel. You got that?"

Diego looked at the clothing.

"This powder in the ..."

"Stabilizer assemblies."

"Yes. It is dangerous?"

The strange Anglo laughed. "No, man. Don't sweat it. Gear's here to keep y'all from contaminatin' the powder, that's all. It just zinc oxide. We sell it to sunscreen companies, but they want their stuff pure. Now—you put the powder in the barrel. Don't drop none, because it expensive, y'hear? And after y'all are done, you close up the barrel with that big, honking wrench—close it tight as it'll go, and then I want you to take the hose, here, and spray everything down. Spray all y'all too. Just soak the joint. Water cheap, you know? Spray it down and wash everything down the drain, because that what keep the clean room clean. You dig?"

Diego nodded. He could see now that, between the edges of the cargo container and the loading-dock doors, pieces of Visqueen had been duct-taped into place. It didn't look like much of a clean room. But maybe they were trying to save money.

"Now here the best part, Dee-ay-go," the strange Anglo was saying. "I got me a hot date tonight, I mean this woman *fine*, and I want to get home and get ready. But I got to go in the office and supervise y'all. You dig?"

He motioned at a video camera on the wall and Diego nodded.

"So here how I see it. I got ten hours' wages budgeted for this here job, and I don't much care how long it take. You finish in three hours, I pay you for ten. You finish in *one* hour, I pay you for ten, and four big strappin' boys like y'all, I should think one hour is all it'll take, particularly if the foreman don't mind workin'. So you finish in an hour, I give you a hundred and fifty cash money – and let's say a twenty dollar bonus on top, you being foreman and all, and we all get to go home early and it's all good. Now what do you say to that?"

Diego accepted his coveralls, looked at his coworkers, and nodded at the cargo container.

"*Andale*," he said.

CHAPTER FORTY-ONE

LOS GATOS, CALIFORNIA

"Hey."

"Hey, yourself." Easton had been calling Angela every weekend, and she was definitely sounding less distant now. The first time, she had obviously read the Caller ID, because she had answered the phone asking, "Who was given the coat of many colors?"

And she only agreed to continue the conversation when Beck had answered, "Joseph."

But she had not agreed to a face-to-face visit. She had, in fact, resisted the idea at every turn. And when Beck had asked, "Don't you trust me?" – she hadn't answered at all.

That had hurt.

And what made it worse was that he couldn't blame her a bit.

But this time, she sounded almost cheerful on the phone. And when she'd asked him, "What are you doing October seventh?" he'd immediately answered, "Nothing. I'm completely open."

She chuckled on the other end of the line. "Don't you want to look at your PDA, check a calendar or something?"

"Doesn't matter. If there's something on my calendar, I'm canceling. I'm open. Why – what's up?"

"Well, there's this wedding here in Wheaton. My cousin. And I'm maid of honor – "

"I'll be happy to take you."

There was a long pause on the phone.

"Maybe you'd better not *take* me, Beck. Not ... pick me up and stuff. But if you would like to meet me at the church and then go to the reception with me afterward ..."

"I'd be happy to."

"But that would be it, Beck. No going home afterward. No ... nothing."

"I understand."

"Do you? I mean, these are an awful lot of hoops I'm asking you to jump through. You'd have to fly out here—"

"That's fine. I need the cross-country hours and the night landings to stay current."

"You're a pilot? You're a pilot."

"Well, yeah."

"Beck, I have to be careful here. I hope you understand."

"I do. Entirely."

"All right, then. And Beck?"

"Uhm-hum?"

"Could you read the New Testament for me, as well?"

"Get the test questions ready, Ms. Brower."

She laughed, and he heard the click as she hung up the phone. Easton wondered how his classmates at Annapolis, how his team-members in BUD/S, would have reacted if they'd heard him talking this way with a woman. They would have made jokes about rings through the nose. They would have talked about giving up your freedom.

Easton walked onto his deck and looked at the developers' small, blue excuse for a "lake," put both hands on the railing, and took a deep breath.

That's what they'd say, and he didn't care. He didn't care a bit.

CHAPTER FORTY-TWO

OCTOBER 7, 2000
WHEATON, ILLINOIS

"So ... what did you think?"

Great-Aunt Eulesta cocked her head and looked at Angela, a thin smile growing on her face. "He can certainly turn a head."

"He can."

"That suit looked awfully expensive, dear. I have always been cautious of men who overdress ..."

Angela laughed and waved a hand at her sea foam-green bridesmaid's dress. "Aunt Eulesta, I don't think *anyone* can be held legally responsible for what they wear at a wedding."

The two women laughed and Angela sighed. Beck *had* looked very handsome in his tailored suit—Gianfranco Ferre, if she wasn't mistaken, and being a design professional, she was not. Her entire family had been abuzz at the sight of him.

And true to his word, Beck had arrived just a few minutes before the start of the wedding and left to go back to his downtown hotel once the reception had begun to thin out. Angela's father had liked him immediately, but Angela's father liked anyone who had a decent haircut and didn't smoke—at least he liked them at first blush.

But Angela had made sure that Beck and Aunt Eulesta had spent some time together because the grand old lady's was the opinion that she coveted. She had arranged to spend the night at Aunt Eulesta's house so she could get that opinion—and have, if she needed it, a reason that Beck could not see her home.

"Now," Angela asked her great-aunt. "What do you really think?"

Great-Aunt Eulesta sat on the loveseat and patted the cushion next to her. Angela sat next to her, so close that she could see the powder on the old lady's cheek. She took her arm and held it.

"First you must tell me, Angela. Are you seeing anyone else?"

Angela shook her head.

"And you haven't been since you met this young man?"

Another shake.

"And this young man; is he seeing anyone?"

"He says he isn't."

"And do you believe him?"

"I do."

The old lady closed her eyes, and when she opened them, she was looking directly at Angela.

"So," she said, "you believe him when he speaks of the state of his heart, but you do not believe him when he speaks of the state of his life. Is that so?"

Angela worked her lips.

"Yes," she said. "No ... I mean, I get the feeling that he has never lied to me. Not ever. But I don't get the feeling that he is telling me the complete truth."

Aunt Eulesta raised her eyebrows. Both eyebrows.

"That is perceptive, Angela. I believe there is a difference between falsehood and concealment. But I do not believe that either has a place between a husband and his wife. Because that is what you are considering him as, are you not? A prospective husband?"

"Oh, Aunt Eulesta ... he hasn't asked me."

The old lady laughed.

"Trust me," she said, "that is simply the drumbeat at the end of the score."

In the parlor, a clock under a belljar began to tinkle and whirr. It began beating a chime, counting to twelve. The sound made Angela think of fairy tales.

"Angela," Aunt Eulesta said, "when you were very small, I remember telling you that God had already picked out the man that you were going to spend the rest of your entire life with and that you would meet him in due time. Do you remember that?"

Angela nodded.

"That was not just a thing one tells children. It is true. Do you understand that?"

Another nod.

"The Bible says, Angela, that the voice of God is like the sound of many waters. We needn't worry about not hearing him. And if God has a man for you, he'll say so. Do you believe that?"

"I do."

"From what you have told me, God hasn't spoken on this young man yet. He hasn't said yes. But he hasn't clearly said no, either. And from what I saw this evening, this is a man willing to go to the ends of the earth for you, and I think he's worth the wait for God's opinion. So let's you and I pray, and hope we hear that soon."

CHAPTER FORTY-THREE

OCTOBER 8, 2000
MIDWAY AIRPORT, CHICAGO

As Beck Easton walked his early morning preflight around the Grumman Tiger, he realized that this was one part of his work life that he was going to miss, once he and Blue Corner had parted company.

The Tiger – a low-wing, single-engine, four-place airplane with fixed gear and a bubble canopy – was registered as a corporate asset, which made it tax-deductible and allowed Easton to bill the insurance to the company. Rodney had already campaigned a couple of times to replace the Tiger with a corporate jet, but Easton had resisted, ostensibly because a piston aircraft was more frugal and would look better to corporate investors, but actually because propeller-driven aircraft were more fun to fly. When you pushed in the throttle on a prop-driven aircraft, it *did* something. When you pushed in the throttle on a private jet, it did something about thirty seconds later. That was all right if you didn't mind thinking of your airplane as a really fast minivan with wings, but Easton liked aircraft that were responsive.

He'd just finished checking the oil when his cell phone vibrated and rang in the pocket of his flight jacket. He fished it out and looked at the ID: "Wm Spalding."

Shaking his head and grinning, Beck flipped opened the phone.

"Bill – it's Sunday morning, you heathen. Shouldn't you be off making recompense for your sins or something?"

"Well, you're sounding chipper. Anything happen last night that I should be aware of?"

"I caught the bouquet," Easton told him. "Now, what's up?"

"Echelon caught a tickle on the lead query. An old one – someone sat on this, I'm afraid, but earlier this summer, a place called Twin Palm Fabricators, in Riverside, received eleven hundred pounds of low-antimony lead."

"Riverside, eh? Your neck of the woods?"

"Would be, but I'm in Maryland. 'His master's voice,' you know. Won't get back to LA until Wednesday."

A Tomahawk rumbled down the taxiway, and Easton looked at his watch.

"Tell you what," he said. "If I leave now, I can make it into John Wayne before the noise-abatement curfew. I'll do that and refile my flight plan aloft. That way I can stop by this fabricator's in the morning and check things out."

"If you think you can. Don't you have a prospectus to file later on this week or something?"

"I'm leaving that to the accountants and Rodney. It's the first thing I've found that the man is actually good at. All I have to do is sign something, and I can do that anytime up to Friday."

"Thanks, Beck. I'll email the address to you. And I owe you my firstborn."

"Not if he looks like you."

"My firstborn is a daughter."

"I'm spoken for."

That got a long pause. Then Spalding said, "I'll see you next week, Beck."

CHAPTER FORTY-FOUR

OCTOBER 9, 2000
SAN DIEGO, CALIFORNIA

"Have you flown a Skyvan before, mister?"

"Some. We operate Otters, mostly."

As he walked around the big high-winged airplane, Ahmed bin Saleen reflected on the fact that at least the first part of that statement was true. He had flown both of the large, twin-engine aircraft that were so popular with skydiving operations around the country. He, in fact, had a logbook under an assumed name that showed that he had better than one thousand hours in type, which was more than an exaggeration, but nothing he was worried about. Americans were very casual about who they let into the cockpits of airplanes. Thus far, this fool had not so much as asked to see identification, let alone a pilot's license. It was a weakness that these softheaded fools would one day regret—Ahmed bin Saleen already had more than two dozen of his Al-Qaeda brethren enrolled in flight schools around the country.

"I've got to tell you, buddy, that this time of year, a Skyvan can be a bit of a handful. If you have Santa Ana winds where you dive, and they come at you from an angle? Man—she'll crab like there's no tomorrow. Where'd you say your skydiving school was again?"

"Tempe." Ahmed bin Saleen smiled. "No Santa Anas there."

He held the smile, masking the start he'd felt when the American had brought the topic up. It was precisely those Santa Ana conditions—hot winds from the desert that blew through the mountain passes east of Los Angeles—that Ahmed bin Saleen was counting on.

While the plutonium in the old Nazi bomb had been plenty potent, the pyrotechnic part of the weapon had long since

succumbed to the effects of seawater. And ever since Oklahoma City, explosives were something that the Americans *did* keep an eye on. There'd been no way to easily acquire enough to disperse the plutonium oxide powder. And even if there had been, it begged the question of how to acquire an aircraft that could drop such a bomb—not to mention move out of range of the explosion's shock wave.

But neither could he simply pour the plutonium out of an aircraft. Even in a fine, powdered form, the heavy plutonium would drop like the proverbial brick in still air. So bin Saleen needed winds—high winds—to disperse the stuff and spread it. He wanted it to spread over miles of freeway and land on automobiles and trucks. He wanted it to blow from Anaheim to Hollywood. He wanted it to waft into the open bags of newspaper carriers, so they could deliver death to suburban doorsteps. He wanted it everywhere.

That took wind, and here, in one of the greatest concentrations of infidels in this part of the planet, God had arranged for a high wind nearly every day this time of year. Just to make sure, bin Saleen had checked the Weather Channel this morning, and the weather maps had told him what he needed to know—that the troughs and ridges were all in position for the winds that brought wildfires. Today would bring even greater calamity than fire.

"Shall we wind her up?"

"Yes. Please." Ahmed bin Saleen led the way into the aircraft, made the step up onto the flight deck, and took the left-hand seat, the pilot's seat. He strapped in, flipped the necessary switches, turned a key, and shouted "Clear!" out the open window before pressing the starter. Then he settled a headset onto his ears and began to taxi. Two minutes after that, they were in the air.

Empty, the boxy Skyvan felt nose-heavy. But once bin Saleen had trimmed it out, it climbed like a kite. Neither man said anything about this—with a load of two dozen skydivers, it would handle like a normal high-wing airplane. That made landings tricky—you always landed these aircraft empty, and they wanted to glide forever—but an aggressive flap setting could handle that.

The infidel selling the airplane was prattling on about time since major overhaul, prop modifications, and other such truck. Ahmed bin Saleen turned down the volume on his headset. As long as the airplane could fly for an hour without bursting into flames, it was more than suitable to his purpose.

He turned, landed, and taxied back to where they'd started. The infidel was smiling now, showing a mouthful of capped teeth.

Ahmed bin Saleen left the props turning and twisted his way. "I forgot to ask about the jump door. It is in good operating condition?"

"Door? Sure. Set the brakes and come on back. Can't go skydiving if the door don't work."

The two men walked back to the flat-floored cabin, where long bench seats were folded up against the fuselage walls. The man selling the plane turned a handle and lifted, and the entire rear end of the airplane seemed to crack and fold inward. A load door, hinged at the top and six and a half feet wide, began to rise toward the roof of the plane.

The infidel secured one side of the door to the overhead, and bin Saleen secured the other, ambling back toward the cockpit as if admiring the vista through the huge, gaping doorway. Taking the cue, the infidel stepped into the center and said, "There you have it. Everything works. Want to go inside and take a look at the maintenance logs?"

"That won't be necessary," bin Saleen told him. "I'll take it just as it is."

And with that, he took a Walther P22 pistol from his jacket pocket and aimed it at the garrulous Westerner.

CHAPTER FORTY-FIVE

RIVERSIDE, CALIFORNIA

Twin Palms Fabricators was hands-down one of the most unusual businesses Beck Easton had ever seen. An armored truck with a futuristic machine-gun turret sat in the parking lot, and in the window was what appeared to be an extensive selection of Japanese samurai swords.

Easton walked in. The assortment of hardware was so extensive and varied that, when a short, goateed man greeted him from behind a long counter, Easton's first question was, "What do you *do* here?"

The short man—he was not a little man; he had arms like telephone poles—laughed and said, "Custom fabricator for film sets, mostly, dude. We're a little ways off in the sticks for that business, but we're low-rent, and it's easier to get materials in Orange County."

"You built the turret for that truck?"

"And the fiberglass armor. You want it, we fabricate it. Half the junk I build here, not even *I* can tell what it's going to be used for. But if you give me a set of prints, or even a pretty good sketch, I can fabricate to order. Why, man? What do you need?"

Easton took out the ID Spalding had sent him. "I'm with the EPA. I understand that you took delivery of just about five hundred kilograms of lead here in August."

The man's face sobered.

"Yes sir, Mister ... Reindel.... I did. But, hey—no worries about that. We're set up for lead fabrication—all the filters in our melt area, everything."

Easton smiled and nodded. "I'm sure you are. We're just here to make sure that all that lead got used or properly disposed of—don't want it finding its way into a landfill, you know? Can you tell me what it was used for?"

The shorter man arched his eyebrows. "Not quite. That was one of those things where I made it, but I'm not sure what I made. You know what I mean? It was like this barrel, stainless steel on all of its outer surfaces, but lead-lined, and the top and the bottom could be joined as a spool, and they were press-fitted."

"Press-fitted?"

"Yeah, like they wanted to make sure that they could be pulled apart again if you put enough torque on them."

"Regular customer?"

"No. Never seen the dude before. Darker skin, frosted hair. Paid cash. And you don't need to worry about disposal of that lead; I used every ounce of it in the fabrication."

Easton looked up at a suit of stainless-steel, futuristic armor. "Can you tell me where this customer is?"

"Sure. We delivered. Here's the address." He opened a file drawer, thumbed through it, and handed Easton a sheet of paper with an Irvine street address.

Easton squinted. "I don't get around here much. Where is this?"

"Barely still in Irvine, man. One of those industrial parks, right across the street from El Toro."

"The Marine Air Station?"

"Used to be. Jets and choppers both. But the government shut it down last year. Nothing out there now but gate guards and some contractors doing cleanup. But hey—you probably know all about that—EPA's supervising most of it."

"Different office," Easton said. He put the paper in his pocket and shook the man's hand. "Thanks for your time."

Easton got back into his rental vehicle – the young woman at Avis hadn't believed it when he'd asked for a Ford Explorer over a Mustang convertible – and started south. He'd been through MCAS El Toro a few times, back in the day. If the place that bought the lead was over there, he'd find it. It was about a one-hour drive.

Plenty of time to think about what the fabricator had described.

Because, while Easton couldn't put his finger on it, there was something about what the man had described that was unsettling.

He got to the industrial park in five minutes less than he'd allowed and drove slowly along its roadways, leaning over to the right of the SUV and peering out the window, looking for the building number. A horn sounded in front of him – not a cheerful double-toot, but a long, angry blare.

Easton looked up. There was a yellow Ryder rental truck, twenty yards ahead of him, taking its half of the roadway out of the middle: obviously a driver unused to the larger vehicle. Shaking his head, Easton pulled to the side and let the driver – mirror Gargoyles, stocking cap, and white coveralls – take his truck through.

Not so much as a courtesy wave. Easton shook his head again and drove on.

He found the number a couple of minutes later, a place that looked barely occupied; no sign on the wall outside, and nothing written on the metal fire door out front.

Parking the SUV, he walked up and tried the door. It opened.

"Hello?" The lobby area was dark. Easton reached for and found a light switch. A set of florescent lights flickered and then came on. "Anybody here?"

He walked through the lobby area and into what appeared to be an office. There was a card table with some Rally bags and cups sitting on it, and a counter with a TV set showing an empty loading-dock area, a joystick next to the TV. Easton walked to a door at the back of the office – the loading dock, he presumed – and found that it was padlocked from this side, no key in the lock.

Strange. Don't they have fire codes here? Easton went to the counter and wobbled the joystick. The picture on the TV moved.

Remote control. He dipped and panned the camera around, and then, on a whim, he pointed it straight down, at the floor below the camera.

Four bodies were piled there, their skin hanging in strands as if it had been burned away, a great ring of dried moisture around them.

Easton looked at the table, at the cups sitting next to the bags. There was wetness on the lower parts of the cups.

Condensation.

He picked up a cup and shook it. Ice rattled.

Someone was just here. But they were gone now. And the only way out besides the front door was locked.

The rental truck.

Easton raced for his SUV.

He drove with one hand and opened the phone with the other, pressing speed-dial for Bill Spalding's number. He got a recording and pressed 2, leaving his cell phone as a call-back number.

The nearest entrance to El Toro was ... right there. He could see an olive-drab guard shack, an olive-drab Humvee parked next to it.

Easton was making the turn-in to the gate when he saw the first body. It was a kid—he couldn't have been more than nineteen—splayed on the drive across from the guard shack, a discrete red-black hole right of center in his forehead. In the doorway of the shack, a second guard was slumped against the doorpost, the back of his head glistening red.

Airplane engines roared overhead and Easton saw a boxy, double-tailed, twin-engine aircraft, white with blue striping, banking in a turn and lining up for a landing out on the tarmac. He took his phone out again and speed-dialed a second number, this time for the confidential switchboard at NSA.

When a female voice answered, Easton gave her a five-digit code number and added two words: "Duty Officer." In two seconds, another voice, also female, answered.

"This is Easton, Romeo Echo—you're taping, so voiceprint this later. Listen up: I am at MCAS El Toro and have two Marines down, presumed dead. Opposition are on the ground, but they won't be for long. They will be exfiltrating in a blue-on-white Shorts Skyvan twin, N number unknown. Do not—repeat—do not fire on Skyvan once airborne. Significant contamination issue. Notify Spalding, Whiskey Sierra. You got that?"

"Sir, I ..." Through the Explorer's dusty windshield, Easton could see a yellow rectangle pulling around a hangar in the distance.

The rental truck.

"I gotta go." Closing the phone, he mashed the accelerator to the floorboard.

CHAPTER FORTY-SIX

"You did *what?*" Ahmed bin Saleen asked in Arabic. Omar took the forklift back to the rental truck while Yasser worked a come-along, inching the lead-lined drum into position on the floor of the Skyvan's flat, open cargo area.

"Ahmed, with God as my witness I will tell you that it was not working," Yasser said. "The Marines were reaching for their radios. They would have called their superiors."

"What of it? Let them call. You had authorization! Signed authorization! The EPA really *is* doing a clean-up on site today. The drum could have passed as a waste container. What did you do with the bodies?"

"We, uh, left them – "

Ahmed bin Saleen struck out with the back of his fist, catching the younger man across the forehead, knocking him back into the wall of the aircraft.

"You left them lying at the guard shack." He was seething. "Where any fool can drive by and see and notify the authorities. Get back to work, quickly! You have probably brought the infidels down upon us. And get your hood up and your mask on. Do you not realize that if one speck of this material lands on your skin you will die in terrible agony?"

"But Ahmed bin Saleen, you are not – "

That was it; bin Saleen lashed out with his boot-tip, catching the younger man in the side. The man curled up, groaning.

"When I give an order, I do not want your commentary," bin Saleen said. "I want your compliance."

He looked up. At the truck, Omar already had his hood on and his respirator over his face.

Easton bounced and jumped over the open ground, keeping the hangar between him and the place where the rental truck had gone. At times all four wheels of the Explorer were off the ground. At other times, his head was hitting the headliner—hard—despite his tightly cinched seat belt. He dimly remembered reading a newspaper report about SUVs and rollovers.

In for a penny ... He kept the accelerator mashed.

He stayed that way until he was almost to the hangar, and then he applied the brakes slowly, trying to keep from squeaking the tires as he made the transition from dusty ground to tarmac. Stopping the SUV next to the old building, he took the key out of the ignition and dropped it to the floormat so the door wouldn't chime, and then opened the driver's door slowly, sliding both feet out and to the ground.

He moved carefully, watching where he put his feet. At the corner of the hangar he dropped to the ground and peeked around. There was the Skyvan, props still turning. There was the truck. A fuel truck was parked out, far from the building, its tires going flat, and there were some barrels standing beyond that. But other than that, the tarmac was empty.

Thin cover.

He looked down at his clothes. His trousers were tan, and he was wearing off-tan boat shoes. But his sport coat was blue, his shirt light blue, the tie red. He took off the coat, shirt, and tie and grabbed a clump of earth off the SUV running-board, rubbing it over his white T-shirt and the backs of his hands and arms. Then he risked a quick look around the end of the hangar one more time and took off running.

He had only taken five steps when he heard it—the worst sound in the world; the crack of small-arms fire. But he didn't hear the clap of bullets breaking the sound barrier around his head, didn't hear the snap of bullets ricocheting off concrete.

They aren't firing at me.

He lifted his eyes and saw a pair of olive-drab Humvees racing toward the airplane from the other side of the base. Maybe in response to his call; maybe they'd seen the airplane land. He couldn't be sure.

It didn't matter. Easton used the distraction to cover the ground to the barrels, then to the fuel truck. Then he ran from behind the fuel truck to the nearest figure, a man in white coveralls aiming an Ingram submachine gun at the oncoming Humvees. Easton leapt through the air like a runner sliding feet-first into third base, both of his feet striking the man behind the knee.

The man was still falling as Easton grabbed his head the way a linebacker would grab a football and twisted forward.

If the man made a sound, Easton didn't hear it over the small-arms fire; and neither one of the terrorist's companions turned.

A Marine fell on the back of one of the Humvees. Easton snatched up the Ingram, aimed it at the other man in white coveralls and pulled the trigger.

Nothing. The magazine was empty.

Frantic, he searched the dead man's pockets for a spare clip but found nothing. He guaged the distance between him and the other two Al-Qaeda. It was a good sixty feet. No way could he cover that distance undetected. Then he looked at the coveralls, the hood, and the respirator. He got an idea.

It took just fifteen seconds to pull the man's body behind the fuel truck, but a full minute and a half to pull off his coveralls and mask, and another minute for Easton to dress himself in them, cinching the hood tightly to hide every trace of his face and his hair. Then he raced forward, but already he saw that he was too late; the third man, wearing khaki slacks and a leather flight jacket, was aiming a metal tube at the oncoming Humvees.

LAWs rocket. Oh, man ... Easton barely had time for the thought to register. He dove to the tarmac as orange flame whooshed over his head.

When he looked up, the nearer of the two Humvees was listing and smoking heavily, the other one was stopped, obviously wondering if there was more where that had come from. The gunfire had stopped entirely.

The other man in white coveralls tossed his Ingram to the ground, and both he and the man in the flight jacket began sprinting for the plane, leaping into the open jump-door at the tail of the fuselage. They yelled at him in Arabic, and Easton realized that he was still dressed like the opposition and there was an entire Humvee full of angry Marines not three hundred meters away. If he stayed here, he'd die—and the plane would get away scot-free.

That made the decision for him. Easton sprinted for the plane and threw himself aboard as the engines roared to full throttle.

The airplane picked up speed. The entire rear end of the Skyvan was an open door, designed to allow whole teams of skydivers to exit the aircraft at once, and the tarmac was scrolling away from it, faster and faster. The two Al-Qaeda were up front, occupying the flight crew's seats.

Easton looked around. Two parachutes were lashed to the bulkhead, and he remembered that it was standard operating procedure for jumpmasters to wear 'chutes on these birds, so he grabbed one and put it on, cinching the chest-strap as tight as it would go. There was also a retention strap secured to the bulkhead behind him, a long nylon strap with two locking carabiners on the tag end, and he snapped this into his parachute harness as an extra measure of security. Then he turned his attention to the stainless-steel drum on the cargo bay floor.

It was so simple it was ingenious. The drum rode on what looked like an industrial-strength version of a mechanic's creeper, a creeper currently attached to the aircraft's cargo-bay deck by means of three stainless-steel quick-releases, clipped off to D-rings sticking up from pockets in the deck.

At the end of the drum nearest the door, attached to the lid, was a wide parachute pack, the kind skydiving schools used for tandem jumps. Its drogue chute pin was missing, and its main chute pin was barely in place, making it obvious how the weapon was supposed to work – you freed the barrel from the floor, pulled the main chute pin the rest of the way out, and rolled the whole contraption out the yawning jump door. The drogue chute would open once the apparatus was free of the plane. Then the drogue would pop the main chute open, the force of the pop would pull the spool assembly out of the drum, and the plutonium dust would spill into the open air. Simple, effective, and – as long as you stayed upwind – it was an attack that its perpetrators could survive.

That was obviously how it was supposed to work. Now all Easton had to do was figure out how to make it *not* work.

The first thing was to fix things so the barrel couldn't leave the plane. Checking to make sure his hood was still cinched around his respirator mask, Easton turned and glanced forward, making sure the two others weren't looking his way. The aircraft tilted and the tarmac dropped away from the open door. Grabbing one of the D-rings, Easton held on as the airplane climbed and banked. Then the plane leveled off for a moment, and Easton removed one of the stainless quick releases and replaced it with a locking carabiner from the retention strap, turning the locking nut until it was firmly jammed into the aluminum of the carabiner gate.

He was looking at the parachute when he heard yelling from up front.

He looked that way. The other man in coveralls, mask lifted, was shouting at him in Arabic and tapping the headset that he wore.

Easton looked behind him. A pale green David Clark noise-attenuating communications headset was resting on a bulkhead hook, its overlong coiled extension cord plugged into an intercom unit. Easton put it on and Arabic erupted from the earpieces.

This was a problem. German, Easton spoke like a native. Spanish, he could pass for local in some dialects. French, he knew enough to get by.

But Arabic?

Beck Easton didn't speak a single word of Arabic.

He pointed to the headset and rocked his hand back and forth in the air.

The coveralled man yelled in Arabic again and made a motion with his hands. Clearly, he wanted Easton to release the retaining straps on the drum.

Easton nodded, bent to the straps, and pretended to fiddle for a second. He glanced out the big door in the back of the plane. Thin cloud scuttled between him and the ground. The airplane, built to carry dozens of skydivers at once, had gained altitude quickly. They had to be around jump altitude, thirteen thousand to fifteen thousand feet. He fiddled with the strapping a little bit more, then looked back at the cockpit and pointed down at the drum, shrugging his shoulders.

The coveralled man shook his head and undid his seat harness, standing up in the space between the seats in the cockpit. His partner in the left-hand seat, aviating through one of the busiest pieces of sky in the western hemisphere, kept his eyes on his instruments and ignored what was going on in back. The coveralled man took a step toward Easton, and Easton gave him a quick once-over.

No parachute: the other man was not wearing a parachute.

Good.

Easton unclipped the retaining strap from his harness and held it out to the approaching stranger, nodding over his shoulder at the gaping door. The man reached out to take the strap and, as he did, Easton dropped the strap, grabbed the man's wrist, tucked, and rolled.

It worked. The white-coveralled stranger was out the jump-door in a heartbeat. If he'd screamed, the sound had been lost in the drone of the engines.

One, back on the ground, and now this one – two down.

Easton looked up. *One to go.* The pilot.

A weapon. He needed a weapon. There was a manual control for the door on the bulkhead behind him, and he could see that the lever section of it was removable, held on by a spring-loaded ball bearing.

He released it. Pretty light, but it would do. Clasping it in both hands, he took four steps forward and then, swinging like he was trying for the bleachers, struck the pilot in the side of the head.

Green bits and pieces of David Clark headset plastic flew everywhere, and Easton swung a second time. He tried for the top of the head, but the low ceiling didn't provide much room in which to swing, so he hit the man in the temple a third time.

It worked. The pilot slumped forward.

Way forward.

The man wasn't strapped into the pilot's seat. He crashed into the controls and the aircraft instantly stood on its nose, sending Easton flying into the center console, where his body shoved both throttles to full power.

Not good. Not good at all.

Easton stood – he was standing sideways, they were diving so steeply, and he could look straight down, out the cockpit windshield and see a tilting spaghetti of freeways. Grabbing the pilot by the leather jacket, he lifted, twisted, grunted, and finally pushed the man's body behind the flight deck, into the cargo area. He wanted to chuck him out the back, but the back was an eighteen-foot vertical wall right now, so Easton squirmed into the pilot's seat, sat awkwardly – there'd been no time to take off the parachute—feathered both props, and began pulling back, ever so gently, on the yoke.

The wings screamed in protest. Easton looked at the airspeed, which was fifty knots above maneuvering range. He couldn't pull back too radically, or he would snap the wings off, but he had to pull back somewhat, because he was low enough now that he could tell the difference between the trucks and the cars on the freeway.

At five thousand feet, the aircraft began to respond. Up at the very top of the windscreen, he could just make out a thin line where ocean met sky. He pulled a little more, and the sky grew by a few inches.

At four thousand feet, Easton had reduced their angle of attack to forty-five degrees, and he could see individual people walking on the Long Beach waterfront. At three thousand, it was thirty degrees, and he was low enough to see some of those people gesturing, pointing his way. At two thousand, the screaming began to let up a little from outside, and at one thousand, his nose was no more than five degrees below horizontal. He pulled the hood back, pulled off the respirator mask, and tossed it onto the empty copilot's seat.

At five hundred feet, he narrowly passed *under* a traffic helicopter, and the Skyvan shuddered as he kept back-pressure on the wheel. They crossed water and cleared the smokestacks of the *Queen Mary* by no more than two hundred feet, nearly skimming the harbor beyond her. Then it was all open ocean ahead of him, and he pushed the throttles forward, pouring the power back on, the aircraft climbing smoothly.

Easton scanned the horizon. He had never flown a Skyvan before and knew they could be tricky to set down. He didn't want to make his first attempt with a hundred kilos of toxic plutonium in the cargo bay.

He could see a dark oblong shape on the ocean ahead. Santa Catalina ... Catalina Island. That would work. The plutonium might prove iffy in a crash, but if he could ditch the Skyvan smoothly enough, and close enough to shore, he should be able to swim away, maybe even grab the last terrorist and tow him in as well. Easton thought it through – the Skyvan's propellers were mounted high enough to keep from flipping the plane when he put it down in the water.

That would work, but it would have to work soon. Beyond Catalina, slowed by the Santa Ana condition, but coming in nonetheless, Easton could see a line of thunderheads building, clouds climbing to – well, higher than this glorified boxcar could probably fly.

Procedure for ditching a Skyvan ...

Easton didn't have a clue. Come in at stall speed and try to stop flying the second the hull touched water, he imagined. But he knew what part of the island he wanted to try for – the far side, off China Point on the southern coast. The Farnsworth Bank was out there, top of an underwater escarpment that plunged off into blue water. That would put the plutonium a decent distance from the most settled parts of the island and deep enough under water to block the radiation if the container broke, but not so deep that a Navy salvage crew couldn't find it. It would mean a huge swim in stiff current; probably more swim than he could do.

Easton pushed the thought out of his head and concentrated on flying the airplane.

He had just put the eastern half of Catalina on his nose when he felt it – a sharp push, as if someone had shoved him in the shoulder. Then a hole appeared in the instrument panel, and blood spattered all over his airspeed indicator.

I never got the chance to check that pilot for a gun.

Easton just had time for that one, fleeting thought, and then his head was ringing as a gun-barrel met it violently from the side. His head rang again, and his arms went limp, as if the power had all been cut off from them.

The next thing he knew, he was being pulled from the pilot's seat. It was the most extraordinary sensation possible—he could feel every bump and jostle as his body was dragged, and he could certainly feel his head, which hurt like there was no tomorrow, but he could not feel his shoulder, except for some warm wetness, and he could not move his extremities at all. He looked up—it took an awful effort to look up—and there was the face of a man. Bloodied, bruised, but recognizable. The face of Ahmed bin Saleen.

So we meet. Easton wanted to say that, but his voice wouldn't work properly either—he just groaned. Ahmed bin Saleen dragged him a few more feet—Easton could tell that the fellow wanted desperately to get him to the doorway and chuck him out—but the terrorist obviously wasn't up to it. The man was barely standing. He let go of Easton, straightened up, gave him a kick in the side for good measure—it wasn't much of a kick—and stumbled forward to the flight deck, leaving Easton sprawled next to the lead-lined barrel.

The barrel. Enough plutonium to murder entire nations. Easton looked at it and marveled that it was right *there*—so close.

He longed to touch it—and found that he could. His hands were working again, after a fashion, and his legs too, just a bit, although standing was out of the question. He pushed with his legs, inching his body closer to the open jump door.

The tandem parachute was attached to the barrel lid right in front of his nose. And next to him was the stout, double-thick, two-inch-wide nylon retention strap, its end flapping out in the air beyond the door.

Turning on his side, his wounded shoulder shrieking in protest, Easton grabbed the strap with his good hand and hauled it back into the airplane. As he did, he saw that they were over cloud now. Ahmed bin Saleen was using the updrafts of the leading edge of the thunderstorm to gain altitude quickly, which was an awfully clever piece of flying for a man with a double concussion.

Easton touched his chest. *Still wearing the parachute: good.* He unclipped the big tandem parachute from the barrel lid. Then he clipped the parachute attachment points to the end of the retention strap. Next, he worked the main chute pin out of its retention slot and reached into the flap beneath it, grabbing the soft, slick coolness of the nylon drogue.

Now the device was still strapped securely to the aircraft's cargo deck, but the only thing the parachute was clipped off to was the strap ...

... the strap that was still secured to the Skyvan's starboard bulkhead.

Still gripping the drogue chute, Easton gave a push with his legs—they were coming back like gangbusters now. He turned the push into a shove and forced his body out the yawning jump door.

The slipstream caught him immediately, the airplane seeming to fly up and away from him as Easton dropped. He kept hold of the nylon drogue until it was snatched out of his hands. The air was filled with a huge "POP," almost like a thunderclap, and then there was this big rectangle of tandem parachute bumping along behind the Skyvan.

Just like that, the airplane stopped flying and canted earthward.

That was when a cold, moist cloud enveloped Beck Easton. He'd forgotten about the cloud, and the cloud posed a problem because he could not see down where the ground was, and he couldn't see up, where the airplane was, and while he did not want to hit the ground, neither did he want to open too early and be overtaken by the falling airplane and its flapping open net of parachute canopy.

Wetness crept down his chest and armpit. Easton wondered if the gunshot had damaged the parachute—if it would open at all.

He waited until the sound of the plane's engine diminished, and then he fished with his working hand and found and pulled the ripcord. There was a *whump*, a sensation like being janked in the air on a huge rubber band, and his wounded shoulder sang out with a pain that he swore he could actually see. But a rectangle of yellow fabric was open above him.

Then he was screaming down out of the cloud, and trees and grass and a hilltop were rushing up at him. It was enough to make him forget the pain. He reached up and grabbed his risers. That turned his downward motion into forward motion; now he was skimming along the steeply sloping hillside, like a man skiing on the tips of the blades of grass.

He stalled the 'chute further and sat, fairly hard, on the hillside, the parachute spilling down around him. He got to his knees just in time to see the Skyvan spin like a maple seed into the ocean about a half-mile offshore. It made a huge white splash, but no noise at all, and a moment after that, Easton realized he was in a herd of huge black, cowlike creatures—were they buffalo?

They were, and he was still trying to figure out why there were buffalo on Catalina Island when the thunder cracked and the rain came pouring down.

CHAPTER FORTY-SEVEN

JANUARY 29, 2001
FORT MEADE, MARYLAND

A dusting of snow covered the landscape rolling past the Town Car's rear windows. Alone in the backseat, Beck Easton resisted the temptation to run a finger under his stiff, red-piped woolen collar and tapped lightly on the sword resting across his knees. He shifted on the seat, gazed absently out the window at the snow, and worked his shoulder, which was stiff, but not as stiff as it had been.

Had Ahmed bin Saleen held the gun just a fraction of an inch higher or lower when he'd pulled the trigger, Easton would still be sprouting surgical pins. Either that or in the ground. The doctors had all agreed on that. But the gun had been at the magic angle, and the bullet had missed bone, missed arteries, missed every single one of the myriad bits and pieces that would have won him the free trip to Bethesda.

He'd not emerged unscathed. There'd been two rounds of arthroscopy to repair ligaments – enough to keep him out of action while the Navy dived on the shredded remains of the Skyvan. But other than the stiffness and an inability to turn his head completely to the right – and the doctors said that both would go away with time – all the incident had left him with was an angry red scar, fading with each passing day.

He touched his uniform, over the wound, and squinted at the half-numb, wooden feel of it.

The salvage divers had recovered the drum of plutonium intact, but found no sign of bin Saleen.

That hadn't surprised them. Sharks, they'd said. Catalina was known for its makos, none too picky about what they ate. But the

Navy had found nothing—no clothing, no tough leather flight jacket, no shoes.

For that matter, Easton knew that there had still been another parachute left on the plane when he'd jumped, and that had never been found, either. But neither had the seats, the flight-deck carpeting, parts of the tail assembly, the cockpit headliner, much of the wings—anything light enough to be carried by the current. Easton would have preferred solid proof that the terrorist was no longer a threat. But he knew life wasn't always like that. You didn't always get to close the book.

He glanced down at the palms of his gloved hands. That was one of the hazards of wearing white gloves, especially in winter—you constantly found yourself checking to see if you'd picked up any dust or lint. *Marines—the few, the proud, the fastidious ...*

Easton had lost count of how many times he'd been summoned to Fort Meade, but he could count on one hand the number of times he'd been asked to report in uniform. And prior to today, he had never, ever, been asked to report in dress blues.

This was also the first time the agency had sent a car to pick him up at BWI. Usually he rented a car and resigned himself to the fact that it would take at least twenty minutes of credentials checking and rechecking to get him onto the yard—the *base*, he reminded himself—and then into the offices of the National Security Agency.

His driver passed the National Cryptological Museum, the only portion of the NSA's considerable facilities open to the taxpaying public. The car barely slowed as it approached the gates to the NSA secure annex; the Army guards at the checkpoint snapped to present-arms as they passed.

Easton reached inside his stiff blue blouse and pulled out the orders that had been brought to him by a signals courier. They had been issued by the agency information officer, a post of whose very existence Easton had been ignorant prior to receiving the one-page communication. And when he had telephoned Bill Spalding to ask what was going on, Spalding had simply told him, "All I can say is I'll be there as well. So clear your calendar, and I'll see you in Maryland on Wednesday, buddy."

The car passed the visitors' lot where Easton usually parked and drove right by the porticoed entrance that he usually used to enter the headquarters building. The driver followed a hedge-lined drive to enter a parking lot beneath the building, stopping before a smoked-glass door, where a young woman in a business suit opened the car door, greeting Easton by rank and name. He stepped from the car, tucking his cover under his left arm.

"Miss, I haven't checked in yet. Don't I need a badge?"

The young woman flashed him a smile. "Not today, Major. You're all set."

She swiped a keycard through a reader slot and the door opened. Easton was just about to ask what was different about "today" when the young woman waved him through. They stepped into a wide corridor, made a turn, and Easton found his bearings; they were approaching, and then entering, the anteroom of the agency director's office.

Easton had been here before, once or twice. It was a place that he associated with long waits, so he moved toward a chair, but the director's administrative assistant, a regal woman with silver hair, said, "That won't be necessary, Major. They're waiting for you. You can go right in."

They're. Plural.

Puzzled, Easton looked around. His escort was gone, her mission having apparently been to deliver him, and nothing more. He walked to the double-oak doors where a young Hispanic man with a flesh-colored earpiece whispered something into his sleeve as he opened the door.

When Easton stepped through, he understood what the mystery was all about.

There, standing as if assembled before the director's desk, were the director, Bill Spalding, three strangers in suits, and a collection of generals and admirals that Easton recognized as the Joint Chiefs of Staff. And in the center of them all was a man in a blue suit, a man whom Beck Easton had seen before, but only on TV ...

... the president of the United States.

Ten minutes later, all of the ceremonies and photographs were over. The Joint Chiefs filed out, and the president asked the director, "Harry, would you mind if Beck and I borrowed your office for a second?"

That had been the cue for everyone else to leave – everyone but a single Secret Service agent who stayed by the door. The president had shooed him out as well, saying, "Give us a minute, Jerry. I think a Marine major can protect us if any bad guys come sneaking out of the curtains."

When the agent had left as well, the president led Beck to a conversation nook, took a seat on the sofa, and motioned to a second sofa opposite him.

Beck removed his sword and sat, silent, waiting.

The president cleared his throat. "You know, Beck – okay if I call you Beck?"

"I would be honored if you did, Mr. President."

That got a nod from the Commander-in-Chief.

"Beck, my father ran a sister agency to this place quite a few years ago, so I know how this works. We just gave you a couple of prestigious medals and took some pictures that anyone would be proud to have on their wall, but both of those medals and all of those pictures are going to be kept here, in a safe. You're gonna have to make an appointment if you want to come back and have a look. And that hardly seems right. I mean, man – you just saved a major city and millions of American lives."

"There's a reason for that, Mr. President. If the opposition ever found out how close they came to succeeding, they might get the idea that they should try it again. We don't publicize those sorts of victories. We never do."

The president nodded.

"You're a good guy, Beck. I knew you'd say that." He picked up a file from the coffee table between them. "I see you've cashed out of your company in Los Gatos. But you're still a young man. I've got a set of silver oak leaves for you today—I don't think anyone will argue with me if I give you those. But that hardly seems like enough, so if it's all right with you, I'd like to talk to the commandant about you skipping a grade next time. If you're interested, two, three years from now, there's a star waiting for you in the Corps."

A star. Promotion to brigadier. Beck swallowed.

"That's ... that is very generous of you, Mr. President. But generals work behind desks, particularly brigadier generals, and I had all the desk time I ever wanted back in Los Gatos. I've purchased some property in Florida, sir. I'm putting a house up there—just a prefab for right now, to get going, and I'm planning on starting a business, guiding and teaching cave-diving. It's what I like. The money I made, selling off some of my stock after the IPO—that made me enough to reinvest and live comfortably for the rest of my life. I just feel like it's time to kick back."

The president nodded and set the folder back on the coffee table.

"You deserve it, Beck. But that brings us back to where we started. A medal in a closet doesn't strike me as much of a 'thank you' for a hero. So what can we offer ... what can I offer ... to do the job properly?"

"Sir?"

"You name it," the president said. "Anything. If it's within my authority, it's yours."

Easton sat there, stunned at the implications in that offer. He searched his Commander-in-Chief's face. The man looked entirely earnest, and Easton leaned forward, toward him.

"Well, Mr. President," he said. "Since you asked, there is this one thing ..."

CHAPTER FORTY-EIGHT

FEBRUARY 16, 2001
WHEATON, ILLINOIS

Fresh from the shower, Angela should have felt invigorated, but she did not. She felt spent. She felt lethargic, and she blew her hair dry and put on her makeup with the absent motions of someone who was there in body only. Selecting the first underwear that her hands landed on when she opened the drawer, she got dressed as if she were clothing someone else, finishing up by dotting perfume on her wrists with the mechanical motions of someone operating out of habit, rather than enthusiasm.

Things had looked better – maybe not really promising, but better – when Beck had flown in from California for her cousin's wedding. But after that there'd been a month – a full month – of silence.

Blue Corner Technologies had gone public in the meantime; Angela had read that much in the business section of the *Tribune*. But when she'd finally swallowed her pride and called Los Gatos to ask for him, she'd been told that he'd left the company.

One *J* gone and the other one nowhere in sight. Angela hadn't even bothered to call Great-Aunt Eulesta for her opinion. She'd known what the grand old lady would say.

And when Beck had finally called, what had been his excuse?

"I've been in the hospital."

"For what?"

"It's nothing I can go into right now."

I believe there is a difference between falsehood and concealment. But I do not believe that either has a place ... Angela could almost hear her mentor's voice. Tears began to well up, and she squeezed her hands into tight fists, trying to push the depression

away. Because that was what she was: depressed. She knew it, and knowing it depressed her further. For months she had been telling herself that she would snap out of it, that there were other fish in the sea besides Beck Easton, but none of her arguments had been successful. Her girlfriends had suggested doctors, and she had resisted. The only thing worse than depression, in her mind, was the idea of taking pills for depression.

Even her work no longer satisfied her. Her clients still loved her, still raved at what she did with color and light, but for Angela it had all become rote: $A = B + C$. It was not that she was searching for the meaning of life – she had found that at age twelve when she had discovered Jesus. But lately she had found it more and more difficult to find a reason to just get up and go through the day.

"Father," she said aloud. "It's time for you to speak. I've waited a long time. I've waited long enough."

Then her face flushed warm as she realized what she had said. Was this what she had come to? Barking orders at God?

"I'm sorry," she whispered, her fingers to her lips. "I'm ... sorry."

She had just slipped on her shoes and was picking up her planner when a knock came at her door. That startled her out of her lethargy – she was not expecting company.

She squinted through the peephole in her condominium door. A young woman in business dress was standing there on her landing. And behind her, at the curb, was a black GMC Suburban – and was that a Marine standing next to the vehicle's passenger door?

Angela opened the door.

"Miss Brower? Miss Angela Brower?"

Angela nodded.

The woman held up an ID. Angela just had time to see a picture, a seal, and the words, "GENERAL SERVICES ADMINISTRATION."

"Miss Brower, I'm from the federal government, and I've been asked to come pick you up. Could you come with me?"

Angela blinked. A lot. "What's this about?"

The woman put her ID away. "You're not in any trouble, Miss Brower. No trouble at all, and coming with me is entirely optional. But it is a matter of national interest, and your presence would be greatly appreciated. That's all I'm authorized to say. Could you come with me? We'll have you back here by noon."

Numb, Angela clutched her planner against her bosom and followed the young woman, barely remembering to close and lock her front door. They got into the Suburban, and the young woman nodded at Angela's planner.

"Do you have any appointments this morning that we can cancel for you, Miss Brower?"

"Um – no. I was ... um, just going in to the office to do some drawings." Angela made a motion as if she was drawing in the air. She wasn't sure why.

"All right. You might want to put on your seatbelt. Things are going to get a bit hectic."

The Suburban, it turned out, was equipped with both flashing lights and a siren, and the dark-suited driver used both once they were clear of Angela's condominium complex. They headed for the tollway, rocketed full-speed through an I-Pass entrance, and got into the carpool lane, where commuters got out of their way like fleeing cats. They drove all the way to I-55 and then headed east, toward downtown. Angela barely had time to register that they were taking the exit for McCormick Place – the Chicago convention center – when they were pulling into a VIP parking area under the center and stopping next to an elevator guarded by three more men in dark suits.

Angela and the GSA woman got onto the elevator, rode up for perhaps half a minute, and got out at a hallway where the woman held Angela's planner while she walked through two pillars, which Angela assumed to be a metal detector, while two more men in suits looked on. One of them appeared to speak into the buckle on his wristwatch, and Angela was ushered into a large room with windows that looked out on Lake Michigan. The room was decorated like a formal living room but with a large conference table at one end and two people, a man and a woman, were standing there with their backs toward her. They turned as she entered and Angela recognized the man.

Did she *ever* recognize the man ...

"Wow," she muttered. "I, um, voted for you ..."

"I appreciate that, Ms. Brower," the president of the United States told her. "And I apologize for the way you were brought down here, but this is supposed to be a surprise drop-in speech here today, and the Secret Service likes to keep it that way. Can we get you something? Have you had breakfast?"

"No, sir. I mean no, I haven't." Her words did not seem to be obeying her. "But I'm fine."

"Maybe some coffee? Some orange juice, Angela? Is it all right if I call you 'Angela'?"

"Yes! Um, juice would be great, sir." Angela said that and marveled at the fact that the chief executive of the United States was fetching her a drink. She accepted it and muttered a thank-you.

"This is Marcia Constantine," the president said, holding an open hand toward the woman next to him. "Marcia is a lawyer with the office of the White House General Counsel and she has a paper for you to sign. It assures us that you will hold everything that we say here this morning in the strictest of confidence, and that you will go to prison for ... well, forever, if you ever reveal it to anyone. Is that okay with you, Angela?"

"Um, yes sir." Actually, it wasn't, but Angela had long since abandoned any idea of control over this situation. It was like being on a roller coaster, and she simply signed the paper and slid it back to Marcia Constantine of the office of the White

House General Counsel, who put it into a briefcase, nodded at the president, and retired to the far end of the table.

The president smiled and motioned toward a set of armchairs arranged in a conversation nook. As they sat, he said, "Angela, I understand that there is a young man named Beck Easton who is, if you excuse my speaking Texan, sweet on you – is that correct?"

Beck? "Yes ... yes sir, that's true."

"And you, in turn, are sweet on him. Am I right?"

Angela nodded mutely, unable to find words.

"Well, that's good. Real good. I have something to tell you, then. Get comfortable, Angela – this is going to take a few minutes."

The president spoke for fifteen minutes without once referring to a notebook or a file. When he had finished, Angela felt as if her head were spinning, and the president was adding, "So that's why your young man wasn't able to tell you what he was up to. He was sworn to secrecy by my office – by my predecessors in this office – and as much as he wanted for you to know the truth, he could not break his oath and tell you. He couldn't even tell you *why* he couldn't tell you. That's how hush-hush this all was. I'm sorry for any anxiety that may have caused you, but trust me, in the short time I've had this job, I have already learned that secrecy and anxiety come hand-in-hand, and I hope that you can appreciate that as well. Can you?"

"Yes, sir." Her voice was small, as if she had never used it before.

The president looked at his watch and then looked back at Angela.

"Angela, the National Urban League is having breakfast downstairs, and pretty soon I need to go down and speak to them while they digest, so I don't have a lot of time. But when I spoke to your young man, he told me that the one thing he wanted, more than anything else in the whole wide world, was to ask you to marry him, and frankly, having met you, I can certainly understand why."

The president held up his hand and, seemingly from out of nowhere, a young man in a business suit appeared and handed him a small, silver cellular phone.

The president looked at Angela and smiled.

"Your young man wants to visit your family and ask your father for permission to propose to you, Angela. May I give him a call and tell him that would be an excellent idea?"

Angela took a breath.

"Yes," she told him, her voice coming back. "Yes, Mr. President. You most certainly can."

BOOK FOUR

LITTLE RIVER

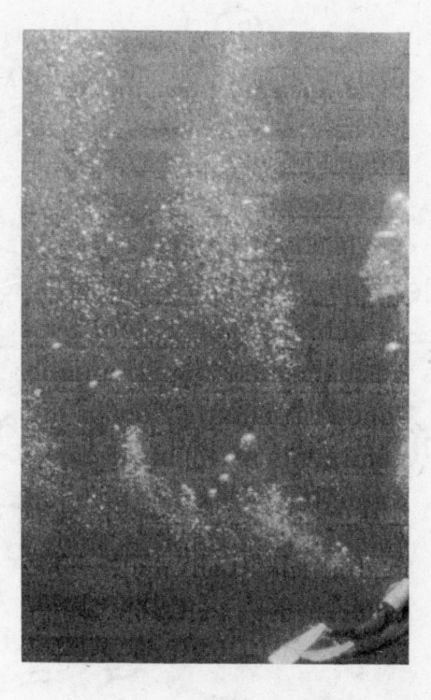

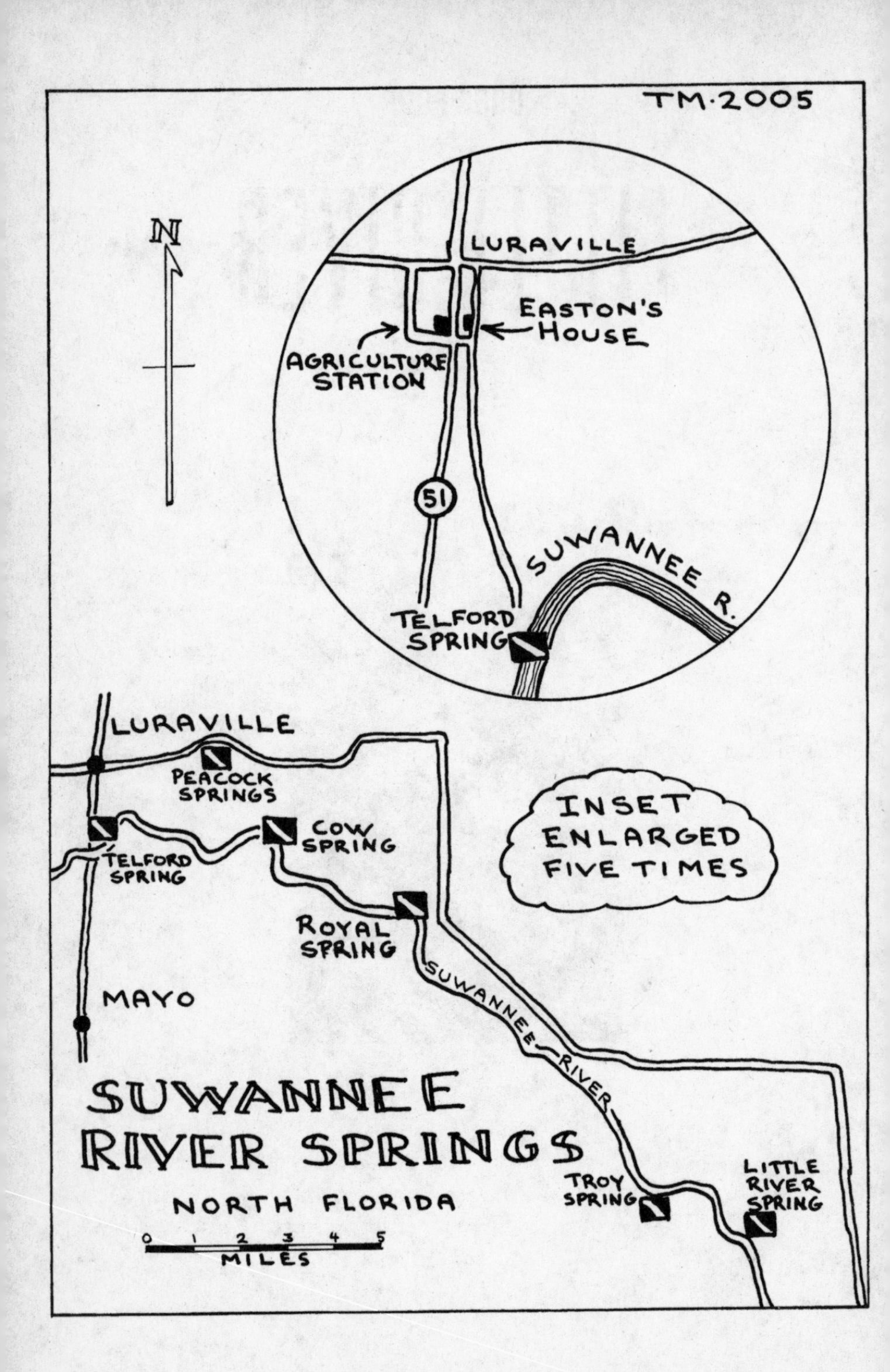
TM·2005
N
LURAVILLE
EASTON'S HOUSE
AGRICULTURE STATION
51
SUWANNEE R.
TELFORD SPRING
LURAVILLE
PEACOCK SPRINGS
COW SPRING
TELFORD SPRING
INSET ENLARGED FIVE TIMES
ROYAL SPRING
SUWANNEE RIVER
MAYO
SUWANNEE RIVER SPRINGS
NORTH FLORIDA
0 1 2 3 4 5
MILES
TROY SPRING
LITTLE RIVER SPRING

CHAPTER FORTY-NINE

SEPTEMBER 10, 2001
LURAVILLE, FLORIDA

Water. Waterfall. Rain. Shower.

The shower. The water was running in the shower in the master bath.

Beck Easton blinked awake and stretched out his right arm, feeling the warmth on Angela's side of the bed. He tapped the sheet with his fingertips; waking up without an alarm clock was supposed to be *his* trick.

It was still dark outside. What time was it, anyhow? Easton checked his watch and laughed aloud. On the back of his left wrist, where he'd worn a heavy Citizen Aqualand dive watch for nearly a decade ... Mickey Mouse beamed down at him.

It was Angela's doing, of course. She'd chaperoned the church's youth group down to Orlando on a day trip on Saturday, and had brought the watch back for him, given it to him at brunch after church the day before.

"Do you like it?" she'd asked. "See? It's a dive watch too. The outside ring ..."

"The bezel ..."

"Okay. It moves, just like on your other one. And look here; it's waterproof to two hundred meters. Do you like it?"

Easton had taken off his old watch and held it next to the new one. Even at discounted PX prices, the black-faced Aqualand, with its built-in depth gauge, had set him back better than $250 when he'd bought it in the Philippines almost a decade earlier. The white-faced Mickey Mouse watch looked as if it'd cost $49.99 at a resort gift shop. And while there were a lot of things Easton liked about Florida, the Walt Disney Company and its midstate enclave of canned and programmed happiness was not one of them.

Easton had hefted the new watch.

"It's perfect," he'd told her, and he'd strapped it on his wrist.

Another sound was coming from the shower now: Angela was humming and singing softly, the way she often did when she was working, making her sketches, or pulling up a floor plan on her computer.

Easton sat up and listened to his wife, imagined her leaning back under the broad fan of water from the showerhead, smoothing her wet hair away from her face with her hands. He thought about that, and then he took that thought a step further, and then he shook his head and got out of bed, heading for the kitchen.

Angela had a big day ahead of her. An important day. She didn't need any distractions. The best thing he could do right now was make her some coffee.

"Yes, I will. Absolutely. Thank you. Thank you very much."

One towel wrapped around her, another twisted on her head, Angela was just hanging up the phone when Easton came back into the bedroom, a mug of coffee in either hand.

"My hero," she said as she accepted a mug.

She looked happy. But Easton obviously did not, because the next thing she said was, "It's just one day, Beck. Out this morning and back tomorrow night."

"I know. I'm good." But he wasn't, and that surprised him. The wedding had been in June, close enough that they still celebrated monthly anniversaries, and the two of them had been out for dinner, observing the three-month milestone, just the week before.

Ninety-some days. It wasn't long. Back before he'd gone covert, Easton had gone on a few missions that had lasted longer than ninety days. But in all of the three-months-and-change of their marriage, Easton and his wife had never passed an evening apart, and tonight was going to change that.

"I hate it too," Angela said. She reached up, touched his cheek. "But Linda and I did the build-out on this guy's space in the Hancock Building, and we're the ones he wants to do his first New York office. It's a really big deal for him, and Linda's making it worth my while."

"Hey, I understand." He touched the back of her hand, stroked it.

She looked up at him, her green eyes searching his.

"Just one day," she said again. "And then I'm coming back here, and I'm staying here. Staying here with my ... family."

"Family?"

"Family." She took his hand and slid it under the towel, against the smooth, warm flatness of her abdomen. "That was Dr. Nichols' office I was talking to on the phone. There are three of us here in this room, Mr. Easton."

The air around them seemed to warp just a little and then straighten back out again. For a long moment, Easton just looked at his wife. Then his arms were around her, holding her.

"I took the EPT last Thursday," she was saying, her voice muffled against his T-shirt. "But I didn't want to tell you until I was absolutely positive, so I went to the doctor Friday. They couldn't get me in until just before they closed, and he couldn't review the results until this morning."

She looked up, her chin against his chest. "Are you all right with this?"

"Are you kidding? I'm *great* with this. You?"

She nodded, her chin rubbing him.

He reached for the phone.

"Who are you calling?"

"Lamar, I guess. I need someone to cover for me tonight."

"Cover for you?"

"Absolutely. I can't let you travel by yourself in this condition."

She laughed and pushed the phone back into its charger. "I'm like two and a half months pregnant, Beck. This early, I can not only ride in an airplane just fine by myself, I could … I don't know. I could skydive if I wanted to."

He held her at arms' length. "You know how to skydive?"

She giggled like a schoolgirl and reburied herself in his arms.

"Were you able to get a reservation at the Crowne Plaza?"

Angela allowed herself a smile. She glanced Beck's way and rubbed his shoulder. His profile as he drove, at ease but not slouching, a relaxed grip on the old Land Rover's wheel—if there'd been light enough to see him this way the night he'd picked her up to go to the New Year's Eve party, she wouldn't have waited until midnight. She would have fallen in love with him on the spot.

"Yes," she told him. "Of course, it's in midtown, foot of East Forty-Second Street, and there's a Hilton right across the street from the client, but what's a trip to New York without a taxi ride, right?"

Easton glanced her way. Eyes fully open, lips slightly downturned, he looked genuinely crestfallen. "The security really is good there," he said. "It has to be. They get a lot of diplomatic traffic from the United Nations. It's right across First Avenue."

"I know." She squeezed his shoulder. "And you're still going to be looking after me and protecting me, even though I'm going to be a thousand miles away. Which is probably …" She blinked and took a deep, slow breath. "Which is probably why I love you so much."

Easton winked at her. "And just think of how much we save on roses and chocolates."

They got to Jacksonville International in ninety minutes flat, exactly what Beck had said it would take, and Angela didn't even bother trying to tell him that he could just drop her at the curb. He would have seen it as an unconscionable breach of responsibility under any circumstances. Now that he knew she was pregnant, there was no way she was lifting anything heavier than her PowerBook, not until she had walked onto the jetway and he couldn't follow her any longer. And even then, Beck had thought ahead. On the way up to I-10, he'd stopped at the bank in Live Oak and picked up fifty dollars in ones – more than enough to assure prompt and courteous assistance from every red cap, taxi driver, doorman, and bell captain that she was likely to meet on her brief, twenty-four-hour trip.

Beck was silent as they walked through the terminal. They'd stopped at the United ticket counter to check her overnight bag and portfolio, and Beck had stood back as she had shown her license and ticket to the counter attendant, stepping forward only to put her bags on the pass-through scale. He said nothing as they passed through security, although he glanced quizzically when the sky marshal asked Angela to turn on her PowerBook.

This silence, Angela knew, was not moodiness. Beck simply wasn't the chatty type. He usually didn't speak unless he really had something to say.

He did speak up, though, once they'd gotten to the gate.

"You'll call me tonight?"

"You bet. I might get a bite first, but as soon as I've settled in, I'll call and give you the room number and everything – just in case you need to reach me. And I'll turn my cell on as soon as we land in New York."

"And your return flight lands at six-thirty-two?"

"That's right. There's an earlier flight, but I was afraid it might cut things too close. Mostly I'm double-checking to make sure that the floor plans are accurate, but I need to meet with the building engineering staff, as well – verify that the wiring and cabling can be done to my specs; otherwise I might have to change some of the lighting selections and workstation locations.

I've got an appointment with them, but they warned me that it could move twenty or thirty minutes if anything urgent came up. Still, I'm betting I'm done by eleven o'clock, latest. And if I am, I'll just treat myself to a leisurely lunch."

"Sounds nice."

She looked up at him. He was standing close enough that she could smell a hint of soap and aftershave.

"Not half as nice as it would be if I had you with me."

"I've got my American Express card. Won't take five minutes to buy a ticket."

"It won't and you won't. But I will … miss you."

She put her arms around him and pulled herself close, and he responded by holding her in those big, strong, lumberjack arms of his. When she looked up, he kissed her, and it was so nice that she kissed him back. Then she squeezed him tightly and looked up, into his eyes.

"Promise me that you'll read the book I brought you from Pastor Jack?"

Beck's arms slackened slightly. The book was one the pastor had recommended because it had adventures and even cave-diving in it. Angela had been impressed that Pastor Jack had made the connection, because the pastor had met and spoken with Beck only a few times, Beck always being ready to use a cave-diving commitment as an excuse for missing church.

The book was from a Christian publisher. It had scriptural commentary that was supposed to resonate with the adventure stories, or something. And Beck had yet to so much as crack the pastor's gift.

It was the greatest irony imaginable. Angela loved Beck unconditionally, and she was absolutely certain that he loved her. The phrase "the real thing" had never made sense, real gut sense, to her until she had fallen in love with Beck Easton. She had no problem at all picturing herself in doddering old age, sitting next to him on the porch in the light of some far-off sunset, every bit as in love with him as she was when she'd told him he was going to be a father. And yet Beck, whom she was certain would lay down his life for her, seemed incapable of giving her the one thing she considered most important. He refused to recognize life's single most important truth.

Part of it was the relentless logic that seemed to be so intrinsically a part of who and what Beck was. That had become especially evident one morning when, over breakfast, she had tried taking the direct approach with him.

"So you think I'm 'lost,'" he'd said, fork poised over his scrambled eggs.

"Yes." That was what she'd said, not trusting herself to interrupt this seemingly promising turn in Beck's spiritual life.

"And because I'm 'lost,' I need to be 'saved'?"

"Yes!"

Easton had lifted a forkful of eggs, chewed it thoughtfully, swallowed, taken a sip of coffee, and then asked, "So how is that not 'found'?"

"Pardon?"

"The opposite of 'lost.' It's 'found,' isn't it? Not 'saved.' I mean, when I think 'lost," I think ... I don't know ... shipwreck or desert islands. The kind of thing where they spot you from the helicopter and pick you up ... or not. 'Saved' sounds like being snatched from the jaws of a shark, or something."

"It's that too."

Easton had nodded, not looking at her, as he'd cleared his dishes from the table, rinsed them in the sink, and set them in the dishwater. Then he'd finally turned and said, "I don't know, Angie. After two thousand years, you'd think these guys would at least have had enough time to get the language right. It makes me wonder what else they got wrong."

On other occasions, when Beck was not so obviously yanking her chain, he'd been considerably more tender, but no less obstinate. The church Angela had chosen in Live Oak, Charis Christian Centre, flew in the face of many of the standards she'd grown up around; denim and khakis abounded in its congregation, neckties were notable by their absence, and the music was more Michael W. Smith than Fanny Crosby. Yet Pastor Jack's theology was every bit as biblically grounded as what she'd heard from her father's pulpit, and in a way the church's numerous and vigorous outreach programs put the mission weeks of her parents' church to shame. So she had joined, hoping Beck would be more amenable to attending, and he had actually accompanied her on a few Sundays. Then, one day, as they'd pulled into Polly's Inn for the Sunday brunch, he'd paused for a moment before killing the engine and said, "You know, I think Jack hit it right on the head this morning."

"You do?" Angela had been unable to contain her surprise. Pastor Jack's message had been on the natures of the seven churches in Revelation. She knew mature Christians, some with theology degrees, who were unable to make heads or tails of the Book of Revelation. "Tell me."

Beck had opened his Bible then, the black, Morrocan-leather-bound study Bible that Angela had given him the year before, back when she had been all but ready to write him off as a hopeless cause. He'd leafed to the end of the New Testament, found Revelation, and scoured the margins until he'd found a lightly penciled "X."

"'I would thou wert cold or hot'" Easton read. "'So then because thou art lukewarm, and neither cold nor hot, I will spew thee out of my mouth.'"

"Uh-huh?" Angela hadn't sounded as enthused then, and she knew that she had shown it. Revelation 3:16 was not her favorite verse in the Bible. She'd seen versions in which the last phrase was translated, 'vomit from my mouth,' which actually made it more troubling.

Beck had closed the Bible and looked at her, his lips set, his eyes steady, but sad.

"Don't you see, Angela? That's me. That's me all over. I'm really trying to give this stuff—" he'd tapped the cover of the Bible—"my best shot. But there's a part of me that strongly suspects it's all just cobbled-together mumbo jumbo."

Angela, feeling that some retort was necessary at that point, had been surprised to find herself silent.

"This is not to belittle or detract from your faith, Angela," Easton had said. "Christianity is the real deal with you; I can see that, and I admire it. But try as I may, I can't emulate it. I really can't. I can't get 'hot' on something I secretly doubt to be true. And if God exists, and Jesus is God, and if this book is his word—three big 'ifs,' as far as I am concerned—then I have it here on divine authority that lukewarm won't cut it, so I have to be cold. And that makes sense. I mean, would you want me to profess to believe something solely on the basis that I love you and think it would please you? What would that be?"

Angela had found her voice then.

"A start," she'd told him, the words coming out almost before she had thought them. "I think that, maybe, it would be a good start."

That was why it pleased Angela so much when, there in the airport, after she'd asked about the book, Beck replied, "Absolutely, I promise. I may not have it finished by the time you get back, but I'll do some reading while you're gone."

Angela stepped back, both of his hands in hers, and smiled as the people in the seats around them began to stand and move. The door to the jetway had opened and a gate attendant had taken his position at the small podium, microphone in hand.

"Looks like we're getting ready to go," Angela said. "And I'll be boarding first."

She hugged him again, and Beck said, "You be safe and hurry back to me, okay?"

Angela blinked back tears.

"I will," she promised. "And when I get home, I'll never go away again. Not without you."

The gate attendant began the boarding call, so Angela pulled Beck close. "I love you, Robert Exeter Easton," she whispered in his ear. Then she gave him one last kiss, picked up her laptop case and hurried for the gate.

CHAPTER FIFTY

LITTLE RIVER SPRING
BRANFORD, FLORIDA

It took many days of intensive training to ready me to dive in a water-filled cave. To ready me for God's forgiveness – for heaven – took only moments. All I had to do was realize that I was a sinner, repent (set my mind in opposition to a sin-filled life and in favor of a Christ-led life), and understand and believe that Jesus Christ paid for my sins when He went to the cross and offered Himself as a sacrifice in my own place. Then, understanding this, I simply had to accept, of my own free will, the gift of eternal life that Jesus Christ had so graciously given to me.

Beck Easton stretched, yawned, and adjusted the Xenon headlamp so the blue-white light fell more evenly on the pages of Pastor Jack's book. He glanced up, through the windshield of the Land Rover, at the darkening gravel turnoff. There was no car turning in; the leaves of the distant trees remained unsilvered by approaching headlights.

One of the beauties of cave diving was that it could be done at any time of the day or night, caves being by their very nature pitch-black twenty-four hours a day. While most cave dives and cave-diving instruction happened during the day, the better divers often preferred to go in at night, when even the most popular cave systems had little or no traffic, and the waters remained clear of silt-raising beginners. So Easton had not been surprised when a pair of New Jersey wreck divers, two guys who had him booked for a trimix class later in the week, had called to see if they could hire him for an orientation dive in the Little River system at nine o'clock. His gear was already in the back of the

Land Rover, fully set up, the twin tanks filled with a nitrox mix that would be more than adequate for Little River, where the evening's dive would be no deeper than 105 feet. And remembering his promise to Angela, he'd brought the book along and improvised the headlamp – which he kept in the SUV for setting up gear after nightfall – as a reading lamp, the Land Rover's interior light being useful for finding dropped keys and little else.

Easton flipped forward a page or two to see how far he had to go to finish the current chapter. The book was composed of short true-adventure stories, followed by italicized commentary that related the accounts to spiritual and moral lessons. And while Easton enjoyed the stories – the one he'd just finished was, in fact, an account of a dive in the very system he'd be diving later that evening – he was finding the commentary a bit obtuse and, in his way of thinking, more than a bit naive.

He reread one line: *All I had to do was realize that I was a sinner ...*

Easton mulled this over. He wondered about the guy who had written the book. What was the worst thing that this writer had ever done? Had he ever shot a man in cold blood on Christmas Eve in front of his children? Was that the sort of thing a person could be forgiven for, free and clear, like the right hand of God reaching down from the clouds with a brushful of heavenly Wite-Out?

Easton seriously doubted it.

Angela had told him, more than once, that "the words of the Lord are spiritually discerned." Easton translated that as, "Once you're in, you'll understand what got you in." It sounded like Catch-22. And for a reason Easton could not quite discern, it made him angry.

Stars were beginning to shimmer in the darkening sky when light rimmed the trees and brush at the entrance to the gravel turnoff. The details on the greenery grew stronger, and twin headlights appeared. The boys from Jersey were pulling in.

Easton flicked off the headlamp, stuck a line-arrow between the pages as a bookmark, and set the book on the passenger's seat. It was time to go to work, and two chapters was a good start. Angela would be pleased when he told her.

"Keep the change, and I'll keep your daughter in my prayers, okay?"

Angela stepped away from the Town Car and smiled as it drove away. It hadn't surprised her that the driver had been willing to unburden himself to a total stranger. It was the sort of thing that happened to her all the time: a concerned father with a daughter about her age – this one's eldest was struggling with an abusive, alcoholic husband – and before you knew it, Angela was a receptive ear for his concerns. Angela thought of it as the Holy Spirit working in her life, and Beck said it was because she had a kind face. She supposed they were both right.

She straightened up and looked down Forty-Second Street. The Art-Deco stiletto of the Chrysler Building reached, floodlit and silver, into an evening sky cottoned with gray light. It was like looking at decades of culture and design, all at the same time, and she stood and took it in, aware that she was gawking like a tourist, chin lifted in rubelike awe, and caring not one iota. It was not that she was a stranger to skyscrapers – Wheaton was, after all, just a stone's throw from Chicago – but skyscrapers in Manhattan were not just buildings. They were art, and art was meant to be appreciated.

Angela took a deep, slow breath, held it for just a moment, and let it out in one satisfied rush. She turned and walked up three low steps, through a revolving door, and into the gleaming mahoganied lobby of the Crowne Plaza.

Her friend, Linda, had made her appreciation more than obvious. She'd sent the chauffeured Town Car to meet her and, when Angela and the bellman got to the desk, she was told that she was all checked in, the room pre-billed to her client's account. She accepted the key card, took the five steps to the elevator, and rode with the bellman up to the third floor.

The room was snug by most standards, but spacious for midtown Manhattan. The bronzed glow of sodium street-lighting fell softly through two sheer-curtained windows and retreated as she turned on the room lights. The bellman put her bag on a folding stand next to the desk, and she smiled, tipped him, and had her suit in the closet and her makeup bag in the white-tiled bathroom by the time he'd closed the door.

Angela set her laptop on the desk and noted with satisfaction that the hotel had broadband Internet and an Ethernet connection. Glancing at the number on an information placard, she pulled her cell phone out of her purse and speed-dialed home. The line burred four times and her own voice answered on the digital message machine. Slipping off her shoes, Angela waited for the tone.

"Hi, handsome." She glanced at the clock on the nightstand. "It's just a few minutes before nine, and I'll bet you're out underwater somewhere. You be safe, okay? I just wanted to let you know that I'm here and all checked in. The number's 212-986-8800, and I'm in room 318. Linda and I met at the Tavern on the Green for an early dinner and then I came back here for a minute, and we're going to have a quick meeting with the client in a little while, and ... and I miss you. I'm going to try to get back to the room early, so call me if you need to, okay? You can call the room, or I'll leave the cell on while it charges. And tomorrow I'll be at ..."

She flipped open her planner.

"... I'll be at Two World Trade Center, Suite 92-200. I don't have a phone number, but that makes sense—they'll have the suite torn out, getting ready to build it back in, so they probably don't have phones yet. Just call me on the cell if you need me, and I'll be home—*we'll* be home—just as soon as we can. God bless you, sweetheart. I love you."

Angela glanced at her watch; time to head out. She put on her coat, slipped the key-card into her purse, and had just reached the door when she remembered her promise to the cabby.

Closing her eyes, she took a deep breath and lifted the stranger's daughter in prayer.

CHAPTER FIFTY-ONE

SEPTEMBER 11, 2001
NEW YORK CITY

Angela stood, just inches from the floor-to-ceiling window, and gazed in awe at the view. The tops of lesser buildings seemed curb-height from this perspective, and Lady Liberty, the folds of her green-patinated robe in shadowed relief from the early light, stood majestically over a broad expanse of blue-green water, the Verrazano Narrows Bridge visible beyond her in the spectacular clarity of this bright September morning. And this was only the ninety-second floor; she could only imagine what the view looked like from the rooftop, a full eighteen floors above.

As a rule, Angela wasn't crazy about heights, but the view from this window didn't bother her. The stainless-steel window surrounds were just a shoulder's width apart, and she remembered something Linda had mentioned at dinner the previous evening: that Minoru Yamasaki, the architect who'd designed the World Trade Center buildings, was an acrophobic and had deliberately placed the window frames close together to give building occupants a feeling of security.

Angela turned around. The office space was open and empty: floor cleared down to bare concrete; ceiling open to bare air ducts and electrical conduit, the lumpy foam fireproofing showing on the trusses supporting the floor above. The only light came from the windows and from a couple of halogen work lights on yellow steel adjustable stands, throwing stark shadows across the ceiling and making the rest of the suite look even darker in comparison. But in her mind's eye, Angela could see a meandering line of wooden workspace dividers, illuminated by soft indirect lighting. The thing about the Trade Center highrises was that the support came from a central core and the latticed stainless-steel skin. The office space was amazingly free of support columns, and she wanted to create a workspace solution that afforded the brokers some quiet and privacy yet preserved the open airiness inherent in the building's design.

The only furnishings on the entire floor were a long folding table and a couple of cheap plastic wire-legged chairs. Angela went to the table, checked a floor-plan blueprint, and opened her PowerBook to make a couple of notes. She glanced at a catalog and looked up.

"Excuse me. Can you tell me the width on these windows?"

The maintenance person, a shy, curly-headed man with *Pablo* embroidered on his Port Authority uniform shirt, took a pamphlet from his uniform shirt and opened it.

"The windows? They are ... um, twenty-two inches, ma'am. That's the actual glass width, not center-to-center on the frame."

"Great! Many thanks." Angela made another note and checked the digital clock in the corner of her computer screen. It was quarter of nine, and at the rate she was going, she'd be wrapped up here by ten o'clock, easily.

Angela was just about to ask about the maximum allowable relief on the sprinkler heads when the halogen work lights dimmed, buzzed, and came back on. She heard a muffled rumble, like a train running at top speed through a distant tunnel. She looked up.

"Is that normal?"

"No, ma'am." Pablo's brow furrowed. "That sounded like it came from outside. Not on the street, but outside."

They both walked to the windows. Typing paper was wafting by in a swirling, confettilike cloud. It fell out of sight, and then a wisp of something black curled by. Angela's heart dropped. She put a hand to her stomach.

"Oh, no ... Is that smoke?"

The maintenance man pulled a black walkie-talkie from the holster on his right hip.

"Control? Can you tell us what just happened?" The radio emitted a puff of static. "Control? Do you read?"

Nothing.

"Uh, ma'am, we'd better leave. Just to be safe. You know?"

"Oh." Angela didn't know. Where had all that typing paper come from? Had something exploded on a floor below them? A water heater, perhaps? But weren't all the water heaters in the center core of the building, well back from the windows? She didn't know, and she shivered involuntarily. "Okay. Let me just get this packed up."

She closed the top on her PowerBook and began gathering up all her papers.

"Um, ma'am?"

Angela looked up.

"You'd better leave that stuff, ma'am." The young maintenance man worked his lip and glanced toward the door of the suite. "If there's a fire, they'll shut the elevators down and we're like—I dunno—a hundred and sixty flights of stairs and three escalators up from the street. We don't want to be carrying anything if we've got to walk all that way. You know?"

"Oh. Yeah. You're right." Angela tapped the top of the computer, looked at the portfolio, and then scooped her purse off the table and passed its strap over her shoulder. "Where are the stairs?"

"There's three sets. Closest one is ... right over here." Another rumble announced itself from outside. "We better get going, huh?"

With one last glance back at her belongings, Angela nodded and followed the man through a steel fire door and into a stark, plasterboard-walled staircase, the door snicking shut metallically behind her.

Beck Easton awoke to the steady *breep-breep-breep* of the clock radio. Its wire-red numerals read "8:50," a silent digital accusation that he was waking better than three hours later than his regular rising time, ninety minutes after he would normally have finished his regular morning workout, and at precisely the time that he would usually be settling, coffee mug in hand, to check his email and update his planner.

Still, he didn't feel that badly about sleeping in. The two divers from New Jersey had been every bit the animals that he'd come to expect New Jersey wreck divers to be, and he had gotten home in the wee hours, having taken them all the way to the Florida Room in Little River, and then followed that up with a shallow dive on the upstream side of Cow Spring for good measure. Either one of those dives would have been a good day, in and of itself, and he'd earned his rest.

He'd humped his hundred-and-twelve pounds of dive gear, plus three steel deco bottles for the group, down the rickety wooden stairs to the Little River basin and then back up again. Then there was the loading and unloading at Cow as well, and while the flow at Cow Spring had been its usual placid creep, Little River had been running at full fire-hose magnitude, a current that had been sufficient to get his pulse up, and then some. So it wasn't as if he had actually missed his workout and, as for his day, he'd kept it open, cave diving having a way of consuming twice the time it was supposed to. Angela's flight was getting in at 6:20 that evening, and Easton had every intention of getting there early. He wanted to be there at the gate when they opened the door to the jetway.

He swung his legs out of bed, sat up, stretched, and glanced at the window. White light painted the slats of the miniblinds, the Sunshine State living up to its name. Easton glanced at the bed linens. He'd fallen into bed only minutes after getting home, so the civil thing would be to wash the sheets before Angela got home. He padded into the bathroom and opened the taps on the shower, turning on the exhaust fan to vent the inevitable steam.

Ten minutes later, freshly shaven and dressed in khaki shorts and a Naval Academy T-shirt, his cell phone snapped into its holster on his hip, Easton started the laundry and then emptied the dishwasher. He spooned Maxwell House French Roast into the filter-lined basket of the Mr. Coffee while he watched a hummingbird flirt with the feeder that Angela had hung outside the window over the sink. Then he picked up a remote, tuned the kitchen TV to CNN with the sound off and noticed that a red "1" was blinking on the answering machine.

Easton pressed "play" and smiled despite himself as he heard his wife's voice, sounding remarkably clear and close on the digital recording. He got to the part where she was telling him that she would be at "Two World Trade Center" when he looked up at the under-cabinet TV and made sense of the picture on the small color screen.

It was the World Trade Center.

Where his wife was.

And smoke was boiling from a gaping hole in its side.

Easton grabbed the kitchen phone out of its wall mount and stabbed at a speed-dial button.

Angela regretted that she hadn't worn lower heels and was glad that she was still so early in her pregnancy. She wasn't all that winded—they'd covered twenty-eight flights of stairs, but all of it had been downhill—but the backs of her calves were already tight, a sure sign that they'd be aching in the morning.

The stairway ended, and Pablo led her out into a bright, airy, high-ceilinged area. She recognized it as the seventy-eighth-floor Sky Lobby.

Angela had learned in her architecture classes at design school that the limiting factor to a skyscraper's height was not its structural mass or its weight, but the necessities needed to support the people in the building.

Chief among these were elevators. In a 110-story building, elevators would occupy better than half the floor space in a conventional plan. So the two towers of the World Trade Center had each been built with three lobbies – one on the ground floor, and one each on the forty-fourth and seventy-eighth floors. Only a couple of express elevators ran all the way from the ground to the uppermost stops – the observation deck here in 2WTC, and the Windows on the World restaurant in its more northerly twin. Most floors were served by "local" elevators that ran from the ground and Sky Lobbies, like local trains running from suburban stations.

Angela smiled and thanked Pablo as he went looking for a phone with which to call his supervisor. People were walking out of other stairwell doors, looking confused but not running or shoving. Most seemed to be thinking the same thing as Angela: *Oh, man! I don't really have to walk all the way down to the ground, do I?*

A young man in a Port Authority security uniform was hanging up a phone as Angela approached the information desk.

"Can you tell me ..."

"From what we can tell, an airplane ran into the other tower, ma'am." He said it without looking up, checking the screens of a dozen TV monitors in front of him.

"An airplane?" Angela dimly recalled that an Army Air Corps bomber had once run into the Empire State Building, back sometime around World War II. But that had been in dense fog and cloud, and the weather was beautiful this morning, not a cloud in the sky. Besides, didn't they have air traffic controllers to prevent that sort of thing these days?

"What kind of ..."

"Don't know, ma'am. All they told me was 'an airplane.'"

"Does anybody need help?"

The guard looked up for the first time.

"The fire department is over there already. I'm not sure what the situation is, but it happened early. Most people don't get into their offices until nine." He gave her a kindly smile. "New York firefighters are absolutely the best in the world, ma'am. My brother's one of them. They'll take care of things. But we might need folks to help guide people down over here if we have to do a full evacuation."

More people were pouring into the lobby.

"So you don't know if we need to evacuate yet ..."

As if in answer, strobe lights began to pulse from the entryways and the corners of the lobby. There was a *whoop-whoop* siren, almost like the red-alert Klaxon in a science-fiction movie, and the two or three hundred people in the Sky Lobby fell silent. Moments later, a man's voice came on the intercom speakers in the ceiling:

"Building Two is secure. Building Two is secure. There is no need to evacuate Building Two. If you are in the midst of evacuation, you may return to your office by using the reentry doors on the reentry floors and the elevators to return to your office. Repeat, Building Two is secure ..."

Conversations resumed, a hundred or more voices that were lighter, but not fully relieved. Angela could tell where their minds were; everyone was thinking about the other building, the one just a few hundred feet away across the plaza. She smiled her thanks at the security guard and joined the throng of people walking toward the elevators, whispering as she walked, praying for the people next door, and for the firefighters who were rushing to their assistance.

The elevator doors opened and the crowd before Angela barely thinned as the doors closed again. She glanced at her watch; only eight minutes had passed since she'd left the empty suite, but already it felt like an eternity. Her calves ached and she felt guilty as she thought about that—had that airplane been just five or six hundred feet off to one side, she could very easily have had a lot more to be concerned with right now.

She was glad that she was pretty much finished with her work upstairs; the streets were going to get congested soon with emergency crews and TV news crews. They didn't need her in their way, and she'd be glad to get away from the building. But first she had to go up and collect her things.

The phone warbled shrilly, three ascending hollow tones. "We're sorry. All circuits are busy. Please try your call again later." The tones sounded again and the recording repeated itself.

Beck Easton resisted the temptation to hurl the phone against the wall. On his hip, his cell phone vibrated. He popped it out of the plastic holster and glanced at the screen; it was a 301 area code—a Maryland call. And the prefix was 688—an NSA number.

"Unbelievable," he muttered at the burring silver phone. He let it buzz and pressed the speed-dial on the kitchen phone again. It was the same busy-circuit recording, and his cell phone stopped vibrating, and then started all over again. He set the cell phone on the counter and speed-dialed Angela's phone a third time.

Angela hadn't realized just how tightly New Yorkers would be willing to pack themselves onto an elevator. She had people pressed against her on all sides; a violation of her personal space that barely left her room to breathe.

The elevator doors opened for the ninety-second floor, not a second too soon. Angela should have felt relieved, but she did not. The crowd of office workers had not spoken a word on the fourteen-floor ride up, yet it was as if there was this angry chorus of voices all around her, voices that she could not actually hear, but that she sensed, an atmosphere of almost palpable oppression. And while she told herself that it was this tragic accident, the fact that this plane had run into the building right next door, a catastrophe that still didn't seem possible, it was something … something beyond that. But what could be beyond that? She didn't know, and she didn't want to know. She just wanted to gather up her things and go home: home to Florida and home to Beck.

Excusing herself, she wriggled through the mass of bodies. It was only as she got to the doors, pass the press of gray flannel and tightly packed people, that she could hear it—the distinctive double-ring of her cell phone, in the pocket of her purse. She dug it out as she stepped into the hallway, the elevator doors rumbling shut behind her.

"Hello?"

"Angela?" Easton could barely get his wife's name out, his throat was so tight.

"Beck!" The connection was clear enough that Easton could hear the strain in her voice. "Oh, Beck … it's awful. This plane hit—"

"I know. I'm looking at it on TV. Are you okay?"

"Oh, yes. Sure. I'm fine. I'm in the other tower, not the one that was hit. They gave an all-clear, and I'm just going back up to the suite to get my stuff, and then I'm going to go downstairs and see if I can find a cab before the fire department closes the streets. But I don't know, I …"

Easton heard a burring sound and looked down. His cell phone was moving, insect-like, toward the edge of the countertop, and he scooped it up, squinting at the matchbook-size screen. It was an agency number again.

"Hang on, honey. Let me get rid of this call, okay?"

He flipped open his cell phone and pressed the "Talk" button. "Easton."

"Beck, listen we've got a – "

It was Bill Spalding.

"Bill, I'll call you right back. I've got Angela on the other line."

"No, don't." Spalding's voice had hardened: the voice of a former Marine officer, the tone of command. "The World Trade Center has been hit – "

"I know, Bill. Angela's *in* the World Trade Center. Now, let me – "

"Wait." Spalding's voice was up half an octave or so. "She's in the tower that was hit?"

"No, no – she's fine. She's in the other one. She's just – "

"Stop. Listen to me." The tone of command was back in Spalding's voice. "The plane strike wasn't an accident. The flight was hijacked. And we've got transponder SigIt that puts three other compromised aircraft in the air right now. Beck, get her out of there. Everything in New York's a target. Get her out of there. Now."

Beck snatched the other phone to his ear. "Angela, listen – "

"Honey, I'm going to have to call you back. The suite door is locked, and I – "

"Angela, listen. Leave the stuff. The plane strike isn't an accident. It's a terror attack – there are other planes in the air."

Angela said nothing. Easton could hear her breathing on the other end of the phone.

"Look around," he told her. "Do you see an exit sign?"

"I'm just a few feet from the elevators."

"Too risky if the power fails. Look for a sign."

"I've got one."

"Good." Easton had never gotten fear-sweats on a mission, but he was sweating now. "Follow it."

"Okay." She paused for a moment. "There are other people in this building. I need to tell them."

Easton gritted his teeth. "If you see anybody as you're leaving, tell them to get out, but don't stop to argue. You've got to leave. Now. Don't run, but keep moving."

"Okay. I'm on the stairs. All the way down to the street?"

Easton thought about this. *Everything in New York's a target*; that's what Spalding had said. Easton screwed his eyes shut, trying to remember his last trip to New York.

"Okay. There's a subway station in the concourse below the Trade Center, right?"

"Yes." He could hear her feet on the stairs now. "I saw the signs when I came in. Go there?"

"Go there. Get below ground. Catch a train if you can. Go to Brooklyn, the Bronx, Queens—anyplace. Anyplace that's not Manhattan. Okay? Are you all right?"

"I'm all right." Angela saw no one else in the stairwell, and she trotted down the stairs steadily, her right hand on the handrail, her left hand clutching the phone.

She took the phone from her ear long enough to glance at her watch. A little over fifteen minutes had passed since the first plane had struck, and she had ninety-two floors to travel to reach the ground. She figured she was covering a floor every fifteen seconds, which was four floors a minute, which meant … wow. Could it really take twenty-three minutes to get down to ground level?

And that was with no one else holding her up. Lower down, there could certainly be more people on the stairway, congestion that would slow things to a crawl. She switched the phone to her other hand and moved to the inside of the stairwell, where she could make the turns on the landings faster. With all that was going on, the last thing she was worried about now was meeting someone on their way up.

"I'm still with you." Beck's voice was clear, assuring on the digital phone.

"Passing the ... eighty-eighth floor," she told him, looking up at the numbers stenciled in white on the fire door.

She was just rounding the landing when a wall of wind lifted her off her feet and threw her back into the handrail. A hollow crack, like thunder, filled the empty stairwell and the whole building swayed to one side, a sickening movement that seemed to last forever. Then the walls collapsed in upon her and she was falling, struck from all sides.

Something sharp hit the back of her head and Angela winced as the world around her dissolved.

CHAPTER FIFTY-TWO

Go. Go. Go. Go. Go. Beck Easton urged Angela along, trying to project his thoughts, his energy to her over the miles, not wanting to say anything on the phone, not wanting to panic her or risk urging her so much that she could stumble and injure herself, stranding her in the tall building.

She had just told him that she was passing the eighty-eighth floor when he heard it over the phone—a loud *whumph*, like a heavy carpet being dropped onto a hardwood floor.

He looked up at the television as a huge orange fireball erupted from the side of the second tower, fragments of the building spilling in seeming slow motion toward the street far below.

"Angie!" He pulled the phone away, made sure the little green display still showed him as connected, and put the phone back to his ear. "Angela?"

An incomprehensible burst of chatter chirped from the cell phone in his right hand. Easton lifted it to his other ear.

"Bill," he said. He willed his voice to be steady. "Angela's not answering. She just told me she was passing floor eight-eight. Repeat: floor eight-eight."

"Stand by," Spalding said, all business.

A low rumble continued to emanate from the landline, the one that Easton hoped was still connected to Angela's cell phone. On the cell phone he could hear Spalding in a muted and indecipherable conversation with someone off-line.

"Angela?" Easton asked. "Bill?"

"Stand by," Spalding said again. Another voice spoke in the background, muffled and incomprehensible. Then Spalding came back on the line. "The strike was between the seventy-eighth and eightieth floors, a good seventy, eighty feet below her, Beck. And that's a good, strong building. It'll contain the fire. We're already calling the cavalry from our end, buddy. We'll send in the pros. You keep trying to raise her."

Easton set the cell phone down and went back to the other line.

"Angela," he said. "Angie, it's Beck. Talk to me, honey. I'm right here. Talk to me ..."

Angela? Come on, honey. Sweetheart, please. Please.

Beck. Beck's voice. Distant. Tinny. Phone. Cell phone. Coughing, Angela tried to open her eyes and winced. There was dust everywhere: in her eyes, in her nose, her mouth. She tried to wipe her eyes, but her arms were weighted down by something that felt like cardboard. Thick, heavy cardboard.

She squinted again, let her tears wet her eyes, then squeezed them shut, trying to wash the dust away. She risked a peek and saw that she was in near-darkness, nothing but vague shapes and shadows. When she moved her head the flat pieces of–plasterboard: it had to be plasterboard–shifted and the back of her head throbbed. She could feel a warm wetness in her hair, just behind the crown of her head, and the base of her skull felt as if a vise were being tightened around it.

Angela. You can do it. I know you can. Talk to me.

Angela moved her shoulders this way and that, loosening the plasterboard pressing down on her. She freed one hand, then the other, and wiped at her eyes, found more plasterboard tented over her head, and shoved it away.

The blackness around her brightened to a deep gray, the dust above her in thick suspension, like a fog.

Angela.

Her watch had a face that lit up at the touch of a button, and she touched it now, turning her wrist and using the watch to throw a thin blue light on the wreckage around her. Through the dust, she saw a glint of metal: her cell phone, Beck's voice calling her insistently from the tiny speaker. She reached for it and as she did, she glimpsed the face of her watch: "9:37."

No way. She'd started for the street at nine, a couple of minutes after. Had she really been unconscious for better than half an hour?

Holding the phone to her ear, she tried to talk, but nothing came out. She closed her mouth and swallowed, wincing at the grit in her throat, but forcing some saliva into her mouth and lips. She tried again.

"I ... I'm ... here, Beck."

"Angela!" Beck Easton felt as if an elephant had just stepped off his chest. "Are you all right?"

"The thing that happened ..." Her voice was unsteady, wavering in and out. "Another plane?"

"Yes." He paused. "Are you all right?"

"I hit ... my head." Her voice grew stronger. "The stairwell is full of ... plasterboard. It came right off the walls. I can just see the top of a door. No. It's not the door. It's the frame to the door. It's sprung. Popped back, out of the wall."

"I've got a guy on the other line," Easton told her. "On my cell. He says there are firefighters in the building. They're reporting that two of the stairwells are blocked with debris. You're in one of those. But there's a third stairwell. It's completely clear, top to bottom. If you can make that, you can get down. Can you get to that door?"

"Think so."

Easton heard her groan softly. There was a crumbling sound, as if something was rubbing against Angela's phone.

"Head hurts ... Wow. I must have a lot of this, this stuff on my legs. They've fallen asleep."

Easton felt the hair rising on the back of his neck.

"I'm going to try to sit up, see what's going on." Easton heard another rustling on the phone. "Honey, I need both hands. I'm going to set the phone down for a sec. Okay?"

"Go ahead," Easton told her, thin lipped. "I'll be right here."

He heard a muffled scraping and a distant grunt, followed by a groan. For thirty long seconds, he heard nothing at all.

Then he heard something so faint that he was not sure he was hearing it at all. It was … laughter? No. Gasping. Sobbing. His wife was weeping. Very, very slowly, he shook his head. He knew what was coming next.

"Angela …"

"Oh, Jesus …" Still distant, but Easton could tell from her tone that it wasn't a curse. It was a prayer.

"Angela."

There was a scraping sound, and then his wife was back on the phone, her voice clear.

"There's nothing on top of them," she told him.

"Your legs?"

"Yes. Beck, there's nothing on top of my legs. There was stuff over my head when I woke up, and my arms were covered, but my legs were free. Even so, I can't feel them, Beck. I can't feel them, and I can't move them. I … can't move."

"Bill?" Easton lifted the other phone. "I've got Angela on the stairwell at the eighty-eighth floor …"

"I fell," Angela interrupted. "I'm not sure … I might be one floor down …"

"Might be the eighty-seventh floor," Easton told Spalding. "She's down and incapacitated. We need assets to extract."

"Copy that," Spalding said. "Stairwell landing, floor eight-seven or eight-eight. Done. We'll relay that to the people on-site."

"'… We need assets to extract …'" Angela said, lowering her voice to imitate his. "I just love it when you get all Marine on me."

Easton was not relieved by the cheery sound of her voice. He'd been in combat enough to recognize the early signs of shock.

"You've got people coming to help you," Easton told her. "You're going to be fine. Just stay with me here."

"I wish I was. You said firemen?"

"Yes, that's right. They're on the way."

The other end of the phone fell silent for a minute.

"Beck … this building." Angela's voice slowed. "It's burning?"

From the corner of his eye, Easton could still see the TV screen, smoke boiling out of both of the twin towers.

"Something is," he admitted. "But that's a steel building. And the fire's contained. You've got a lot of fireproof floors between the fire and you."

"I don't know how contained it is, Beck. I smell something like … kerosene. Like at the airport – jet fuel. That and a smell like trash burning – paper and plastic."

"They've got crews working on it." Easton glanced up at the television and looked at the gaping impact zones, at the dense, brown-black smoke. He wondered how they could ever get firefighting equipment, a ladder, up that high.

They can't.

"Do me a favor?" Angela asked.

"Anything. You name it."

"Do you have your Bible handy?"

"I can get it." Cordless phone to his ear, Easton walked into the bedroom and got the black leather-bound book out of the drawer of the nightstand.

"I've got it," he said, walking quickly back to the kitchen, where he'd left his cell phone. "What would you like me to read?"

"Um … the Twenty-Third Psalm."

"Okay." Phone still to his ear, Easton began leafing through the unfamiliar book: *Genesis*, *Exodus*, *Leviticus*. He tried the back: maps, some kind of glossary, *Revelation*. No. He went farther in: *Matthew*, *Mark*, *Luke*.

"Honey," Angela's voice said gently from the phone. "Just close your Bible and open it up right in the middle."

Easton juggled the phone and did that. "Oh. Okay. Top of the page says, 'Proverbs 6:22.' "

"Back up a little. About fifty pages."

"Okay ... Here we are. 'Psalms.' Which one?"

"Twenty-three."

"All right ..." He leafed back a few pages. "Ready?"

"Ready."

Easton took a deep breath.

" 'The Lord is my shepherd,' " he read. " 'I shall not want ...' "

Angela closed her eyes and listened to the old, familiar Scripture: listened to her husband's steady, tender, warm voice. She imagined the two of them sitting out on the patio some warm, Florida evening, years in the future. She imagined him reading this, not because she had asked him to but because he wanted to. She imagined him filled with the same Spirit that filled her.

Somewhere, far, far beneath her, the building groaned, a metallic *uangh*, like the death agonies of a sinking ship.

"... and I will dwell in the house of the Lord for ever," she said aloud with Beck, finishing the wonderful old psalm.

Easton fell silent. He had suddenly recalled something that he had not thought about for years: his mother, reciting that same psalm from memory when he was small, six or seven. He remembered she said that she had memorized it for ... some special occasion. A class. A confirmation class; that was it.

Easton tried to picture why his mother had shared the psalm. Were there other people there? Had she recited it for him, or had he merely overheard her?

He couldn't recall. But he did remember her saying it. He remembered the part about the confirmation class.

His mother had been raised, then, in church. Yet his family had rarely attended. He wondered what had happened.

"Beck?"

"Here, sweetheart," he said. "The firemen – are they there?"

"Not yet. But you got quiet on me there for a moment."

Easton looked up at the television set. Smoke continued to pour from both towers as helicopters orbited at a respectful distance.

The world has gone crazy.

"Sorry," he told her. "I just spaced out for a second."

He heard her sigh.

"You okay?"

"I'm ... yeah, I'm fine. I'm just sorry. Sorry I had to come here. If I'd just stayed home with you, none of this would have – "

"Angela, stop that." Easton's voice came out firmer than he'd intended. "You didn't do anything. You were ... we were attacked. It was the people who hijacked that airplane that did this. Not you."

She sighed again.

"You're right," she told him. Then: "Beck. Sweetheart, I want to see you again."

"They're coming for you. You will."

That sound. The same sound. Almost like laughter, but deeper. Sobs: she was weeping again.

"Angela." Easton kept his voice low. "Don't you dare give up on me. You hear?"

"Beck." He heard her take a deep breath. "Beck, I have never, ever, given up on you. Not once. I never will. But if I don't get out of here – "

"You will."

"Maybe I will. And then maybe I'll get hit by a car on the street below. Or my plane won't make it back to Florida. Or I will come home, but you'll be diving, and somebody will get in trouble and you'll go being a hero – "

"Not me."

"Right. As if. But Beck, if I leave this life, I know where I'm going. I know *exactly* where I'm going. And I don't know the same about you."

Easton didn't say anything.

"Beck, heaven is more than a nice story. It's more than a comforting wish. It's real. As real as right now. More real than right now. And if something happens that I ... that I don't get home to you, then I know where I'm going to be. Jesus is absolutely real, Beck, and I am going to be with him, and I don't know that you will, and that's the worst thing – the very worst thing. Worse than where I am right now."

Easton took a breath. He stared at the TV, at the newsperson mouthing noiselessly, at the burning buildings in the inset shot, at the "Breaking News" banner on the bottom of the picture.

He wanted to say something, but he had no words.

Holy Spirit, speak through me.

Angela squeezed her eyes shut. Another groan rose from the depths of the building.

"Beck ..." Angela took a breath. Her cell phone interrupted her with three loud beeps, and she opened her eyes, glancing at the tiny green-gray display. "Beck, I don't have a lot of time; the battery's going in my phone. Sweetheart, I need to know ... have you thought about this?"

"I ..." She could almost hear him thinking, trying to find an appropriate answer. "Last night, I read some of that book ... the one your pastor sent."

Something told Angela to say nothing.

"... And I have no problem thinking of myself as a sinner," Beck told her.

"Me either."

"Well, me especially, okay? But that's really the first problem I have; I mean, there's sin, and then there's ... *sin*."

Like what? Angela thought it, but she didn't ask it. Her phone beeped again.

"Beck—Jack the Ripper, Son of Sam, Adolf Hitler: any of them. If they accepted Christ—accepted the fact that his death on the cross paid for their sins, and decided that he was the purpose of their lives—then they are with him right now. Now I'm 99.9 percent certain that you have not done anything worse than any of those people, and even if you have, the same principle applies. It's not our criteria. It's God's criteria. Jesus died to pay for the sins of *all* those who accept him, not just some."

Angela's phone beeped a third time, and Beck was still silent.

"Beck—my phone's getting ready to go. If there's something more, something else that's stopping you, I need you to tell me."

More silence.

"Beck, please."

"It's just ..." More silence.

"Yes?"

"It's just that I'm not sure."

Angela squeezed her eyes shut again. *Please give me the words. Please...*

"About God, you mean," she finally said. "You're not sure about God. Whether he actually exists."

"That's it. Angie, I've got to tell you; I want him to exist. I want there to be ... something. Something after all this. I can't tell you how much I want that, how much I want to have your ... your certainty. But I won't lie to you, Angela. I never have and I won't start now. And I can't say I believe something that I still have my doubts about."

Angela's phone beeped again. *I don't have much time. Please, please, please, please tell me what to say.*

Then she knew.

"Beck, listen. In the Bible there's a story of a man who comes to Jesus asking for help for his son. And before Jesus does this, He asks, 'Do you believe I can do this?' And the man replies, 'Lord, I believe; help me in my unbelief.' He wants to believe, but he needs help to do it. So try that, Beck. Ask Jesus to help you. To help you in your unbelief."

Easton hesitated. His professors at the Academy would have called this a fallacy of logic. How can you ask something you're not sure you believe in to help you to believe in it?

But what had he said earlier when Angela had asked if he'd do something for her?

Anything. You name it.

So he had to do this.

"Jesus," he whispered aloud. "I'm not a religious man. I'm not nearly the same caliber as ... as Angela, here. I want to believe that you are real, and that you are God, and that you paid for ... for what I have done. I want to believe in you so I can trust you, and trust that what you did has made up for everything I've done, and I want to turn my life around and live it for you. But I need your help to do that, and I'm asking for it. I'm asking for it – right now."

The room seemed to grow incrementally brighter, the air incrementally sweeter. He closed his eyes and it was as if someone was washing a dirty window before him, a window with the accumulation of a lifetime of grime, and the more it was washed, the clearer the image became, and on the other side of the window was truth.

"Thank you ...," Easton muttered.

"What?" Angela asked. "What did you say?"

"I said ...," Easton gasped, "thank you."

On the other end of the phone, his wife sobbed again, but in between her sobs, he could hear her repeating what he had just said, "Thank you … thank you … thank you."

Easton shook his head as if he had just taken a punch. Things were just so … clear.

"Beck!" Angela's voice on the phone, excited.

"What is it?"

"Firemen! Beck, I can see them through the crack around the door!" She raised her voice. "Here! Can you hear me? I'm in here! Yes, right here!"

Easton squeezed his eyes shut in gratitude. He could hear sounds of digging, men's voices, a snatch of conversation, and then the phone fell silent. There were sounds there one moment, and then nothing.

The battery. The battery on Angela's cell phone has finally gone dead.

But when he opened his eyes, he saw that it was not the battery.

On the television screen in front of him, Tower Two of the World Trade Center was falling, collapsing into itself. It was there one moment, and gone the next. After that, all that was left was a pillar of smoke and ash, smoke that mingled and swirled, like the lingering ghosts of the building and the people within it, of his wife and their unborn child.

EPILOGUE

DECEMBER 16, 2001
LURAVILLE, FLORIDA

Beck Easton pulled the old Land Rover into the driveway, cocked his head and squinted at the car parked in the turnaround, off to the side of the drive. It was a gray Lincoln Continental, relatively new and squeaky clean; not exactly a cave diver's ride.

The car had Florida plates, Broward County stickers – practically a sure sign of a rental. Nothing too unusual about that; many of Easton's customers arrived in rentals. But customers generally showed up at the beginning of the weekend, not on Sunday morning. And he didn't have anyone booked for the rest of the day.

He pulled further into the drive, looking the Continental over as he switched off his ignition. There was an Avis bar code on the Lincoln's rear-door glass, driver's side – definitely a rental.

Easton left the Land Rover in gear so it wouldn't roll. He went around to the back, opened the hatch, and swung a twinned pair of steel 104s out of the load area and onto the concrete drive. Lifting the eighty-one pounds of scuba tanks by the manifold, like a ponderous, overlong briefcase, he carried them down the walk between the two-car garage and the house, toward the back of the garage, where he kept his shop – not really a retail establishment, but a staging area for his gear – and the gas-blending station where he filled his tanks.

He had just cleared the corner of the house when he saw Bill Spalding standing on the patio, dressed in khakis, penny loafers, a golf shirt, and a linen sport jacket. He was wearing sunglasses, the aviator style, and a saddle-leather portfolio was resting on the patio table next to him.

"Bill ..." Easton nodded. "You know, a jacket like that might fly in West Palm, but you wear it around here, you might just as well take a Magic Marker and write 'Yankee' on your forehead."

Spalding took off his glasses and looked genuinely disappointed. In the NSA, a contingent of the federal government as yet unreached by the custom of 'casual Fridays,' his manner of dress was probably only barely more civil than pajamas. But he didn't comment on that. What he said was, "I was wondering whether you were traveling."

"Phone still works."

"I thought of that. But I figured if I called first, you would *definitely* be traveling. Just back from a dive?"

Easton shook his head.

"Church." He saw Spalding glancing at his jeans and faded polo shirt, and added, "Our pastor is pretty much a come-as-you-are kind of guy. And I had some people in who wanted to make a dive and still get twelve hours of surface time in before they flew home tonight. So we went into Peacock about three in the morning, and I went straight to church from there. You need to get in the house? Use the head or anything?"

"Thanks. Not right now. I'm good."

"Let me get my gear hung up, then. If I leave it in the truck, it'll turn into a biology experiment."

Spalding nodded and Easton made four more trips to the driveway, carrying back stage bottles, a mesh bag full of regulators, reels, and back-up lights, a Dive-Rite Trans-Pac II soft harness and a battery-pack-powered halogen light, and a DUI dry suit with its polypropylene undergarment. He set his tanks next to the blending equipment, hung the suit in a shaded gear locker, put the light on its charger, and stowed the rest of the gear on peg racks, checking each item for wear as he did so. Only after this ritual was complete did he turn to his guest, nod toward the house, and ask, "Want some coffee?"

"Please."

Easton let the two of them in through a sliding patio door and unloaded his pockets on the kitchen counter: keys, wallet, pocket Bible, some folded bills and change, and a small matte-black semiautomatic pistol in a black leather Hedley pocket holster.

Spalding bent forward for a closer look. "What's with the poodle-shooter?"

"Kel-Tec," Easton said. "Company down in Cocoa makes 'em."

"Thirty-two?"

"Three-eighty." Easton opened a narrow door under the counter and punched four buttons on a small safe. A compartment swung out and he put the gun in and closed it. "Regular joe okay with you? I don't have decaf."

"Regular's fine." Spalding said nothing as Easton rinsed a coffee pot, filled it with cold water, and poured it into the coffee maker. Spalding cleared his throat. "So why're you packing, Beck?"

Easton spooned coffee into the filter compartment, looked up, and grinned. "What? You don't trust me with guns now?" He switched the coffeemaker on.

Spalding grimaced. "I didn't say that. I just ... I didn't know you ever carried off-mission. You never did in Los Gatos."

Easton got a couple of mugs out of the cupboard. "You get stopped carrying in California, and you're going for a ride with the Chippies. You get stopped carrying in Florida, you show the cop a permit, and it's, 'Have a nice day.'"

He opened the refrigerator, took out a quart of half-and-half, and set it, a canister of sugar, and a spoon next to the mugs. Then he raised his head just a bit, looking directly at Spalding. He wasn't grinning anymore.

"And it's not like it was in Los Gatos, Bill. You know what I mean? World's a more dangerous place."

Spalding pursed his lips and nodded, and the two men stood there, saying nothing, while the coffeemaker gurgled and gasped. Finally there was enough in the pot for Easton to fill the two mugs. When he nodded toward the table out on the patio, Spalding picked up his cup and said, "By all means. It was forty-five degrees and drizzling when I left Fort Meade."

Easton led them outside.

"Place looks nice," Spalding said, sitting down.

"It's coming along. I'm putting in a bunkhouse." Easton motioned with his mug toward an area behind the dive shop, where a concrete pill had been poured. "If you can give people a place to crash after they dive, it makes the guiding service more attractive. I was going to add a wing to the house, but Angela vetoed that. We started planning it back when ... When she was still ..."

He fell silent and sat there, looking at the concrete, white in the Florida sun.

"Good idea." Spalding finally said. "I mean, I've never been cave diving myself, but ... Seems like a good idea."

"So ..." Easton tented his fingers and leaned back in his chair. "What's up, Bill?"

"I dunno." Spalding lifted both hands, dropped them. "I haven't seen you since the memorial service."

Easton waited, saying nothing.

"We've got fresh intelligence on the nine-eleven attacks," Spalding said. "We know a little more about who was behind it."

"CNN seems pretty sure it was Al-Qaeda."

"But do you know who quarterbacked it?"

"Osama bin Laden."

Spalding shook his head.

"It's his checkbook," he agreed. "But we've got three other Saudis who weighed in heavily on logistics. And ... well, Beck ... you know one of them."

One by one, Beck Easton could feel the hairs rising at the nape of his neck, on the back of his head, all the way up to the crown of his scalp.

"I knew it," he finally said. "I *knew* it."

Spalding took a deep breath. "I have no idea how he survived that crash, Beck. There wasn't a piece of that plane bigger than a suitcase – I saw the Navy salvage tapes. But we have three separate acoustic recordings – a cell-phone call placed from Canada, another from Germany, and a satellite phone call that originated in Afghanistan just last week. The voiceprints match the ones from the SigIt over here last spring. There's no doubt at all, Beck. It's him. It's Ahmed bin Saleen."

Easton closed his eyes, opened them, and exhaled slowly.

"Why are you telling me this, Bill? I'm not inside any more."

"You still hold your commission ..."

"Inactive."

"But not resigned."

Easton let another breath out in a huff. "Don't go there. I'm not objective. I'm ... it's personal."

Spalding folded his hands. "We've thought about that, Beck. Nine-eleven was personal. I mean, I didn't have anywhere near the kind of loss you had, but still – no way could I be objective on this thing. There isn't a limb in the world I wouldn't go out on to nail this guy. Same story all over the division. All over the agency. But what I was thinking was ..."

Gazing off at the far edge of his property, Easton became aware that Spalding had stopped talking. The trees at the end of the long yard blurred, and he blinked. Blinked again.

Spalding put his hand on Easton's arm. "No, Beck. I know what you're thinking. We've considered it too, and the odds are infinitesimally small. Besides, the other tower was hit first."

"They were both hit."

Spalding shook his head, eyes closed. "Uh-uh. No. He didn't know she was in there. It was ... It was just the way it worked out."

Easton leaned back. "Then why are you here, Bill? I've got dead skills. I haven't been on a rifle range in better than a year, not even to spot."

"We don't want bin Saleen dead, Beck. We want him taken. This guy knows names, places, all the assets. The information he carries in his head can take the whole thing apart. And you know how he thinks. You found him last time, and this time ..." He pulled a red-bordered manila file folder out of his portfolio. "... We have much more current intelligence."

"I thought I'd stopped him last time. Thousands of people died."

"Millions, if not for you."

Easton sat, silent, while a mockingbird called from a tree at the far end of the property.

Spalding glanced at his watch.

"All right," he finally said. "It's not like I can't see your side of this. I can certainly understand your, uh ... wanting some ... distance here. And I'm sorry I stirred this up. But I had to try. I hope you understand that. You got us close."

Easton turned away just a little, a clenched hand to his mouth. He shook his head, a small movement.

"Beck – I'm sorry, man." Spalding stood, slid the file back into his portfolio, and cleared his throat. "I'd better get back up north. Task force meeting in the morning ... Um – you take it easy, Beck. And you need something, you call. You hear me?"

He held out his hand, and Easton shook it without standing, without looking up.

"I mean it, Beck. You need something, you pick up a phone."

Easton nodded. "I'll do that. And Bill?"

"Yeah, buddy?"

Easton looked up, his eyes clear.

"You'd better leave the file."

AFTERWORD

AUTHOR'S NOTE AND ACKNOWLEDGMENTS

As any fan of Steven Spielberg's movies knows, *nurflügel* or flying-wing aircraft actually were in development by Nazi Germany near the end of World War II, and some examples of these aircraft were built, tested, and flown. Likewise, transshipment of materiel, key personnel, blueprints, and the like by submarine from Europe to Japan actually was attempted by the Axis near the end of the war.

But the Ho-18 *Amerikabomber*, while under development by Horten in the last year of the war, was never actually built, and the transport submarines used to attempt to smuggle technology were invariably destroyed in transit or captured.

It is true, however, that the Allies captured and brought to fruition a wide variety of captured German technology after the end of the war; the American space program was begun with such technology, and so were the early Northrop flying-wing bombers – distant predecessors of today's Northrop Grumman B-2 "Spirit" Stealth Bomber.

The use of airburst ordnance to disperse warfare agents was also a reality by the end of World War II, although the developing country – Japan – created such weapons with biological, rather than nuclear, warfare in mind.

So the opening premise of this novel, while fiction, is not that great a departure from reality.

That said, a question I hear all the time from readers and other writers is, "Where do you *get* this stuff?" And here, for the record, is where I obtained my material for this novel …

Selection of materials for the *Amerika*'s hypothetical bomb was made with the help of physicist and novelist Randy

Ingermanson. This selection was done primarily by email, with most messages containing red-flag keywords like "bomb," "plutonium," and "New York City," and I am trusting that the intelligence agencies have decided by this point that Randy is harmless and that they are no longer monitoring his communications.

Randy was also my source for information on the care and feeding of computer programmers and writing Beck's job description at Blue Corner. Sounds as if I owe Randy *two* Christmas cards this year ...

Captain Luther Alexander, chaplain with the United States Navy, helped me keep Beck's military promotions record just barely within the bounds of credibility. During his previous billet as head chaplain of the United States Naval Academy, Captain Alexander did me the honor of inviting me to speak, and while I was not there to do research, I was impressed nonetheless with the character, intelligence, and integrity of everyone I met at Annapolis—I hope Beck reflects at least some fraction of my admiration for those who serve the cause of freedom.

On the history, culture, and day-to-day life of the Island of Bermuda, I had assistance from a number of sources. They include:

- Ty Sawyer and his staff at *Sport Diver* Magazine for their pre-trip suggestions and insights ...
- Terri Gallagher, Mary Ramsay, and the rest of the media-relations professionals at Lou Hammond & Associates for helping me to hit the ground well-informed ...
- Joy Sticca and the Bermuda Ministry of Tourism for opening so many Island doors ...
- Elbow Beach Club Resort, and Grotto Bay Resort, for hosting me during my travels ...
- The Bermuda Underwater Exploration Institute, Blue Water Divers, and Triangle Divers, for introducing me to the watery parts of their world ...

- Detective Inspector Oliver Bean (Ret.) of the Bermuda Police Service for his insights into law enforcement and daily life on the Island …
- Graham Maddocks and Ken Vickers for teaching me the finer points of wreck-hunting in Bermudian waters, acquainting me with Bermuda's World War II history, and teaching me authentic Bermudian phrases, my favorite being "Where are your gates?" ("Where do you live?") …
- James Tyson, managing director of Atlantic Mine Holdings, Ltd., for giving me a businessperson's perspective of the Island, and for reading this novel in manuscript, with an eye toward accuracy on both the Bermudian and the securities fronts …
- And of course I would like to thank in general the wonderful people of Bermuda, who were uniformly kind, cordial, and generous far beyond expectation and truly made me feel at home during my visit.

A number of my fellow cave divers have contributed over the years to my knowledge of cave exploration in general and Florida springs in particular. Jim Bowden, Dustin Clesi, Bill Rennaker, and Karl Shreeves (of the Professional Association of Diving Instructors) are four names that immediately come to mind, and I would be particularly remiss if I did not also thank Lamar Hires, president of Dive Rite.

I visited Ground Zero shortly after the World Trade Center attacks and spoke with many of the volunteers involved in recovery and cleanup. For particulars on the attacks as experienced by those within the buildings, I depended on a variety of media accounts, most notably the WGBH-Boston Nova television documentaries on the 9/11 attacks.

And now, two quick thank-yous before I take my leave:

The first is to all the people who were involved on the development of this book, yet selflessly allow the illusion that it was solely the result of my labors. They include: Karen Ball, Zondervan executive editor of fiction; Dave Lambert, my content editor; Bob Hudson, copyeditor; Cindy Davis and Curt Diepenhorst, who provided what must be – in my humble opinion–the coolest and most brand-sensitive art-direction in fiction today (don't these covers *rock*?); and to the sales, marketing, publicity, and author-relations people at Zondervan, who help keep any small light I provide from being hid under a bushel.

The second thank-you is to *you*. In the value chain of publishing, the most important person is not the publisher, nor the editor, nor the sales managers and marketing directors, and certainly not the author. It's the reader; without you, all the rest of us are doing is killing trees. I cherish your support, I read every one of your letters, and I especially covet your prayers, because if you find anything good in my books, it does not mean that I am a skilled writer – it just means that during that particular session at the keyboard I did a better than average job of staying out of the real Author's way. His glory is the light of my life.

A hundred thousand blessings on you and yours.

Tom Morrisey
www.tommorrisey.com

READ AN EXCERPT FROM

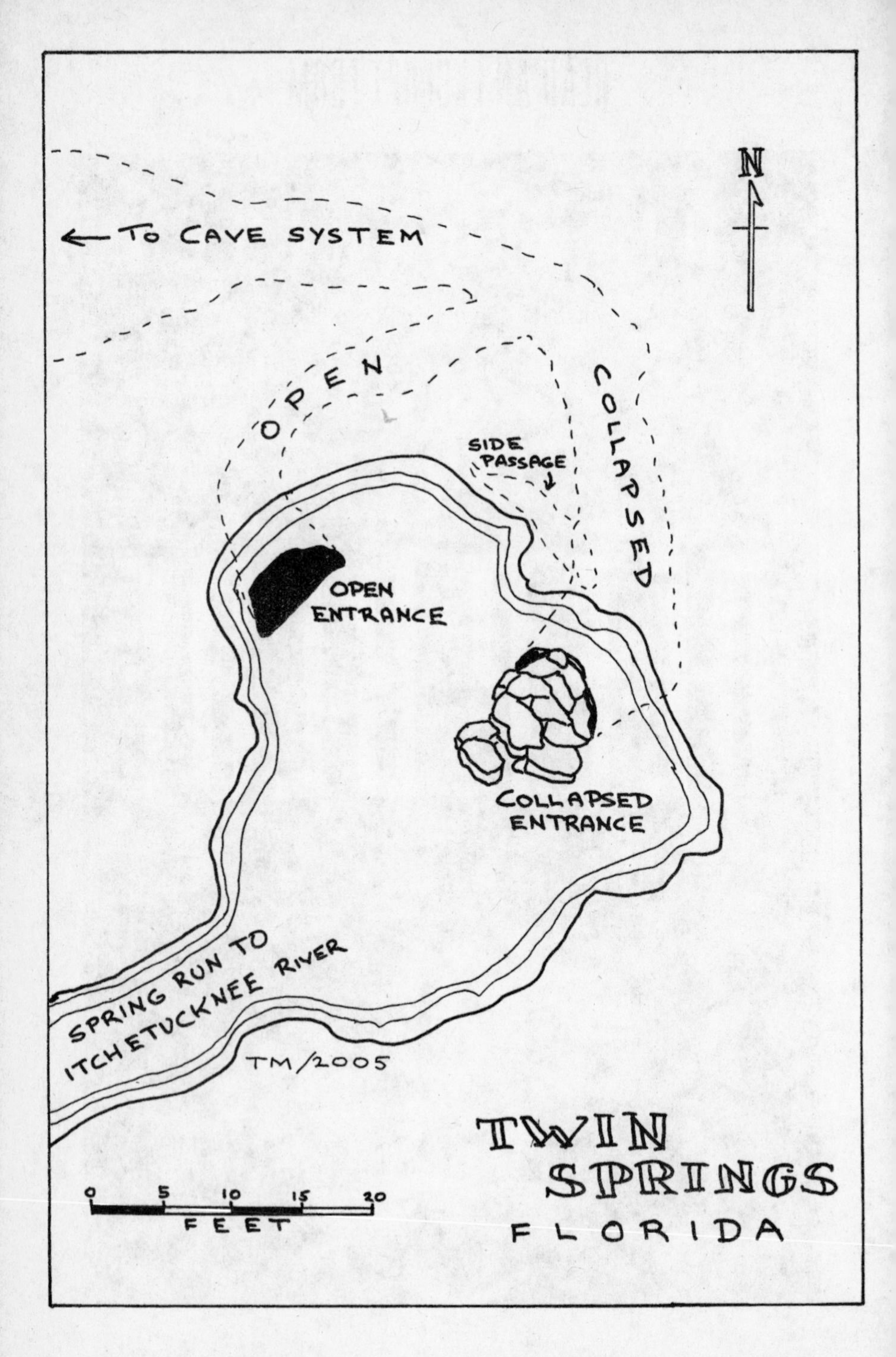
N
← TO CAVE SYSTEM
OPEN
COLLAPSED
SIDE PASSAGE
OPEN ENTRANCE
COLLAPSED ENTRANCE
SPRING RUN TO ITCHETUCKNEE RIVER
TM/2005
0 5 10 15 20
FEET
TWIN SPRINGS
FLORIDA

CHAPTER ONE

JULY 14, 2005
LURAVILLE, FLORIDA

The single-story house was plain and pale yellow, about as architecturally distant from a Miami-Beach art deco as one could imagine. The vegetation across the road was pulp pines, not palm trees, and there was no beach littered with bronzed bodies. In fact, there was no beach, and no body, at all.

Jennifer Cassidy had been to Florida before – she'd come here for spring break at the insistence of a persuasive college roommate. But this nondescript house, sitting alone on a minimally landscaped lot, didn't offer a hint of the glitz and glamour she'd come to associate with the Sunshine State. In fact, were it not for the Bermuda-grass lawn and the palmettos planted along the drive, it wouldn't have appeared Southern at all.

Jennifer slowly drove the fifty yards of concrete driveway and stopped the rental car in front of a detached garage. She moved the shifter to "park," turned the rearview mirror her way, and took a quick glance.

She looked . . . efficient.

Her blonde hair was cut short, short and tufting every which way in a responsible sort of punked-out style. She twisted the mirror down, and her eyes, clear and vibrant blue – the kind of blue that made people ask if she wore colored contacts – peered back at her. The rest of her face had that no-makeup look, like the face of somebody who'd gotten up while it was still dark out, made the thirty-five-minute drive to Detroit Metro Airport in something more like twenty, and had still only barely caught her flight.

All of which was absolutely true.

This was no time for the full treatment. She dug the essentials out of her purse and made two quick passes with her blush

and just the barest hint of mascara. But that still looked too unfinished, so she got out her lipstick, squinted at the mirror, and applied two smooth, stay-between-the-lines strokes. Then she finished the job with a soft-chomp on a napkin fished from her Burger King bag.

The face in the mirror still looked efficient, younger than her twenty-four years, and vaguely boyish, mostly because of the hair—what there was of it. She turned the mirror back to where it was supposed to be and put her makeup away. On the journey to "beautiful," "cute" was about as far as she'd ever gotten, and she'd learned to comfort herself with the sentiment that things could be worse. She turned the key, silencing the engine, and then rummaged in her bookbag for the webpage she'd printed out back in Ann Arbor; the address was the same as the number on the eave of the garage. This had to be the place.

Jennifer opened the car door and grimaced at the heat. *Okay, maybe I am in Florida, after all.* But it sure wasn't the Florida they put in the tourist brochures. The largest body of water she'd seen on the drive down from the airport was the Suwannee River. And the landscape had consisted mostly of stands of scrawny pine trees and open fields dotted with cattle—not the polled Herefords she'd grown up with on the farm in Ohio, but scrawny, humped and wattled creatures that looked as if they belonged in India.

The yard was quiet; no breeze. Just a few birds, probably asking one another for sunscreen. Slipping on her sunglasses, Jennifer took note of a sign that said "SHOP," and followed the paved walk around the side of the house.

Then she stopped in midstep and wished she'd spent more time with her makeup.

Because there was a man seated at a table on the brick patio, and he wasn't just any man.

This guy was a hunk: nice, strong profile, good jaw, and a head of brown hair that was just coming due for a cut and going light at the ends from the sun. He was wearing khaki shorts, aviator sunglasses, and a faded blue T-shirt that fit snugly enough to show that he was in shape and then some. His arms, tanned and garnished with blonding hair, looked almost too muscular for the tiny, bent-nose pliers in his hand. He looked older than Jennifer, but not much. She guessed that he was in his thirties, early to mid.

Probably early.

He was working on something with black rubber hoses and shiny metal fittings. It looked like a piece of scuba gear, one of those things divers used to get air from a tank. Jennifer searched for the word ... *regulator.* He was working on a scuba regulator.

"I'll be with you in a second," he said without looking up. "I'm at one of those points in this rebuild where you have to hold your tongue just right ..." He tinkered with the device for the better part of a minute, and then he set it aside and stood, wiping his hands on a shop towel. "Sorry about that. I'm Beck Easton. Call me Beck."

"Jennifer. Uh, Cassidy."

They shook hands and Easton stepped back, giving Jennifer a long, slow look from head to toe – long enough to take her from flattered to mildly irritated.

"Let's see," he said. "Five-two?"

"And a half."

"And what? A hundred and fifteen pounds?"

Jennifer lifted her chin. "A hundred and fourteen, actually."

Easton nodded and walked around to her side. "Good tone. Do you run? Work out?"

"I bike a lot, swim when I can." Jennifer considered a quick sprint back to the car.

"That's great. Strong leg muscles help. We can put a 104 on you for the intro section and go to steel 72s, maybe even 95s for the Full-Cave."

"Huh?"

"Not that you have to do it all in one shot," Easton told her, hand up. "Take your time. Work your skills between courses. Do you have your C-card and logbook with you?"

"My what?"

"Your certification card and logbook."

Jennifer removed her sunglasses and squinted. "My certification card certifying what?"

Easton cocked his head and looked at her. "Well, that you're a trained diver, of course."

"Oh. I'm not. You see . . . that's why I'm here."

He removed his own sunglasses. Green eyes – nice. "I'm sorry. You want open-water lessons, then? I can do that, but I've got to tell you, a group class down at Ginnie Springs will be a lot cheaper . . ."

"No." Jennifer waved her hands and cut him off. "No – I'm not here to learn to dive. I'm here to hire you to do some diving for me."

"Research diving?"

"Exactly." In fact, that was all she wanted him to put on the credit-card receipt. One word: "Research."

"Well, sure." Easton nodded. "I do some of that. Although I've got to tell you, for hydrology, things like that, there's better people. What sort of research do you have in mind?"

"I need you to find something."

Easton rubbed his nose, crossed his arms. "Find what?"

"I . . . I don't know."

Easton looked at her in silence. When he spoke again, his voice was low. "Can I ask how you found me?"

"Well, I did a Google search on 'cave diving' and 'Live Oak,' and found an equipment company called Dive-Rite. When I called there, I talked to a man named Lamar, and told him I needed a good diver who won't blab what I'm doing. He said I should come see you."

"O-kay . . ." Easton smiled, just a bit, and glanced at the patio table. "Here, let me get this stuff out of our way. Can I get you something to drink?"

"Sure." Jennifer grinned. *Man—is this guy good-looking.* "That'd be great. Would you have a beer?"

Easton shook his head. "Soaking suds and blowing bubbles doesn't mix," he told her, tapping on the regulator. "I've got Coke, Diet Pepsi, root beer, and I think maybe even some Dr Pepper—had some locals diving with me last week. Or I've got some iced tea that I just made up. But I've got to warn you—it's sweet."

She grinned even more. "Sweet tea's fine."

"Great. Grab a seat. Facilities are in the shop if you need 'em."

The tea was still a little warm, so Easton heaped two heavy glass tumblers full of ice, added a stout wedge of lemon to each one—he never had figured out what good it did to slide a wafer of lemon onto the rim of a glass—and poured the tea in, the ice crackling as he did it. A car door slammed out in the driveway as he did this, and when he slid open the door to return to the patio, he saw why: his visitor now had a large black-nylon catalog case next to her and was removing thick file folders from it.

"Looks like this is going to get involved." He set a glass on a paper napkin in front of her and took a seat on the opposite side of the table.

"Well, it's . . . complicated." The young woman took a sip of tea and smiled her approval. "Where do you want me to start?"

Easton glanced at the sky. "Plenty of daylight left. Start at the beginning."

"Okay." Jennifer wiped a bead of condensation off her glass and then looked up at Easton. "I'm a graduate student at the University of Michigan, the School of Information Science."

"Like IT – information technology?"

"That's part of it." She grimaced just a little as she said it. "But information science deals more with application than infrastructure. It's about sleuthing out facts, finding where the information is hiding."

"Like being a detective."

"More like a librarian." Jennifer laughed. "Sometimes both. Anyhow, I'm a second-year MS candidate, but this is my first year at U of M; I transferred in from Case Western. That put me low on the totem pole for any kind of assistantship work over the summer, but I was trying anyway – so I could keep my apartment and, you know – avoid going home and waiting tables in Wapakoneta."

Easton nodded and wondered if she was going to ramble. True, female customers at a cave-diving operation were few and far between, and this one was cute as the proverbial button, but he preferred to deal with people who could get to the point.

"Anyhow, it was starting to look as if that was just what I was going to be doing. But then my department head called me in, and there was this attorney in his office, looking for research help." She handed Easton a business card:

LOUIS F. SCARVANO

ATTORNEY AT LAW

SCARVANO, MARTOIA AND WOODWARD, LLC.

1 PEACHTREE CENTRE – STE. 3459, ATLANTA, GA 30309

"I know the address." Easton handed the card back. "High-rent. I'd expect that anyone who hangs a shingle there could afford to keep his own paralegals on staff."

"He can and he does. But he didn't need legal research. He needed a family history."

"He traveled to Michigan to have you do his family tree?"

Jennifer shook her head. "Not *his* family history . . ." She pulled a glossy photograph out of an envelope and handed it across to Easton. ". . . Hers."

Easton took a look and straightened up just a bit. The picture was obviously a copy of a much older image. Yet even rendered in shades of gray, and partly obscured by creases, the woman in the image was a stunning, raven-haired beauty with eyes that seemed to reach out and lock with his.

"Who am I looking at?"

"Cecilia Sinclair, although she was still Cecilia Donohue when that picture was taken. Daughter of Cameron Donohue, who owned a plantation near Branford. That's near here, right?"

"About half an hour away."

Jennifer returned the photo to its envelope. "That was shot the day they announced her engagement to Augustus Baxter— "

Easton shook his head. "You said her married name was 'Sinclair.'-"

"Henry John Sinclair was her second husband, originally from Baltimore, although he and Cecilia moved to Ann Arbor after the war. That's why Mr. Scarvano came to U of M for his research; Cecilia Sinclair's personal documents are kept in the archive library there, and you need a stack pass to access them."

Easton nodded. This was making sense. "And you, being a grad student, have a pass."

"Exactimundo. Cecilia's first husband was originally from Georgia."

"So that's the Scarvano connection—his client is from Georgia, one of Baxter's descendants?"

Jennifer's face went to something that was halfway between a grimace and a scowl. "I asked him, and he wouldn't say—attorney-client privilege."

Easton nodded for her to go on.

"Anyhow, Augustus Baxter's father was a plantation owner, like Cecilia's, and apparently that's how they met; their fathers knew one another; Baxter was invited to Cecilia's cotillion – her coming-out ball – chemistry happened and they got engaged. Baxter even took a job at a bank in Jacksonville, to be nearer to Cecilia. They were only engaged three months, which would have been scandalous back then, except for the fact that this was 1861. Florida had already seceded from the Union, and Baxter had accepted a commission as a captain with the First Florida Cavalry. There were a lot of hurry-up weddings down here that year."

"You seem to know a lot about the period."

Jennifer smiled. "I was a dual-major undergrad – English and history. And I've always been interested in the Civil War. Not so much the battles, but the culture. How it affected people."

She took a sip of her tea. "Cecilia was a diarist, and she wrote every day, even when paper got scarce during the war. I read her journal – pretty sad story. Her father was in the war as well, and he got injured, came home, lingered, and eventually died of his wounds. Then Augustus Baxter was killed outright in a skirmish in Virginia, and that left Cecilia alone to run a plantation that was drowning in debt and hadn't cleared a dime in more than four years."

"So she lost it to banks up North?"

Jennifer nodded. "You've got it. Northern banks bought up the loans from failing banks down here. Then the banks up north hired traveling agents who went around selling off estates, liquidating the assets. And that's what happened with Cecilia. They swooped down and sold her home right out from under her."

Easton took a sip of his own tea, lemony and sweet and satisfying. He couldn't believe he'd grown up drinking it plain. "So where does Sinclair come in?"

"I don't know." Jennifer frowned. "In the journals that I have, August of 1865 shows her destitute and scraping for a living. That's how that volume ends. Yet when the next one starts, it's later in the same year – 1865 – and she's up in Michigan, happily married, comfortable and living on an apple farm. That's one of the mysteries."

"One?" Easton shifted in his chair. "There's more?"

Jennifer nodded, eyebrows up.

"There's a big one." She opened a thick three-ring binder and leafed through photocopies of pages covered with a refined and feminine handwriting. She stopped, read a little, and tapped the page. "On the night before their wedding, Baxter is staying down here, at the Donohue plantation. He comes to Cecilia after dinner and tells her something. In fact, she says that by the time they get done, it's midnight. She doesn't record exactly what it is that Baxter tells her, only that it is a secret important both to them and to their country – which was the Confederacy at the time – and that he is entrusting it to her in case something happens to him after the war."

Easton looked at the binder. It had to be a good three inches thick. "And she doesn't say any more about it in all of that?"

"I think she was so concerned that she was afraid to even mention it in her own journals," Jennifer told him. "In fact, she doesn't bring it up again until it's pretty clear that the South's goose is cooked." She leafed to a section near the back of the binder. "When she gets the news of Lee's surrender at Appomattox, she wonders if 'our Secret may yet save us.' And a few months later, when the war officially ends, she wonders 'what may become of our great Secret, for which so many lives were given, and if it has not yet saved our nation, may it perhaps save us?' Meaning herself and a freed slave she calls 'Uncle Jonah,' who was the only other person left on the plantation at that point. And then she mentions it one more time."

"Which is?"

Jennifer leafed to the last few photocopied pages. "August 6, 1865 – Cecilia's just about at the end of her rope. The house has been all but emptied: furniture, paintings, even any clothes of value. And now she's two days away from having to leave the house itself. She's kept this secret, whatever it was, hidden throughout four years of war. Now she's about to be cast—well, she doesn't know where. And she doesn't see how she can keep the secret safe anymore, so she confides in the only friend she has left: the former slave, Jonah. And she adds in a postscript that Jonah has come up with a plan that gives her hope."

Easton tapped the table. "But she doesn't say what it is. Am I right?"

Jennifer glanced up from her binder. "You are. Cecilia's sick with worry. Too afraid to even confide in her diary, for fear that somebody might find it in the days to come. But the next day, she has no such worries. Jonah is dead, drowned in an underwater cave where he was hiding whatever it was. He was trying to breathe off these . . . like sacks of air that he took down with him. And something went wrong. He drowned. So now Cecilia's last friend is dead, the secret is gone, and she has no way of getting to it. She closes with, 'All is lost and I am alone.'-"

Easton leaned forward and looked at the binder. "And that's where it ends?"

"That's where this volume ends." Jennifer closed the binder. "As I said, when the next one starts, it's Christmas of that same year, and she's married and living on the farm in Michigan."

"Poor farmers or rich?"

Jennifer frowned at the material on the table. "I'd have to say very rich. When Cecilia died in 1931, she left a lot of money to charity—half a million each to the drama departments at U of M and Eastern Michigan University, more than a million, all total, to various missions organizations. She even left eight hundred thousand dollars in trust to help restore Ford's Theater. Pretty odd for a daughter of the Confederacy, but I guess she decided it was time to bury the hatchet. She didn't have any heirs—she and Sinclair had a son, but he died in a streetcar accident in Chicago in 1893. And Sinclair himself had died years earlier, in a shipwreck on the Great Lakes in . . ." Jennifer checked her notes. " . . . 1868."

"So Sinclair—did he come from money?"

"I don't know. His Bible—not a family Bible, but the one he carried—is with the papers that were left with the university, and it has lots of marginal notes in it. Looks like he memorized verses, kept notes on what he was working on. But the only personal information I can find in that is their wedding date: October 14, 1865. And the first public record I've found of him is in the social pages of the *Ann Arbor Beacon* in November, announcing that they've set up housekeeping and are receiving visitors."

She paused, her shoulders sagging a bit as she looked at Easton. "You think they came back and got it, don't you? Got the money, or jewels, or the deed or whatever it was, cashed it in and went up to start a farm in Michigan . . . a hundred and forty years ago."

"It's sounding like it." Easton reached over and tapped the binder. "Does it say in here what spring they used as their hiding place?"

Jennifer searched the binder and read for a moment. "Here it is. Cecilia only mentions the name one time: Twin Springs."

Easton sat back in his chair.

"What?"

"Well . . ." Easton put his hands atop his head, fingers knit. "It's sounding even more like it. There are springs down here that aren't often dived, but Twin's not one of them." He wondered why a researcher wouldn't have caught this, and then shook it away. The world of cave-diving was so closed that you'd almost have to be part of it to be privy to the information. "It's on private property, but even so, over the years there've probably been two, three hundred divers through that spring and the system behind it. If anything is down there to be found, I've got to think they would have found it by now."

Jennifer Cassidy looked as if someone had pulled the plug on her. She rubbed her forehead, reached for her tea, and looked absently at the empty glass.

"Here. Let me freshen that."

Easton picked up both glasses and headed back into the house. He glanced out the window at Jennifer, chin on her palm, the picture of defeat. All of his life, he'd thought of himself as a "ready, aim . . . fire" sort of person. But Jennifer Cassidy seemed like more of a "ready, fire . . . aim" – the sort he'd long since learned to avoid.

So why was it that he felt so badly for her and wanted to find some way to give her hope?

He wasn't sure. But as he was filling the second glass, he remembered something that might let him do just that.

When Easton reappeared from the house, a fresh glass of tea in each hand, he was smiling. Not just smiling – grinning.

Jennifer scowled just a bit. *The cave-diving business must do pretty well. Here this guy has just talked himself out of a job, and he looks happy as a clam.* Finally, her ire got the better of her. "So what's got you so cheerful?"

"Twin Springs," he said, still smiling as he handed Jennifer her glass. "It isn't 'twin springs.' Not really. There's only one aperture – one way into the cave system. There used to be another spring head; you can see where it was and still feel some flow coming out of it. But it's collapsed – the entrance and a fair amount of passage behind it."

"And that's good because – ?"

"Because the passage didn't collapse until sometime in the 1890s."

"Are you sure?" Jennifer straightened up a bit.

"Positive." Beck sat down, ignoring the drink in front of him. "As I said, Twin Springs is on private property. And most times, you take what a landowner tells you with a grain of salt. I mean, people tell you they have a 'spring' on their land, and, half the time, you go out to see it and it's not a spring at all. It's usually a sinkhole, no water coming out. But the guy that owns Twin Springs? The land's been in his family for more than a century; they probably picked it up from whatever bank it was that seized it from your Southern belle, there. And because Twin Springs was once obviously two springs, I once asked the owner if he knew what happened to the second one."

"Did he?"

"He did." Easton looked straight at her. "It was dynamited."

Jennifer lifted her head a bit. "Why would somebody want to blow up a spring?"

"To relieve boredom, I guess. Back in the 1890s, there was even less to do around here than there is now. The locals' idea of a good time on a Sunday afternoon was to head out to a spring with a picnic lunch and a barrel of beer. And then, for after-dinner entertainment, they'd chuck sticks of dynamite into the water, watch it geyser up. Only a matter of time before somebody made a lucky shot, landed their stick in the aperture, and the explosion collapsed the cave."

"So there's a fifty-percent chance that what I'm looking for is behind all that rock?"

"I wouldn't go counting your chickens just yet." Despite what he'd just said, Easton leaned forward, one arm on the table, obviously warming up to the idea. "But you can tell, even today, that the second aperture – the one that they blew – was once much larger than the first."

Jennifer waited for a moment, then asked, "And that's important because . . . ?"

"Because of something called Bernoulli's Principle." Easton held up both hands, the fingers of his left in a tight circle, the fingers of his right touching loosely. "If you figure that the same cave system is feeding both apertures, and one is smaller than the other, the water coming out of the smaller one will have to accelerate to balance the flow. It's the same thing that happens when you turn a shower head from a coarse to a fine setting–it sprays harder, because the flow is coming through a smaller opening."

"Okay." Jennifer nodded slowly. "I follow that. But why would that mean that the larger opening is the one we want?"

"Because . . ." Easton's grin grew larger ". . . if I were diving in that cave on a breath-hold, I'd want to go against the lowest resistance possible on the way in."

Jennifer could actually feel her eyebrows rise. "The one that was collapsed."

"In the 1890s." Easton nodded twice. "They had diving suits back then, but I've never heard of anyone using one in a spring. Scuba wasn't invented until the Second World War. And the exploration of these cave systems around here didn't really get going until the sixties. Yeah, if your information is right–and if this secret, whatever it is, is waterproof–I'd say there's a chance that whatever your man put in the cave is still in there."

They sat back, looking at one another. In the distance, some bird asked another about sunscreen.

"Where are you staying?" Easton asked.

"I haven't gotten around to finding a place yet."

He laughed. "You really planned this out, didn't you?" He stood up and reached for her catalog case. "I've got a bunkhouse built onto the other end of the shop for people taking lessons. Nobody's in there right now. Let's get you settled. We can dive in the morning."

We want to hear from you. Please send your comments about this book to us in care of zreview@zondervan.com. Thank you.

ZONDERVAN.COM/
AUTHORTRACKER